PENGUIN BOOKS

Mirage

Clive Cussler is the author or co-author of over fifty international bestsellers, including the famous Dirk Pitt® adventures, such as *Crescent Dawn*; the NUMA® Files, most recently *Zero Hour*; the *Oregon* Files, such as *The Jungle*; the Isaac Bell adventures, which began with *The Chase*; and the highly successful Fargo Adventures, such as *Lost Empire*. His non-fiction works include *The Sea Hunters* and *The Sea Hunters II*: these describe the true adventures of the real NUMA, which, led by Cussler, searches for lost ships of historic significance. With his crew of volunteers, Cussler has discovered more than sixty ships, including the long-lost Confederate submarine *Hunley*. He lives in Arizona.

Jack Du Brul is the author of the Philip Mercer series, most recently *Havoc*, and is the co-author with Clive Cussler of the *Oregon* Files novels *Dark Watch*, *Skeleton Coast*, *Plague Ship*, *Corsair*, *The Silent Sea* and *The Jungle*. He lives in Vermont.

Find out more about the world of Clive Cussler by visiting
www.clivecussler.co.uk.

Mirage

CLIVE CUSSLER
with JACK DU BRUL

PENGUIN BOOKS

PENGUIN BOOKS

Published by the Penguin Group
Penguin Books Ltd, 80 Strand, London WC2R ORL, England
Penguin Group (USA) Inc., 375 Hudson Street, New York, New York 10014, USA
Penguin Group (Canada), 90 Eglinton Avenue East, Suite 700, Toronto, Ontario,
Canada M4P 2Y3 (a division of Pearson Penguin Canada Inc.)
Penguin Ireland, 25 St Stephen's Green, Dublin 2, Ireland (a division of Penguin Books Ltd)
Penguin Group (Australia), 707 Collins Street, Melbourne, Victoria 3008, Australia
(a division of Pearson Australia Group Pty Ltd)
Penguin Books India Pvt Ltd, 11 Community Centre,
Panchsheel Park, New Delhi – 110 017, India
Penguin Group (NZ), 67 Apollo Drive, Rosedale, Auckland 0632, New Zealand
(a division of Pearson New Zealand Ltd)
Penguin Books (South Africa) (Pty) Ltd, Block D, Rosebank Office Park,
181 Jan Smuts Avenue, Parktown North, Gauteng 2193, South Africa

Penguin Books Ltd, Registered Offices: 80 Strand, London WC2R ORL, England

www.penguin.com

First published in the United States by G. P. Putnam's Sons 2013
First published in the UK by Michael Joseph 2013
Published in Penguin Books 2014
001

Set in 12.5/14.75pt Garamond MT Std
Typeset by Jouve (UK), Milton Keynes
Printed in Great Britain by Clays Ltd, St Ives plc

ISBN: 978-0-241-95712-7

www.greenpenguin.co.uk

Prologue

Off the Delaware Breakwater
August 1, 1902

By the time the echo from the first knock on his door rebounded off the back of his cabin, Captain Charles Urquhart was fully awake. A lifetime at sea had given him the reflexes of a cat. By the second knock he knew through the vibrations transmitted by his mattress that the ship's engines had been shut down, but the hiss of water flowing along her steel hull told him the *Mohican* had not yet begun to slow. Dishwater-coloured light leaked around the curtain pulled over the room's single porthole. With the ship heading north and his cabin on the starboard side, Urquhart estimated it was coming up on nine in the evening.

He'd been asleep less than a half hour, following a gruelling twenty hours on duty as the cargo vessel ran through the tail end of an early-season hurricane.

'Come,' he called and swung his legs off his cot. The deck was covered with a carpet of such thin pile that he could feel the cool of the metal plates beneath it.

The cabin door creaked open, light from a gas lantern marking a wedge across the threshold. The ship had an electrical generator, but the few lights it powered were reserved for the bridge. 'Sorry to bother, sir,' said the third officer, a Welshman named Jones.

'What is it?' Urquhart asked, the last vestiges of sleep sloughing off. No one woke the captain unless it was an emergency, and he knew he had to be ready for anything.

The man hesitated for a second, then said, 'We're not sure. We need you on the bridge.' He paused again. 'Sir.'

Urquhart tossed aside his bedcovers. He thrust his feet into a pair of rubber boots and threw a ratty robe over his shoulders. A Greek fisherman's cap finished his ridiculous outfit. 'Let's go.'

The bridge was one deck above his cabin. A helmsman stood mutely behind the large oaken wheel, his gaze not over the bow as it should have been but fixated out the port door leading to the ship's stubby bridge wing. Urquhart followed the gaze, and although his expression didn't change, his mind whirled.

About two miles away, an eerie blue glow clung to the horizon and blotted out the dying rays of the setting sun. It wasn't the colour of lightning or St Elmo's fire, which had been the captain's first suspicion. It was a deeper blue, and a colour he had never seen before.

Then all at once it expanded. Not like a fog boiling up from the ocean's surface but like the beat of a gigantic heart. Suddenly they were inside the luminous effect, and it was as if colour had texture. Urquhart could somehow feel the glow on his skin as the hairs on his arms raised up and the thick pelt of man fur that covered his torso and back prickled as if the legs of a thousand insects were crawling on his body.

'Captain,' the second mate called plaintively. He was pointing at the big compass ball mounted above the main bridge windows. Inside its liquid gimbal, the compass spun like a child's toy top.

Like any good seaman, Charles Urquhart lived by routine, and when routine was broken, it was to be reported in the ship's log. His next glance was to the chronograph, hanging on the back wall above a chart table, so he could record the time of this strange phenomenon. To his dismay, the two hands pointed straight down.

Not like it was six thirty, where the shorter hour hand would rest halfway to the Roman numeral seven, but straight down.

He crossed to it to check the mechanism and accidently dislodged its metal winding key. As if snatched by a force greater than gravity, the key dropped to the deck like it had been hurled at great speed. The key didn't bounce but seemed to adhere itself to the metal deck. He stooped to retrieve it but couldn't even wedge a fingernail between the key and the deck.

He again looked to the west, but the cobalt light cut visibility to just a few dozen yards. He did notice that the sea around the ship was so still it appeared solid, as though it had frozen as smooth as a skating rink, only it remained as black as anthracite coal.

A few crewmen down on the main deck spotted Urquhart's silhouette in the bridge wing door. One cupped a hand to his mouth and called, 'What's all this, Captain?'

The voice reached him like the man had yelled from the bottom of a well.

Other men appeared, and Urquhart could sense their nervous apprehension. He knew sailors were a superstitious lot. Each one of them carried talismans of various kinds, miniature dream-catchers, rabbits' feet and lucky marbles. He'd once served with a fellow who kept a small jar of alcohol in his pocket with the preserved remains of his severed pinkie finger. He claimed losing the digit proved it was lucky. Urquhart had never pressed for the details of exactly why that was.

In order to get their minds off the strangeness of the situation, he pointed to some loose chains left haphazardly on the *Mohican*'s forward hatch cover.

'Stow that chain properly,' Urquhart said in his most commanding voice, 'or there'll be hell to pay.'

The four men moved from the rail at double speed, as eager to have something to do as the veteran ship's master had suspected. But like his experience with the key, the brawny seamen could not move so much as a link of the chain. Had someone welded the entire mass of rusted steel to the hatch, they couldn't have done a better job of adhering the chain to the ship.

It was just occurring to Urquhart that his ship had turned into a giant magnet when he heard the scream, an unworldly peal of anguish that keened higher and higher without let-up.

The noise galvanized him because he recognized the voice despite the agony tearing through it, and he knew what was happening to the man.

The chief engineer, a Scotsman, had his cabin down the hallway from Urquhart's own. Urquhart reached McTaggert's door and burst through it only seconds after hearing him scream.

In the beam of the brass hurricane lantern Urquhart had snatched from the second mate, he saw the shirtless Scot atop his bed with a look of terror etched upon his face. He was pawing at his chest, or, more precisely, at the big scar that bisected his left pectoral muscle. The scar was a souvenir of a boiler explosion some twenty years back, and behind it, as McTaggert liked to brag, was a piece of pot metal the ship's cook who'd stitched him up at the time had been unable to remove.

'Flip over, Conner,' Urquhart shouted, but knew he was too late.

A fresh scream exploded from the engineer, a sound so sharp and so full of pain that Urquhart winced. And then a sputter of blood bubbled from Conner McTaggert's lips. The two men's eyes locked, and a silent message passed between them. Good-bye, it said.

The sputter turned into a continuous gout of rich arterial blood as the shard of metal lodged in his chest tore through his heart and lungs as it was drawn inexorably deckward by the powerful magnetic forces at play. The pain that had transformed his face into an ugly mask had passed, and the crimson stain running from chin to chest was the only testament to the man's last horrifying seconds.

A moment later came a wet sucking sound, then the metallic ting of the chunk of shrapnel hitting the deck after passing all the way through McTaggert's body.

Urquhart closed the cabin door before any of the other crew members saw the corpse. He returned to the bridge, his face ashen and his hands a little unsteady. The glow still spread over the ship with its eerie light, while the men on deck had given up their task of stowing the chain and peered anxiously toward where the glow had first emanated.

The sea remained glassy, and not a breath of air stirred the ship's rigging. The plume of smoke from her still-fired boilers shot straight into the sky and hung over the *Mohican* like a pall.

For twenty minutes nothing changed, and then, as if a light had been switched off, the glow vanished entirely. In the next instant, a chop returned to the ocean's surface, and the smoke began drifting aft as a wind swept across the ship from out of the north. To the west, where the phenomenon had first appeared, lay nothing but darkened skies sprinkled with a scattering of stars. A night at sea had never appeared more normal.

Urquhart huddled with his remaining officers in the back corner of the pilothouse while they detoured west to see if another ship had been at the epicentre of the otherworldly aura. He gave them orders to have Conner McTaggert sewn into his blankets and for his body to be slipped over the side. They were close enough to making Philadelphia that the engineer's death could be concealed, and his absence, once they left port, could be explained away as him jumping ship.

They found no evidence of any other vessels in the area, and after an hour-long search Urquhart determined that they had wasted enough time. Still, when they reached Phili, he planned to report the incident in case any other ships had suffered from the strange effect. McTaggert's death would remain a secret for the simple reason that it would delay them for days, or weeks, as statements were taken and investigations launched.

He wasn't pleased at the disrespect he was showing his friend, but he felt certain that the unmarried McTaggert would understand.

As he'd promised himself, Charles Urquhart did report the incident to the Coast Guard, and his story was picked up by a local paper. No mention was made of the dead engineer. Nor was there any mention of another ship that had experienced the phenomenon. The *Mohican* managed to limp back to Philadelphia. But another ship, and its five-man crew, had vanished without a trace.

I

North Siberia
Present Day

It was the landscape of another world. Towering black crags rose above vast glittering snowfields. Winds that could shriek out of the stillness blasted the air at over seventy miles per hour. A sky that was sometimes so clear it was as though the earth had no atmosphere. And sometimes clouds would cling to the land with such utter tenacity that the sun remained hidden for weeks on end.

It was a landscape not meant for human habitation. Even the hardiest natives avoided this location and lived far down the coast in tiny villages that they could pack up in pursuit of caribou herds.

All this made it the ideal spot for the Soviets to build a supermax prison in the early 1970s, a prison meant for the most dangerous criminals – the political kind. God and a few bureaucrats alone knew how many souls had perished behind the bleak concrete walls. The prison was built to hold five hundred men, and until it was shuttered in the years following the collapse of the Soviet Union, a steady stream had been trucked in on the isolated access road to replace those who had succumbed to the cold and deprivation and brutality.

There were no graves to mark men's remains, only a pit of ashes from their cremated bodies – a very large pit – that now lay buried in the permafrost a short distance from the main gate.

For twenty years the facility remained abandoned and left to the vagaries of the weather, though Siberia's notorious winters could do little to erode the cement-and-steel structure. When people returned to reopen the prison, they found that it was exactly as it had been when it closed, immutable, impenetrable and, most of all, inescapable.

A lone truck painted in matte green military livery wound its way toward the penitentiary that sat in the shadow of a singular mountain that looked as if it had been cleaved in two, with a sheer vertical face to the north, the Arctic Ocean some thirty miles away. The road was heavily rutted because in the summer parts of it turned into a swampy morass, and if crews didn't smooth it before the frosts came, it retained a corrugated texture. Blowing snow drifted across it in places where the plows hadn't opened the pathway far enough.

The sun hung low on the horizon, cold and distant. In a few weeks' time it would make its final plunge over the rim of the world and not reappear until the next spring. The temperature hovered just a tick above zero Fahrenheit.

The truck approached the slab-sided prison fortress, with its four guard towers rising like minarets. An outer ring of chain-link fence with razor wire circled the entire two-square-acre building. A sentry box sat just inside of the fence to the right of the access road. Between the box and the prison sat a humpbacked heavy-transport helicopter painted arctic white.

Only when the truck had come to a stop did a guard, bundled against the cold, waddle out of his little heated hut. He knew the truck was expected, but peering through the windshield he didn't recognize the drivers. He kept his AK-74, the updated version of Mikhail Kalashnikov's venerable AK-47, within easy reach on the strap dangling from his shoulder.

He motioned for the driver to step out of the cab.

With a resigned shrug, the driver opened his door, and his boots crunched into the compacted snow.

'Where's Dmitri?' the guard asked.

'Who's Dmitri?' the driver replied.

It had been a test. The regular drivers of the prison transfer truck were named Vasily and Anton.

The driver continued, 'If you mean Anton or Sasha —' Vasily's nickname — 'Anton's wife had her baby, another boy, and Sash is down with pneumonia.'

The guard nodded and felt less ill at ease at having strangers coming out to the secret prison. They obviously belonged to the same squad as the regular crew. 'Show me your papers, and have your co-driver come out with his.'

A few moments later, the guard was satisfied with the men's bona fides. He swung his assault rifle farther onto his back and keyed open the gate. He pushed the gate outward, its mass of concertina wire jangling with dark resonance.

Exhaust burst into a white cloud as the driver accelerated through the gate and under an open portcullis that gave access to the central courtyard, around which the four blocks of the prison had been built. Ahead were steps leading to the entrance, itself a door more befitting a bank vault than a building. Two guards in white camouflage were waiting by the door. The truck turned in a tight arc, then began backing slowly toward the men. When one of them judged it close enough, he held up a hand. The driver hit the brakes. It was against protocol for him to leave the engine idling, on the off chance a prisoner might manage to steal the truck, so he killed the ignition and pocketed the keys.

It was a separate key on a different fob that opened the rear doors. The two guards had their AKs at their shoulders when the doors creaked open.

Inside was a single prisoner, shackled at the wrists and ankles and chained to the floor. He wore prison blues, with a thinly padded jacket to ward off a little of the arctic air. At first, it looked as though he had tightly cropped dark hair, but, in fact, his head was perfectly shaved. It was the intricate design of interlacing tattoos covering his skull that made it look like he had hair. The tattoos continued around his throat and disappeared into the V of his prison shirt. He wasn't necessarily a big man, but there was a feral intensity to his glacial blue eyes that made him seem dangerous.

'Okay, my friend,' the driver said with mocking jocularity, 'you're home.' His tone darkened. 'Give us any trouble and you die here and now.'

The prisoner said nothing, but the ferocity of his glare eased like he'd dialled down some personal rheostat of rage. He nodded once, a signal that he would cooperate.

The driver stepped up into the truck and unlocked the chain that secured the prisoner to the windowless truck's floor. The driver backed out, and the prisoner shuffled after him. The prisoner winced when he jumped to the ground. He'd been locked in the same position for the past six torturous hours. The transfer would not be complete until he had changed out of the shackles he wore, so all four men mounted the stairs and stepped into the prison.

The cinder-block walls of the receiving hall were painted a sickly green favoured by all Soviet institutions. The floors were bare concrete, and the ceiling lofted ten feet. The room was little warmer than the outside air, but at least there was no wind. There was a barred cage to the right of the door. Inside were two additional men. They weren't dressed in uniforms but wore clothing not unlike the prisoner himself.

Both of them were massive, standing at least six foot six, with hands like sledgehammers and biceps and chests that strained the fabric of their shirts. Also like the newly arrived prisoner, their necks were adorned with prison tattoos; one had a strand of barbed wire inked across his forehead that denoted he'd been sentenced to life with no possibility of parole.

The new prisoner was shepherded into the caged room. One of the armed guards handed his assault rifle to his companion and pulled a set of shackles off a peg above a bare desk. Together with the driver, they entered the enclosure and closed the barred door. The lock engaged automatically.

'This is a rather ugly new fish you brought us,' said the prisoner doing life. 'We were hoping for something prettier.'

'Beggars can't be choosy, Marko,' the prison guard told him. 'And with you, they are never pretty for long.'

The mountainous man shrugged as if agreeing. 'Let's see where you've been, little fish. Take off your shirt.'

Tattoos were like a résumé inside the Russian penal system, telling others how many years a man had been inside, what kinds of crimes he'd committed, who he had worked for on the outside, and all manner of other information. A cat tattoo meant the man had been a thief, and if he had more felines inked on his body, it meant he worked with a gang. A cross on his chest was usually applied involuntarily and meant he was some-one's slave.

The driver glanced at the guard, who nodded at this slight deviation from procedure and proceeded to unlock the leg and wrist irons. When he was free, the prisoner stood as still as a statue, his eyes never leaving those of Marko, the lifer who sat at the apex of prison hierarchy and actually ran it for the guards.

'Take off your shirt or you won't leave this room alive,' Marko said.

If being threatened with death a second time in as many minutes intimidated the prisoner, it didn't show.

He remained motionless and unblinking for a beat of ten seconds. Then, with slow deliberation, as if it were his idea, he unzipped his thin jacket and languidly unbuttoned his shirt.

There were no crosses on his chest, though nearly every square inch of skin was decorated with ersatz prison ink.

Marko pushed himself from the wall, saying, 'Let's see what we have.'

The prisoner, one Ivan Karnov – though he had many names over the years, and, given his southern rather than Slavic features, this too was no doubt an alias – knew what was coming. He knew prison culture, understood every subtext and nuanced meaning, and the next few seconds would determine how the rest of his time here would be spent.

Marko towered over Karnov as he sidled up behind him, and the stench of garlic that oozed out of his skin despite the chilled air was overpowering.

Ivan Karnov gamed it in his head, watched angles and postures, but mostly he kept his attention on Marko's consigliere. When that man's eyes widened just the tiniest amount, Karnov spun and grabbed at Marko's wrist an instant before he almost powered his massive fist into Karnov's kidney with a hammer blow that would have likely ruptured the organ. Next, Karnov's knee came up as he forced Marko's arm downward. The two bones, the radius and the ulna, shattered upon impact, and their sharpened ends erupted through the skin as the forearm was bent in half.

Karnov was in motion before Marko's nervous system told his brain of the massive damage. He was across the room in two strides and slammed his forehead into the other prison trustee's nose. The angle wasn't optimal because of the man's height, but the nose shattered anyway.

In a fight, this move accomplished one critical goal. No matter how big an opponent, or how strong, the eyes watered copiously as an autonomic response. For the next few seconds, the man was effectively blind.

Marko's agonized roar filled the room as his mind finally reacted to the trauma.

Karnov pounded the second man's nose. Right, left, right, and then he slammed a stiffened hand into the guy's neck, shocking the muscles so they clamped down on the carotid artery. Starved of blood, the man's brain simply shut down, and he collapsed.

Elapsed time: four seconds.

More than enough for the driver and the prison guard to react. The driver had stepped back a pace while the guard had come forward, his hand on the lacquered black nightstick fitted through a ring on his utility belt. The guard was concentrating on making it a clean cross draw, knowing once he had the weapon out all advantage swung to him.

That was the mistake of thinking a weapon gave you an advantage before it was deployed. His concentration was on his own actions and not on those of his opponent.

Karnov got his hand on the nightstick's tip just

before it pulled free of its restraining loop and crashed into the guard while his arm was drawn awkwardly between their chests. Both were solid men, and the impact when they hit the cage wall was more than enough to pop the ball joint at the top of the guard's humerus bone from the glenoid socket of his scapula and tear several connective muscles and fibres.

The guard outside the caged room had his rifle up to his shoulder and was shouting incoherent orders but had the presence of mind not to fire into a confined space where only one of the five men was a threat.

Karnov whirled to face the driver and had eight pounds of steel shackles swung at his head and nowhere near enough time to avoid them.

The blow sent him staggering as blood sprayed from where the sharp manacles had flayed open skin at his temple. The driver was on him even before he collapsed to the floor, not quite unconscious but not all there either. In quick, practiced moves, he had Karnov fully cuffed at the wrists and ankles.

Karnov began pressing himself up from the floor.

The driver stepped back and said softly, 'Good luck in here, my friend. You're going to need it.'

The outside guard finally thought about the alarm and tripped a switch under the desk. The klaxon brought a half-dozen men within seconds. Karnov was on his feet now, but the defiance that had made his face such a mask was gone. He'd done what he needed to do – establish himself quickly. He was not a man to mess with, but his fight was with the other prisoners, not their guards. The dislocated shoulder was collateral damage only.

'I am done,' he said to the guards frothing to tear him apart. 'I will resist no more, and I am sorry for your man here.'

The first guard finally opened the door, but despite Karnov's words and passivity, the men wouldn't be denied. Karnov was only grateful as they swarmed him and began a vicious pummelling that they were using only their fists and not their nightsticks. And then a guard kicked the crown of Karnov's head with a steel-toed boot, and the beating faded away from his consciousness.

Time was meaningless after that, so Karnov had no idea how much had elapsed before he came to. His body ached all over, which told him the beating went on long after he'd been knocked out, but that was to be expected. He couldn't imagine mercy being a job requirement for a guard at a supermax prison at the ass end of the world.

His cell was tiny, barely big enough for him to stretch fully across its freezing floor. The walls were unadorned cinder blocks, and the door was solid metal, with a slot at the bottom for food and another at eye level for observation.

He was locked down in solitary.

Perfect, he thought.

He was still fully shackled, and in the confusion the guards hadn't realized that he still sported the transport manacles he'd had on at his arrival.

Perfect, he grinned.

Also in their anger and their desire to see the prisoner punished, the guards hadn't performed the customary full body search, otherwise they would have taken away his prosthetic leg.

Perfect. He knew he was home free.

Juan Cabrillo had busted out of more than one prison in his life, but this was the first time he'd ever busted *into* one.

The whole purpose of the fight had been to get himself thrown into solitary as soon as he arrived. Marko and his goon buddy had made perfect targets, but if necessary Cabrillo would have taken on the guards just as easily. None of them here were upstanding citizens doing a needed but dismal job. They were handpicked thugs who were pretty much part of a private army commanded by Pytor Kenin, a fleet admiral and perhaps the second-most-corrupt man on the planet. Cabrillo's whole plan was to bypass the prison indoctrination process entirely.

He touched the spot where he'd been hit with the shackles. The bleeding had mostly stopped. He looked down at his chest. The tattoos did look real, even though they had been applied in four-hour-long sessions over the past week aboard the *Oregon*. Kevin Nixon, a former Hollywood special effects artist who'd painted on the special ink, had warned him that it would begin to fade quickly. Hence Cabrillo's desire to get himself tossed into solitary as soon as he arrived at the prison.

Juan rolled up his trouser leg and checked the artificial limb that attached just below his knee. It was neither the most realistic of his collection of prosthetics nor even the most functional. This one was specially built for this mission to allow him to smuggle in as much equipment as possible. The leg was almost a perfect cylinder, with only a slight indentation for an ankle. Had a guard slapped on the shackles, he would have been suspicious right away, but the driver who'd done the cuffing was on Cabrillo's payroll for this mission. Throughout the entire incident, only he had manacled Cabrillo's legs, as they had planned and choreographed over and over.

Juan fingered his bloody temple and wished they'd rehearsed that bit a little more.

Not knowing the prison's routine, he decided it best to wait for a while before making his move. It would also allow him some time to recover from the beating. The first part of the operation, hijacking the truck carrying the real Ivan Karnov, had gone off without a hitch. The two drivers and their prisoner were trussed up in an abandoned house at a largely forgotten port town that was the closest to the prison.

When this op was over, a call would be placed to the village's authorities, and Karnov would once again be headed to whatever fate awaited him here.

The second part, getting smuggled into the prison, had gone as well as to be expected. It was the third phase that gave Cabrillo pause. Max Hanley, Cabrillo's closest friend, second-in-command of their 550-foot freighter *Oregon*, and all-around curmudgeon, would call it insane.

But that's what Juan Cabrillo and his team did on a routine basis – pull off the impossible for the right reasons. And the right price.

And while this mission had a personal component for Cabrillo, he wasn't above accepting the rest of the twenty-five million dollars they'd been guaranteed.

Over the next thirty-six, frigid hours, Cabrillo figured out the routine for solitary confinement. There wasn't much to it.

At what he guessed was near noon, the slit at the base of his door was opened and a metal tray with thin gruel and a hunk of black bread the size and consistency of a hand grenade was passed through. He had as much time to eat as it took the jailor to feed the other prisoners on this level and empty the slop buckets the men passed out to him. Judging by the sounds of the guard doing this dreary work, there were six others in solitary. None of the prisoners spoke, which told Cabrillo that if he tried, there would be reprisals.

He remained silent, ignoring the food, and waited. A hairy hand reached back for the tray. The guard muttered, 'Suit yourself. The food ain't gonna get any better,' and the slot slid closed.

Knowing now that no one checked on the men down here other than the once-a-day feeding, Cabrillo set to work. After removing his artificial leg and opening its removable cover, he carefully set his equipment around him. He first used a key to unshackle himself from the irons. The key was a duplicate made from the original the driver carried. Not clanking around like the ghost of Jacob Marley was a relief unto itself. Putting on the shirt and jacket that had been dumped into the cell with him was sublime. Next from the leg came nearly a dozen tubes of a putty-like substance – the key to the whole operation. If this didn't work as advertised, if Mark Murphy and Eric Stone, Cabrillo's crackerjack researchers, had messed up, this would be the shortest prison break in history.

He strapped his leg in place and uncapped one of the tubes and applied a thin bead of the gel to the mortar seam between two of the cinder blocks nearest the floor.

All manner of horrible thoughts flashed through Cabrillo's mind when the gel didn't react as it had when they were experimenting back on the *Oregon*. But the brain can think up scary scenarios in fractions of seconds. The chemical reaction was a tad slower.

Stone and Murph had deduced the chemical make-up of the mortar used here by reading through thousands of pages of declassified documents in Archangel, where the company that had built the facility back in the '70s was located. (In truth, a team from the *Oregon* had broken into the facility and scanned the documents over a three-night period and fed them into the ship's mainframe computer for translation, and then Eric and Mark had gotten to work.)

In less than a minute, the acidic putty had completely broken down the mortar. Cabrillo then attached a probe to the tube, so he could stick it into the narrow slit he'd created, and applied more gel to etch away the remaining mortar on the far side of the block. When he was certain it was clear, he kicked the block into a narrow crawl space between his cell's wall and the prison's exterior basement wall. He peered into the gloomy space and saw that the next obstacle was a preformed slab of concrete resting on poured-cement footings. Each section probably weighed ten or so tons.

The mortar acid wouldn't work on it, but the pack of C-4 plastic explosives would more than do the job.

2

It took Cabrillo nearly an hour to enlarge his one-block hole into an aperture he could crawl through. On the off chance of a random inspection through the peephole, he stacked the blocks in front of it with just enough room to squeeze behind. In the cell's dismal lighting it would give the optical illusion of a solid wall.

Next, he attacked the wall next to the cell door. Rather than use the acidic putty to remove individual blocks, he first eroded all the mortar he could reach in an area just wider than his body. Again, this was a precaution in case a guard or the warden came around. Only when he was ready to make his move would he blow through the rest of the mortar.

The second-to-last item in his prosthetic limb had been a tiny transmitter. Once he hit the button and its burst signal was sent to the men waiting on the ship, he had six minutes to get the man he had come here to rescue, blow the C-4 he'd already planted, and make it up to the surface.

Yuri Borodin had been imprisoned here for just a few weeks. While the man ate like a bear, drank like, well, like a Russian, and exercised every third leap year, he was still in pretty good shape for a man of fifty-five. But the guards could have done anything to him in that time. For all Juan knew, he'd find a broken and shattered man in Yuri's cell, or, worse, Yuri'd already been executed and his ashes added to the mound outside.

No matter what he found, Cabrillo's six-minute deadline was carved in stone.

He went to work on the last of the mortar, committed now beyond all shadow of a doubt. When he was done, he got his lock picks ready, the last trick to come from his cache, and kicked his way through the cement blocks. They tumbled to the floor in a chalky heap, and Juan dove through headfirst.

'Yuri,' he called in a stage whisper when he got to his feet.

He was in a long corridor with at least twenty cell doors. At the far end he could see where the hallway bent ninety degrees. From his study of the construction diagrams, he knew there was another door just around the corner and, beyond that, stairs that rose to the prison's first floor. It was like Hannibal Lecter's cellblock without the creepy acrylic wall.

'Who's there?' a voice he recognized from their years of dealings called back just as faintly.

Juan went to the door where he thought Yuri was being held and drew back the observation slit. The cell was empty.

'To your left,' Yuri said.

Juan drew back that slit, and there in front of him was Admiral Yuri Borodin, former commandant of the naval base in Vladivostok. It had been at Borodin's shipyard that the *Oregon* had been refitted and the sophisticated weapons systems integrated after the original ship had outlived her usefulness and was nearly scrapped. The fitting of her revolutionary magneto-hydrodynamic engines had been carried out at another shipyard Yuri controlled. Both jobs had neared a combined cost of one hundred million dollars, but with Juan's former boss at the CIA giving him the go-ahead to convert the *Oregon* into what she was today, financing had not been an issue.

Borodin's normal helmet of bronze hair lay limp along the sides of his open face, and his skin had an unnaturally sallow mien, but he still had the alert dark eyes of the canny fox he was. They hadn't broken him yet, not by a mile.

He had a look of wary confusion as he regarded the man before him, as if he recognized him but couldn't place him. Then his face split into a big toothy grin. 'Chairman Juan Cabrillo,' he exclaimed loudly before moderating his voice to a whisper again. 'Of all the prisons in all the towns in all the world, why am I not surprised you are in this one?'

'Proverbial bad penny,' Cabrillo said, deadpan.

Borodin reached through the observation slit to rub Juan's head. 'What have you done to yourself?'

'Making myself pretty just for you.' Juan started working the lock picks.

'Who sent you?'

'Misha.' Captain Mikhail Kasporov was Borodin's longtime assistant and aide-de-camp.

'God bless the boy.' A sudden dark thought occurred to him. 'To rescue me or kill me?'

Juan glanced up from the lock, which he almost had open. 'Does your paranoia know no bounds? To rescue you, you idiot.'

'Ah, he is a good boy. And as for my paranoia, Mr Chairman of the Corporation, a look at my present surroundings shows that I was not paranoid enough. So what is new, my friend?'

'Let's see. The civil war in the Sudan is winding down. The Dodgers again have no pitching staff. And I think half the Kardashians are getting married while the other half are divorcing. Oh, and once again you've managed to anger the wrong guy.'

On his ruthless rise to power within the Russian Navy, backed by hard-right political cronies, the mercurial Admiral Pytor Kenin had left a trail of destruction in his wake – careers ruined and, in one instance, a rival's suspicious death. Now that he was one of the youngest fleet admirals in the country's history, rumours abounded that he would soon turn to politics under the guiding wing of Vladimir Putin.

Yuri Borodin had become one of Kenin's enemies, though he was too well positioned among the general staff to be dismissed outright and had been arrested on trumped-up charges and sent to this prison to await trial – a trial that he would most likely never survive to see. A company Kenin controlled ran the prison on behalf of the government in a public/private cooperative much like the ones that gave rise to the oligarchs in the days after Communism's demise. His death could be easily arranged and would likely happen after the initial flap over his arrest died down.

That Borodin was corrupt was an open secret, but singling him out was like arresting only a single user in an overcrowded crack house. Corruption in the Russian military was as much a part of the culture as itchy uniforms and lousy food.

'And you do this out of the goodness of your heart?'

'Of course,' Cabrillo said. 'And about a tenth of your net worth.'

'Bah. My Misha is a good boy, but he is a lousy negotiator. You love me like a brother for what I did to that oversized scow of yours. We had good times, you and me, while the men at my shipyard turned your tabby cat into a lion. To honour those memories alone you should rescue me for free.'

Juan countered, 'I could have charged double, and Mikhail would have paid because even he doesn't know all your Swiss bank account numbers.' With that, he twisted the picks and sprang the lock.

The first thing Yuri Borodin did was grasp Cabrillo in a big bear hug and kiss him on both cheeks. 'You are a saint amongst men.'

'Get off me, you crazy Russian,' Juan said lightly as he extricated himself from Yuri's grip. 'We're not out of this yet.'

Borodin turned serious. 'There is a great deal we

need to talk about. The timing of my arrest was not coincidental.'

'Not now. Let's go.'

They crawled back into Cabrillo's cell. Juan took up the microburst transmitter, set a mental timer in his head, and activated both. He then keyed the plastic explosives he'd earlier moulded to the prison's exterior wall a good distance from his rabbit hole. The blast was muted by the intervening cinder blocks but could still be felt in every corner of the large facility. The guards would be swinging into action almost immediately.

Juan ducked down to enter the claustrophobic space between the prison's inner and outer walls. He turned back to Borodin. 'No matter what happens, just stay with me.'

Yuri nodded grimly, his normal bonhomie replaced with real concern for his fate.

They moved laterally along the cramped space and had to squeeze by pipes that rose through the floor. These were part of the passive ammonia cooling system that kept what little heat maintained by the prison from melting the permafrost on which it was built. The air thickened with the burned chemical stench of the explosives as they neared the breach through the outer foundation.

The C-4 had blown a ragged hole through the concrete slab about the size of a manhole cover. Chunks of smashed cement shifted under his feet as Cabrillo boosted himself through the opening. On the far side he found himself standing in a moat that encircled the prison's basement level. This dead space acted as a thermal buffer to again prevent the building's latent heat from melting the frozen ground.

Twelve feet overhead were panels that hid the moat from the surface. The panels had dozens of holes punched through them so that air could circulate freely and were supported by metal scaffolding. Clots of snow jammed some of the holes, and some drifted down on the men as a result of the blast.

'Come on,' Juan called over the sound of a doppleringjsiren. They ran away from the hole in the wall, as the blast had surely been seen by the guards in the towers. It was like running through a maze. They had to twist and contort their bodies around the countless struts that made up the scaffold. And yet only a contortionist could have moved quicker than these two. Once they rounded a corner, Cabrillo led them a few more feet and then began climbing upward. The metal was so cold, it felt like his hands were being scalded. The panels were secured from above with threaded bolts screwed into receptors on the steel framework. A final tube of concentrated acid formulated to dissolve steel ate through the rust-stuck nuts and even the bolts themselves.

Cabrillo's six minutes were almost up. He levered himself into position so he could use his back and legs to shove the panel up and off the scaffold.

'Remember, stay with me, and we'll be fine,' he warned again. 'Half of what's about to happen is for show.'

He pressed with his shoulders to test how hard the panel would resist after so many decades and, to his surprise, the section of perforated steel plate popped free almost before he was ready.

The prison alarm continued to keen, but over it came another sound, the unmistakable *whop-whop-whop* of a fast-approaching helicopter.

The timer in his head touched zero, and Cabrillo heaved the panel aside. He scrambled up and out of the earth, knowing that his blue prison uniform stood out starkly against the foot-deep snow that lay in drifts all around him. A dedicated guard could spot him in an instant, but he was banking on human instinct to keep from being spotted. The guards should be watching the approaching helicopter.

He could see the chopper out beyond the security fence, an olive drab insect that grew in size until he could recognize it as an ungainly Kamov Ka-26. With two main rotors set one above the other atop the hull, and spinning in opposite directions, the craft had no need for a tail rotor on a long, tapering boom. This made the six-passenger helo resemble a flying moving van with two stumpy rudders bolted to its rear bumper.

In seconds, Yuri was at his side, and both men stood with their backs pressed against the prison's featureless wall.

Now that it was closer, Juan saw the small wings that had been attached to the chopper's hull just aft of the pilot's door.

A jumpy guard let loose a long burst with his AK

even though the chopper was well out of range. In response, a single rocket shot off one of the winglets and streaked toward the perimeter fence while a heavy machine gun on the opposite side roared to life, spitting a tongue of flame that shot out past the cockpit bubble. Shell casings the size of cigar tubes rained from the weapon as the newly fallen snow between the perimeter fence and the building came alive under the blistering assault of lead.

'Run!' Juan shouted over the hellish din.

To Yuri's utter astonishment, Cabrillo charged into the maelstrom kicked up by the machine gun as though he were a member of the Light Brigade riding into the Russian guns at Balaclava.

'No matter what, follow me,' the man who called himself Chairman had said, and, to his greater amazement, Yuri let out a full-throated bellow that was unheard over the siren and chopper and still-pounding machine gun and took off after his friend.

The rocket detonated at the base of the fence, throwing up even more snow and clumps of frozen soil. Borodin expected to be cut down at any moment while geysers of snow erupted all around him, tossed high by bullets he had yet to hear cracking past.

Then he felt a small hit to the bottom of his left foot. It wasn't enough to toss him to the ground, but it did make him stagger. It was the clue he needed to tell him he wasn't immune to the massive amount of bullets pouring down from the chopper's machine gun, for, in truth, there were no rounds. The Kamov was firing blanks, and the detonations of snow that created a ten-foot-high fog were small explosive charges that Cabrillo's team had likely sown during the last snowstorm by simply tossing them over the fence.

But their luck couldn't last forever. Bullets from autofire by the men in the guard towers began searching them out, the micro supersonic booms ripping the air near his head. Borodin wished Cabrillo wasn't so soft. Had *he* planned this escape, the first missiles off the Kamov's rails would have taken out the guards' lofty perches. But Juan was different. Though a mercenary, as tough as any, he loathed killing when it wasn't necessary, even if that put his own life at risk. Juan also didn't know these men, didn't know that they were Kenin's private army, paid more for their loyalty to the admiral than to Mother Russia. They wore the uniforms of their country, but they were no less mercenary than Cabrillo himself.

With more and more real bullets stitching the ground, Cabrillo and Borodin made it across the open killing field with neither man being hit. The rocket had blown apart a section of the fence near one of its support stanchions, leaving a gap wide enough for them to run through but forcing them to angle to the left to avoid the mound of deadly razor wire lying on the ground.

Now clear of the shooting gallery and much closer to the chopper, they saw that ropes dangled from each side of the Kamov that were long enough to trail on the ground.

Juan led them to the ropes, and he quickly found the loop for his foot and another for a hand. 'Hang on,' he shouted over the jarring rattle of rotor and gunfire.

The chopper's downblast was a maelstrom of Category 5 proportions.

The pilot must have seen the two men take their places, for no sooner had Yuri slipped his shoe into one of the loops and his hand through another than it felt as though his stomach was trying to leave his body through the soles of his feet.

The Kamov lifted and whirled, swinging both men like pendulums and leaving the ground a good hundred feet below them. The wind, as the chopper gained speed, clawed at their exposed bodies like stinging needles that numbed skin and turned eyes into streaming torrents.

Borodin fought to cling to the twisting, sinuous rope and prayed that Cabrillo's plan called for them to land soon and crawl into the nice warm cabin – and knowing Juan's style – where a good bottle of brandy awaited. He wasn't sure how long he could hold on, but looking down at the snow and stone racing by below, he knew he could last for the rest of his life because a fall would certainly kill him.

The chopper thundered due east and deeper into the mountains, the pilot flying as close to the earth as he dared with his two passengers dangling below the helo's tricycle landing wheels. Each dip and rise and swooping turn sent shocks through both men's bodies. Dusk was beginning to settle over the landscape, but the pilot didn't turn on any landing lights. Borodin suspected he had some night vision capabilities to be flying so recklessly through these uncharted canyons.

After an eternity of ten freezing minutes, the beat of the rotors changed when they neared a copse of pines sheltered under yet another granite cliff. They were finally landing. Borodin would curse the Chairman for such a torturous flight, but only after he stopped shivering.

The chopper dropped lower and lower until both men could simply step out of the loops and duck under the wind screaming at them from the whirling blades. Borodin expected the Kamov would continue to the ground, but instead the engine's whine increased, and once again the ungainly aircraft was shooting eastward, leaving the two men alone in a frozen wasteland. He knew that they'd both be dead of hypothermia within the next hour, if not sooner. He also knew that Juan Cabrillo hadn't yet finished dipping into his bag of tricks.

Borodin pointed to where the helicopter had vanished around a cragged tor. 'Decoy, yes?'

Juan switched from Russian, one of the four languages he spoke, but said in Russian-accented English to mock Borodin's syntax, 'Decoy, *da.*'

'What about the pilot? Will he be okay?'

'Why wouldn't he be? He's sitting at a console aboard the *Oregon.*'

Juan enjoyed the range of emotions that played across Yuri's wind-chapped face as he absorbed that information. Incomprehension morphed into under-standing, and then horror at the implications, and then outrage at the potential consequence.

'You mean while we were whizzing by mountains and skimming the ground, there was no pilot? He could have killed us while he sat safe and secure on your ship?'

Juan couldn't help but taunt him a bit more. 'My pilot, Gomez Adams, so nicknamed for a dalliance he had with a woman who looked remarkably like Carolyn Jones, the original Morticia, had less than a week to practice tele-flying the Kamov after we bought it and installed the remote controls.'

'You're mad.'

'Barking,' Juan agreed with a grin. 'Come on.'

He led them a short distance into the trees, where Cabrillo's team had another surprise waiting. It was a Lynx Rave RE 800R snowmobile painted a matte white that perfectly matched the snow. With its massive cater-pillar tread and double runner skis, it was the perfect machine for crossing any arctic terrain. Bundled next to it was a bag containing helmets and white snowsuits, one helmet battery-powered and the other able to jack into the Lynx's electrical system, as well as insulated boots and gloves.

'Put these on. There's a chopper at the prison, and they'll soon be in pursuit.'

As they dressed Yuri said, 'That was why we didn't change direction when we flew off. You wanted them to follow the Kamov.'

'And while they head east in pursuit of an empty

chopper, we go north to where the *Oregon*'s waiting for us.'

'How long?'

Juan threw a leg over the sled's saddle seat and flicked the 800cc Rotax engine to life. Over the whine of the two-stroke he replied, 'About an hour.'

He jacked a cord dangling from his helmet into a satellite phone that had been secreted with the rest of the gear.

'This is Edmond Dantès calling.' His code name referenced the famous prisoner who escaped a life sentence in the Dumas masterpiece *The Count of Monte Cristo*. 'We have gotten out of the Château d'If.'

'Edmond,' came Max Hanley's happy reply. 'Ready to go find your treasure and exact your revenge?'

'The treasure's going to be sent to a numbered account as soon as we're back aboard, and revenge has never been my intent.'

'How'd it go?' Max asked, dropping all pretence that he hadn't been concerned for Juan's safety.

'No problems as yet. The squib bombs worked better than we'd hoped, and Gomez could have threaded that chopper through a needle if he'd needed to.'

'You're on speaker here in the op centre, Chairman,' George Adams drawled. 'I heard that and won't disagree for a second.'

Juan could picture the handsome Texan, with his drooping gunslinger moustache, sitting just behind and to the right of the command chair in the middle of the *Oregon*'s high-tech nerve centre. While Cabrillo was being transported to the prison, Adams had flown the drone Kamov from the ship and pre-positioned it near the complex with another of Yuri's loyalists waiting to fire up its engine when he received Juan's signal.

'We're in position and standing by,' Hanley cut in.

'Okay, Max. Yuri and I will be there in about an hour.'

'We'll keep the light on for you.'

Juan patted the seat, and Borodin legged over to straddle the sled just behind him. Two handholds had been sewn into the back of Cabrillo's snowsuit for him to hold on to, saving both men the ignominy of the Russian clutching Juan's waist. Juan could have jacked Borodin's helmet into the snow machine's onboard communications set, but that would mean he would miss any incoming calls from the *Oregon* as they tracked both the drone Kamov and the prison's big Mil chopper in hot pursuit.

The Lynx accelerated like a rocket and shot out of the pines with the swift agility of a startled hare. In minutes, they were blasting over the snowpack. Because of the sophisticated suspension and the heated suits, the ride was remarkably comfortable. The deep core chill Cabrillo had suffered was soon replaced with enough warmth that he had to dial down his heater. He barely felt the vibration of the sled cutting through the snow, and the whine of the two-stroke engine was a muted purr in his helmet.

If not for the fact an armed Russian helicopter would soon be hunting for them, he would have enjoyed the ride.

It was only fifteen minutes into their dash for the coast that Max Hanley called to report their drone helicopter had been shot down and that its cameras had survived long enough to tell them the Russians knew the aircraft was unmanned.

Cabrillo cursed silently. He'd hoped for a half-hour or more. The Mil must have been kept at ready status to have caught their bird so quickly. Now it would be doubling back, and a sharp-eyed pilot would see the snowmobile's trail like a scar across the virgin crust of snow.

Juan slowed just enough for him to open his visor and crank his head around. He shouted over the wind, 'They're on to us.'

Yuri understood the danger and gave Cabrillo a double tap on the shoulder in acknowledgement.

It was a race not only against the chopper now searching for them but also against the setting sun. The Mil doubtlessly had running lights, so once it found their spore, they could keep it lit up as they ran the fleeing pair to ground. On the other hand, Juan couldn't switch on the Lynx's headlamp because it would be the only source of light in the otherwise desolate plane, and the pursuing chopper could cut a vector onto them if they spotted it. He dared not back off the throttle, and he cursed the decision to go with a tinted visor. He could just barely see the white snow through the darkness.

When it got too dark, he thought he could ride with the visor popped up. He tried an experiment. The wind stung like daggers thrust deep into his eye sockets, and he quickly lowered the protective shield. For several seconds he was completely blinded by the tears. So much for that.

They'd just have to trust his reflexes as they continued screaming across the open ground.

Out here it wasn't that big of a deal, there was very little by way of obstacles, but they had to cover several more miles of frozen ocean to reach the *Oregon*.

On they drove, Borodin clinging to the straps while Juan hunched over the handlebars, and the sun sank below the horizon to the west. Somewhere to the east a chopper was hunting them as surely as a hawk searches for prey.

They rapidly approached the coastline and entered a jumbled mess of icy hummocks and crushed leads in a nightmare landscape that appeared impassable. Juan was forced to slow, and no matter how badly it stung, he also had to open his visor. It was just too dark to see through its tinting, and almost too dark to see anything, period.

Despite the Lynx's superb suspension, both men were tossed about as the machine lurched and rolled over the fractured ice. Yuri was forced to loop his arms up to the elbows through the straps and clutch at the seat with his thighs as though he were trying to break an untamed stallion. But still he maintained the presence of mind to scan the sky around them so that the Chairman could concentrate on the path ahead. A particularly bright star caught his attention, and he gazed at it in exhausted wonder.

He'd been so cold for so long – his prison cell never rose above fifty degrees, making sleep nearly impossible – that the warmth of his heated suit was dulling his senses and making his mind drift to near unconsciousness. Only the jarring ride was keeping him awake. The day of his arrest, he'd been in his six-thousand-square-foot apartment in the company of a Burmese courtesan, sipping Cristal. His last real physical ordeal had been basic training when he'd joined the Navy. Brezhnev had been president.

He craved sleep the way a drunk craved alcohol.

But there was something bedazzling about this one particular star that held his attention. It didn't have the cold aloofness of its celestial neighbours, as it straddled the razor's edge between the earth and sky. It pulsed and seemed to grow, almost calling to him, like the way the Sirens called to Odysseus when he was lashed to the mast of his ship. They had tried to draw him to the rocks.

To danger.

To his death.

Stars don't grow!

It was the Mil!

3

Borodin came out of his warmth-induced torpor. He slapped Cabrillo on the shoulder, his shout of warning muffled by his helmet but his urgent squirming making his consternation well understood.

Juan cranked up the throttle, heedless of the rough terrain.

At the same time, a call came over his satellite link. Juan heard Max: 'Bogey just appeared on your six. He came out of the backclutter of the mountains and is flying nap of the earth. We never saw him coming.'

'Are you jamming?'

'Across everything but this frequency,' Hanley replied.

Juan did the calculations in his head and came up short every time he ran the scenario. The chopper would catch them before they reached the ship. He was just about to order Max to shoot the advancing chopper out of the sky when Yuri pounded on his back again more urgently than before. Cabrillo chanced a look over his shoulder to see the sky light up around the Mil like the corona of a black sun.

Multiple launch, most likely from a UB-32 rocket pod suspended off the side of the Mil's fuselage. The range was extreme, and the unguided missiles had a tendency to flare out in a wide swathe, but their explosive warheads were designed to come apart like shrapnel grenades.

Even as he turned to face forward again, Cabrillo could hear Max over the radio link giving the order to fire.

Two miles ahead of them, and still hidden by the ice hillocks, the hatch covering one of the *Oregon*'s multiple 20mm Gatling guns snapped open and the already-spinning pack of six barrels poked from its redoubt. With the sound of some hellish industrial machine, the gun spit out a solid curtain of tungsten rounds. The ship's weapons control systems were so accurate that there was no need to include tracers in the mix of munitions. The chopper and its pilot and crew never saw what was reaching out from the night for them.

The five-second burst filled the air with four hundred rounds, and nearly all of them hit the Mil dead-on or plowed into the flying debris as the aircraft came apart. Then the Mil bloomed as its volatile fuel erupted in a fireball that hung in the sky for many long seconds before gravity took hold and slammed it into the ice like a shooting star coming to earth.

Two rounds had managed to hit the small incoming rockets by pure chance, but still thirty more arced over the ground, fanning out and bracketing the Chairman and Yuri Borodin in a deadly box.

In those last frantic seconds, Cabrillo tried to steer them out of the deadly inbound swarm, but it was as though the ice was actively trying to thwart his efforts. To either side, ridges rose shoulder high and were too

43

steep for even the Lynx to power over. They were trapped in a shallow canyon with no means of escape but through sheer speed.

In an ironic quirk of design, snowmobiles don't do as well on ice as on snow. The tread tends to heat up and cause excessive wear, but at this moment Juan couldn't care less if the track came apart just so long as it did so after they reached the ship.

The first explosions rang out behind them and were muted by the walls of ice, but almost immediately other rockets began landing all around the Lynx, each detonation a bright flower of fire and ice. And steel shrapnel.

The sea ice was shredded by the blasts in a continuing rush of mini-eruptions that turned the air into a whirling boil of snow. More rockets came, in what seemed to be an unending assault. Juan felt the odd tugging as bits of shrapnel passed through his bulky snowsuit, and he had his head thrust to the side when one careened off his helmet's tough plastic shell.

That same moment of impact, Yuri gave a choking, wet gasp and slumped heavily against Cabrillo's back.

Juan knew his friend had been hit but had no idea how badly. The last of the missiles were exploding in their wake as they motored out of the Kill Box. He reached a hand behind him, feeling along Borodin's side, and when he brought his hand back, the white nylon appeared black with blood. With the chopper down, he flicked on the Lynx's headlight. In its glow, he looked more carefully at his hand. The blood was loaded with tiny bursting bubbles, like a thick cherry soda.

Borodin had been lung-shot.

They had a mile to go.

'Max, do you copy?'

'We're right here. Tell me you weren't anywhere near those rockets.'

'Smack-dab in the middle of them. Yuri's hit in the lungs and is hemorrhaging badly. Get Julia down to the boat garage.' Julia Huxley, a Navy-trained physician, was the *Oregon*'s chief medical officer.

'You still want to transfer to the RHIB?' Max asked.

'No time. Move the ship as close as you can to the edge of the ice.'

'That's gonna leave a gap of about two hundred feet.'

Juan didn't hesitate in his reply, 'No problem.' Secretly he thought, Big problem.

The wind had eroded the ice into a ridge that ran eastward in a long arcing curl, as if one of the rolling breakers off Waikiki had been flash-frozen. Juan took the Lynx into it, the throttle cranked until his wrist ached. He could feel Yuri's weight shift down as the machine climbed the ice chute and then was straightened again by the centripetal force of their speed. They dropped out of the flume at its end. The ice became as rough as corrugated steel, forcing Juan to slow fractionally. Every bump and jostle wracked his body like he was being worked over by a prizefighter. He hoped that Borodin had lost consciousness if only to spare him further pain.

He shot the Lynx between two icy hummocks, around a third, and there before him, so tantalizingly close, lay the *Oregon*, every light ablaze so that she looked as cheerful and festive as a cruise ship. Wisps of sea smoke coiled up from the water trapped between the ship and the ice.

From this low vantage he couldn't see that Max was using the ship's bow and stern thrusters to edge the 550-foot vessel closer to the ice sheet, but he knew his old friend was doing everything he could to close the gap.

Terrain be damned, Juan pushed the snow machine until its motor screamed in protest and a rooster tail of ice particles burst from under the studded tread. It looked like they were roaring out of a fogbank of their own creation. He aimed amidships, where a large, garage-style door had been opened. This was the bay where they could launch any number of small watercraft, from eight-man RHIBs to sea kayaks. Light filled the space within, a beacon to Cabrillo and his gravely injured passenger.

'Hold on,' Juan said unnecessarily as they neared the end of the ice pack.

There wasn't a sharp delineation from ice to ocean but instead a gradual fragmentation of the surface below the machine. What was once solid turned into bobbing chunks, and thinned further until the machine was supported by mush the consistency of a convenience store Ice-E. The tread's metal studs found no purchase. It was only their momentum, and what little thrust the track got from skimming across the slurry, that kept them afloat.

And then they were over clear water that was as still as a millpond and hazed by vaporous fingers of fog. Still, the Lynx kept them going, its wake of icy mist turned into a proper tail of creaming water. Juan leaned back as far as he dared to keep the skis from plowing into the sea, a real possibility that would cartwheel the two of them like rag dolls. He saw they were drifting a point or two from their destination and compensated by shifting his body, mindful that Yuri's weight would also factor into the manoeuver. Cabrillo had been snowmobile skipping, as this move was called, a few times, but never with a passenger on the back of the sled and never with the stakes so high.

The Lynx's Rotax engine performed flawlessly, and they skimmed across the water, not with the jerky hops of a flattened stone skipped by a child but with the even power of a craft seemingly built for the task. As they drew closer, the ship loomed larger and larger until it completely blocked Cabrillo's view of the ocean beyond. He realized that speed had become a factor in another way. They were going much too fast to hit the Teflon-coated ramp into the garage. At their current velocity, they would fly up the ramp like a water-skier and crash into the far wall with so much force that the safety netting would tear them to shreds. Yet if he backed off too soon, the Lynx would drop off plane and sink like a brick.

He eased the throttle slightly to get a feel of how the machine would react and a panicked second later opened the taps to full again as the tips of the skis dipped sharply. There were no calculations he could perform. In truth, there were, but he'd need a super-computer or Mark Murphy's brain to do it. This was by gut alone.

To those on the *Oregon*, it looked as though the Lynx's driver was hell-bent on suicide as the sled flew across the water at fifty miles per hour, shooting for the steel side of a freighter that towered over them like a castle over a pair of riders on a horse.

Juan felt he'd left it a moment too late and instinc-tively tensed his body for a crushing hit. In fact, his timing was perfect. Just yards shy of the ramp, he eased off the accelerator and let the Lynx slow until it was pushing a heavy bow wave that ate up even more momentum. The craft entered the hull as it began to founder, and then the skids hit the submerged ramp, and she crawled out of the sea with such perfect control that Cabrillo barely had to tap the brakes to bring them to a gentle stop.

There was a half-second pause, when everything seemed still in his mind, before a team began swarming from behind bulkheads and equipment, wading through churned-up water that sloshed across the ramp and still cascaded off the snowmobile like a gundog shedding water after a retrieve. A warning alarm went off, indicat-ing the garage door was closing. Hands reached for Yuri Borodin to move him onto a waiting stretcher. No sooner was he disentangled from Juan's snowsuit than Juan had flung his helmet aside to check on his friend.

Julia Huxley – Hux or Doc to most of the crew – was

already standing over Borodin while an orderly kept the Russian from falling off the gurney. Dressed in scrubs, and heedless of the freezing water in which she stood, the Navy-trained physician first flipped up the visor of Yuri's helmet.

As if held back by a dam, a wall of blood poured out of the visor opening and down the lower part of his helmet and splashed like a wave across his chest. The helmet had been so tight that whenever Borodin coughed up blood from his punctured lung, it pooled around his jaw and steadily rose with each violent paroxysm. She unstrapped his helmet, certain he had already drowned. But as soon as it came free, dripping more blood into the water still sluicing around her feet, he coughed, spattering her medical face shield and chest.

Juan gave them room as an orderly slapped a scalpel into Julia's hand. She began cutting away the bulky white snowsuit while another aide prepped an IV, ready to refill Yuri's nearly drained veins with Ringer's lactate, as a stopgap until they could get him transfused from the ship's blood bank.

The heavy-duty arctic gear fell away under Hux's knife until Yuri's painfully thin and pale chest was exposed and one arm was laid bare for the IV drip. Froth oozed from the hole in Yuri's skin every time his chest fought to expel air from his body and seemed to suck back into the obscene little mouth on each inhalation. The rest of his exposed body was a sea of welts and mottled bruises from weeks of beatings.

From the red medical case on a nearby rolling tray

Hux grabbed an occlusive patch and tore away the wrapper. This type of battle dressing allowed air to be expelled from the wound but would not let air back in, giving Yuri's collapsed lung a chance to reinflate. She and her team gently rolled Borodin onto his injured side. This position made it easier for the uninjured lung to function. Only then did she whip the stethoscope from around her neck and check for Borodin's heartbeat. She hunted across his bruised and whip-scarred chest like someone with a metal detector sweeping a beach. And like the beachcomber, it appeared she hadn't found what she was looking for.

'BP?' she asked.

'Barely registering,' replied the orderly monitoring the cuff.

'Same with the heartbeat.' Julia looked up to see the Ringer's were flowing wide-open and knew she could do no more here. 'Okay, people, let's get him to medical.' Her voice had the crisp command of a person who was in complete charge.

She exchanged a glance with Cabrillo, her sombre dark eyes telling him everything he needed to know.

'Nyet,' Borodin wheezed. Somehow he levered open his eyes.

'Sorry, no nyet yet,' Hux said, laying a hand on Yuri's arm. 'Let's move it!'

'Nyet,' Borodin managed to rasp again. 'Ivan?' He called to Juan, using his Russian name.

Juan leapt forward so he stood over Yuri's supine body. 'Easy, my friend. You're going to be okay.'

Borodin smiled a bloody smile, his teeth stained crimson like a shark's after a meal. *'Nyet,'* Yuri said a third time. 'Kenin.'

'I know all about Pytor Kenin,' Juan assured him.

'Chairman,' Hux said edgily.

'One second.' Juan didn't want to look at the rebuke on her face. He knew as well as she did that every second counted. He also knew that Yuri Borodin understood this fact even better than them.

Borodin coughed, and the effort seemed to tear something deep within his body. He winced, his eyes screwed tight as he rode a wave of pain. 'Aral.'

The word dribbled from his lips.

'The Aral Sea?' Juan asked. 'What about it?'

'Eerie boat.'

'I don't understand.' Juan could see – all of them could see – that Borodin had seconds left.

'What about the Aral Sea and an eerie boat?'

'Find Karl Petrov – Pe-trov –' The syllables came further and further apart. Juan bent down so his ear was barely an inch from his friend's bloody mouth. 'Petrovski.'

The effort to get the name out was the last gasp of a dying man. His skin, if possible, looked even paler, more translucent, like the waxy rind of one of Madame Tussauds' dummies.

'Yuri?' Juan called with a desperation he knew would go unanswered. 'Yuri?'

Borodin's Adam's apple gave one final thrust, one more attempt to speak. With his lung so full of blood, there was hardly enough air to form his dying word. It whispered past his unmoving lips already laced with the icy touch of death. 'Tesla.'

Julia pushed Juan out of the way, rolled Borodin onto his back, and leapt atop the gurney so she was astride her patient like a jockey on a horse. She was a curvy though petite woman, but when she started chest compressions she did it with strength and vigour. The orderlies took up positions to guide the rolling stretcher to the Level 1 trauma centre within the labyrinthine corridors of the *Oregon*'s secret passages.

Cabrillo watched them disappear through a watertight door, blew out a long breath, and then moved to an intercom box mounted on a wall. He barely noticed the crewmen securing the boat garage from battle stations.

'Op centre,' came the voice of Max Hanley. Not knowing the situation, Max wisely kept his usual repertoire of bad humour and sarcastic remarks to himself.

'Max, get us out of here,' Juan said, as if leaving the scene of the act could somehow bury the fact. 'This mission was a bust.'

'Aye, Chairman,' Max replied gently. 'Aye.'

4

He sat slouched against the corner of his desk for the next fifteen minutes, his cabin lights dim, his eyes pointed at the floor but seeing nothing. The space had been his home for years. Its current inspiration was the set of Rick's Café from the movie *Casablanca* and had been pulled off with some of Kevin Nixon's Hollywood set-designing friends. Usually it was a place of solace for Cabrillo. Today, until the phone rang, it was merely a void.

The replica Bakelite phone trilled, and he snatched up the handset before the first ring ended. He said nothing.

'I'm sorry, Juan.' It was Julia Huxley. 'I just called it. He's gone.'

'Thanks, Hux,' Cabrillo said in a monotone. 'I know you did all you could.'

He settled the heavy handset back onto its cradle.

From the brief exchange of looks he'd shared with the ship's physician back in the boat garage, he'd known the inevitability of Yuri's death but couldn't motivate himself to do anything until he'd received verification. He'd failed. It didn't matter that he'd busted Yuri out of the prison and got him to within a mile of the *Oregon*. Juan blew out another long breath.

Cabrillo stripped off the remains of his snowsuit and stuffed it and his prison garb and the bloody boots into a plastic bag for incineration. He strode into a green-marble bathroom and hit the brass taps of a multiheaded, glass-enclosed shower that was big enough to hold six. As steam began pouring over the top of the enclosure, he unstrapped his artificial leg, gave the toughened skin of his stump a quick massage, and then stepped into the hot spray.

There were usually just two items in his shower, a bar of plain soap and generic shampoo. Though Juan was a bit of a clotheshorse, like most men his personal grooming was minimalist.

Today there was a third item and from it he poured some yellowish gel into his palm and felt its chemical burn over the heat of the water. He smeared his hand across his bald head and began working it into his skin. Kevin Nixon had explained the chemical process that would dissolve the ersatz tattoos he'd painted across half the Chairman's body, but formulae and reactivity coefficients were meaningless when the solution felt like it was not only melting off the ink but his skin as well.

The water sluicing off his head turned grey as the ink began to run.

It took fifteen minutes of searing agony to remove the tattoos to the point they looked like faint, week-old contusions that would fade away completely in a couple of days. He could have spared himself the pain and let them wane on their own, but having them on his body somehow reminded him of the mark of Cain.

He towelled off and swiped clear a spot in the mirror over the vanity, deciding at first glance that for a while, at least, a hat was in order. The baldness was shocking enough – he usually sported thick blond hair trimmed neatly by the ship's barber – but the faint blue cast left by residual ink made him look like a reject from Dr Frankenstein's lab.

He looked past the faded ink and decided that if his hairline ever did go into retreat, as it had with two uncles on his mother's side – an ill omen – he would shave it all off. With his broad swimmer's shoulders and height, he thought he could pull it off. He thought he looked more Yul Brynner than Telly Savalas.

He hopped through his cabin to the closet. The leg he'd worn on the mission would go down to the Magic Shop for cleaning and maintenance. Lined up like boots at a shoe store, the back of his walk-in had a selection of artificial limbs for any number of occasions. Some were designed to mimic his real leg right down to the coarseness of his hair, while others were metallic monstrosities out of science fiction. He chose a flesh-coloured plastic limb and snugged the top sock over his stump, making sure there were no wrinkles that would later chafe his skin.

It had been more than five years since a shell fired from a Chinese gunboat had severed the limb below the knee, and not a day went by that the missing portion of his leg didn't hurt. Phantom pain, doctors called it. To those who suffered through it there was nothing phantom about it.

He dressed in a pair of jeans, an Oregon State sweat-shirt and a pair of sneakers. He'd gone to UCLA for his undergraduate degree. The Oregon shirt was a hat tip to the ship. He slipped on an original L. A. Raiders baseball cap that had belonged to his grandfather, a season-ticket-holder for the twelve years they were in the City of Angels, and worn only at home games. He hadn't worn it in so long, he had to reshape the bill.

It was only as he turned away from the walk-in closet that he noticed the plastic bag containing his soiled clothes had been removed and a silver server had been placed on the white alabaster bar in the corner of his cabin. Next to it was a single glass of wine that glowed like liquid ruby in the subdued lighting.

He chuckled a little ruefully.

An hour ago he'd been so hyper-aware of his surroundings that he still retained the muscle memory of every turn, bounce and shudder of the ride from the forest until the moment the snow machine came to rest in the *Oregon*'s boat garage. Yet now, back in what had been his home for so many years, his guard had so dropped that he hadn't noticed when one of the ship's stewards, most likely the septuagenarian chief steward Maurice, had padded into his cabin as he was in the shower and removed the dirty clothes while bringing Cabrillo his supper. Had the man been an assassin, Juan wouldn't have stood a chance.

He plucked the silver dome off the serving tray and was greeted by a rich, spicy aroma. He justified to himself that if there was any safe place for him on the planet, it was aboard the *Oregon* surrounded by her amazing crew. The embossed card resting on the plate said the meal was bison chilli served in a French bread *boule*, and the wine was a Philip Togni cabernet sauvignon.

Maurice, who'd spent his career in the Royal Navy as the personal steward for at least a dozen admirals, was a superb sommelier, and Juan was certain the wine paired beautifully with the dish, but tonight wasn't a wine night. There was a minifridge tucked under the bar, and from it Cabrillo slipped out a bottle of plain Stolichnaya vodka and two chilled shot glasses. No sooner had he filled them than there was a knock on the door. Max Hanley came through without being invited.

'In the movie,' Max said, crossing the room to take the barstool next to Cabrillo, 'Bogie eventually asked Sam to play "As Time Goes By". Just so you know, I can't even play "Chopsticks".'

Juan smiled a bit. 'Truth is, I didn't have room for a piano in here anyway.' He handed one of the shot glasses to Max and hoisted the second. 'To Yuri Borodin.'

'To Yuri,' Max echoed, and they both downed the vodka.

Max Hanley was the first person Cabrillo hired when he'd formed the Corporation on the recommendation of his CIA mentor Langston Overholt IV. Hanley had been running a scrapyard in Southern California at the time and had given Juan's offer less than a minute's thought before accepting. Prior to that he'd been involved in marine engineering and salvage, and before that he'd commanded Swift Boats on nearly every navigable inch of river in South Vietnam.

Heavyset, with a florid complexion, a crescent of ginger hair ringing the back half of his skull, and a nose that had been broken enough times that he could have been mistaken for a professional boxer, Max was the details man of the outfit. No matter how crazy the scheme Cabrillo dreamt up, Max was there to see it pulled off.

'I already broke the news to Misha Kasporov,' Hanley said without looking Juan in the eye.

That task rightly fell to the Chairman, but Cabrillo was grateful his number two had told Mikhail Kasporov of his boss's fate. He toasted Hanley with a refill and downed it with a little shudder.

'He asked that we bury Yuri at sea with Russian military honours,' Max went on. 'I had Mark pull up the appropriate ceremony off the Internet.' He handed Juan a piece of paper.

Cabrillo scanned the ceremony. Typical Russian, it was maudlin and somewhat bombastic but with a dutiful sense of patriotism, which, he supposed, summed up Yuri. 'Tell the crew we'll hold the ceremony at 07:30.'

'And not that you particularly give a damn tonight,' Max continued, 'but Misha held to the contract to get Yuri out of jail. The rest of the money's been transferred to our temporary account on the Caymans.'

Juan raised another shot. 'Honour amongst thieves.'

'Amen.' Hanley pointed at Cabrillo's dinner. 'Are you going to eat that?'

Cabrillo pulled the plate closer. 'Actually, I am. I'm starved. You can have my wine if you want.'

Max went around the bar to retrieve two fresh icy shot glasses from the fridge and refilled them from the bottle of Stoli. 'Pass.'

'Misha knows his life isn't worth a plug nickel,' Juan said as he dipped a spoon into his chilli.

'We discussed that. He knew the score and is already on the move. He says he has a bolt-hole someplace in Africa where Kenin will never find him.'

Cabrillo nodded noncommittally. He knew of dozens of dead or jailed fugitives who thought they'd never be found. But Kasporov wasn't his responsibility. 'Any word from Linda?'

Linda Ross was the *Oregon*'s number three. An elfish woman who had hit the glass ceiling in the Navy, she was currently on another assignment with one of the Corporation's regular clients.

'She and the Emir have left Monaco on his yacht and are en route to Bermuda.'

The Emir of one of the United Arab Emirates insisted that he travel with members of the Corporation whenever he left his native land, even though he was always accompanied by a virtual army of bodyguards. Usually he insisted that the *Oregon* shadow his 300-foot mega-yacht, *Sakir*, but the ship was needed to rescue Yuri, so he'd been mollified by having Linda as his travelling companion.

Max went on, 'We'll have no trouble catching up

with them once we clear some of the ice still floating around up here.'

When Juan converted the *Oregon* into the hybrid warship/intelligence-gathering vessel she was today, the modifications included the ability to break through ice nearly three feet thick. However, in these northern waters, drifting bergs posed the most serious threat, and the *Oregon*, even with her armoured sides, could be torn open as easily as the *Titanic* by a glancing blow. It wouldn't be until they were clear of the danger that they could open the taps on the most powerful engines afloat. Her revolutionary magnetohydrodynamic engines could push the ship through the water at a rate not much below some offshore power racers.

'Is the Emir behaving himself?' Juan asked with fatherly concern.

'He's eighty. Linda says apart from a few perfunctory passes, he reminds her of her grandfather.' Max had a bulldog face, a canvas of a lifetime of experiences writ large. Suddenly his jowls seemed to grow and his brow furled until it was corduroyed. 'Something tells me that Linda's going to be on her own for a while longer, yes?'

'Not sure,' Juan said, tearing a hunk of crusty, chilli-soaked bread from the *boule* and popping it in his mouth. 'Just before Yuri died, he implicated Admiral Pytor Kenin –'

'No surprise there,' Max interrupted.

'No,' Juan agreed. 'Kenin is behind the frame-up, but I don't think that's what Yuri was talking about.'

'What, then?'

'He mentioned the Aral Sea and someone named Petrovski. Karl Petrovski.'

Max leaned back into his barstool, his bullet head cocked to the side. 'Never heard of him.'

'Me neither. Then Yuri said something like "eerie boat".'

'Eerie boat?'

'Eerie boat. Don't ask. I have no idea. But his last word was "Tesla".'

'As in Nikola?'

'I have to assume so. The Serbian inventor who basically created the modern electrical grid.'

'And a heck of a lot more,' Hanley added. 'Everyone knows about Thomas Edison and his contributions to modern society, but few have ever heard of Tesla. Well, apart from the new electric sports car named after him. Tesla was an über-genius. Some of his ideas –'

Juan cut him off, a classic case of who knew more about what. 'I saw a documentary on cable about how Edison tried to convince people that his DC theory was safer than Tesla's alternating current by electro-cuting elephants in New York City.'

'This was the dawn of a new age,' Max said. 'The stakes couldn't have been higher.'

'But, come on. Electrocuting elephants to prove a point?'

'In the end, showmanship did pay off, in a way. AC won out over Edison's DC system, yet we all know Edison's name, and Tesla remains a footnote in history. Sometimes history favours the activist more than the activity.'

'So where does this leave us?'

'Trondheim,' Juan replied.

'Excuse me?'

'Trondheim, Norway. I need to get to the Aral Sea as soon as possible. I assume Trondheim is the closest city with an airport. You can drop me off on the way to the North Sea, and eventually the Atlantic and Bermuda.'

Max took in Juan's suggestion for a second, his jaw drooping. When he spoke, he chose his words very carefully. 'Eerie boat. Aral Sea. Karl Petrovski.' He waited a beat. 'You see a connection?'

'No. I don't. But Yuri did.' Cabrillo wiped his mouth with his napkin and set it on the bar next to his mostly cleared plate. He crossed to his desk phone, checked his watch, and dialled an extension. He found Eric Stone in his cabin as he'd expected.

'What's up, Chairman?' Stone was another Navy veteran, but an R and D guy, not a blue water sailor.

'Is Mark with you?' Stone and Mark Murphy were practically conjoined twins.

'Yeah, we're moderating a debate on the Net between *Hunger Games* fans.'

Cabrillo was vaguely aware those were a series of books and movies but had no idea what they were about or how two of his crewmen could be involved in an online debate. Nor did he particularly care. But Eric added, 'Mark got his masters with the studio wonk charged with Internet promotions.'

'You have my sympathies.'

'We need them. I had forgotten how catty teenage girls can be, and they use language that certainly makes this sailor blush.'

'I need you two to do some digging for me. First, though, I want you to book me the fastest flight from Trondheim to the airport closest to the Aral Sea.'

'That would be Uralsk Airport in Kazakhstan,' Eric interjected.

How Stone retained such arcane information was a mystery to Cabrillo, but it made him one of the best researchers in the business. 'Next, I want you to dig up everything you can find on a Karl Petrovski.' Cabrillo spelled it out for him. 'That name won't be too uncommon, so concentrate on anyone connected to the Aral Sea, Admiral Pytor Kenin, or Nikola Tesla.'

'I get Kenin's name thrown into the mix, he's the guy behind Yuri Borodin's arrest. But what does Tesla have to do with anything?'

'Haven't a clue, but it was the last thing Yuri said before he died.'

Eric paused to absorb this information. 'I'm sorry, Juan. Mark and I knew he'd been hit but we didn't know he died.'

'You guys are off duty and couldn't have known.'

'Just so you understand, with the sea state and all, I won't have an ETA into Trondheim for at least twelve hours.'

'I know. Do your best.' Cabrillo hung up and rejoined Hanley at the bar. He accepted another shot of vodka.

'What's your gut telling you?' Max asked.

'One, that if I do too many more of these,' he downed the drink, 'I'm going to feel it in the morning.'

'And two?'

'The timing of Yuri's jailing wasn't coincidental. I think he discovered something about Admiral Kenin and that something has to do with Nikola Tesla and the Aral Sea.'

'But what?'

'Until Stoney and Murph come up with some information, I have no idea. But because Yuri died passing this on to me, I intend to find out.'

Those who knew Juan Cabrillo understood that when his mind was set on a task, there wasn't much in the world that would stop him. And anyone who tried would come to understand the true nature of determination.

5

The boat was rigged for ultraquiet. They were fifteen miles off California, and there was an American Coast Guard cutter cruising lazily on its way south to San Diego. The cutter was less than four miles away, and while the submarine wasn't actively pinging with her sonar, her crew couldn't afford being detected. Though they were in international waters, the presence of a diesel-powered attack submarine so close to the American coast would bring a swift and deadly response.

While the cutter herself didn't have much in the way of armaments to take out the Tango-class submarine, they could dog the sub using their sonar until a strike aircraft could be called in from any number of naval air stations. They had come too far to blow it this late in the mission. If it meant an hour or two delay to lurk quietly under the surface until the cutter was out of range, so be it. Patience and silence were the two cardinal virtues of a submariner.

The trip north had taken them more than a week, most of that time spent well outside normal shipping routes and running at snorkel depth so the boat's three diesel engines could draw air. Only when sonar reported a nearby ship, usually one headed inbound from Asia as they came abreast of ports along the US and Mexican west coasts, would they retract the snorkel and dive out of sight.

While normally crewed by seventeen officers and sixty-one seamen, this particular sub had only two dozen men aboard, and the captain couldn't have been prouder of them.

'Sonar, sit-rep,' he whispered. He was standing behind the man hunched over the antiquated passive sonar system.

The sailor slipped off the one headphone he'd had plastered to his right ear. 'The cutter's still moving away at eight knots. I put him at five miles distant.'

In relative terms, five miles was a tricky distance. It was only a five-minute drive by car or it was a two-hour walk. At sea, with sound able to travel so far through the vastness, five miles could be considered shouting distance.

'Any indication he's towing an array of his own?'

'No, sir,' the sailor whispered back. 'If he was, he'd cut his engines to drift. Otherwise, he couldn't hear anything over his own propellers.'

The man suddenly tightened the headphone to his skull once again. It was as if speaking of it made it happen. 'Captain! His screws just went silent. He's drifting!'

The captain placed a restraining hand on the younger man's shoulders. 'Steady, son. He can't hear us if we don't make a sound.'

The boy looked sheepish. 'Yes, sir.'

'We're nothing but a three-hundred-foot-long quiet spot in the ocean. Nothing to hear here. Just move along.'

The captain looked across the confined conn. The low-ceilinged room was as claustrophobic as a crypt, and with the red battle lights glowing the men appeared demonic. In the centre of the space the periscope hung from the ceiling like a metallic stalactite. Around it were clustered the helm station, the engineering monitoring space, the captain's chair, and several other work-stations. The sub was so old that all its readouts were on analogue displays and simple dials, not unlike those of a World War Two-era boat. The air was somewhat chilly, and with the sub running off her batteries, amps weren't squandered on extra heating. And yet several men still had sweat on their faces. The tension was palpable.

'The cutter is still drifting, Captain.'

'That's okay, lad. Let him drift. He has no idea we're here.'

They had been running ultraquiet for the better part of an hour since first detecting and identifying the cutter from a database of acoustic signals stored on magnetic tapes – another piece of antiquated technology that illustrated the Tango-class's '70s roots. So when an internal alarm sounded, it was especially shrill and piercing.

The seaman closest to the alarm held true to his training. Most men would have remained frozen for a few crucial seconds as their brain processed the source of the intrusive noise, but he moved with the speed of a cat and hit a toggle that muted the klaxon. Half of the red battle lamps began to pulse as a visual cue that an emergency was under way.

Time seemed suspended as the men exchanged nervous glances. They now faced two dangers: one, the American cutter that had been listening for sounds in the abyss with a towed sonar array that could pick up the slightest anomalous noise – one Cold War story told of how a Soviet sub had been tracked for its entire four-thousand-mile journey because one crewman popped his gum whenever he was alone – and, two, whatever the boat's sensors had detected was life-threatening enough to warrant a tripped alarm.

The answer to that second danger came moments later when a wisp of smoke coiled from one of the overhead ventilators. Even as the crew turned to watch, that wisp became a white, opaque torrent.

More than drowning, submariners feared fire.

And it was obvious that the boat was burning.

The captain's gaze swept the bridge, pausing for only the briefest moment on one particular figure before moving on. There would be no help there. He focused on his executive officer. 'XO, lock down that fire no matter what it takes. Silence must be maintained.'

'Sir,' the man said, and rushed forward where the smoke seemed to be thickest.

'Sonar, sit-rep?' the captain asked with studied disinterest. He needed to show his crew there was no need to panic. Inside, his guts felt oily.

'Contact still drifting,' the sonarman replied, one hand pressing the headphone so tightly, his fingers had gone white.

'Did he hear us?'

'He heard, all right. He just doesn't know what he heard.'

'If you were him, what would you do?'

'Sir?'

'Answer me. If you were listening on his passive array and heard that alarm, what would you do?'

'Um,' the sailor hesitated.

'Simple question. Tell me. What would you do?'

'I would turn my ship to our bearing and tow the array once again, hoping to pick up another transient emission.'

The captain knew the correct answer, the one his young sonarman had given, but his instincts told him to abandon the bridge and follow his XO. The fire was the immediate emergency. The American cutter was secondary. And yet training dictated otherwise. He must remain on the bridge. It was a good leader's ability to acknowledge the disconnect between instinct and training that kept crews alive. The most immediate threat to the sub wasn't the fire at all. It remained the Coast Guard vessel.

He waited with the rest of his men, his eyes glued to the big clock over the planesman's station. The cutter continued to drift and listen on her passive array.

At the six-minute mark, he let out a little of the breath he felt he'd been holding since the alarm sounded. At seven minutes, he exhaled the rest.

'I think he's missed us, boys,' he whispered.

Just then, the XO returned.

'Sir, it was a small grease fire in the galley. Nothing's been damaged.'

'Captain, the cutter's engines just came back online. She's gaining seaway.'

'Is she turning?'

The wait seemed endless, but the young sailor suddenly turned to look at his captain, a big grin splitting his face. 'She's headed due south and is already up to eight knots.'

'Well done, everyone,' the captain said in an almost normal tone of voice. He looked over at the stoic face of Admiral Pytor Kenin. He wasn't sure what to expect, so he was pleasantly surprised that the man gave him a grudging nod of respect.

Kenin had been leaning against a bulkhead and suddenly pushed himself erect and called out, 'Evolution complete.'

The red battle lights clicked off, and overhead lamps bathed the sub's control room in stark white light. Technicians who'd been unseen moments before entered the space to check on equipment, while the sailors manning the various stations got up from their seats. Their bodies were as exhausted and tensed up as if this had been a real encounter and not a training exercise. And yet there was a feeling of self-satisfaction among them for a job well done.

'Congratulations, Captain Escobar,' Kenin said when he reached the man's side, a hand extended for a shake. He spoke English, the only language the two men shared.

'For a moment I thought we had failed,' Jesus Escobar admitted. 'A most inopportune time for a simulated fire.'

'A good sub captain can handle one crisis at a time; the great ones can handle more.'

Escobar allowed himself a smile at the compliment.

Kenin continued, 'This completes your training, Captain. You and your men are ready to put to sea.'

'The cartel will be pleased to hear that. They've spent a great deal of money on this venture, and it is now time that our new toy be put to use.'

'Didn't you tell me when you arrived here at Sakhalin that you would need just two runs up to California from Colombia for your cartel to turn a profit?'

'Yes,' Escobar replied, smoothing down his dark moustache. 'With just a skeleton crew and enough fuel for the trip up and back, we can load several hundred tons of cocaine into this boat.'

'You've proven to me that you will manage much more than two runs, my friend.' Kenin threw an arm around Escobar's shoulder, which emphasized the physical difference between the two men. Where the Colombian narco-trafficker was built like most sub-mariners, five foot six and lean of muscle, the Russian admiral brushed the ceiling at six foot three. He was a typical bear of a man, solidly built and possessing an iron constitution. 'Tonight I will hold a celebration in honour of you and your men and the three long months you've trained here. Tomorrow you will sleep that off, and tomorrow night, under cover of darkness, we will release your boat from the floating dry dock and you will head home.'

'You do us an honour, Admiral.'

'Debrief your men, Captain, and I will see you later.'

Kenin turned to climb the ladder up into the Tango's sail, where one of his men waited to open the outer hatch. The simulation had lasted for nearly five hours, and Kenin was desperate for some fresh air, but he would have to wait a while longer. The 300-foot sub lay in the bowels of a fully enclosed floating dry dock nearly three times its size, which itself was docked at a near-derelict Navy station that Kenin used as his own private domain. He dropped down an exterior ladder and crossed a movable ramp to a catwalk that ran the length of the dry dock. The cavernous space smelled of the sea on which the Tango floated, oil, and rust. Powerful lights on the ceiling could do little to dispel the gloom.

He walked with a long-legged, hurried stride, as was his custom, and reached a flight of stairs that would take him to an exterior hatch. It was only when he passed through that door and stepped onto the open deck that he filled his lungs with air. The sun had long since set, and the breeze was freshening. The temperature stood at about forty degrees, and he knew from experience that once winter hit, minus forty would be the norm.

Another ramp led to the old Navy pier. The dock was failing concrete and frost-heaved pavement with gnarls of weeds growing wherever the cracks allowed. Obscuring his view landward were dilapidated warehouses whose paint had long been scoured off by the winds that shrieked down from Siberia. A car was waiting for him, its driver standing erect at the first sign of Kenin's emergence from the dock.

The man saluted smartly and opened the rear door. Kenin slid into the rich leather seat and immediately pulled his encrypted cell phone from his pocket. There was no signal inside the sub, and he'd missed a dozen calls. For now he'd return just one, from his aide-de-camp, Commander Viktor Gogol.

'Gogol, it's Kenin.'

'Admiral, how did it go?'

'They'll sail tomorrow night.'

'I've been assured by the dockworkers that the device is ready,' Gogol said.

'How the Colombians ever thought I would allow them to buy a surplus submarine to haul cocaine to America is beyond me. Escobar seems capable enough, but the US Navy would be on him five minutes after he left South America. It takes years to properly train a crew to evade American sonar. These fools actually think they've mastered their boat in just three months.'

'If you recall, Admiral, originally they wanted just a week of instruction before they took possession of the boat.'

'I do recall. They wouldn't even have known how to get her out of dry dock. Like I said, they're fools. It's better this way. The cartel will make their final payment to me just before the sub sails, and then when it dives to a depth of two hundred feet, the ballast intakes will jam open and it will sink to the bottom of the Pacific. No witnesses, and no blowback from the cartel. So tell me, Viktor, why did you call?'

'We have a problem,' Gogol said in such a way that Kenin leaned forward.

'Go on.'

'Borodin has escaped.'

Kenin went from contentment to rage as though a switch had been thrown. 'What? How did this happen?'

'A new prisoner was brought in, part of a routine transfer. It appears that this man was an impostor sent to free Borodin. He somehow smuggled in explosives. They blasted their way out of the prison and had a helicopter waiting to pick them up.'

Rage couldn't describe the emotions welling up from the void in his chest where normal men had a heart. 'Go on,' he said with his teeth tightly clenched.

'The prison launched their own chopper in pursuit and shot down the first aircraft. When they investigated, they discovered that the helicopter was remotely piloted. There was no sign of Borodin or the fake prisoner. When they backtracked, they discovered a set of snowmobile tracks heading north. The last anyone heard from them was during the pursuit.'

'What do you mean "the last anyone heard from them"?'

'Sir, this happened three hours ago. There has been no word from the flight crew. Another chopper has been searching, but there's been no sign. They fear it either crashed or was shot down over water and sank.'

Pytor Kenin hadn't achieved the rank of admiral or created for himself a private army within Russia's military without being both bold and ruthless, and never was he at a loss for decisions. 'The guards who let the prisoner smuggle in explosives, I want them jailed immediately. Put them in general population, and let the inmates mete out justice on them. I want the warden replaced immediately, and I want that man in my office when I return to Moscow.'

'Yes, sir,' Gogol replied.

Kenin went on. 'We have to assume Borodin made it aboard some waiting ship. Track all known vessels that were in the area, where they came from, who owns them, everything.'

'Yes, sir.'

'If Borodin's alive, that puts the Mirage Project at risk. He has no proof of anything, so it will just be his word. We need to ensure that he can't find proof. Do you understand?'

'I believe so, Admiral.'

'I want every loose end, no matter how tenuous, eliminated.'

'Do we inform the Chinese?'

'Absolutely not. We can contain this. We need just a few days. Then we will hold our demonstration, and after that it's up to them.' Kenin allowed himself to settle back into his seat as the car crossed the defunct base and headed to the prefab house he had been staying in whenever he visited the Colombians. They were paying him thirty million dollars for the sub and the training of its crew, the least he could do was give them some face time every once in a while. As soon as the Tango departed, the dry dock would be towed back to

Vladivostok and the prefab home dismantled and returned there as well.

'Viktor, one more thing.'

'Sir?'

'The next time you have news of this importance, do not ask me questions about how training went. It wastes my time.'

'Yes, Admiral. I am sorry, sir.'

'Don't be sorry, just don't do it again.' Kenin had another thought. 'I assume Borodin's rescue was arranged by his little bootlick, Misha Kasporov. See to it that he dies as well.'

'That order went out as soon as I heard about the escape. He'd already gone to ground, but we'll find him.'

'There's hope for you yet.'

6

Nukus, Uzbekistan

In the end, Eric Stone's odd knowledge of regional Central Asian airports proved ineffectual. Cabrillo wasn't headed to the reasonably stable nation of Kazakhstan but rather to its more rough-and-tumble neighbour to the south. Uzbekistan had an abysmal human rights record, no freedom of the press, and when the nation's large cotton harvest – its principal cash crop – was ready to be brought in from the fields, forced labour was often employed. While it was not as corrupt as other former Soviet states in this part of the world, given a choice, Cabrillo would have been happy to avoid coming here.

According to Eric Stone's research, Karl Petrovski had been forty-two when he died in a hit-and-run accident and had been a respected hydrologist with degrees from both Moscow University and the Berlin Institute of Technology. His most recent employment had been with the government of Uzbekistan, copying the success Kazakhstan was starting to show in reversing the devastation wrought by the Soviets and their ill-conceived irrigation projects of the 1940s and '50s.

Prior to the Soviet intervention, the Aral Sea had

77

been one of the world's largest, with an area greater than lakes Huron and Ontario combined. The Aral supported a vibrant fishing and tourist industry and was the lifeblood of the region. In an effort to boost cotton production in the surrounding deserts, the Soviet engineers diverted water from the two rivers that fed the Aral, the Amu and Syr, into massive canal networks, most of which leaked more than half the water forced through them. By the 1960s the lake level began to drop dramatically.

The Soviets knew that this would be the result of their engineering, but a centrally planned government gave short shrift to the environmental impacts of their scheme. A half century later, the Aral Sea, which meant 'the Sea of Islands,' had so shrivelled it was now several separate bodies of brackish water that could scarcely support life. In fact, its current salinity was three times that of the world's oceans. The once great fishing fleets now stood rusted and abandoned upon a barren desert. The shrinking of the Aral Sea changed local weather patterns, heating the air and diminishing seasonal rainfalls. Dust, salt and pesticide runoff from the cotton fields further poisoned the land until all that remained was a vista as desolate as the moon.

The one bright spot in the sad history of the area was that the Kazakh government was working to redirect water back into the North Aral Sea in an attempt to revitalize the lake. Already, the lakeshore was creeping back toward the main port city of Aralsk from a maximum distance of some sixty miles. Commercial fishing was beginning to return, and microclimate changes were occurring that saw an increase in rain.

In a belated attempt to emulate their northern neighbours, the Uzbeks were now looking at the feasibility of a similar scheme. Karl Petrovski had been a member of the team that first saw success in Kazakhstan and had been working for the past year to duplicate that success once again.

Cabrillo doubted Petrovski's work in this field was what had gotten him killed. It was something either connected to Nikola Tesla, which seemed unlikely, or to the mysterious eerie boat, which no amount of research had unearthed even a hint of.

That brought the Chairman to this loveless, windswept outpost that had to be considered the hind end of the globe. Stepping out from the glass-fronted airport after a flight south from Moscow's Domodedovo Airport, Cabrillo hit a wall of seared air and salty dust. He quickly slipped on a pair of sunglasses and hiked his shoulder bag a little higher on his back. The passport he'd used for this trip identified him as a Canadian photojournalist, and the papers he carried stated he was working on a piece he hoped to sell to *National Geographic* magazine.

While transiting through Russia, he'd worn a sports coat, an open-necked white shirt and scuffed dress shoes, but he'd discarded that look in favour of the *de rigueur* of photographers the world over: khakis, boots, and a vest festooned with countless equipment pouches. He carried a second bag that contained a Nikon SLR, a few lenses and enough other paraphernalia to complete the cover.

There were pluses and minuses for such a disguise. In a nation like Uzbekistan where the media was heavily repressed, snapping pictures to one's heart's content invariably drew the attention of the authorities. Since Juan had no intention of removing the camera from its bag near any government buildings or military bases, it shouldn't be a problem.

On the plus side, thieves usually understood that photographers rarely had anything on them worth stealing other than their cameras, and they always reported such thefts to the police, who in turn usually knew who was responsible and, not wanting to give their homeland a bad name, made quick arrests.

Safe from the government, safe from would-be muggers. He ignored the shouted plaints of taxi drivers promising good rates to the nearby city and focused on a battered UAZ-469. The utilitarian Russian jeep had probably rolled off the assembly line about the same time Cabrillo was being potty-trained. The bodywork was a blend of bare metal patches, matte dun paint and dust, and was so dented and wrinkled it looked like the skin of a shar-pei.

The young man standing next to it holding a cigarette in one hand and a handwritten placard with the name Smith on it in the other watched the crowds exiting the terminal with the predatory patience of a hunting falcon. When he saw Cabrillo break from the pack of travellers negotiating cab fares and stride toward him, he ditched the smoke and plastered on a tobacco-stained smile.

'Mr Smith, yes?'

'I'm Smith,' Cabrillo said, and accepted an outstretched hand for an enthusiastic shake.

'I am Osman,' the young man said with an almost impenetrable accent. 'Welcome to Uzbekistan. You are indeed most welcome. I am told to meet you here with my most fine desert truck, and, as you can see, she is a beautiful.'

Russian was the universal tongue among the various tribes and subtribes in the region, and Cabrillo could have saved the rental representative from speaking tortured English, but there were few Canadian photojournalists fluent in it, so he stuck to English.

'She is beautiful,' Juan replied, casting a sidelong glance at the small trickle of oil that oozed from under the chassis.

'I am not told that you will need driver, yes?'

That was the guy's angle, Juan realized. Hiring out a 4×4 was one thing, a non-negotiable fee listed on the company's archaic website. Osman wanted the lucrative contract to be Cabrillo's driver and personal tour guide for the four days Cabrillo had contracted for the UAZ.

'You were not told that because I do not need a driver.'

Then Cabrillo threw him a bone. 'I would be happy to pay you if you can get me extra cans of gasoline.'

'So you go deep into desert?'

'Not so deep that I cannot return.'

The Uzbek thought this was a grand joke and laughed until he coughed. He lit another smoke.

Juan enjoyed an occasional cigar so didn't begrudge anyone a hit of nicotine, but he couldn't imagine smoking cigarettes in a dust bowl, choking with so much grit that his teeth felt like sandpaper and his lungs like two half-empty bags of cement.

'Okay,' Osman replied decisively, then asked, a bit shier, 'Maybe after you drop me at my office in town?'

It was something Cabrillo had always enjoyed about the Middle East and Central Asia, everyone was always fishing for something more out of a deal. Didn't matter how insignificant so long as the other guy gave up just a fraction more than you. To most Westerners, it was seen as deceitful and greedy, but, in truth, such negotiations were a test of each other's character. Accept too quick and you were dismissed as a rube; push too hard and you were a snob. The balance defined what kind of person you were.

'Agreed.' Cabrillo nodded and held out a hand to finalize the deal, then said, as their palms touched, 'But only if you have a glass of tea for me back at your office.'

Osman's smile returned, and it was much more genuine than the salesman's smarm he'd displayed before. 'I like you, Mr Smith. You are A-OK.'

The diversion of having tea with Osman would only take up a few minutes, but being called A-OK by this young Uzbek hustler made Juan smile for the first time since Borodin's death.

The road north to the former seaside town of Muynak was a kidney-jarring ribbon of cracked asphalt, made worse by the UAZ's nonexistent suspension.

The terrain was flat, windswept desert with the occasional clump of faded vegetation. The only thing Cabrillo saw of any interest were double-humped Bactrian camels. They were shorter than their single-humped cousins and had tufts of heavy fur along their necks and crowning each fatty hump. He wasn't sure if these belonged to anyone or were wild. But by the way they passively regarded him as he drove along the lonely highway, it was obvious they were used to man.

Muynak was only a hundred and twenty miles from Nukus and yet the trip took almost four hours. Evening was still some time off, so the air remained hot and acrid, and the closer he got to his destination, the more it tasted of salt – not the refreshing sea air he enjoyed from the bridge wings of the *Oregon* but a dry bitterness like vinegar.

The town had once been the Uzbeks' major port on the southern reach of the Aral Sea. Now that the lake was some hundred miles farther north, Muynak was an isolated speck of civilization with no right to exist today. Once thriving with commerce, it was virtually dead, its population a fraction of what it had been. Driving past abandoned houses and commercial blocks, Cabrillo came to what had once been the main wharf. A tower crane set on rails stood sentinel over a weedy trench that had once been the harbour.

Rusted husks of fishing boats littered the basin in

the most otherworldly display Cabrillo had ever seen. He'd once discovered a ship buried in the sands of the Kalahari, but somehow the juxtaposition of a harbour without water and the derelict hulls really jarred the senses. Like Salvador Dalí's painting *Persistence of Memory*. Adding to the surrealism was the presence of yet another camel, this one nibbling grass that grew out of a hole in the side of a sixty-foot trawler.

Around him were abandoned fish-processing plants, slab-sided metal buildings that the elements were slowly dismantling. Each had strips of siding missing like smiles lacking a few teeth. It was obvious the town had died slowly, as though it were a cancer patient withering away until all that remained were skin and bones and despair.

There were few people about and they moved with the listlessness of zombies. Cabrillo saw no children playing in the street, a first for him in any Third World town.

Somehow, the sun seemed harsher here, brassier, as though it were a hammer, the desert an anvil, and the town was being pounded between the two.

Across the border, at Aralsk, Kazakhstan, they had tried to keep the town connected to the lake by dredging a channel that eventually stretched twenty-odd miles, but here it looked like the citizens of Muynak had succumbed to their fate without a fight.

There was so little left inhabited that it took him only a couple of minutes to find his destination, the home of Karl Petrovski's widow, a Kazakh woman. His timing had been fortuitous because in another week, he'd learned, she was moving back to live with her family.

The house was a single-storey cement block of a building that had once had a stucco veneer, but wind had eroded it until it resembled flaking skin. The yard was weed-choked, though a scrawny goat was doing its best to keep ahead of the growth. The place looked like a snapshot out of the 1920s, with the glaring exception of a satellite dish mounted on a pole stuck in the ground. Getting out of the truck, Cabrillo noticed that even this modern convenience was wearing away. Bare wires were exposed at its receiver hub, and wooden pins revealed its primary function now was to act as a rack for drying clothes.

He took off his sunglasses as he approached the door. It swung open before he had a chance to knock.

Mina Petrovski had once been a beautiful woman – it was there in the structure of her face, and she still retained a slim and firm body, but the sheer effort of living had taken a toll on her. She no longer stood erect but had the slouch of a woman thirty years her senior. Her skin was sallow and her face heavily etched with lines. Her hair was more salt than pepper and had the dry, brittle texture of old straw.

'Mrs Petrovski, my name is John Smith,' Cabrillo said in Russian. 'I believe a Mr Kamsin told you to expect me.'

Arkin Kamsin had been Petrovski's boss with the newly formed Bureau of Reclamation of the Aral Sea. Eric Stone had traced the widow through the agency he headed. As she had no telephone of her own, negotiating this meeting had taken some doing.

A man appeared over her shoulder, older than her, with dark, intense eyes and a tobacco-stained moustache. He wore the uniform of a government functionary in this part of the world: black slacks made of some indestructible poly blend and a short-sleeved white shirt so heavily stained at the collar and under the arms that even a bleach bath couldn't clean it.

'Mr Kamsin?' Cabrillo asked.

'Yes, I am Kamsin. Mina asked me here today.'

'I want to thank you both for taking the time to speak with me,' Juan said with a warm smile. Kamsin's presence was a wild card. As a man who could have made a comfortable living playing poker, Cabrillo hated anything that shifted the odds.

'Please,' Mina Petrovski said in a timid voice, 'won't you come in? I am sorry about the house . . .'

'My associate explained you are moving home soon,' Juan said to cover her embarrassment at a parlour stuffed with packing boxes and furniture covered in protective plastic wrap. If anything, it was hotter in the room than it was standing under the blazing sun.

'Let me first say how sorry I am for your loss.'

'Thank you,' Mina said perfunctorily.

Just then, two little girls entered the room from someplace farther back. One was about eight, the other six. It was clear by the amount of wear and fading of her clothes that the youngest was forced to wear the elder's hand-me-downs. They gaped, wide-eyed and open-mouthed, at the bald stranger.

'Sira, Nila, go back into the kitchen,' Mina Petrovski said sharply.

The girls dawdled for a few seconds, giving Cabrillo an opening. He reached into his shoulder bag and removed two semi-melted Hershey bars, in their distinctive brown-and-silver wrappers. The power of American advertising had even reached this remote outpost, and both girls' eyes widened to impossible dimensions when they recognized the candy.

'May I?' Juan asked, and knew immediately that Eric Stone's in-depth research that showed Karl Petrovski had two children had paid off.

The saddened widow gave a smile that showed she hadn't exercised those particular muscles in months. 'Of course. Thank you.'

He presented one bar to each of the little girls and received an over-the-shoulder thanks as they scampered out of view. Melted or not, every last molecule of chocolate, he suspected, would vanish in moments. If there was such a thing as a chocolate atom – *chocosium*, perhaps – the very last one would likely be licked clean from the inner wrapper.

'Please, sit,' Mina invited. 'May I get you some tea?'

'I find tea upsets my stomach,' Juan said. It was a lie, but he didn't want this woman putting herself out on his behalf, and an outright refusal was considered rude. 'And I just finished off a bottle of water.'

Mina nodded neutrally.

Arkin Kamsin offered a pack of Pakistani-made cig-arettes to Cabrillo. Refusing this wasn't a gesture of rudeness but unmanliness. One-upping the man, Juan produced a pack of Marlboros, a currency as universal as gold. He plucked one for himself and handed the pack to the Uzbek, then made a cutting gesture when Kamsin wanted to give it back after taking one for himself. The gesture brought a small smile to the func-tionary as he tucked the pack into a shirt pocket.

Cabrillo let the cigarette smoulder in his fingers while Kamsin dragged deep on his and allowed feathers of smoke to drift from both nostrils.

Hospitality rituals complete, the man leaned forward so his belly spilled over his imitation leather belt. 'Your associate was somewhat vague about why you wanted to meet with Karl's widow.'

That reality still hadn't sunk in because Mina flinched at the word.

'Why was he in Moscow?' Juan evaded the question with one of his own.

'Research,' Kamsin replied.

'What type?'

'Technical research on the old Soviet systems of canals. Much of that information is archived in Moscow.'

Cabrillo had to take a gamble. He didn't know if Kamsin was here to protect his employee's widow or his own ministry, and without laying cards on the table, he and the Uzbek could verbally spar for hours without getting anywhere.

'May I be blunt?' he asked. Kamsin made an inviting gesture with his hands and leaned back into the plastic-covered sofa. It crinkled like old newsprint. 'I represent a Canadian environmental group. We believe that Mrs Petrovski's husband was deliberately killed because of something he found here and was researching in Moscow.'

Cabrillo had played his hole card. It was up to Kamsin to finish the game.

He and Mina exchanged a look, and Juan knew immediately that this possibility had been discussed already and that it was most likely the truth.

'How is it that you speak Russian so well, Mr Smith?' Kamsin asked when he'd glanced back at the Chairman.

'I have an ear for languages,' Juan told him truthfully. 'Give me a few weeks and I will be able to speak Uzbek.' That too was the truth.

'But you do not speak our language now?'

'No.'

'I will trust you.'

He then turned to Mina, and the two of them spoke for several minutes. It was clear the conversation was distressing the widow. What was less clear was Kamsin's tones and intentions. Was he telling her to keep quiet and get this foreigner out of her house or was he being convinced by her that they finally had an ally who believed her husband's death had been anything but accidental?

Finally, it was Mina who took up the thread of the

conversation. 'We don't know what Karl found. A few days before he went off to Moscow he had been surveying the lake bed north of here as part of his job. He came back very excited about something but wouldn't tell me what he had found until he had verified his discovery.'

'He wouldn't tell me either,' Arkin Kamsin added. 'But he managed to convince me to authorize the travel expense. Karl was like that. I trusted him completely. Any man who spent five minutes with him would.'

'How far north?' Juan asked. With the Aral Sea shrunk to a quarter of its size, there were tens of thousands of miles of exposed seafloor between here and the Kazakh border.

'We do not know.'

That statement hung in the hot air for several seconds.

'But there is someone who might,' Mina said.

Juan cocked an eyebrow in her direction.

'He often travelled with old Yusuf,' she explained. 'He was once a fisherman on the Aral before the waters went away. Now he is just an old man, but Karl claimed that Yusuf knew the lake bed as sure as he'd once known its surface.'

'Did you question him about where Karl had gone?'

'Of course,' Kamsin said. 'But like many of the old-timers, his directions were vague. He talked about certain islands and winds and how the earth felt. He could give us nothing concrete.'

'And you didn't want to go out and look for your-selves?' Juan asked, already suspecting the answer.

'If what Karl found got him killed . . .' Kamsin replied, his voice trailing off.

'I understand,' Juan said to both of them. Kamsin had a job, a life he would not want to jeopardize, and had probably been living in fear that his ignorance might still not keep him safe. Mina's motivation for not investigating further was nibbling chocolate in the next room. 'What about Yusuf? Would he be willing to go back?'

Kamsin had to think for a moment. 'It is possible. He didn't volunteer when Mina and I first questioned him, but we didn't exactly ask to be shown either.'

'Of course,' Juan said, knowing both were embar-rassed by not following through on what had gotten Karl Petrovski murdered.

The Uzbek people had only been independent from Russia for twenty years. These two were old enough to remember what life was like under a Stalinist regime. People didn't ask questions, didn't make eye contact with strangers and never made themselves noticeable to anyone else. It was the only way to stay safe. As much as Karl's death hurt both Mina and Kamsin, they wouldn't – couldn't – do anything but accept the offi-cial ruling from Moscow and move on.

'Does the term "eerie boat" mean anything to either of you?' Cabrillo asked in the uncomfortable silence.

The pair exchanged perplexed looks. 'There are many

boats out on the lake bed,' Kamsin replied. 'I know none called *Eerie*.'

'Karl never mentioned it to me either,' Mina added. 'Is this what Karl died for?'

'I don't know, and it is perhaps best if you forget I asked.'

They nodded knowingly.

'Why don't I take you to meet Yusuf?' Kamsin offered. 'I am sorry, but he speaks only Uzbek. I would be more than happy to translate for you.'

'You are most kind,' Juan said, getting to his feet. He pulled two more Hershey bars from his satchel and handed them to Mina Petrovski. 'For your daughters. For later.'

Wherever his investigation took him was a place she could not visit. Karl was dead. Knowing why would not bring him back. Ideology was for the others, her look said to him. I must be pragmatic.

As soon as they were outside, Arkin grabbed Cabrillo's arm and stared into his eyes. 'Will there be justice?'

Juan glanced back at the house, an already-empty shell, only its occupants hadn't moved on. 'For Mina?' he threw the question back at the academician.

'For any of us?'

'No.'

'Then why are you here?'

Juan took a second, which surprised him. 'Because a friend died in my arms and I thought that I could at least give him justice. Is that enough?'

'For us? Here? I guess it has to be.'

The two remained mostly silent on the drive to find Yusuf, the only words exchanged were directions as Cabrillo steered through the empty city. The buildings seemed little more than façades and lifeless husks.

Yusuf lived down by the harbour in the rusted carapace that had once been a fishing boat. Arkin didn't think the old man had owned this particular one, but he'd moved into the hulk nevertheless. The boat, like all the others in the harbour, sat on the ground, sand piled up to the gunwales in some places. Juan scanned a couple of the nearby craft and guessed the old fisherman had chosen this particular one because it sat a little more level than the others, many of which were canted over onto their sides.

Cabrillo stopped in the dust next to the boat. The two men stepped out.

Kamsin shouted a greeting to the derelict boat, and Cabrillo spotted movement through a porthole in the cabin below the pilothouse. Methuselah was a teenager compared to the man who trod out onto the craft's broad rear deck. He wore robes and a head scarf and leaned on a cane made of gnarled wood. Wisps of pure white hair coiled from under the scarf while the lower part of his face was covered in a beard befitting a fairytale wizard. His cheeks and eyes were sunken. One eye was a dark brown, almost black, while the other was covered with the milky film of cataracts. He had an ancient AK-47 slung over one buzzard-like shoulder.

It wasn't until Yusuf reached the railing and was peering through the four feet of space separating him from his two visitors that he finally recognized Arkin Kamsin. He gave a toothless smile, and the two men began speaking in Uzbek. Cabrillo knew how things worked in this part of the world and waited patiently while they went through the longish greeting custom: asking about family, presuming either man had any, commenting on the weather, recent town gossip, and the like.

Ten desultory minutes passed before Juan detected a change in the conversation's tone. Now they were discussing Cabrillo and his reasons for being here. Occasionally, Yusuf would glance his way, his withered face as blank as a cipher's.

At last Arkin turned to Cabrillo. 'Yusuf says he is willing to help but he himself isn't certain what had so interested Karl.'

'Did you mention the eerie boat?'

'I did.'

'Please ask him again.'

So Kamsin interrogated the old man further. Yusuf kept shaking his head and holding out his empty palms. He knew nothing, and Juan began to see that this trip had been a complete waste of time. He wondered if somehow his meaning was being lost in the translation. He was well versed in interrogation techniques and knew how to draw details out of the dimmest memories, but without being able to speak Uzbek, he was powerless. And then it hit him, and for a moment he was back aboard the *Oregon*, cradling Yuri Borodin as he uttered his last words.

He'd spoken in English.

'Eerie boat,' Juan said in the same language. Yusuf shot him a blank look. *'Eerie lodka,'* he said, this time using the Russian word for 'boat.'

All of a sudden that toothless grin was back, and his one good eye glittered piratically. *'Da. Da. Eerie lodka.'* He turned back to Kamsin and unleashed a long monologue in Uzbek. This time, his skinny arms waved around as though he were being swarmed by wasps, the tip of his walking stick arcing dangerously close to his two guests.

Arkin finally was able to translate the verbal onslaught. 'The eerie boat is out on the Aral Sea, a hulk like all the rest, but Karl told Yusuf that there was something special about it, something "magical", is how he described it. It was a couple of days after they explored the wreck that Karl made his request to go to Moscow.'

Cabrillo asked, 'Can Yusuf show it to me?'

'Yes. He said if you two left at first light, you can reach it by the afternoon.'

Juan wasn't keen on roughing it out in the desert, but he realized that there was no help for it. He had a counterproposal and asked through Kamsin if they could leave now and camp on the way. The old man seemed reluctant until Juan pulled a wad of cash out of his pocket. Yusuf's one good eye lit up again, and he nodded until Juan thought his head might roll off his scrawny neck.

Twenty minutes later, with Arkin's help getting provisions, which included a fifth of what passed for premium vodka in these parts, and which set Cabrillo back the equivalent of eighty cents, the two of them drove out across a wasteland that had once been the bottom of a lake, a wake of dust, not water, boiling into the air behind them.

7

As the name implies, the Aral Sea, the 'Sea of Islands,' once had thousands of peaks that dotted its windswept waves. Today, they poked up from what had once been the seafloor like mesas in the American Southwest, lonely sentinels on an otherwise desolate plain. After a near-sleepless night in which the temperatures plunged into the forties and Cabrillo was forced to wedge himself into the rear cargo area because Yusuf had passed out in the backseat, the empty vodka bottle clutched in a bird-like claw, they were up again shortly after the sun.

Yusuf navigated using his vast knowledge of the islands. He had been a fisherman as the water levels ebbed and recognized the shape of each one even now that he had to look up at them from their very bases. As they passed each former island, he would point to a new heading, as sure of himself as if he were reading a map and consulting a compass. There was no need for GPS in your own backyard, and for sixty-plus years all of the Aral Sea had been the old fisherman's domain.

Again, Juan was struck by the surrealism of their situation each time they drove by what remained of a sunken ship. Often they would be surrounded by debris fields of fishing gear and kitchen utensils. One wreck was a car ferry, and, judging by the shapes of the rusted-out cars still atop her deck and strewn around her keel, she had sunk sometime in the 1960s or '70s. The vehicles had that boxy, no-frills utilitarianism that the Soviets so coveted. Yusuf pointed out that they should go slower, so Cabrillo guided their UAZ until they were abreast of one particular car, a sedan that had once been tan but now showed more rust than anything else. Its tyres were deflated puddles around each wheel, though remarkably all the glass was still intact.

Yusuf swung his skinny body out of the SUV and indicated Juan should follow. Not knowing the old man's interest, Cabrillo moved cautiously, scanning the distant horizon and the hump of what had once been an island a mile to the west. Out here, the bitter taste of salt swirled up by the wind was even harsher than it had been back in Muynak. He took a pull from a water bottle before leaving the truck and had to spit out the first mouthful. It tasted of the ocean. The second was brackish, and it was only the third swig that tasted fresh.

The old Uzbek stood next to the sedan's driver's-side window. He'd used the sleeve of his robe to clear a small opening in the dust that crusted the car and peer inside. He was motionless for a minute before gesturing for Juan to take his place. Juan felt a chill of superstitious dread climb his spine. He pressed his face to the hot glass. Enough light filtered through the filthy windshield for him to see the remnants of a body laid out on the passenger seat. Not much was left but bits of cloth and bleached white bones. The skull remained intact but was at such an angle he could only see the rounded hump of its occipital lobe.

Cabrillo shot Yusuf a questioning glance. He said something in his native language and then dredged up the Russian word. 'Brother.'

Juan grunted, thinking what it must have been like to lose a brother at sea only to find his body years later as the waters that had claimed him slowly evaporated to nothing. He wondered too why Yusuf hadn't given the remains a proper Muslim burial but realized that this had been his tomb for decades and to disturb him now would be a sacrilege. There were no words he could say, so he gave the old man's bony shoulder a squeeze and walked back to their idling truck. Yusuf joined him a minute later, giving his brother what Cabrillo sensed was one last long look, and pointed off to the north.

For six more hours, as the temperature climbed and the sun beat down harder and harder, they pinballed their way toward their destination, zigging and zagging from one island to the next as they followed the map Yusuf carried in his head. At least once an hour they had to shut down the UAZ and let the engine cool. At one such stop, Cabrillo prudently added a gallon of water to the radiator at the same time he topped up the gas tank from the spares they carried.

Of course he couldn't understand a word of what Yusuf said as they drove along, but the old man kept up a running monologue. He could only assume the Uzbek was recounting stories of fishing trips he had taken to the spots off the islands they passed. He pointed out a great depression in the ground that had once been an undersea trench. At its bottom were dozens of rocks, and fanning away from them were the remains of countless large fishing nets spread across the ground like fallen spiderwebs.

Yusuf spoke passionately about the spot, his voice terse with anger until he couldn't help himself, gave one final curse and spat. Juan understood that he must have lost more than one trawling net to the trench's traitorous bottom. He couldn't help but smile. Yusuf caught the grin, and his scowl deepened until he too saw the lunacy of blaming unseen rocks for lost catches from so long ago.

The laugh they shared was bittersweet at the prospect that no fisherman would ever lose a net there again.

The desert stretched forever.

A little past noon, a shape started to form on the horizon, shimmering out of the desert heat. Beyond it was another island, a palisade of rock that rose sheer and vertical like the walls of a fortress. As they drew nearer, the image resolved itself from an amorphous lump on the desert floor to yet another ship, this one a little larger than the typical fishing boats they'd stumbled upon, though smaller than the car ferry. Judging by its condition, it was older than many others too. The sea had been given much more time to erode steel, and the underwater creatures had had plenty of time to eat their way through the ship's wooden decking. Yusuf thrust a crooked finger at the derelict hull with finality.

'*Eerie lodka?*' Juan asked.

'*Da.*'

Cabrillo swung the truck until it was parallel to the old ship, which he judged to be a hundred feet in length and quite beamy. She would have handled the seas well, and he wondered what had sunk her. The island was close enough that on a moonless night a careless navigator could have slammed into a rock peaking above the surface and holed the hull.

This side showed no such damage. Some plates were buckled from when she hit the seafloor, but that was all. She had the remains of an A-frame crane over her rear deck and a sloping stern that would have allowed her to deploy and then reship her nets. The bridge was a glassless cube hunched over the bows, the open window frames like mouths caught in terrible screams.

Juan killed the UAZ's engine and stepped to the ground. At his foot, embedded in the salt and dust, was a ceramic coffee cup, a substantial piece of pottery befitting the harsh life aboard a fishing boat and the big hands of the men who worked her.

Yusuf joined Cabrillo, and together they walked around the ship, inspecting its hull. On the far side, Juan saw the evidence he thought he would: a long gash below the waterline that ran for nearly a third the ship's length. She had hit some rocks near the island, and this amount of damage would have capsized her in moments. It might have been possible that some of the crew managed to swim to the island a quarter mile distant. It all depended on the weather. A rough sea would have crushed them against the unforgiving stone.

The old Uzbek suddenly threw up his hands and made a strangling sound in his throat. He jerked a thumb at the fishing boat. *'Nyet eerie lodka.'*

He pointed to a long depression in the ground a hundred yards farther on. Like some mythical monster climbing out of the earth, the remains of another ship looked like they were rising from the shallow trench as though the rim was a wave and the vessel was struggling to crest it. *'Eerie lodka,'* Yusuf announced.

This one looked to be much older than the ship behind them. Her length was impossible to determine because only her first thirty or so feet rose above the lip of the trench. She was narrow in the beam. She had a good amount of foredeck, which was surprising for a fishing boat since all the work took place at the stern, and her superstructure looked more befitting a yacht than a commercial vessel.

Rather than circle back around to the truck, Cabrillo strode across the desert toward the other ship. Yusuf trailed him, using his walking stick to steady his uneven gait.

The old ship had a sharp prow and dual anchors still tucked tight against their hawseholes. Her entire skin was of a uniform rust colour, not a fleck of her original paint remained. Juan reached the edge of the ravine and looked down. Her single funnel rose out of the sand ten feet from where her hull disappeared into it, the metal flakey from erosion. Using the funnel as a reference, Cabrillo guessed she was about seventy feet long in total. She had the straight vertical lines of a ship much older than the nearby fishing boat. She reminded him of a turn-of-the-century luxury cruiser, something out of the end of the Victorian age.

This wasn't the workboat of the local fishing industry or a ferry to bustle peasants across the Aral. This was a rich man's toy, perhaps belonging to a member of the old royal family who had vacationed along the inland sea's shores. But that made little sense. Why would the tsar and tsarina want to vacation in this backwater of their kingdom?

A local oligarch? Someone from before the revolution who made a pile of money and had the ship built on the Aral? The boat was much too big to have been transported here whole, even by rail, and there were no oligarchs left after the Bolsheviks were finished.

Juan suddenly saw this ship as an anomaly. There was something to her presence here that had piqued Karl Petrovski's interest, and he felt it too. This wasn't the type of vessel to be plying these waters. He looked around at his surroundings. She shouldn't be here in a desert either, he thought.

The ship's bow was undamaged, so he had to assume that whatever had sunk her showed up in the parts of the hull that the sands had swallowed.

Yusuf finally shuffled up and tapped Cabrillo on the arm to guide him around the prow to where someone, presumably Petrovski, had piled stones up against the hull high enough for him to climb over the gunwale.

Juan scaled the cairn and gripped the metal skeleton that was all that remained of the rail and pulled himself up, twisting his fists as he pivoted and leaving skin behind as he managed to throw a leg over and gain the deck.

There was little left of the original wood – teak, he supposed – so he was forced to step across the metal ribs that had survived the ravages of time. Below him he could see an empty space that had once carried cargo, or it could have been a forward cabin. Now it was a mound of windblown dust.

A narrow passage between the rail and superstructure allowed him to gain access to a single watertight door that had been wrenched from its hinges and lay drunkenly against its jamb. Crawling through was a tight fit, and halfway into the ship itself Cabrillo paused, his back pressed against the sandy floor. Yuri Borodin was a lot of things, but he was not a details man. He embraced the big picture, the larger view, the grand scope. He saw strategy, not tactics. Minutiae bored him. Why the hell would he waste his last words leading Cabrillo to drag himself into a derelict ship in a barren no-man's-land?

This was wrong on so many levels that Juan skidded himself back out so that he was hard against the gunwale again. Yusuf stood below him, looking up with his one good eye.

The shot hit perfectly, blowing a cone of tissue out of the old man's neck so that his head fell to his chest and then obscenely dropped again as if there were nothing holding it to his body. A cloud of blood hung in the air, the sniper's proverbial pink mist. Yusuf folded to the ground. It was as if he had dropped to his knees in prayer, but with his face planted in the sand there would be no supplication to Allah. He was dead long before he hit the ground.

Then came the sharp whipcrack of a rifle shot and the echo of the round as it passed through Yusuf's throat and pinged off the ship's hull.

8

A second later, Juan was back under the ajar door, all doubts erased. He went from being contemplative and analytical to survival mode in as much time as it took the auditory aspect of the gunshot to catch up to the visual.

He was in a narrow space no bigger than a phone booth with an iron ladder that led up to the bridge. Sunlight filtered down from above, showing how exposed he would be up there as well, but, with no choice, he climbed. A layer of sand coated the deck when he emerged in the wheelhouse. Most of the fittings had long since been scavenged. The wheel and binnacle were gone, as were the engine telegraph and the chart table. What little brightwork remained behind was blackened and pitted, and what he assumed had been teak panelling was nothing more than a papery veneer turned grey with age.

Cabrillo stayed low under the large window openings that ringed three sides of the bridge. The fourth wall was blank except for some metal brackets, which had perhaps held a fire extinguisher or other such gear, and a door leading aft. He crawled to it and peered into the hallway beyond. The passage was also lined with blanched wood, and there were bits of rotted carpet still attached along the crease where wall met floor. A mere three feet aft of the bridge door, the entire space was filled with sand all the way to the ceiling.

He was trapped.

He went back out to the bridge and cautiously peeked over a window frame in hopes of spotting the sniper. A round slammed into the metal an inch from his head, punching a hole through the eroded steel as though it were no more solid than gauze. Four sizzling holes appeared where Cabrillo had crouched a second before. And four tiny geysers of sand erupted from the floor next to his prone form as the bullets struck the deck.

Cabrillo slithered to a new position, knowing the sniper couldn't see him, because he'd figured out the man was halfway up the side of the nearby island/mesa, though he wasn't sure of the exact location.

Another fusillade raked the bridge, punching holes through its thin metal skin, as the sniper hoped for a lucky shot hitting his quarry. Juan had tucked himself up close to the forward wall, where the corner frame member offered better protection. The hot air on the bridge was filled with dust kicked up by the rounds plowing into the floor.

He remained motionless, not thinking yet about the why of his predicament. That would come later. Now all that was on his mind was survival. The rounds were coming in from the port side of the ship, so he could leap through the starboard window and hide behind the bulk of the ship, but a hundred yards of open desert separated him from the 4×4. He'd be picked off the instant he emerged from under the vessel's shadow.

He had nothing he could use to distract the sniper. His bag was back in the UAZ, and the artificial limb he had was basically a commercial model since he hadn't thought the risk of smuggling a weapon through Moscow was worth it.

He considered waiting out the other man until nightfall. Cabrillo was an excellent shot but lacked a sniper's special training. He knew from talks with Franklin Lincoln, the ex-SEAL crewmate who was the Corporation's sniper, that a skilled marksman could remain immobile in a blind for days. The man above him wouldn't just pack it in, and with a thermal scope Juan's body heat would appear like a vaporous apparition against the desert backdrop. If anything, an easier target at night than during the day.

A trio of shots rifled into the bridge, mangling steel and kicking up more sand.

The sniper didn't know if he'd hit his target. He was trying to keep Cabrillo pinned, which likely meant he had more men with him, and they were sneaking up under covering fire.

Juan couldn't move and he couldn't stay.

He snatched off his sunglasses and held the mirrored lens up and just over the windowsill, moving so slowly that it looked as though it was nothing more than a creeping shadow. In its convex reflection he could see the plain separating his position from the sniper's. He breathed a small sigh of relief. There was no assault team threading their way across the desert. Another shot cracked. The round passed through a window well aft of Cabrillo. The sniper hadn't seen the glasses and was just firing for effect, but now Juan had his blind pegged thanks to a tiny spark of fire from the weapon's muzzle.

The gunman was a little above Cabrillo's first estimate, tucked into a fold in the hillside. Juan wondered how long the man had been up there. This situation was obvious proof that there was something important about Karl Petrovski's eerie boat, though Cabrillo had yet to discern any significance. It was just another rusted hulk littering what had once been the seafloor.

If there were no additional troops coming, why keep an unarmed man pinned down? Why not come yourself and finish the job?

One explanation popped into Cabrillo's mind and jolted him into action. The sniper was about to get his wish, but Juan had a trick up his sleeve. He was certain that the vessel had been rigged with explosives. The sniper had been out here eradicating all traces of Petrovski's discovery. From the sniper's point of view, either his prey died when the bombs detonated or he would make a run for it and the sniper would pick him off from his eyrie. Mission accomplished.

'Like hell,' Juan spat as he reached the door leading to the aft compartments.

The hinges were located inside the hallway, so he had to crawl through and partially close the metal door. Protected from the wind, the steel was as hard as the day it had been forged. The hinge pins had bulbous caps that made pulling them out easier for the ship's crew if the need ever arose. The centre one eased out of the hinge as easy as a weed from the ground. The next one came much harder, but Cabrillo managed to free it as well. It was the bottom pin that refused to budge no matter how hard he pulled, and sweat quickly slicked it so he couldn't find purchase.

Cursing, Juan pulled up his trouser and peeled back the sock holding his prosthesis in place. The top of the leg where it met his flesh was smooth and rounded to prevent chafing, but there was a hard ridge down by the articulated part of the ankle. He wedged this ridge under the stubborn hinge pin's cap and hammered on the leg's heel with his hand. The pin remained rusted in place as though it had been welded.

He had no idea how much time he had but could imagine the clichéd image of a digital timer ticking down so only seconds remained. He slammed his palm into the leg's heel again. And again.

'Come on.' Again. And again.

Rust particles puffed up from the pin, and then the pin itself moved upward ever so slightly. Each blow to the leg raised it more and more. An eighth of an inch. The next shot pushed it another quarter inch. And then a half.

Cabrillo's palm was numb by the time the recalcitrant pin finally popped free and fell to the deck.

The door dropped against him, bashing his good leg

on the shin hard enough to break skin. He estimated the door weighed at least a hundred and fifty pounds.

He dropped to the deck and refitted his artificial leg.

The unattached door loomed over him, a deadweight that was about to become both his best friend and his worst nightmare.

Grasping the hot metal, Cabrillo wrestled the door back onto the bridge, making sure to keep his improvised shield between him and the sniper. It took only seconds for the gunman to figure out something was wrong because a pair of quick shots slammed into the door. It felt like someone had swung a sledgehammer with everything he had. The double impacts staggered Juan back a pace so that he was hard up against the pilothouse's starboard wall.

He crawled through and heaved the door over the sill after him. The sniper fired two more rounds but could not reach his prey. Juan thrust his shield hard over and jumped down to the main deck. As he intended, the door hit the ship's outside rail and crushed it flat before falling all the way to the desert floor.

He had no idea how long it would take the sniper to figure out his plan, so he moved quickly, jumping the ten feet to the ground. He manhandled the door into position so that he could drag it backward while he crouched in its shadow. His fingers barely grabbed hold, and the door drove its trailing edge into the loose gravel.

In seconds, lactic acid was already building in Cabrillo's thighs and back, and his fingers were going numb.

He continued inching forward, dragging the door behind him and staying low so as not to show himself to the sniper. A moment after he emerged from under the side of the derelict ship, the sniper zeroed in and triggered off three shots in rapid succession. Each one hit the door in almost the exact same place.

The kinetic force of the high-powered rounds made Juan lose his grip, and the door fell down on top of him. He quickly scrambled back to his feet, heaving the door nearly vertical. The sniper fired again, and again his round ricocheted off the door. The metal was dimpled by each hit, and energy transfer made the steel scalding hot, but the rounds just wouldn't penetrate.

Juan knew now that the race was really on. The sniper couldn't shoot him so he'd have to come after him. Cabrillo had to cover a hundred yards to reach his sport utility vehicle. The gunman had almost a quarter mile, but a lot of that was downhill. He was unencumbered while the Chairman had to lug his shield all the way back to the truck or else the sniper would stop charging, raise his rifle, and shoot Cabrillo as he fled.

Juan hauled the heavy door across the open plain like an anchor he could not drop. Gravel and sand built up where the metal hit the ground, and it felt like he was dragging half the desert with him. His back was screaming by the time he was a quarter of the way to his destination, and his legs shook like jackhammers, yet he didn't slow or pause. Pain was the body's way of telling a person to stop doing something. Holding a hand to a candle hurt, so the instinct was to pull it away, but the mind ultimately controlled the body, and you could leave your hand there until the flesh roasted off.

Cabrillo's body was telling him to drop the door and rest, but his intellect knew something his body didn't. If he abandoned his shield he would die, so he bulled through the pain and kept dragging the door. All the while, the gunman was surely out of his hiding place and running with everything he had.

As if to verify his suspicion, the sniper fired at him again. The sound of the rifle was much closer – too close – and the impact felt much stronger as the bullet had lost little of its power over the shortened distance.

Juan craned his head around. The fishing boat he had first thought was the eerie boat was only twenty yards away. The gunman? A hundred? Two? Juan had no way of knowing and risked getting his head blown off if he peeked around the door.

For perhaps the tenth time, he lifted the door slightly higher onto his shoulders so it would skip over the mound of debris accumulating at its base as he was dragging it along. Juan decided to shift position, lowering the door so that it glided easier across the sand but more than doubling the strain on his arms, legs, and back. His teeth ached from clenching his jaw so tightly, but he somehow managed to quicken his pace.

Sensing that his quarry was escaping after all, the sniper fired off a wild volley of shots on the fly, triggering his semiautomatic as fast as he could cycle it. Several rounds hit the door, but most peppered the ground to either side of the Chairman.

Like any race, the last leg was the hardest fought, and both men were pushing with their all. Cabrillo gave a primal shout as he towed the heavy door, his legs pistoning against the stony ground. He looked again and saw the prow of the fishing boat was a tantalizing five yards away.

He let the door drop to the ground and started sprinting. The sniper was forty yards back and running flat out and was caught off guard by Cabrillo's sudden change in tactics. He didn't have the time to bring his rifle up, so he fired from the hip just as Juan lunged out of view around the boat's bow.

Juan felt a wasp sting of pain on his neck as the hastily fired shot hit the steel hull just as he crossed around it, and he was stung by flecks of dislodged metal. The truck was just a dozen paces away.

He launched himself over the UAZ's hood just seconds before the sniper reached the boat and fired at him again. The driver's-side window shattered. Juan hit the ground on the far side of the truck, rolled to his feet, and reached through the open passenger window, his eyes now on the gunman for the first time since the battle began. The man wore khakis from head to toe, but not the clothes of a native Uzbek or Kazakh. He looked like he'd stepped from a Beretta clothing catalogue.

The man stopped less than twenty feet away and started swinging his rifle up to his shoulder for the kill shot.

Cabrillo's hand found the familiar shape of Yusuf's old AK-47, the weapon he insisted they bring along because smugglers used the old seabed to carry contraband into and out of the country. He pulled it out of the passenger footwell enough so that he could swing the barrel toward the sniper.

The stock of the sniper's rifle was just six inches and a half second away from the optimum firing position when Cabrillo found the safety and trigger and loosened a twenty-round burst through the shattered driver's window. Several of the shots never made it out of the SUV, but enough did, and his spray and pray worked.

The sniper shook as if he'd grasped a live electrical cable when eight of the erratically fired bullets raked his body from hip to head. Juan didn't have the strength to stop the AK barrel's inevitable rise on auto, and his last shots punctured the UAZ's roof. He finally willed his finger off the trigger as the gunman collapsed in the sand.

He let the AK drop from his hand and he sagged to the ground, his back leaning against the truck. He gulped lungfuls of air. He had no concern about the sniper miraculously coming to get him. This wasn't a movie. The man was clearly dead. Still, Juan gave himself only ninety seconds before levering himself back to his feet.

He rounded the SUV and then staggered to the sniper. Like his clothes, the sniper didn't have the facial features of a native. He looked –

The explosion knocked Cabrillo off his feet, and the concussive wave blew rust scale off the old fishing boat as if it had been hit with a hurricane-force wind. The sound echoed and rolled across the desert like thunder, and, seconds later, bits of rock and stone and steel rained from the sky. Cabrillo lay on the ground, his hands clamped behind his head to protect it until the hail of debris stopped and just dust and smoke drifted over him.

He stayed on his hands and knees and crawled over to the fishing boat and looked beyond. The prow of the eerie ship was simply gone. All that remained was a smoking hole in the desert floor, a crater the size of an Olympic pool. Thermite, he thought. The sniper had used thermite and a timed detonator to do this much damage. Juan realized now that the largest piece of the ship remaining was the door he himself had used.

He went to it now and gave it an affectionate pat. 'Didn't know I was saving you while you were saving me.'

It was only then he noticed the small brass plate that had been affixed near the door's lower side. He hadn't seen it when he was unpinning the hinges because the passageway was so dark, and the inside of the door had faced the sniper the entire time he'd used it as a shield. He had to wipe away a smudge of dirt to read what had been etched on the old identification tag.

Stamped into the little piece of brass were just a couple of words. It would be days before he understood the implications of what he read, and a few weeks for the ramifications to be felt, but in those first few seconds all he had to go on was his own confusion.

C. KRAFT & SONS SHIPYARD
ERIE, PENNSYLVANIA

9

Manhattan had once been ringed by piers, like spokes projecting from the axle of a bicycle tyre, and nearly every inch of the island's coast was given over to maritime commerce. The advent of containerization and the booming value of the city's property had closed all but a few anchorages, and those were reserved mostly for cruise ships. So for the *Oregon*, there was no triumphant trip up the East or Hudson rivers to dock before the most famous skyline in the world.

Instead, after passing under the Verrazano-Narrows Bridge, she found herself berthed in Newark, New Jersey, amid acres of metal containers and rows of cars that had been offloaded from the factories of Europe. By today's commercial standards, she was a wilting flower amid oceangoing behemoths. At 550 feet, she was dwarfed by the panamax and super panamax ships that lined the docks, and her appearance was that of a hag next to a group of beauty queens.

Her hull was a mismatch of paint colours that was peeling so badly it looked like the ship had some hideous skin condition. Her decks were littered with trash and old machinery that no longer worked. She had a central superstructure, with a large funnel, just aft of amidships. Bridge wings thrust out port and starboard from it. The pilothouse's glass was filthy with dried salt, and one small pane had been patched over with a piece of delaminating plywood. Three cranes serviced her forward six cargo hatches while another pair of cranes aft could load and unload her remaining two holds. There was just a trace of champagne-glass grace to her fantail, while her bow was a blunt blade that looked as if it fought the sea more than thrust it aside. From outward appearances, she looked like an old tramp steamer that should have been scrapped many years ago.

As Cabrillo made his way across the quay following a taxi ride from JFK, he couldn't imagine a more beautiful vessel in the world. He knew that her dilapidation was artful window-dressing, a ruse that gave her such anonymity that she went unnoticed in any of the Third World ports she frequently called upon.

The *Oregon*'s papers were in order, and a customs inspection turned up nothing suspicious. Her bills of lading said she was carrying rolls of paper from Germany to various ports in the Caribbean, and when the hatches were popped, the inspectors did see the curving tops of enormous paper drums, each weighing more than eight tons.

Of course, the paper drums, like the ship's rough façade, were just that: a façade. The rolls were only a foot thick and covered over the top of the hold like the false bottom of a spy's briefcase and weighed less than a thousand pounds.

He climbed up the ship's gangplank and looked aft, as was his ritual. The ship normally flew the flag of the

Islamic Republic of Iran, one more ruse on top of all the others, and it was his tradition to give it the one-fingered salute. To make their stay here less problematic, the *Oregon* carried Panamanian registry, and that nation's quartered and starred white, blue and red standard hung from the jackstaff.

The interior of the ship's superstructure matched that of her exterior, with gloomy passages, peeling paint and enough dust to fill a child's sandbox. The floors were mostly bare metal or cheap vinyl tiles. Only the captain's cabin had carpet, but this was an indoor/outdoor variety that was about as plush as burlap. Secreted throughout the accommodations block were doors that led to the hidden and much more opulent spaces where the crew actually lived and worked.

Juan went to one such door, passing through the grease-laden galley and seedy mess area. The secret door opened using a retinal scanner hidden in the belly button of a bikini-clad beauty adorning a travel poster plastered to the wall with other cheap decorations that would be seen to amuse a crew of misogynist seamen.

As the door slid open seamlessly, Juan entered the luxurious interior of the *Oregon* proper. Here, the carpets were plush, the lighting discreet and pleasing, and the artwork the labour of some of the world's masters. This was the secret her outer disguises masked – this, and the fact that the ship was armed to the teeth.

She sported launchers for surface-to-surface and surface-to-air missiles, as well as 20mm Gatling guns and a monstrous 120mm cannon hidden in the bow that could be deployed through clamshell-type doors. Of the dozen old oil drums sitting on the deck, six held remotely controlled .30 caliber machine guns that were operated from the *Oregon*'s high-tech op centre. These were used to repel pirates, and more than a few off the Somali coast had felt their sting.

The *Oregon* also possessed a sophisticated suite of sensors that made her optimal for intelligence-gathering operations in places the United States could not send in her own spy ships. They'd lingered near any number of adversarial nations, such as Iran and Libya before its fall, gathering signal intelligence that satellites couldn't detect. One recent mission had them posted off the coast of North Korea, armed with an experimental high-energy laser 'loaned' to them by Sandia National Laboratories. The result had been the spectacular though inexplicable, at least to them, failure of that reclusive regime's test launch of its Unha-3 long-range missile.

Juan chatted up a few crew members as he made his way to his cabin to shower off nearly twenty-four hours of travel. He still had grit from Uzbekistan under his nails. He dressed in charcoal slacks with a striped button-down shirt and custom-made shoes from Otabo.

He had time to enjoy a Cobb salad in the dining room, surrounded by overstuffed leather furniture and a gentlemen's club's cozy atmosphere, before heading to the *Oregon*'s boardroom for a status meeting with his senior staff.

The room was rectangular in shape and done in a

sleek modern style, with a glass table and black leather chairs. Had they been at sea, portals would be opened to give the room natural light, but since they were hard against the Newark pier it wouldn't do to give dock-workers a glimpse of the ship's true interior.

Seated at the table were Max Hanley, Eddie Seng – another CIA veteran like Cabrillo – who headed up shore operations, along with the big former SEAL at his side, Franklin Lincoln. Across from them were Eric Stone and Mark Murphy. Stone had put in his five after Annapolis and retained a Navy man's bearing, though he was still trapped in a nerd's gawky body. Murph was one of the only civilians on the crew. Possessor of several PhDs, a near-photographic memory and the paranoia of a true conspiracy theorist, he usually dressed like he'd picked up last night's laundry from the floor, and his wild dark hair was an unkempt bush. He'd been a weapons designer for one of the big defense contractors and had joined up with the Corporation on Eric Stone's suggestion.

Absent from the meeting was Linda Ross, who was still with the Emir on his yacht, and the ship's medical officer, Julia Huxley, who was visiting her brother in Summit, New Jersey.

'Welcome back,' Max said, lifting a cup of coffee. 'Good flight?'

'Why do people still ask that?' Murph interrupted. 'It's not like flying is so rare these days that the answer is important. The plane landed. Good or bad, who cares?'

Max shot him a look. 'For the same reason people pick up a ringing phone as quickly as possible: it's a polite social convention.'

'It's a waste of time,' Mark countered.

'Most of the good social conventions are,' Max replied with a dismissive wave. 'Only, your generation's in too much of a hurry to appreciate them.'

'For the record,' Juan said loud enough to take control of the meeting, 'my flight was fine, much better than trying to backtrack out of the Uzbek desert following my old tyre prints.'

'Good piece of work,' Linc said, his voice rumbling out of his deep barrel chest. 'Make you an honourable SEAL one of these days.'

'Any blowback for Petrovski's widow?' Stone asked. 'It's clear someone was sanitizing his discovery, and she would be another loose end.'

'When I got back to Muynak,' Juan said, 'I told Arkin Kamsin what had happened. He promised to get her and her kids out of the country as quickly as he could. As soon as they were gone he was taking some time to visit friends in Astana, the capital. It's the best we can do.'

He went on. 'Bring me up to speed on your research.'

Mark Murphy wore a pair of fingerless gloves with wires jacked into his laptop, which itself was linked to the ship's mainframe Cray supercomputer. He moved his hands through the air, and on the big flat screen his moves shuffled aside data windows in a way similar to a science-fiction movie. It was the latest generation slide-screen technology that he was beta-testing for a friend's start-up company.

'Here we go,' he announced as an aerial photograph of an industrial site alongside a body of water came up on the display. 'This is a shot of the C. Kraft and Sons shipbuilding facility taken in 1917, only three years before it was destroyed by fire. The company was founded in 1863 by Charles Kraft to build iron case-ments for the Union's ironclad fleet. After the Civil War, they started constructing iron ships for the Great Lakes, mostly coastal ore carriers. At its peak in 1899, it was the prominent shipbuilder on the lakes.

'After Charles Kraft's death, his two sons, Alec and Benjamin, squabbled over control. Alec, the elder son, eventually bought out his brother's shares, but the debt he incurred doomed the company. Rather than expand, it grew smaller and smaller as Alec was forced to sell off assets to cover his expenses. It didn't help matters that he had a severe drinking problem.

'The fire that destroyed the yard was deemed suspi-cious, although the insurance company couldn't prove arson. Alec Kraft died in 1926 from chronic liver dis-ease. Benjamin Kraft hadn't stayed in Erie after his buyout but moved to Pittsburgh with his family. He lived a quiet life off the proceeds of the sale. Neither man has any children alive today, but there are four grandchildren and eleven great-grandchildren, mostly in Pennsylvania or Upstate New York.'

'Any record of the company ever selling a ship to anyone in Russia?' Juan asked the question that had been burning in his mind since discovering Karl Petrovski's eerie boat, in fact, had been a boat built in Erie.

'No direct overseas sales at all,' Mark said. He flicked his hands, and up came a list of the ships they had built. 'I found this on a database of the Great Lakes Maritime Museum.'

He then highlighted several on the long list and explained as he went. 'Going on your description, I've narrowed down the vessels that could be the one you found.'

The pages showed more than two dozen craft that fit the rough dimensions and approximate age of the ship Juan had seen.

'Any pictures?' Juan asked.

'Yeah, hold on a second.' Murph worked more of his magic, and soon they were looking at sepia-tone photographs dating back more than a century.

Most of them were designed to carry cargo of one type or another. One of them was a ferry built to haul railcars on tracks laid onto the deck, with an arch over the bow to support the wheelhouse. More pictures clicked by.

'Stop!' Juan shouted. 'Go back one. That's her.'

'The *Lady Marguerite*,' Murph said after checking his laptop. 'Built in 1899 for, get this, George Westinghouse, and named for his wife.'

Cabrillo studied the picture, not paying much attention to Mark's commentary. She wasn't a commercial vessel but rather a pleasure boat. She was painted snowy white with a dark-coloured band around her plucky funnel. Her rear deck was mostly open, but partly covered by a sunshade to protect her passengers from the elements. In the picture, she was moored close enough to shore for a tree to be seen in the foreground. He couldn't see her in great detail, but he could just imagine her lavish appointments.

'What do we know about her?' Juan asked, imagining himself cruising the Great Lakes while listening to tinny music from a gramophone. 'And what's so special about George Westinghouse owning a pleasure yacht? He was one of the richest industrialists of his age.'

Eric Stone had been polishing his wire-framed glasses and slipped them back onto his nose. 'To answer your question: Westinghouse is significant here because he partnered with Nikola Tesla to build the Niagara Falls power station, and together they basically invented the electrical grid we use today.'

Tesla, Cabrillo thought, Yuri Borodin's last word. This wasn't a coincidence. It looked as though they had peeled the first layer off the onion of his cryptic death confession. The crazy Russian hadn't died in vain, of that Juan was certain, but right now he had no idea what his friend had stumbled into.

'Mr Murphy?' he prompted.

'Hiram Yaeger at NUMA gave me his master passwords to their mainframe. I'm accessing it now, but there isn't much in the archives about the *Lady Marguerite*. Let's see. It says here that she was moved from the Great Lakes to Philadelphia in 1901, and lost at sea in the summer of '02.'

'Was she insured?'

'Yep, I've got the Lloyd's of London claim right here. She went down with five people aboard. There is no list, but there were no survivors.'

'Storm?'

'Doesn't say. I'm cross-checking the date for any other losses. No, nothing else was lost. Hold on. Checking NOAA's archives for the weather. The night of August first, 1902, was clear for the entire Atlantic seaboard.'

'What else could have sunk the ship?' Eddie Seng asked, his fingers steepled under his chin.

Linc quipped, 'How about a white whale?'

'Not a white whale,' Eric Stone said, looking up from his own laptop. 'A blue cloud.'

'Come again?' Juan invited.

'There's a report from a freighter, the *Mohican*, about a strange blue cloud, like an electrical aura, that enveloped their ship as they were approaching Philadelphia. It lasted for about thirty minutes, and vanished as mysteriously as it arose. The *Mohican*'s captain, a Charles Urquhart, reported strange magnetic anomalies while his ship was enshrouded. Metal objects adhered to the deck as if glued, and the ship's compass just spun in its mount.'

'Any other ships report this effect?' Cabrillo asked.

'Nothing else. Just the *Mohican*.'

Mark Murphy gasped as he was struck by a sudden revelation.

'Hold on to that thought,' Juan warned, knowing

when Murph was about to steer the conversation into a conspiracy-laden dead end. 'No need to get ahead of ourselves. This sounds to me like a straight insurance scam. Westinghouse claims the boat sank, takes the money, and then sells it off to some Russian guy who parks it on the Aral Sea. And if there was ever a place an insurance investigator wouldn't look, it's there.'

Mark was practically bouncing up and down in his seat.

'Okay,' Juan conceded, 'go ahead.'

Murph grinned wolfishly. 'According to the Lloyd's report, the insurance was just a token amount to satisfy a bank over liability issues. The ship itself wasn't covered.' When no one reacted to his statement, he went on in a rush. 'Come on, guys. It's all there. Westinghouse's money, Tesla's genius, a weird blue aura with strange magnetic properties, and a ship found ten thousand miles from where it vanished.'

'Are you talking teleportation?' Linc asked dubiously.

'Exactly! What was it Sherlock Holmes said? If you eliminate all other factors, the one which remains must be true.'

'How do we know we've eliminated all the other factors?' Eddie asked.

Mark had no immediate answer to that.

'Insurance issues aside,' Seng continued, 'I think the more likely scenario is, the ship was sold off. The new owners sailed it to the Black Sea, where it was disassembled, transported to the Aral, and put back together.'

Cabrillo turned his gaze to Murphy, an eyebrow

arched. 'You have to admit that makes a lot more sense than your science-fiction idea.'

Mark looked like a child who'd just had his favourite toy taken from him.

'I hate to be the one to say this,' Max Hanley said with a resigned shake of his bulldog head, 'but Mark might not be wrong.'

'Excuse me?'

'At the turn of the twentieth century, the only way to reach the Aral Sea was by caravan, probably using camels rather than horses. It's a thousand miles from any navigable water, and we're talking about a ship that weighed a couple hundred tons and was not designed to be easily broken down. Anyone know the pack load of the average Asian double-humper camel? Can't be more than a few hundred pounds. A bit more, using carts. How many trips would it take? How many animals? It would be easier, and cheaper, for our fictitious Russian guy to build a boat right there on the Aral rather than lug one in. But here's the kicker: Where would they reassemble it? You'd need a dry dock or a large shipyard, and I'm willing to bet dollars to doughnuts that you won't find either anywhere in the region as early as 1902.'

Eddie chimed in immediately. 'She could have been used on the Black Sea for years and only later transported to the Aral.'

'That window slams closed after the Russian Revolution,' Max countered. 'No more rich men and, therefore, no more rich men's toys. Mark can double-check, but

128

I doubt the facilities I mentioned were around in 1917 either.' He looked at each Corporation partner in turn. 'I think Murph's idea is screwy too, but it can't be dismissed out of hand.'

Juan nodded but was far from convinced. 'Murph, anything in your research into Tesla indicating he was working on teleportation?'

This time, it was Mark's turn to look frustrated. 'Nikola Tesla is such a shadowy figure, especially in his later years when he became destitute, that there's no way of ever knowing what he actually worked on. There's talk of death rays and earthquake machines and mind control. It's impossible to know what was true and what's speculation.'

'Who would know?'

'Glad you asked.' Mark waved his gloved hands through the air, pushing aside the picture of the *Marguerite* and the insurance information and bringing up the head shot of an older, balding man fitting the stereotype of the absentminded professor. In the photo, he wore a tweed jacket and large black-framed eyeglasses. His features were weak and his expression bemused. His comb-over seemed to be his only concession to vanity. 'This is Professor Wesley Tennyson, a theoretical physicist formerly with MIT. He retired to Vermont five years ago. He's the author of the definitive Tesla biography, *The Genius of Serbia*.

'Eric and I have hacked into this guy's life every way possible. Since leaving MIT, he's basically gone into hiding. He has no phone number listed, no email account, and just a PO box address, though we did track down an actual address for him in Vermont's capital city, Montpelier. By modern standards, he's off the grid.'

'Why are you telling us this?'

Eric replied, 'It's our excuse for why we haven't actually questioned him.'

Cabrillo leaned back in his ergonomic chair, lacing his fingers behind his stubbled head. 'So the dynamic duo failed.'

'Using technology to find a Luddite is like trying to catch a moth with an anvil,' Mark countered.

Max chuckled when Juan couldn't come up with a suitable rejoinder.

'Looks like someone's going to Vermont,' he said, looking at the Chairman. 'Be sure to bring back some maple syrup.'

'Oh, and Ben and Jerry's ice cream,' Eric added. 'Hux loves their Cherry Garcia.'

Juan looked around the room. 'I think Vermont is famous for granite too. Anyone want some of that?' He got no takers. 'Okay, so I'll head north. Mark and Eric, I want you two to find a more plausible explanation for how that ship ended up in the Aral Sea. Max, you came up with a good point about a dry dock or shipyard. Pore through whatever archives you can and see if there's any mention of either of those on the Aral. To be safe, cover from 1902 until they started the irrigation work that eventually drained the lake. Also, Max, when are we finished provisioning the ship?'

Max had slipped on a pair of cheater glasses and now peered over their top with a look of mock disdain. 'You want to pursue what could be the greatest scientific discovery since man started making fire and you're asking me about provisions? Are you that dismissive of the idea?'

'Quite frankly, yes. Linda's waiting for us. What's our ETA in Bermuda?'

Max pulled off his glasses and studied Juan. He waited a beat and finally said, 'When Nikola Tesla started his studies, he had no peer. Nothing was off-limits because, well, because the nascent field of electricity was so new, no one knew there even *were* limits. A lot of modern scientists stop themselves from looking into certain things because they have the preconceived notions, based on those who came before them, that some things are simply impossible. The thing is, Tesla had no such limitations because he was the first. He was the pioneer who would set the limits. Who's to say he didn't investigate teleportation and death rays and earthquake machines? And just because he never published his findings doesn't mean he wasn't successful.' He looked down the table to Mark and Eric. 'Who was the guy who said teleportation was impossible?'

'Werner Heisenberg,' they said in perfect sync, and then both added, 'The Heisenberg uncertainty principle.'

'Right. You can know the location of a subatomic particle or its spin, but not both.' Max made it sound like a question, and when he got a pair of nods from the resident geniuses, he went on. 'This came out decades after the timeframe we're talking about. Tesla didn't know the uncertainty principle, so he wouldn't have been constrained in his thinking.'

'But Max,' Juan said, 'the principle still stands, whether it had been discovered or not. For example, no one went faster than light before Einstein proved you couldn't do it, and no one's done it since.'

Hanley had laid a logic trap, and Cabrillo had walked right into it. Max pounced, 'A couple of months ago you got a telephone call from a computer based on quantum entanglement that relies on subatomic particles communicating with one another at a speed faster than light. Impossible, you just said, and yet your call happened. All I'm saying is that when it comes to technology, yesterday's impossibility is tomorrow's IPO. Go to Vermont, keep an open mind, and Murph, Stoney, and I will come up with an alternative theory that fits your gestalt.'

'Gestalt?' Cabrillo smirked.

'Word-of-the-day toilet paper,' Max chuckled, 'don't mock it. Just to keep things in perspective, your cell phone has more computing capacity than the lunar lander that put men on the moon. And both of those things were considered impossible less than ten years before they were invented.'

'Fine, consider my mind open. Getting back to my original question, when is the ship's provisioning over?'

'Ten tonight. We're waiting for a shipment from a liquor wholesaler, and the flight from Anchorage with our king crab legs lands at Newark at eight thirty.'

'An army travels on its stomach,' Linc said.

'And liver, apparently,' Eddie Seng added. 'It will be nice to have real bourbon again. Max, that African swill you bought in Madagascar was beyond rotgut.'

'What do you expect for a dollar a bottle?'

'I'm just grateful that stuff didn't blind us all.'

'If you go blind, it'll be for other reasons,' Hanley shot back. He looked to the Chairman. 'We've got a pilot scheduled to take us out at eleven.'

'So you meet Linda and the Emir in Bermuda the day after tomorrow?'

'Actually, they've made good time. We're going to have to kick the old girl into high gear and reach Bermuda in twenty hours in order to meet them.'

Juan considered timing for a moment. 'Once I'm done with Professor Tennyson, I'll fly commercial to Hamilton and have Gomez pick me up in the chopper. We shadow the Emir like we're contracted to do, but I want the ship ready to bug out at a moment's notice.' He looked at each of his top people. 'Yuri Borodin died to reveal a secret Pytor Kenin is keeping. We're not going to stop until we find out what it is.'

He saw the punch coming from the way his opponent torqued his hips. It gave him the third piece of the puzzle. In any fight, a good boxer could deduce from where and how the punch was coming. The great ones figured out the big question: when it was coming. When he saw the shift, he had perhaps half a second to react. The left came at his head with everything the man had to throw. It wasn't a knockout blow. It was a killing strike.

For him, that half second was a lifetime, and he actually used a portion of it to admire his opponent's daring.

To throw such a punch meant you knew that when it landed, the fight was over. It was an act of supreme confidence.

Or, in this case, arrogance.

He brought his right around just enough to deflect the punch and leaned back, his opponent's glove taking off a layer of skin from the tip of his nose. It was all his opponent would ever claim – a tiny patch of skin – because his left came up in a hammer strike that hit with the force of a hurricane. He no longer had the wind for a long match, age had robbed him of that, but he could exploit an opening. His punch, fired from close range and out of defence, still shattered his sparring partner's nose as though they were fighting bare-knuckle.

Blood flew in a spraying arc as the other man cork-screwed to the canvas, his brain so short-circuited that eight sticks of ammonia would be needed to rouse him.

Three hours in a surgeon's care would be needed to restore his appearance.

Pytor Kenin didn't even wait for the ring workers to wake this morning's sparring partner. He ducked under the ropes and held up his gloves for a trainer to unlace them from his hands. He'd only been in the ring a few minutes, but, as part of his training program, the gym's owner kept the facility near eighty-five degrees. Sweat poured through the dense coils of hair that covered his chest, back and shoulders.

'Where ever did you find that man?' Kenin jerked his head back to indicate the prone figure still lying on the canvas.

His trainer, a veteran of the Olympics back when the Soviet Union dominated the games, shrugged. 'He claimed to be the champion boxer at the truck factory where he worked. I'd never heard of him but took his word for it.'

'Fateful boast,' the admiral remarked as his second glove came free and his trainer went to work on the tape. 'He had power, but that man telegraphed his moves like Samuel Morse.'

The trainer chuckled at the turn of phrase. 'He had you by two inches and twenty pounds, but, as we've both learned over the years, youth and vigour are no match for age and treachery.'

It was Kenin's turn to smile. 'All too true.'

The admiral was bent over a sink in the gymnasium's bathroom, razoring his face, a towel wrapped around his waist, when a newly assigned aide came through wearing his full uniform. Kenin cocked an eyebrow at the young sailor, who was seeing the scar that ran down Kenin's rib cage for the first time. It was a souvenir from a helicopter crash early on in Kenin's career.

'Sorry, sir,' the aide stammered. 'Commander Gogol's compliments. He would like you to phone him right away.'

Kenin had a good idea what the call was about, so he quickly rinsed away the little lather still on his face with a double palmful of water. 'Thank you. Go back to the car and tell the driver we'll be going back to my apartment rather than the office.'

Kenin put on his uniform, adjusting several of the decorations that covered a sizable portion of his jacket, and strode out of the bathroom, an encrypted phone to his ear. In the boxing ring, the trainers had his sparring partner on one of the corner stools with a mess of bloodied towels at his feet and a fresh one pressed against his face.

He only noticed the smell of the gym when he first stepped into its heat or when he stepped out onto the Moscow streets. The city air was not clean by any stretch of the imagination, but he drew air deep into his lungs to purge them of the smell of sweat and blood and old leather.

'Viktor, it's Kenin. Are the men in place?'

'They just called. They're ready.'

The admiral ducked into the backseat of his

Mercedes limo, and his veteran driver closed the door. The young aide rode in front with him. So confident of his position within the government, Kenin didn't bother with a coterie of security men.

'Good. I'm on my way home to make the call. Meet me there so we can make our plan.'

'I'll be there in thirty minutes, Admiral.'

Kenin's luxury apartment was only a ten-minute drive from the gym where he regularly trained. The palatial flat had its own exercise room equipped with the latest gear, but he preferred to work out in the dank gymnasium surrounded by other men whose single dedication to the pugilist arts was an inspiration.

He could never have afforded the ten-thousand-square-foot floor of the high-rise building overlooking the river. His was but an admiral's salary, after all. No, the apartment had been a gift of one of his many benefactors, an oligarch who had made his fortune in the Wild West days following the collapse of the Soviet Union and now backed several political and military up-and-comers in order to preserve it.

In the building's lobby, he slotted his key into the elevator controls, telling it to take him to his private floor. There, the doors opened to the apartment's entry foyer, a marble-and-gilt affair that looked like it had been stripped out of the palace at Versailles. Kenin ignored the opulence. He was a man interested in only one trapping of wealth and that was power. The material side of the equation meant nothing to him.

A moment later, he was in his office, staring at a

flat-panel monitor mounted on a wall to the left of his desk. Most of the screen was black, though one corner showed an image of himself taken from a camera placed to make him appear massive behind his desk. He hit a button on his desktop computer when he was satisfied with how he looked on the monitor.

The screen came to life. In the foreground sat a man behind his own desk. Behind him was a casement window, looking out over the ocean. The weather appeared cloudy where the man was; the sky leaden, and the ocean churned as it raced for shore. Kenin had spoken to this man enough over the years that his physical form was something he no longer noticed.

No one knew the origin of the fire that had robbed the man of so much. Some claimed it was an assassination attempt, others said his mother deliberately set him on fire when he was a child. Still others said it was an accident from the days when he made bombs for Turkish separatists on Cyprus. His left hand was nothing more than a pair of lobster-like pincers, though the right had been spared. He had no hair. The scar tissue that covered his skull had the tight sheen of a Halloween mask pulled too tight. Both ears were burned away, as was his nose. The skin on his neck looked like the scaly hide of a desert lizard. One eye was covered with a simple black patch, though the other glittered with intellect.

'Admiral Kenin, so delighted you wished to call me this fine morning,' the man known in intelligence circles as L'Enfant said.

Kenin was certain that Yuri Borodin and his boot-lick, Mikhail Kasporov, hadn't used a Russian team to break him out of prison. Kenin knew all the groups capable of such a sophisticated operation and all of them eventually reported to him. That meant Kasporov had gone to foreign operators for the extraction. There were few such groups, and each of them guarded their identity well. These weren't the big security contractors that had gained notoriety during America's forays into Iraq and Afghanistan. No, these were smaller elite forces that operated far beneath the radar. But there was one constant in the shadow world and that was if anyone needed discreet information, they would eventually have to deal with L'Enfant.

'How are you, my old friend?' They were not friends, and the levity Kenin put into his voice was for appearances only. L'Enfant was as happy to take this call as he was to discuss his own funeral arrangements with the undertaker.

'I can complain, dear Admiral, but would you really like to listen?' The fire and smoke had damaged L'Enfant's lungs so he spoke in a gravelled rasp. An oxygen cannula ran under the ruin of his nose, held in place by surgical tape, and every few minutes he took a hit off a separate clear-plastic mask. The damage also garbled any accent the man might have spoken with. Details of his national origin were as elusive as the cause of the disfiguring fire.

Kenin gave him a disingenuous smile. 'Your well-being is always in my interest.'

L'Enfant inclined his misshapen head. 'Strange thing,' he croaked. 'Your name came up just the other day.'

'Really.' The information broker had spies all over the globe who siphoned up more intelligence than the CIA. Kenin had no idea in what context his name would have come up to interest L'Enfant other than Borodin's escape, and it was too early in the conversation for either man to mention the true purpose of the call.

'Indeed. It seems some Colombian gentlemen reportedly purchased a decommissioned submarine, and its crew has missed two scheduled reports on their return voyage.'

Kenin's expression didn't change. He was too good for that, but inside he was seething at the fact this little toad knew about that operation. The leak had to have come from the Colombians, but the fact that it was out there was a severe blow.

'I hadn't heard Colombia wanted to purchase a sub for their Navy,' he said evenly.

'Oh, you misunderstood me, Admiral. It wasn't their Navy at all. Just some businessmen who'd formed a . . . let's call it a syndicate. I believe they had some unusual cargo to transport and thought the submarine would make their job a little easier. I only mention this because one member of the syndicate who was responsible for procuring the sub was killed by his partners over its loss, and upon his death he said the queerest thing. He said he got the boat from you.'

Kenin smiled. 'There you go. How can you trust

anything said under duress? He must have heard of me when I helped broker the deal for the Chinese to buy a few of our old Kilo-class subs and, most recently, the aircraft carrier *Varyag*.'

'I bet that's it,' L'Enfant agreed readily. 'I do recall your prominence in that transaction, and I bet this poor fellow blurted out your name by mistake.'

Both men nodded at the lies given and accepted. This was just L'Enfant's way of showing off his knowledge and reminding Kenin that he knew where every body was buried and in which closet every skeleton had been hidden.

'Shall we get down to business?' L'Enfant invited.

'Very well.' The fake bonhomie vanished from Kenin's expression, and his voice hardened.

'Before you say anything, let me assure you I had nothing to do with Yuri Borodin's escape.'

'So you know of it?' Kenin asked.

L'Enfant didn't deign to answer.

'I believe that you didn't broker his rescue, but I wager you still know who pulled it off.' When L'Enfant didn't protest, Kenin continued. 'As a sign of our long-standing dealings, I would please ask that you tell me.'

This was a line one never crossed. L'Enfant had been so successful for so many years because he kept confidences with the vigour of a Swiss banker. To even ask to divulge something like this was a mark of disrespect, and both men fully understood that their relationship was over from this moment on.

L'Enfant sucked off his oxygen mask, his chest

heaving to fill his damaged lungs. 'An unusual but not unexpected request. How do you wish me to respond?'

'By answering another question first.'

'By all means.'

'Who do you fear more? Me or the man who master-minded Borodin's escape?'

'I fear neither, though in all candour I admit that I admire and respect him more.'

'That is the wrong answer.' Kenin looked down at his keyboard and typed a quick IM. When he spoke, a little of the earlier brevity was back, but now it was more genuine. 'The secret to your success has always been two things. Your discretion, which I can do little about, and your physical location, which I can.' Kenin paused as if something occurred to him. 'Actually, three things. There is what is referred to as a dead man's switch. Upon your death, information that you've gathered over the years will be disseminated to interested parties. I imagine it will ignite assassination after assassination, and perhaps even trigger a few wars. I guess I should have said switches, since there are four separate people tasked with carrying out your final orders should any harm befall you.'

Had L'Enfant's scarred visage been able to show emotion, fear would have crept across his face. That he had a dead man as protection against betrayal was known to all. That he had four was not.

The video monitor both men could see split into four quadrants at a command from Pytor Kenin. In each, a man dressed in black tactical gear and wearing a dark mask held a pistol to the head of another person – three men and a woman. Two were dressed in suits, and it looked as though they had been at their offices or commuting to them. Of the other two, the woman wore workout clothes, and behind her were several pieces of fitness gear in a home gym. The third man was next to his bed and wore nothing but a pair of boxers, his gut sagging over the waistband by a good six inches.

All four were lawyers. None of them lived on the same continent or knew one another and yet all had been hired in secret by L'Enfant to divulge upon his death all of the information he'd gathered on his clients and their enemies.

'My only real risk,' Kenin said airily, 'is that I'm not certain if these people have people of their own who will carry out your final command. But I think I'm safe.' He then turned deadly serious. 'As to your location, my friend, you are currently in the southeast corner of the one hundred eighteenth floor of the Burj Khalifa tower. The ocean vista behind you is a live webcam from Italy's Amalfi Coast, and while you own the floors immediately above and below yours, I have packed the suite on one sixteen with enough explosives to take down the entire building.

'I will now repeat the question. Who do you fear more, me or him? And let me remind you that I will trigger the charges in, say, twenty seconds.'

L'Enfant took a draw off his oxygen mask. 'If this was a level playing field, I would still fear him more than you.'

'The playing field is no longer level,' Kenin said, waving at the monitor to indicate how his men held weapons on L'Enfant's people.

'I see that.'

'Here's how this is going to work. You are going to give me his name and the name of his outfit, and then we will never speak again. You will not warn him. Maybe your betrayal will become public and maybe not. It is possible you will be able to salvage something of your career after this. The choice is yours, and you now have five seconds.'

L'Enfant hesitated for as long as he dared and then for the first time in his life he gave up one of his clients. 'Juan Cabrillo. He is the chairman of the Corporation. They are based on a ship called the *Oregon*, although that name is rarely painted on her fantail.'

'See? That wasn't so hard.'

'Screw you, Kenin.'

Kenin ignored that remark. 'Now, my good friend, tell me everything you know about this Cabrillo and his ship.'

11

One of the things Juan loved about New York City was that enough money could get you anything no matter day or night. Thus he found himself headed north at seven the next morning behind the wheel of a Porsche Cayman S. Because he was at sea year-round, he had little opportunity to drive, so when it became clear the night before that flying and driving times to the Vermont state capital were about the same, he opted to rent the sports car. The dealer in exotic cars could have gotten him a Lamborghini or a GT3 Porsche, but all those fins and spoilers were like a toreador's red cape to cruising police.

Speed traps weren't much of a concern since the radar and lidar detector he'd taken from the ship's stores would give the car's ceramic-composite brakes more than enough time to slow down.

Before setting out, he'd checked the Cayman's GPS to map out the most efficient route, and when he saw it involved mostly sticking to highways, he programmed it to find quiet back roads instead. Once through the snarl of congestion that surrounded New York and its environs, he found himself on two-lane blacktop that saw little traffic other than farm tractors and locals running errands.

The six-cylinder engine directly behind his low-slung seat thrummed with eager anticipation as he worked the gears and steering wheel to throw the nimble sports car around rolling turns, first in Connecticut and then the western Massachusetts Berkshire Mountains. Prudence made him take it easy when passing through little towns that clung to the road in clusters of tired storefronts with only a few cross streets before opening up again to vacant farmland. Black-and-white Holstein cows dotted the fields as if placed there for tourists to photograph.

Though his concentration was fully focused on keeping the Cayman glued to the asphalt, he still could mull over ideas about what exactly the Corporation had stumbled into. It was a secret Pytor Kenin was willing to kill for, he knew that much. Yuri, Karl Petrovski and the old man Yusuf were dead because of it. From what Cabrillo knew of Admiral Kenin, this had to be tied to some Russian defence project. If Yuri supplemented his meagre naval pay by selling off military technology, he was quite certain Kenin was doing it too. The other fact he was reasonably certain of was that this technology was based on something Nikola Tesla had invented more than a century ago.

He put little stock in Mark Murphy's teleportation theory, despite Max's limp endorsement, or at least not outright rejection of the idea. Juan felt sure that their research would turn up a more plausible explanation as to how George Westinghouse's yacht ended up halfway around the globe.

Montpelier sits in a bowl of mountains along the banks of the Winooski River, Vermont's central artery. Crossing the river on one of the numerous bridges that serviced the city of eight thousand, Cabrillo quickly found himself facing the impressive Greek Revival statehouse building, with its granite façade and gilded domed roof. A little farther along he found himself in a downtown district out of a Norman Rockwell painting. There were no buildings of more than four storeys, and each had exacting architectural details. He pitied any modern developer having to face design-review committees.

When he was still two streets shy of his destination, he parked in the lot of a small apartment building and used the hood of the car to shield him while he slipped on a shoulder holster and then shrugged into a black single-breasted blazer tailored to hide the telltale bulge of the FN Five-seveN semiautomatic pistol. Beneath it he wore a white broadcloth oxford with the collar open. He clicked the holster's lower loop around his belt to secure it in place and carefully closed the Porsche's hood.

A minute later, he rolled up to a Queen Anne-style house that was all brightly painted gingerbread, narrow dormered roofs and peaked turrets. Had it actually been made of gingerbread, he wouldn't have been surprised. The hundred-year-old house had an attached garage that was an obvious add-on, but whoever had done the work had strived to match the original building's delicate architecture. In a word, the place was 'charming'. And it looked to be the perfect hole-up for a retired MIT professor.

Cabrillo slid from his seat and walked across the stone path to the front porch and the door. There was an electronic bell, but it felt right to use the ornate brass knocker instead.

'One moment,' a muffled voice called from within.

If Juan could pin down exactly how long a moment lasted, that's how long it took for the door to swing open.

'Yes?'

Professor Tennyson had gained some weight since the photo Cabrillo had seen was taken. His face was fleshier, but with a healthy glow. Atop his head he wore a wide-brimmed straw hat, and he sported rubber boots and had a pair of gardening gloves tucked into his belt. That he'd left a trail of dirty footprints from his open back door and across the polished cherry floor of his living room was lost to the man.

'Professor Tennyson?'

'Yes,' he repeated. 'May I help you?'

'I certainly hope so, Professor. My name is John Smith, and I'd like to talk to you about Nikola Tesla.'

Tennyson blinked and looked a little guarded. 'Are you writing a book?'

'No, sir. I'm doing research purely for myself.'

'And what do you do, Mr ah . . . ?'

'Smith, Professor Tennyson. John Smith. I'm an analyst with a think tank that consults with the government on foreign policy and security.' This could go one of two ways, he thought. Either Tennyson would abhor anything to do with the government and would shut him out or he would like the opportunity to talk about his favourite subject no matter who was listening.

'Security, eh? Are you one of those people who believe that some aspect of Nikola's work could be turned into a weapon?'

'Actually, sir, I'm here to make sure someone else hasn't already done it.'

That seemed to pique Tennyson's interest. He opened the door fully. 'Sure, we can talk, for a bit, but it will cost you.'

Judging by the size and age of the house, Tennyson didn't look like he was wanting for money, so the comment threw Cabrillo until the man went on.

'I've cut down a small elm tree out back, but I'm afraid I'm not up to the task of digging out the stump. A strapping young man such as yourself can have it out in no time.'

Juan grinned. 'I think we have a deal if you let me use your restroom first. It's been a long drive.'

'You drove all the way from DC?'

'I'm based in New York,' Cabrillo said as he stepped into the house. The furnishings were spotlessly clean and looked as if they were the original contents of the home. An ornately carved banister rose up to the second story. Juan noted that, as in many homes of this era, there were two-foot-square grates set between the floors to allow heat from the main hearth to reach the bedrooms above. To the right of the entrance was a hallway with a small table next to the door that would lead to the garage. He saw that the bowl sitting on the spindly legged table appeared to be an antique Tiffany.

Tennyson noted Cabrillo's interest in the furnishings. 'This house belonged first to my grandparents and then a spinster aunt,' he explained. 'She kept it exactly as it was as a personal shrine to her father and mother, and when she passed a few years ago, I couldn't bring myself to change it either.'

'It's beautiful,' Juan remarked.

'And a nightmare to maintain,' Tennyson said with a small laugh. 'I often wonder if I am the house's occupant or its servant.'

The fixtures in the bathroom looked like they'd come out of a plumbing museum. After using the toilet, with its tank mounted high up on the wall, Juan shrugged out of his coat and removed his holster. There was no way he could dig out a stump wearing the rig without Tennyson spotting it, and it was his experience that civilians were wary around firearms. He folded the pistol into his jacket, placed the jacket under his arm, and joined Tennyson on the back brick patio. The gardens were just starting to bloom and by summer would be a riot of colours and aromas.

'Is gardening a hobby?' he asked.

'Yes. Unfortunately, it was my aunt's, not mine. I personally hate it, but what can one do?'

He led Cabrillo over to the left side of the fenced-in yard, where a three-inch-diameter stump stuck up through the grass. Next to it was a shovel and an axe.

A pair of robins were building their nest in a nearby tree and squawked at their approach.

Juan set his hidden gun bundled in the jacket a short distance away and took up the spade.

'So tell me, Mr Smith –'

'John, please.'

'And I'm Wes. What sort of weapon do you think Nikola invented?'

Cabrillo liked how Tennyson used Tesla's first name, as if he were a friend and not a long-dead stranger. 'That's just it. We're not sure. We think his research is tied into a defence program, but we don't know exactly what.'

'He was a remarkable man – Tesla, I mean. Mad in the end, and destitute, the poor bugger, but he was a certified genius. I'm sure I don't need to give you a primer on all of his accomplishments in the field of electrical research – the induction motor, radio control, wireless communications, spark plugs. It was said that his ideas and inventions came to him fully formed in a flash of inspiration.'

'What about weapons research?'

'There is talk that later in his life he wanted to build a direct-energy "peace beam", but it is mostly known as the death ray. His treatise on the subject, *The Art of Projecting Concentrated Non-dispersive Energy through the Natural Media*, is in the Tesla museum in Belgrade. I've read it and it's pure drivel. His theories are interesting, but the device would never work. He spent time trying to develop an aircraft that flew by ionizing the air under it. Perhaps that is what you're looking for.'

As he dug, Juan couldn't see a fit between an ion-powered plane and George Westinghouse's boat ending up in Uzbekistan. 'He and Westinghouse were friends?'

'Oh yes,' Tennyson nodded vigorously. 'Though he was already a wealthy man, Westinghouse added to his vast fortune on their collaborations.'

'Can you think of any experiment that Tesla would have performed aboard Westinghouse's yacht, the *Lady Marguerite*?'

'No,' Tennyson said quickly.

Too quickly, to Cabrillo's trained ear. 'Something on or about August first, 1902?'

'Nikola was working on the Wardenclyffe Tower in 1902, out on Long Island. It was intended to transmit electricity wirelessly.'

'Funding for that project was pulled a month earlier,' Cabrillo shot back, silently thanking Murph and Stone for the briefing paper they'd prepared for him. 'Please, Professor Tennyson, this is important. I found the *Lady Marguerite* buried in a desert that used to be the Aral Sea just a few days ago.'

Tennyson went ashen, and he laid a hand on his chest, taking a couple of steps back. 'My God.'

'What happened that night?' Juan pressed. 'What were they working on?'

Tennyson moved to an Adirondack chair and lowered his bulk into it. 'It was only a secondhand account. That's why I never put it in my book.'

'What was he trying to do?' Juan laid the shovel aside to give Tennyson his full attention.

'It was an experiment they were going to show the US Navy, had it worked. The idea was to use magnetism to bend light around a ship in such a fashion that anyone looking at it would not see light reflecting off of its hull. Their field of vision would pass over the ship and on to the other side.'

'Optical camouflage?'

'Exactly. They rigged the system to the *Marguerite* and sailed out from Philadelphia, where the work had been carried out in a dockside warehouse Tesla owned. Another ship went with them, for the observers. It was from a story handed down from one of the observers, a Captain Paine from the War Department, that I know any of this.'

'What happened?'

'No one was really sure. They were still steaming out past the shipping lanes when the *Marguerite* suddenly lit up the night sky with a strange blue aura. It lasted for about thirty minutes and then winked out. When they went to investigate, the yacht was gone. They assumed she had sunk.'

'Did they report any anomalies on their ship? Anything to do with magnetic fields?'

'You're referring to the story of the *Mohican*?'

Cabrillo nodded.

'Of course I investigated that tale as best I could. Nothing like what that crew experienced happened on the observers' boat, but, in full disclosure, I must say they were in a wooden-hulled sloop. The Aral Sea, you say?'

'Yes. What do you think happened?'

Tennyson went quiet. His eyes behind the tortoise-shell glasses had gone vacant as he stared into the middle distance.

'What is it, Professor? What are you thinking?'

'I'm not sure,' Tennyson finally admitted. 'The *Lady Marguerite* vanished that night. Of that, there is no doubt. And you say you found her in Kazakhstan.'

'The Uzbek side of the Aral,' Juan corrected.

His gaze still fixed on an object only he could see, Tennyson said, 'Nikola died in January of 1943. There was a rumour of a story that came out of Philadelphia later that same year – October, to be precise. It involved another Navy project using the ship the USS *Eldridge*.'

Cabrillo knew enough of the subject, thanks to Mark Murphy's rantings, to say, 'You're not talking about the Philadelphia Experiment, are you? That was completely debunked.'

Tennyson turned his gaze on Cabrillo, his eyes fierce. 'Debunked? You just found the *Lady Marguerite* in Uzbekistan and you're willing to discount the story of a Navy ship vanishing from Philadelphia and reappearing in Richmond, Virginia? The tale goes on that the ship then returned to her home port with some of the crew fused to the deck in grotesque tableaux while others were driven mad by their experience.' He paused to get a grip on his emotions. 'I'm sorry, John. This is all so overwhelming. There was so much more to Nikola than I could ever write about. He was a genius in the way Einstein was a genius except history has completely forgotten him because so much of what he accomplished has been dismissed as speculation and rumour.'

'So what happened in Philadelphia?' Juan said softly to prompt the professor along.

'Right . . . Philadelphia. Not long after Nikola's death, the FBI took control of part of his estate under the direction of J. Edgar Hoover himself. They raided the hotel room he lived in in Manhattan and also seized property he owned on the Philadelphia waterfront. The story of the USS *Eldridge* is bull. But it remains the basis of what they discovered in that waterside warehouse. What happened to the *Eldridge* wasn't the story. What they found in Nikola's warehouse was.'

Without a doubt, Tennyson had Cabrillo's full attention. 'What did they find?'

'Another ship. One that had been modified. It was an old Navy mine tender that Tesla had purchased with the help of Westinghouse. He had claimed that he had a new concept to make his optical camouflage work this time. But he never had enough money to complete the project, so the ship languished in the harbour for years until the FBI raided the facility.

'They took every scrap of paper they could find, but they left the ship behind. Nikola died owing a great deal in taxes, so the ship was turned over to the War Department as scrap in order to pay off his debt.'

'How do you know all this and why haven't I read about it before?'

Tennyson smiled. 'Because of a little-known pact

made during World War Two between the US government and the Mafia.'

'Excuse me?'

'You heard me right. You see, the mob controlled the port facilities in the Northeast, from Boston down to Wilmington, Delaware. In order for the docks to run smoothly for the war effort, certain concessions were made to organized-crime figures, including Lucky Luciano, who was paroled from prison after the war for his cooperation.'

'And how does this pertain to Tesla's boat?'

'Dockworkers first tried to fire up the ship's boilers to move it to a wrecking facility on the Delaware River. They succeeded, and one worker inadvertently powered up the equipment Tesla had left wired to the ship's hull. Two men were in the room when the machine went live. One of them was cut in half by an unknown force and his lower extremities vaporized. This is where the rumour of men fused to the deck of the *Eldridge* originates. It's said the dead man's torso was found erect and propped up on his hands as though he was lifting himself out of the deck.

'The second man looked perfectly fine, but he too was dead, his skin turned as white as a sheet. It was later determined that the iron in his blood had been ripped free of its binding protein, and toxic shock killed him. These two men happened to be pretty well connected with the local mob boss – I can't recall his name at the moment – but, needless to say, the workers were spooked and refused to work on the ship. They discussed a general dockwide strike until the Navy agreed to tow the ship out into the Atlantic and sink it.'

'Did they?'

'They had no choice. Philadelphia was one of the Navy's most important facilities for both shipbuilding and repair. It wasn't worth the scrap value of one old mine tender to put that in jeopardy.'

'Why didn't the Navy investigate the machine that killed the men?'

'I'm sure they wanted to, but with twenty thousand workers threatening to walk off the job at the same time the Allies were marching up the spine of Italy, and material was being amassed for the eventual invasion at Normandy, they took the prudent course to keep the peace on the home front.'

'How did what you just told me become the story of the USS *Eldridge* and the Philadelphia Experiment?'

'In 1953, the author of an obscure book about UFOs named Morris Jessup received a letter from a man identifying himself as Carlos Allende. Allende singled out Jessup because in his book he speculated that UFOs were powered by electromagnetism and that during the war the Navy had experimented with such forces on a ship in Philadelphia. Allende claimed the research was based on Einstein's unified field theory, though Einstein never could reconcile all the forces of nature into one elegant formula like he had for relativity.

'They corresponded for a time until Jessup realized Allende was some kind of crank and stopped all contact. Who Allende really was has never been established, but I believe he was aboard Nikola's old mine tender when those two men were so mysteriously killed and spun an even greater tale for a gullible dupe.

'Interestingly, the Office of Naval Research contacted Jessup a few years later about an annotated copy of his book they'd been sent. He informed them that the cryptic notes were written by Allende. Then, in 1959, Jessup set up a meeting with Dr Manson Valentine, the man who later discovered the limestone formation called the Bimini Road in the waters off the Bahamas. Jessup never made that meeting. He was found dead in his car in Miami, with a rubber hose stretched from the exhaust to his closed window. That last detail is the lifeblood of conspiracy theorists the world over. They say it wasn't suicide but that he was killed by French operatives.'

Cabrillo scoffed. 'French?'

'It's a conspiracy theory, after all.' Tennyson chuckled. 'Why not the French?'

'Where did you get the story about the mine tender and why didn't you put it in your biography?'

Before answering, the retired academic hauled himself to his feet. 'I'm thirsty. Let's get something to drink and then finish up with that stump. You almost have it out of the ground.'

Picking up his jacket and securing the holstered gun when Tennyson had his back turned, Juan followed him across the lawn and patio. The house's kitchen was tucked into the back corner overlooking the garden, and while there were 'modern' appliances, the fridge looked like it had been converted from an icebox, and a box of extra-long matches next to the stove meant its pilot had to be lit by hand.

Tennyson pulled two Cokes from the fridge and handed one over. 'I'm sure you'd prefer a beer, but I don't drink.'

'This is fine.' Cabrillo popped the can and took a long draught, not realizing how dry his throat had become.

The doorbell buzzed, and Juan's thirst vanished as his mind flashed to the bullet striking Yusuf out in the desert where no assassin had a right to be.

'Are you expecting anyone?'

'Not really. But my birthday is this week, and I've been getting gifts from old students and colleagues,' Tennyson said as he ambled from the kitchen. Juan brushed passed him and looked out the front window. A delivery van was parked next to his Porsche on the street, its side emblazoned with a bouquet of flowers. His pulse slowed.

'Looks like someone sent you flowers.'

'Probably my old secretary. She sends peonies every year.'

Cabrillo shifted his angle to see the driver standing on the stoop. He could only see a sliver of the man and just a hint of the colour of the flowers he carried. And then he took a second glance at the truck. The name under the painted bouquet: EMPIRE FLORISTS.

The connections came as fast as the synapses in his brain could fire. Vermont was the Green Mountain

State. It was its neighbour, New York, that carried the Empire nickname. No way would a florist deliver this far out of state. They would have called a local business to drop off a bouquet of whatever the customer requested. Someone coming all the way from New York wasn't here to deliver flowers. Pytor Kenin's name popped into his head, and he knew that if Kenin used local talent to kill the world's foremost expert on Nikola Tesla, they would be based out of Brighton Beach, New York, aka Little Odessa.

'Wes!' Cabrillo shouted, turning to see that Tennyson was already reaching for the front door. 'No!'

12

Tennyson started to pull on the heavy brass handle when the door burst against his face as the florist kicked it in from the outside. The professor fell backward onto the floor only seconds before the muted buzz of a machine pistol on full automatic filled the parlour followed by two muted blasts from Cabrillo's silenced FN pistol that sent the phony florist reeling into a bed of rosebushes.

Tennyson's fall had saved him. He had dropped to the floor below the volley that sprayed the air above him. Cabrillo cursed himself for being two seconds too late to stop the attack on the professor, yet he was thankful that Tennyson did not appear to have stopped a bullet. He barely had time to tell him to play dead.

In the eerie silence that followed, Cabrillo heard two men speaking in Russian as they rushed across the backyard and into the kitchen. When they reached the parlour, it was empty but for Tennyson's body and a small yellow carpet of scattered daffodils. Only the shattered front door showed any sign of splattered crimson. Unknown to the men, Cabrillo was hiding behind coats in the hall closet as he stared through a crack in the door.

'That him?' one of the killers asked.

His accomplice nodded. 'Right here. Vermont driver's license issued to Wesley Tennyson.'

In the closet, Cabrillo held his breath, hoping that Tennyson was savvy enough to play a good corpse. The only hitch was, there was no blood on him.

As if suddenly thinking of something, one of the killers stood and looked out of the doorway. 'Where's Vladimir?'

'He probably went to the van to get the gas cans to burn the house.'

'I can see through the van's windshield. He's not in it.'

'I'll check the front,' the man standing in the doorway muttered. 'You go upstairs and search the bedrooms. I'll take the downstairs after I find Vladimir.'

'Don't forget to turn on the gas on the stove.'

The man stepped out in front of the house while his co-conspirator climbed the stairs.

He only took five steps past the front door when he spied Vladimir's remains lying in a bed of roses, his dead eyes staring into the sun. He whirled around and ran back into the house, shouting his colleague's name. As soon as he burst into the entryway, he saw a man sitting on a nearby divan. Surprise cost him the three microseconds Cabrillo needed to put a bullet in his forehead precisely between the eyes.

Too late, the man on the stairs realized something was wrong. Cabrillo fired a second time, and a red hole appeared in the Russian's neck.

Cabrillo looked down on the body that had fallen across Tennyson's feet. Then he hoisted the corpse and dropped it on top of the other. Only then did he kneel beside Tennyson.

'Are you all right, Professor?'

Tennyson raised his head and stared into Cabrillo's eyes. 'No, I'm not all right. I lead a quiet, dignified life, and within five minutes I have three dead men in my flower bed and entryway. What am I going to tell the police?'

'Not to worry. Have you got a wheelbarrow?'

'I have one in the tool shed.'

'May I borrow it?'

Tennyson looked at him. 'What for?'

'I'm going to haul the bodies out to the van and hide them. Do you have any ideas for a nice secluded area?'

Tennyson thought a moment. 'There's an old gravel pit that's filled with water. Sport divers don't go into it because of chemicals left over when it was abandoned.'

'Where can I find it?'

'About ten miles south of town. It's rough going. It runs through a thick wooded area. The road to it hasn't been used for thirty years.'

'Sounds perfect,' said Cabrillo. He handed Tennyson the keys to his car. 'You lead me to the gravel pit as soon as you pack.'

'Pack?'

'Yes, pack. Your life isn't worth two cents if you stay here. My corporation owns a nice little condo on the island of Antigua. You can go there and relax on the beach until I let you know it's safe and there will be no more attempts on your life.'

Tennyson asked the obvious question: 'Why do these people want to kill me?'

'You know too much about Tesla.'

Without further talk, Cabrillo loaded the van with the cadavers while Tennyson quickly threw clothes and a shaving kit into a suitcase.

It took forty minutes to drive the ten miles. Cabrillo took the lead, followed by Tennyson in his rented Porsche. The professor honked the horn once for a right turn and twice for a left. Once they left the main road for a barely visible dirt track through the woodlands, their speed dropped to fifteen miles an hour. Three times they were forced to stop and heave dead branches off the old road. Finally, they reached the abandoned gravel pit.

Old rusting equipment lay scattered around the edge of the pit. Battered and rotted wooden buildings were all that were left of the offices and crew's mess hall. Cabrillo stepped from the van and stared over the lip of the pit. The water looked yellowish brown and smelled like sulfur. He could only guess how deep the water was and hope it was enough to cover the van.

He put a rock on the accelerator, shifted the transmission into drive, and watched as the van jerked forward, dropped over the brink, and impacted the water with a formless splash and slowly sank into the watery ooze.

Then Cabrillo sat on a large rock, deep in thought, as he waited for the van to sink out of sight. He knew who hired the assassins and why, yet there were other questions.

Amateurs, he said to himself. Why did Pytor Kenin send a trio of amateurs?

13

When the mast rose out of the sea like a shark's telltale fin, it barely cut through the water and left no trail of churned oceanic phosphorus, no presence other than a tiny blip undetectable to all but the most trained observers. Leviathan showed itself yet remained hidden in its watery realm.

Forty feet below this thin stalk of metal lay one of the most devastating weapons ever devised by man. Named Akula, or shark, this class of Russian fast-attack submarine was a true predator of the sea. Measuring more than a football field in length and displacing some twelve thousand tons when submerged, the hunter/killer boasted multiple torpedo tubes, rocket launchers, and a sonar suite that could detect the minutest sound over vast distances. She carried a crew of seventy-three led by one Kapitan Anton Patronov.

Patronov was so fair-haired and pale-skinned that he almost appeared albino, and with an upturned nose that looked like the double barrels of a shotgun, he was considered porcine as well. His wet lips were overly large, and he had a cauliflower ear from his days as a boxer in the old Soviet naval academy. He wasn't particularly tall, but had wide shoulders that sloped up to a bullet head that he kept trimmed in a half-inch buzz of pure white hair. What he lacked in mannish charm he made up for in capability and utter ruthlessness. He'd turned down promotions twice so that he could stay at sea, and because many years ago he was the youngest sub captain in modern Russian history, he had more experience as a submariner than anyone else in the Navy.

Patronov was just stepping from his cubicle-sized cabin when the flash traffic came off the comm line. Over the Tannoy came the cry, 'Captain to the shack. Secure transmission for your eyes only.'

'Clear the way,' he growled as he made his way aft to the radio room. He possessed a low, rasping voice with a dark inflection that commanded instant respect. Seamen and officers alike pressed themselves against the tight companionway walls to ease his passage.

The radio shack was a confined space made more hospitable to electronics than man. Yet somehow two young techs were shoehorned into the room, one with headphones draped around his neck while the other sat back as far as the confines would allow and translated the burst transmission.

'We had an Ohio on the plot,' Patronov said as he entered the space. 'Tell me this is more important.'

The Akula had been trailing an Ohio-class submarine, one of the legs of America's defensive triad of nuclear deterrent, when she was called to the surface by a ULF summons for immediate data download. 'It's in code,' the radioman said without meeting his captain's glare. He held the flimsy paper over his shoulder in

166

hopes it would be snatched away and his culpability in ending the sub chase was at an end.

'Damn.' Patronov ripped the thin piece of paper out of the sailor's hand, snapped it so he could inspect the type, and cursed again. 'Kenin. He's been the pain in my ass since the academy.'

'Sir?' It was obvious from his tone that the young radio operator hadn't expected such disrespect from his captain for the fleet's commanding admiral.

'Relax, Pavel. When the time comes for them to pin captain's bars on your shoulders, you will curse my name ten times worse than I curse my first commander.'

'Yes, sir. I mean, no, sir. I mean . . .' The young radioman wisely stopped talking and kept his stare riveted on his equipment. The second radio operator swivelled in his chair and asked, 'Will we reacquire the Americans?'

Patronov shot him a look that twisted the tech back in his seat so that he too stared at the radios. 'It took us a week of searching the first time,' he said as he left the room. 'It will probably take me that long just to decrypt this damn message.'

It took him the better part of an hour to decode the page-length missive. Because this was a private communiqué between the two men and not an official order, he had to use a private codebook that Kenin had given only to his most loyal followers. Patronov knew that such a book was in the possession of senior captain Sergei Karpov. Karpov was currently on deployment aboard a Typhoon-class missile boat with a complement of twenty nuclear-tipped ICBMs. Patronov knew Sergei well and knew that if Kenin ever ordered a secret launch, Karpov would press the button as fast and as hard as he could.

Truth told, Patronov admitted, so would he.

With China ascending as a world leader and America no longer willing to fulfill its role as a superpower, a void was opening that a man like Admiral Kenin could exploit. The dragon and eagle would eventually fight it out in some form, but it would be the bear that would emerge victorious.

Patronov read through the decrypted message for a second time before hitting the comm button on his desk that connected him to the bridge. 'Emergency order. XO to the captain's cabin. Helm, make your course two three-five. Course to be corrected later when plot is resolved. Speed all ahead full. The American boomer is no longer a target. Repeat, the American is no longer a target.'

Seven seconds later, the sub's executive officer, her second-in-command, knocked on Patronov's cabin door.

'Enter.'

Paulus Renko stepped through the door and stood as stiff as a ramrod until his captain waved him into a chair. The younger man was the opposite of Patronov physically. He was as handsome as a model on a recruiting poster, a hair's breadth shy of the maximum height allowance on a submarine, and had a fencer's lean build, with broad shoulders and a tapered waist and hips.

Patronov eyed him for a moment, his ugly countenance giving away nothing. He sighed as if reaching a weighty decision. 'I've been tasked with telling you, Commander Renko, that you will never deploy as an executive officer ever again.'

Renko's blue eyes widened in shock and his mouth gaped.

'Admiral Kenin has communicated to me that following this mission you will have a boat of your own.' Patronov stood and struck his hand across the small desk that took up a quarter of his cabin's floor space. 'Congratulations.'

Renko's face went from ashen fear to flushed jubilation in the blink of an eye. He shook his captain's hand, his grin widening until he could no longer contain himself, and he whooped aloud.

'I can't believe this,' he said when he could finally speak. 'I didn't know I was even up for promotion.'

'You weren't,' Patronov said as he retook his seat. His chilly tone cooled the room by twenty degrees, and Renko's smile turned a little sickly.

He fumbled back into his chair. 'Sir?'

'Let me tell you a story,' Patronov said in a disarming tone, as if the frostiness of the past few seconds had never happened. 'Eighteen months ago, before you joined this crew, we were tasked to act as a dive platform on a salvage job. It took place close to the eastern seaboard of the United States, though not in her territorial waters. We were on-station for a week, and the divers recovered items of a technical nature from a sunken ship.' He forestalled his subordinate's obvious question by adding, 'Admiral Kenin never cleared me, so I have no idea what they took off the derelict. All I know is, the wreck was about a hundred years old, and Kenin felt the reward justified the risk of discovery by America's Coast Guard or Navy.

'I just got a message from the Admiral that he's learned that another group is showing unusual interest in the derelict and may dive on it soon.'

'Who is this group?'

'American mercenaries,' Patronov said with obvious distaste. 'It was decided the first time we were there not to destroy the wreck so we wouldn't draw attention to it. Now Kenin wants us to blow it off the bottom with a couple of torpedoes. To do that, I need your authorization as XO to fire live shots as per procedure.'

'And if I go along with this, I get promoted?'

'Quid pro quo.'

Renko rubbed his lantern jaw. 'I take it neither this act nor the original dives were authorized by the Navy High Command?'

'I'm sure a few know about it, those closest to Admiral Kenin, but, no, this operation is strictly off the books.'

'What about the mercenaries?'

'According to Kenin's source, they aren't capable of detecting us, let alone fighting us. We'll sneak in low and slow, pop two USET-80s into the wreck, and be gone before they know we were there. If they happen to have divers on the bottom, well, that's just bad luck for them. So what do you say, Paulus, do you want to be a captain at the age of thirty-one? That would, by the way, give you a two-year head start on breaking my service record.'

Renko stood and reached across the desk to shake his captain's hand. 'I'm your man, sir.'

'Very good, alert the torpedo room that we will be loading two tubes with the antisubmarine fish. We have a good three days' sailing to get into position, but I want them prepped down there.'

'Aye, sir.'

Patronov jotted some coordinates onto a piece of scratch paper. 'That's the GPS location for the wrecked ship. Refine and plot our new course. Remain at full speed.'

'Aye, aye, sir.' Renko pivoted on his heel and left the cabin.

Patronov could tell his subaltern was excited about his future prospects, but, then again, all deals with the devil promised much. It wasn't until much later you learn the costs.

14

'You are the very picture of boredom,' Max said, stepping off the elevator at the rear of the op centre.

Cabrillo settled his coffee cup into a holder built into the Kirk Chair, the central command platform in the middle of the electronics-packed, low-ceilinged space. On the main view screen was a murky video feed coming up from a tethered probe poking around the bottom of the Atlantic nearly three hundred feet down. Details were hard to come by as the unmanned submersible ran its cameras over the hull of an unidentified ship.

'Got that right,' he replied. 'Twenty-two wrecks checked and twenty-two consecutive goose eggs.'

'So what are we looking at?' Max asked as he crossed the room with a plate of food in his hand. He set it next to Cabrillo's elbow. 'Fish tacos, by the way. Fresh pico de gallo, but the chef hid a ghost chilli in there, so watch yourself.'

'Thanks. I'm starved.' Cabrillo ate half of a taco in a single bite, managing to not ruin his shirt when the shell inevitably collapsed. 'What we are seeing, if my five days of experience has taught me anything, is a Boston long-liner that sank in 1960 or so.'

'Not our target?'

'Not even close. Do you know how many wrecks there are off the East Coast?'

'About thirty-five hundred,' Max replied. 'And most of them are clustered between Richmond, Virginia, and Cape Cod. Less than a quarter of them are identified. Which leaves us searching a lot of haystacks for a single needle.'

'You are the paragon of the understatement.'

In the days since Cabrillo's return to the ship after his ill-fated meeting with Wesley Tennyson, the *Oregon* had been scouring the seafloor with side-scan sonar looking for the mysterious mine tender that the professor said had been modified by Nikola Tesla. Murph and Stone had worked out the search parameters and overlaid it with a grid of shipwrecks in the region. There was good news. Since these waters were so heavily fished, all bottom obstructions, like boulders, outcroppings, and sunken ships, were clearly marked, though rarely identified by name.

That left them with forty possible candidates to explore with their remotely operated vehicle, named *Little Geek* after a similar-looking ROV from the movie *The Abyss*. They could safely ignore wooden-hulled ships and natural rock formations by first verifying each target with a magnetometer to detect the presence of metal. Once they did have a steel-hulled wreck, it was a laborious process of lowering the suitcase-sized robot through the moon pool to the bottom and visually inspecting each wreck. Identification was more difficult because many of the vessels were festooned with nets torn off fishing trawlers as they plied the seas. Nets that not only obscured the wrecks but made it easy for an ROV to get trapped.

Juan hit a button on the arm of his command chair. 'Cabrillo to Moon Pool. This one's a bust, Eric. Reel in *Little Geek*, and we'll check out target twenty-three.'

'Roger that, Chairman.'

'Helm, as soon as the ROV's aboard, steer one eight-five at twenty knots.' That was far below the ship's best speed, but with the waters so busy, it wouldn't do to show off the *Oregon*'s true potential. In fact, twenty knots seemed out of reach for a rust-streaked old tramp like her, but that was all part of her elaborate deception. 'Next potential target is twenty miles away.'

Juan rubbed his eyes. 'I can't believe Dirk Pitt did this kind of stuff for a living. Talk about boring.'

'Different strokes,' Max replied. 'And you and I both know there isn't a whole lot of boring on that man's résumé.

'By the way, how is it that the Emir isn't screaming his head off that we're not there to protect him?'

'We lucked out. He's rafting with a Saudi prince and some Mexican telecommunications billionaire, if you can call three mega-yachts lashed together rafting. Linda tells me they're trying to outdo each other on hosting lavish dinners. She says each of them has had chefs and food flown into Hamilton and choppered out to them. She Googled one of the wines and saw it sold at auction four years ago for ten grand.'

'Per case?'

'Bottle. And the three of them and their nubile guests went through eight of them at dinner.'

Max cocked an eyebrow. '"Nubile"?'

'My adjective. Linda's description of them was less kind. I think she even used the word "floozy."'

Hanley chuckled. 'There aren't too many women who can make her jealous in the looks department.'

'Well, six of them are with her now and she's not too happy about it. She says we have two more days before they break up their little party and the Emir heads to Bermuda. If we don't find the wreck by this time tomorrow, we'll call off the search, nursemaid our esteemed friend on one of the safest islands in the world for two weeks, and then head back here to keep looking.'

'What do you think we'll find?'

'I have no idea, but if Pytor Kenin is interested, it can't be good.'

Eric Stone's voice came over the speakers built into the ceiling. '*Little Geek*'s back aboard, and the keel doors are closed.'

'Helm,' Cabrillo prompted.

'On it, Chairman.'

Juan flipped the main view screen to the bridge cameras and expanded it so he had an almost panoramic view of the ocean. The seas were choppy and leaden under a grey sky, and in the distance there were dark curtains of rain squalls. He could see the silhouettes of two ships along the horizon, one heading north and the other south. As the *Oregon* picked up speed, her ride stabilized, and the constant rolling she'd endured while hovering over the old sunken trawler faded away.

He wolfed down the second taco and gave a sudden gasp. His face reddened, and he began panting.

'Ghost chilli?' Max asked mildly.

'Yes,' Cabrillo managed to wheeze with tears streaming from his eyes.

'I hate to be the one to tell you this,' Hanley breezed, placing a hand on Cabrillo's shoulder as the Chairman tried to suck air past his tortured tongue, 'but this is payback for adding salt and pepper to your meatloaf last night. Chef said it was seasoned perfectly, and if you want his food spicier, he's more than happy to oblige. Enjoy.'

He sauntered from the op centre, leaving the Chairman literally unable to reply.

An hour later, they were over the spot where the charts indicated an obstruction on the seafloor. They lowered the side-scan sonar, a towed array that hovered just above the seabed, and took acoustical pictures of its surroundings. More often than not, the obstruction, whether man-made or natural, was exactly where the charts said it would be, but ocean-floor mapping wasn't the *Oregon*'s primary, secondary, or even tertiary mission. As a result, their sonar unit wasn't up to par when compared to outfits like NOAA or NUMA, and it took time to find the target. In this case, they spent an hour running lanes north and south over a swath of the sea, much like a weekender mowing the lawn. It was this tedious back-and-forth scanning that tested Cabrillo's patience.

Finally, after their second hour of fruitless search, the display screen showed an object that began reflecting sonar waves back to the array.

Juan felt the initial spike of adrenaline that any hunter does at the first sign of the quarry. It turned to bitter disappointment when the sonar revealed an object at least five hundred feet long and so oddly shaped that it could only be a stone outcropping on the otherwise barren continental shelf.

Another bust, he said to himself. He keyed the intercom. 'Eric, to paraphrase Charlie Brown on Halloween, we got a rock. Go ahead and leave the sled deployed, our next target is only five miles away.'

The cable for the towed sonar was much stronger than the ROV's umbilical, so they could leave it in the water as they transited to the next grid mark, but they would need to keep their speed below fifteen knots so as not to stress it too much.

'Okay.'

'Helm, next target is five miles away on two nineteen.'

'Making my course two nineteen at fifteen knots.'

Mark Murphy strolled out of the elevator wearing a seemingly blood-stained T-shirt with the words 'I'm fine' written out over his chest. The young tech genius had his face buried in an iPad as he walked.

'About time,' Juan said. 'You were supposed to spell me ten minutes ago.'

'You and I both know you weren't going to leave the op centre until you identified this latest target, so I monitored communications and came up when you pegged it.'

Juan frowned at being so easily read. 'All right. I'll give you this one. Just so you know, the array is still deployed.'

'Hello. Monitored communications. I knew that.'

'You're in a mood,' Cabrillo remarked.

'Sorry, boss. I've been asked to peer-review an article by a friend at UC Berkeley and his conclusions are all wrong, and no matter how I try to help him see his mistakes, he's just not getting it.'

'He doesn't like being out-nerded?'

Murph grinned. 'Nobody does.'

Juan spent the rest of the day on paperwork, had dinner with Eddie Seng and Franklin Lincoln, and watched a movie in his cabin before turning in for the night. They'd checked five more targets during Mark's watch, and, like all the others before, they hadn't found Tesla's ship.

They had one more day before heading south for Bermuda. In the great scheme of things, a two-week hiatus guarding the Emir wasn't a big deal, but Juan felt the spectre of time looming over him. Kenin was covering his tracks, first in Kazakhstan, and again with Professor Tennyson. It followed that he would try to destroy Tesla's experimental ship, if he knew about it, which Juan felt sure the Russian admiral did.

It was little wonder his sleep was restless.

The ringing of his bedside telephone roused him.

'H'lo,' he muttered. Cleared his throat and tried again. 'Hello. This is Cabrillo.'

'Chairman, it's Eric.'

'Yeah, Stoney. What have you got?'

'I think we found her.'

Juan noted it was five o'clock. Weak sunlight spilled around the curtains drawn over his cabin's portholes.

'What time did you guys start this morning?' he asked, swinging his legs out of bed.

'We ran all night. Figured we're searching so deep that we need halogens on the ROV anyway, and shipping traffic's been light.'

'Where are we?'

'Target thirty-two.'

Juan knew that put them about twenty miles due east of Ocean City, Maryland. Almost the exact centre of the search grid Eric and Murph had drawn up.

'Nicely figured,' he said.

Stone knew what Cabrillo meant. 'Truth told, it wasn't rocket science, but thanks.'

'You've got a visual?' Juan had clamped the phone with his shoulder and was working the sock of his prosthetic leg over his stump.

'*Little Geek*'s down there now, and it looks to be a small, thirties-era warship, with some weird modifications. It looks like a cage was built over the entire deck up to and over the superstructure and bridge.'

'What's the condition of the wreck?'

'She's sitting pretty much upright on the bottom. There's been some collapse, but, on the whole, she's in better condition than you'd expect. Only problem is, she's got a couple of nets snagged over her, so I don't want to get *Little Geek* in too close and snarl the umbilical.'

'Okay. Alert the moon pool that I'm coming down, and wake Mike Trono.' Trono was the butt of a lot of jokes on the *Oregon* because he was the only ex-Air Force member of a crew dominated by Navy veterans. He'd been a pararescuer, one of those tasked to go behind enemy lines to save downed airmen, and he'd made his bones first in Kosovo and later in Iraq. He was also the only diver besides the Chairman certified to dive on trimix gas, which they would need to reach the mine tender's depth.

'You're going swimming?'

'Can't risk *Little Geek*, but we can risk me. Also roust Eddie. I want him down there with us in the Nomad.' Cabrillo hung up the phone, threw on yesterday's clothes, and made a quick pit stop in his bathroom.

The largest single space aboard the *Oregon* other than the main hold is the sub bay, where they stored the two submersibles, and the moon pool, where they were launched through large doors cut into the ship's keel. It was lit with stark-white lights that flashed reflections on the surging black water sloshing in the swimming-pool-sized hole. A prep crew was working on the Nomad 1000, the larger of the two mini-subs and the only one equipped with an air lock. The Nomad looked like a white lozenge with three small, forward-looking portholes mated to an industrial framework of ballast tanks, thrusters, battery packs, and a pair of nasty-looking mechanical arms equipped with feedback pincers that could collect the most delicate sea fan or rip apart a sheet of steel. The mini was rated to carry six people and could dive to a thousand feet. The smaller Discovery submarine was a sports car compared to its delivery-van cousin and could make this dive depth, but Cabrillo wanted the air lock as a contingency if anything went wrong. He and Mike could lock into the chamber and decompress inside if the sub had to make a quick ascent. Cabrillo's natural pessimism was what made him an excellent contingency planner. Max always liked to tease him about his plans C, D, and E, and a lot of them were nuts, but they'd saved more operations than Hanley would ever admit.

Off in a corner of the cavernous room, engineers readied the most high-tech dive gear in the *Oregon*'s inventory. The more dangerous the environment, the more equipment man needs to survive. Put someone on a tropical isle and he can get away with little more than a grass skirt. Where Cabrillo was headed was as inhospitable to human life as the hard vacuum of outer space. Because of the increased pressure below a depth of about four hundred feet, the nitrogen that makes up the vast majority of air would saturate the blood and cause nitrogen narcosis, or rapture of the deep. It was a debilitating sense of euphoria that made even the simplest tasks impossible. To counter this, most of the nitrogen in the air Cabrillo and Trono would breathe had been replaced with undissolvable helium gas. The mix was called trimix because it did contain some nitrogen to prevent another debilitating problem called High Pressure Nervous Syndrome.

On top of that they would carry small cylinders of argon gas to inflate their dry suits. Argon conducted heat much more slowly than either helium or regular air, and the bottom temperature was less than forty degrees, so hypothermia was always an issue. All told, each man would be burdened with over a hundred and fifty pounds of gear.

'Morning, Juan,' Mike Trono greeted. Trono was in his mid-thirties, with a slender build and thin straight brown hair. 'I haven't had a chance to ask, how'd you like Vermont?'

Trono was a native of the Green Mountain State.

'Beautiful, but the roads are atrocious.'

'Ah, potholes and frost heaves – oh, how I don't miss thee.'

'You up for this?'

'Are you kidding me? I live for wreck diving. I spent my last vacation exploring the *Andrea Doria*.'

'That's right. Didn't Kurt Austin lead that trip?'

'Yeah. It was his second time down to her.'

A new voice, one with a refined English accent, intruded. 'There are simply too many type A personalities aboard this ship.'

'Hello, Maurice,' Juan greeted the *Oregon*'s chief steward.

182

It didn't matter that it was barely past five in the morning or that news of the discovery was less than fifteen minutes old, the retired Royal Navy man was dressed as elegantly as ever in razor-creased black slacks, a snowy white button-down shirt, and shoes so polished they'd shame a Marine honor guard.

He had a white towel draped over one arm and carried a domed silver serving tray. He set down a carafe of black coffee and removed the dome. The tempting aroma of scrambled eggs and country sausage beat back the briny scent of the sea that permeated the sub bay.

After they ate, both men stripped down and donned thermal diving underwear and socks. Then came the Ursuit Cordura FZ dry suits. These suits were of one-piece construction that left only the face exposed. That would be covered with dive helmets outfitted with integrated communications gear. A computerized voice modulator would null some of the effects of breathing helium, but both men would still be left sounding like an alto-voiced Mickey Mouse.

While they were suiting up, Eddie had performed his pre-dive checks, and the Nomad submersible was lowered into the water. Additional trimix tanks were attached to hard points on the hull so the two divers wouldn't need to use their own supply until they were on the bottom.

'How you coming?' Cabrillo asked his dive partner.

'Good to go.'

Juan flashed Mike the universal OK sign for divers,

pressing index finger to thumb, and pulled his helmet over his head. Mike did the same. The two took a couple of tentative breaths and made adjustments as needed.

'And a very good morning to the Lollipop Guild,' Max Hanley called from his station in the op centre.

'Very funny,' Juan retorted, but his irritation went unheard because of his comical voice.

'Just so you know, the forecast is for light wind, and a sea running barely two feet. But be advised, you've got a five-knot current out of the south on the bottom. Get careless and you'll be gone.'

'Roger that,' the two men acknowledged at the same time.

'Bus driver, you ready?' Cabrillo asked Eddie Seng.

'Say the word.'

'We're going in.'

Juan and Mike threw each other another OK sign and unceremoniously rolled into the Atlantic's cool embrace. Both were quick with inflating their suits and adjusting their buoyancy so they hovered like dark jellyfish just below the surface. They found handholds along the side of the Nomad and switched their air feeds to the spare tanks attached to her.

'Let's go.'

'Hold on tight. Nomad, release.' A pause. 'We are clear.'

Bubbles erupted around the submersible as Eddie purged her tanks and the thirty-foot mini-sub began its descent to the seafloor and whatever lay hidden on the derelict mine tender.

Cabrillo could feel pressure building on his suit and knew it would approach two hundred pounds per square inch when they reached the wreck. He continuously added argon gas to keep the material from crushing in on him. The cold temperature wasn't a problem now, but it would eventually start seeping through the protective layers and leach heat first from his skin and then his very core.

Down they dropped, the blue-grey water of a dawn dive giving way to midnight blue and finally true black as they settled deeper and deeper. There was no sense of movement to their descent except for the steadily building current that swept tropical waters out of the Caribbean along the East Coast and eventually to Northern Europe.

Juan kept a constant vigil over his equipment, checking valves and his dive computer for time and depth and other details. He also checked in with Max and Eddie at regular intervals and maintained visual confirmation that his dive partner was okay. Laxity anywhere is dangerous. On a dive, it is deadly.

'Bottom coming up in fifty feet,' Eddie announced. 'I'm going to switch on the lights.'

As powerful as they were, the xenon lamps mounted on the forward part of the submarine could throw a corona of light only twenty feet. It showed the ocean was full of snow – tiny particles of organic matter that continuously rained down from the surface, only this was much worse because of the current. Cabrillo had experienced this phenomena many times, but this trip was like trying to peer through a blizzard.

'Visibility sucks,' Mike complained.

'Say again,' Max radioed.

'No visibility,' Juan enunciated slowly.

'Copy that. Poor vis.'

'We're coming down about fifty feet off the ship,' Eddie said. 'I've got it on lidar. The vessel itself is eighty feet long, but she's trailing a good two hundred feet of old fishing nets that're snagged around her hull.'

A burst of silt erupted around the hull when Eddie gunned the sub's motors a bit too hard. 'Oops. Sorry about that.'

The submersible crawled out of a billowing cloud of sand that seemed to be flushed away by the Gulf Stream. Cabrillo got his first look at the wreck with his own eyes. The old Navy ship appeared as haunted and forlorn as any wreck he'd seen, and with the rotting nets waving in the current, she looked like an old castle draped in cobwebs. He felt a shiver run up his spine that had nothing to do with the temperature.

The ship itself was a slender, arrow-bowed craft, with good proportions to her superstructure and a single up-and-down funnel placed just aft of amidships. She had no name, but under the accumulated rime of sea growth the number 821 could be seen painted next to her main anchor hawsehole. It appeared that she'd settled evenly. There were no crushed hull plates, but the superstructure was showing signs of decay as portions of some decks had collapsed after nearly seventy-five years of the ocean's corrosive assault.

'Would you guys turn on your helmet cams so we can get a visual up here?' Max prompted.

Juan turned on both his camera and his own lights while Mike Trono did the same.

As they edged closer, more details emerged, and Juan saw the odd frame built around the ship that Eric Stone had mentioned. The metal trusswork looked like it extended to just below the waterline and covered the entire ship in what was essentially a cage with openings of about two feet square. It was going to be a tight fit to get through the frame and actually explore the ship.

There was something really strange about the structure, whose purpose he couldn't begin to guess. And then it occurred to him. While the rest of the ship was rust-streaked and matted with marine growth, the frame was shiny, and not a single organism had tried to make it their home. No clams grew there, like the colonies infesting the ship's deck, no starfish clung to it, not even a stray coral polyp. It was as if the sea creatures shied away from the metal scaffold.

'Mike,' Juan called, 'take a sample of that frame. Priority one.'

'Copy. You want a sample of the frame,' Trono repeated back so there was no confusion.

Eddie settled the Nomad onto the seafloor about ten feet from the wreck. Cabrillo and Trono switched over to their own trimix tanks, waiting a minute to make certain they had regular airflow, then they pushed off from the mini-sub.

Eddie had positioned them so that the Nomad's hull blocked the worst of the brutal current, and it was an easy swim over to the wreck. While Mike got busy with a diamond-toothed saw on one of the frame members, Cabrillo managed to ease himself through one of the square openings by first taking off his main tank and pushing it through ahead of himself. Once he had the tank strapped back in place, he swam over the open aft deck, where the ship had once deployed and repaired mines. Now that he was out of the Nomad's protection, he kept one hand on part of the ship at all times. The cage would prevent him from being carried clear off the ship, but impacting the trusswork, should he slip up, could damage equipment or break bone.

He reached a door that led into the ship's interior. Before doing anything, he rapped on it with the steel butt of his handheld dive light to test the metal's strength. Near the edge of the door, the door flaked some, but its integrity seemed good.

'I'm going in,' he announced.

'Roger,' Max said. Standard procedure would have been to have Mike stationed at the door should anything go wrong, but the Chairman's dive partner was only seconds away.

The passage was a standard hallway, with doors leading left and right. Each room was inky black until Cabrillo swept his light across the walls. It looked as though the ship had been completely stripped as part of her being scrapped. There was no furniture in any of the rooms, and he could tell by the plumbing that toilets and sinks had been removed from the enlisted men's head.

He came to a stairwell, and his light caught a sudden movement that made him rear back. A silver fish, he had no idea what species, blasted past him in a blur of fins and tail.

'What happened?' a concerned Hanley asked. As bad as it was for Juan, the jerky video wouldn't have shown what had so startled him.

'Just a fish.' Normally, Juan would have made a lame joke, but communicating humour in a helium-induced falsetto was next to impossible.

He figured that whatever equipment Tesla installed would be on a lower deck rather than up above, near the bridge. He swam down the stairs – really, a steeply canted ladder – and came upon a room where mines had once been stored. Rather than being empty as he'd expected, most of the compartment was taken up by an odd piece of machinery. Juan snapped some pictures with his high-res camera.

'What am I looking at?' Max asked in frustration because of the poor video quality despite the equipment's expense.

'A machine,' Juan told him. 'Never seen anything like it.'

It was a boxy contraption, with wires running from various parts in a dizzying whirl of loops. Some of the machine had been attacked by sea life, while other parts, much like the cage surrounding the ship, hadn't been touched. Thick cables ran out of the top of the machine and up through the ceiling where they probably attached to the frame. Behind the machine was an electrical dynamo with exposed copper coils now rendered to verdigris-coloured ruin. He could see no evidence of what Professor Tennyson said transpired in this room nor did he really expect to.

And while he was no engineer, Cabrillo was versed enough in technology to know he was looking at something completely new. That this was Tesla's work wasn't in doubt, but its purpose certainly was. Optical camouflage? Teleportation? Death ray? Rumours all, but this thing had definitely scared people enough to see it buried in a watery grave. He also saw evidence that someone had dived this wreck before because it looked as though parts of the machine were missing.

It was at that moment, when he realized that his mind was drifting from the technical aspects of the dive, that he heard a shrill alarm over the comm. It was coming from the *Oregon*.

'Max?' Seconds passed and there was no reply. So again he cried in his helium-altered voice, 'Max!'

15

The alarm's wail was followed up with red flashing strobes as the *Oregon*'s automated systems went into combat mode. A sultry female voice came over the intercom. 'All crew to battle stations. All crew to battle stations.'

'Report,' Hanley barked from the command chair.

Mark Murphy was seated at his normal position toward the front of the room, where his primary job was to monitor the ship's vast array of weaponry. He was there this morning to watch the dive.

'Second.' He typed furiously, his skinny fingers moving with the virtuosity of a concert pianist. 'Oh damn.'

'What is it?'

'Passive sonar detected the sound of a submarine opening two of its outer hull doors.'

'Distance and bearing?'

'Eight thousand yards off our starboard side.'

'Whose is it?'

'Coming up now.' The United States Navy kept a database of identifiable noises made by nearly every submarine in the world so that individual boats could be identified during combat situations. Mark had happened to work with one of the data specialists who updated the lists and who had lousy computer-security skills. 'It's a Russian Akula-class. Hull number one five-four. She must be just creeping along, because there are no machinery or screw noises.'

Max glanced over at the radar plot. There were no ships within twenty miles of the *Oregon*. That meant there were no other targets if the submarine's intentions were hostile. The fine hairs on the back of his neck began to prickle.

'Chairman, we've got a Russian sub parked about four and a half miles off our starboard beam. She just opened two torpedo tubes.'

'Get out of there,' Juan ordered.

'Shot fired!' Mark yelled. 'Torpedo in the water.'

It would take a few seconds to accurately calculate the torpedo's course, but all the men listening knew instinctively that the torpedo was on a course towards the *Oregon*. The only real question was whether she was the target or they were gunning for the derelict ship she was hovering over.

Max wasn't the strategist Juan was. He was a nuts-and-bolts kind of guy who left planning to others, so he took his cue off Cabrillo's last order. 'Helm, flank speed.'

The inertia of eighteen thousand tons of steel idling on the ocean's surface was a massive force unto itself, but it was no match for the magnetohydrodynamic engines. The cryopumps spun up and went infrasonic as they pumped liquid nitrogen around the magnets that stripped free electrons from the water forced through the drive tubes. A creaming explosion of froth erupted at the *Oregon*'s fantail, and within ten seconds of Max's command the big former freighter was moving.

That they were under way also meant that within seconds they would be beyond their radio's limited range to communicate with the divers or Eddie in the submersible.

'Max, just before you gave the order I heard a second torpedo launch,' Mark told him. With the ship under way, the passive sensors were deaf to everything except the noises the *Oregon* herself produced, the shriek of her engines and the building hiss of water against her hull.

'Juan, did you catch that?'

'A second torpedo.' Cabrillo didn't hesitate before issuing his orders. The underwater radios weren't encrypted, so the Russian captain knew there were people on the wreck. What he'd done was cold pre-meditated murder. 'Sink 'em.'

There were only about seven minutes until impact. The *Oregon* would be safely outside the torpedoes' sonar range, but the wreck was a sitting duck.

'You got it. Mark, let's tell this guy he picked the wrong dance partner. Hit him with the active sonar, maximum gain, and keep hitting him until I tell you to stop.'

Murph gave a wicked grin and fired off sonar pings. The returns showed the Akula hadn't yet started to make her escape.

'She's still sitting there, and her torpedoes are staying deep.'

'Waiting around to see her fish hit the wreck. Bad mistake, my friend,' Max said. 'You should have high-tailed it the moment you fired. 'Course, you couldn't know that we were listening or know that we can track you.'

Eric Stone rushed into the op centre and took the helm seat next to Murph. With the exception of the Chairman himself, young Mr Stone was the best helms-man aboard and could thread the *Oregon* through the eye of a needle if necessary.

'Eric, bring us about and let's get him within range of our torpedoes.' The Akula could take such a rela-tively long shot because she was firing at a stationary target, but to hit a moving opponent required a short-ening of the distance. 'Wepps, get our own fish readied.'

'Roger that. Looks like the sonar woke 'em up. The Akula's starting to move. The continental shelf drops away about twenty miles from here, and once she goes over, she'll dive like a stone and we'll lose her for sure.'

The *Oregon* began cutting a long arc through the sea as she chased the fleeing Russian sub, and with her vastly superior speed, there was little chance the sub would get away.

'Tubes one and two are flooded,' Mark announced moments later. 'Outer doors are still closed. And, just to remind you, we need to slow to twenty knots for them to open. Otherwise, we can damage the torpe-does.'

'Noted,' Max replied.

They'd cut the range down to six thousand yards,

and Hanley kept at them. Five minutes had elapsed since the first shots were fired. The torps would hit the wreck in about two more. Max needed to end this quickly if he was to get back on-station and coordinate any necessary rescue operation.

'Contact!' Mark shouted. 'He's fired on us! Torpedo coming straight in.'

'Helm, full reverse. Slow us to twenty knots. Wepps, open those doors as soon as you can and fire. Eric, once the torpedo's away, take us back up to thirty knots.'

At that speed, they wouldn't be travelling much slower than their own weapon. The two men didn't understand Max's strategy but carried out his orders nevertheless.

The ship physically shuttered as the impellers went into reverse, glasses rattled on tables, and crewmen were forced to brace themselves against anything solid due to the massive deceleration.

'Twenty knots,' Eric called out.

'Firing.' Mark pressed the key to fire their own torpedo and flipped the toggle to close the doors.

Eric Stone had watched him and reversed the engines once again. Again, the ship gave a mighty shiver as if all that power was trying to tear her apart.

'Sorry, old girl,' Hanley said under his breath and patted his seat's armrest. He then spoke aloud. 'Prepare autodestruct of our torpedo as soon as it's abreast of the incoming Russian fish.'

'Ah,' Mark said with understanding.

Because they were still blasting the sea with active

sonar pulses, they could track the two torpedoes in real time, unlike the Russian, who wasn't pinging but relied on passive listening to find its prey.

In one corner of the main view screen, Hanley brought up a computer-enhanced sonar 'picture' of the seas ahead of them. Between them and the Akula, the two torpedoes were hurtling toward each other at a combined speed nearing ninety knots.

'Helm, be prepared to slow again for another shot. The explosion's going to ruin his ability to listen to us. When they blow, come right five points, so if he pops off a blind shot, he won't get lucky.'

The two torpedoes raced at each other with mindless abandon and would meet less than a half mile off the *Oregon*'s bows. Just a few seconds more. Murph's hand hovered over the autodestruct button, his eyes unblinkingly on the screen. If this didn't work, they would have little time for evasive manoeuvers.

The Akula's captain never would have suspected his quarry would dare to keep charging at them. But there was a truism he obviously wasn't aware of: Never play a game of chicken with a man you don't know.

'Now!' Max, Eric and Mark shouted at the same time.

Stone set about changing their course while ahead of the ship, a mushrooming ball of water was thrown twenty feet into the air.

Both torpedo icons disappeared from the screen, replaced by a hazy cloud of distorted acoustical returns.

'Okay, Helm, slow us down to twenty. Wepps, fire at will.'

Moments later, the *Oregon* unleashed her second torpedo, and the range was so close that the Akula didn't have a chance. She was racing along the bottom, eking everything she could out of her machinery in hopes of reaching the edge of the continental shelf. The cacophony of sonar pings the *Oregon* was throwing into the sea would overwhelm the Akula's displays should she try to go active herself.

They all saw it simultaneously. On the sonar screen they could see their torpedo racing in the Akula's wake when the sub came to a stop in a little less than half her length.

Hanley reacted fastest of any of them. 'Wepps, autodestruct now!'

Mark peeled his gaze from the monitor and typed in the appropriate command. The torpedo was so deep that there wasn't even a ripple on the surface when it exploded less than five hundred yards from its target.

'What happened?' Eric asked.

'She hit something, a seamount of some kind, a boulder. Something,' Max posited. 'Back off the engines so we can listen on passive.'

'Why'd you blow our torpedo?'

'Because when and if that sub is ever found, the investigators will conclude, rightly, that this was an accident. No need to advertise that they were being chased when they did a nosedive into the seafloor.'

By the time the ship slowed enough for the sensitive microphones to be deployed, the Akula was as silent as the grave.

Max roused himself. 'Helm, get us back to the wreck ASAP.' He shot a glance at the battered Timex on his wrist. 'Their torps would have hit eight minutes ago. The Chairman and the others are on borrowed time.'

He wouldn't let himself think about the more likely scenario that they were all dead.

16

Panic kills divers. That was the first lesson from his crusty dive instructor when Juan had earned his scuba certification as a teenager. That was the last too. Panic kills divers.

He and Mike and Eddie had between six and eight minutes to get away. Plenty of time. No need to panic.

Cabrillo shoved his camera back into the dive bag strapped to his waist, took one last glance at Tesla's remarkable contraption, and headed back towards the staircase.

'Mike, are you on your way to the Nomad?' Cabrillo asked, irked that the helium made him sound like a little girl.

'Yes. I even got a sample from the frame.'

'Good. Eddie, we're going to have to jam ourselves into the air lock. Once we're in, emergency ascent.'

'Roger. Emergency blow once you and Mike are aboard.'

That's going to cost me, Juan thought.

In an emergency ascent, the cylindrical hull of the submersible disconnected from the rest of the craft, all the motors, battery packs and ancillary equipment. The crew compartment would shoot to the surface like a cork, taking them out of the blast range, but it also meant that about a million dollars' worth of sub components would be left behind to be blown into oblivion.

Cabrillo misjudged as he moved up the staircase and bumped his trimix tank into a bulkhead. It wasn't much of a hit, but to the old derelict it was a deadly punch. Steel bracings, weakened by decades of immersion, gave way, and the walls around the staircase collapsed in a slow pirouette of destruction. The water filled with an impenetrable cloud of rust particles that turned the light from Cabrillo's lamps into a meager brick-coloured glow.

He managed to push himself away from the worst of the collapse, saving himself from being sliced apart by the avalanche of plate steel.

His careless action had to have caused a chain reaction because he could hear additional rumblings as the old wreck tried to find some new equilibrium.

He remained curled in a ball until everything finally settled down. A piece of steel had landed across his back. His tanks had protected him, but now as he tried to push it off he realized it was either heavier than its impact indicated or it was wedged in place.

'Chairman? Are you there? Juan?'

'I read you, Mike. I might be in trouble.'

'What happened?'

'A wall gave way when I hit it. I'm in a stairwell and I might be trapped.'

'I'm coming.'

'Negative. Get to the Nomad. I'll get myself out.'

'We've got five minutes.'

Cabrillo ran the odds through his head. 'Okay. I'll

give you three. If you can't reach me, get the hell away from here.'

Eddie Seng had been monitoring the divers and knew what he had to do. He powered up the Nomad and swung it around so that he was facing the wreck. He eased in closer, reaching across the tight cabin to switch on the manipulator arms at the copilot's station. He could see Mike, working to remove his tank so he could fit through the frame surrounding the wreck, and radioed to him.

'Hold on, Mike. I've got a better idea.'

Trono had to have seen the sub's dive lights shift toward him. He looked up and saw the craft practically looming over him, its arms outstretched like skeletal limbs. He quickly got out of its way.

With a deft hand on the thruster controls to keep the Nomad in place against the current, Eddie grasped one of the metallic bars with a manipulator hand and tore it completely free. He backed off to allow Mike to swim through the larger aperture.

Mike swam across the aft deck and reached the door Cabrillo had entered only minutes earlier. Rust particles billowed from inside the ship like smoke from a burning building. It only cleared when it was borne away by the current, again like smoke on the wind.

He groped like a sightless man along the passageway, sensing that there wasn't much he could do until visibility improved.

'The stairwell is the fourth door on the right,' Juan said as if reading his mind.

Mike counted doors, and when he'd shown his light in through the correct door, he saw an open shaft that had once been a stairwell. The steps themselves had collapsed, and steel plating had peeled away from its internal structure. He realized that the rivets that had once held them in place had failed, allowing the plating to fall free.

The rust was settling out of the water, and he could just see Cabrillo's leg peeking from the debris one deck down. The leg moved when Juan tried to free himself, but each upward thrust locked the tangle of junk even tighter.

'Hold on,' Mike said.

'I'm not going anywhere,' Cabrillo replied.

Trono swam down, careful not to tear his gloves, and began moving some of the plating. The sections weren't large, but it was like the old game of pick-up sticks. He didn't want what he was doing to cause additional cave-ins. He tore into the pile with repressed frenzy, wanting to work faster but knowing he had to be careful. All the while, he knew that Juan would order him away at any second.

He shoved away enough of the old bulkheads for Cabrillo to try to free himself one last time.

'It's up to you.'

Juan gathered his energy, channelled it, and pushed with everything he had. Mike had done just enough so that the plate that had kept him pinned shifted and ground against the others but didn't jam up. He heaved again and finally dragged himself out of the pile.

Mike was there with a hand to steady him.

'I owe you.' Juan meant it to sound solemn, but the helium lessened the sense of import. 'Now, let's get out of here.'

The two men swam back up to the main deck and finned down the corridor. They burst out of the superstructure to see that Eddie had used the manipulators to tear apart more of the old framework and had the submersible practically parked on the deck.

Mike reached the air lock door first and spun open the wheel lock. The space was tight – a phone booth, really – and he and Cabrillo would need to stay in it for quite some time. They'd been at depth long enough to need almost two hours to decompress. The cramped space would act as a decompression chamber once they reached the surface, but they would need the *Oregon* supplying power since the Nomad's batteries would be left behind.

Getting away from the wreck was only the first part of their ordeal. If they didn't link up with the *Oregon* in time, both divers would run out of trimix, and the Nomad had no internal supplies of the gas. To make matters worse, Juan and Mike had to be decompressed before Eddie could leave the sub via the air lock.

Trono dove headfirst through the hatch and disappeared inside. Juan waited a beat, letting his dive partner get settled, before he swam into the air lock chamber. His feet were on Mike's tanks and his head was still outside the sub when he felt a vibration through the water. He knew immediately what it was and ducked at the last second.

He managed to get the hatch closed but not fully secured when the torpedo slammed into the old mine tender up near her bow. Nearly a thousand pounds of high explosives detonated in a blast of energy that swept through the uncompressible water and pummelled the mini-sub so that she crashed into the remains of the metal framework. Steel tore and shrieked. The ship's superstructure was peeled back and collapsed at the same time.

Inside the air lock, the Chairman and Mike Trono were so tightly wedged that neither man was injured but both were severely disoriented as the sub tumbled end over end. Yet even before they had settled, Juan was working to secure the hatch's lock. His head rang with the concussive force of the explosion, and his hands felt leaden, but he managed to spin the lock down, sealing the two of them in the tight chamber.

'Eddie, emergency blow.'

Seng had already seen the indicator light in the cockpit telling him that the hatch was secure. He'd hit the button even as the Chairman's voice came over the radio.

With a clunk, the Nomad detached from its lower frame and began a wild rise to the surface. Only it didn't. It rose less than two feet before it became enmeshed in the mine tender's dislodged radio mast and an old, rotted fishing net.

Juan knew he should feel the cylindrical hull rocketing up from the depths the way one feels in a high-speed elevator. That wasn't happening. They had cut loose the heavy sled but weren't rising.

There was at most thirty seconds between the torpedoes, and he reacted without thought.

'Seal the hatch after me,' he said to Mike Trono and opened the air lock.

Cabrillo launched himself out of the mini-sub, flashing his light along its length, searching for whatever had snagged it and prevented its ascent. He saw the mast that had fallen across the sub's hull, but it wasn't big enough to have stalled their rise. Instead, it was the tangled mass of fishing nets that kept them stuck in place.

His titanium dive knife was honed to a razor's edge, and the buoyancy of the submersible cabin kept the net's lines taut. He attacked them like a ninja wielding a samurai sword, slashing and hacking the lines with abandon. The mini-sub rose fractionally as more of the tendrils binding it fell free. Cabrillo kept at it. The water filled with tiny bits of old sisal and a maelstrom of disturbed marine growth.

Then all at once, as he knew it would, the submersible erupted from the net, freeing itself of the last of the ropes and vanishing upward in the blink of an eye.

Cabrillo wasted no time watching it. He swam over to the far side of the wreck, dropped down to the bottom, and crawled as far from the ship as he could. He had to thrust his hands into the silt to keep from being blown away by the current.

The second torpedo augered into the seafloor well short of its target. Because he was shielded by the ship's hull and was lying flat on the bottom, the pressure wave mostly expanded over him, but he still caught enough to have the air forced from his lungs in an explosive breath that almost unsealed his dive helmet.

He thought he'd survived the worst of it when a second pressure wave hit, and this time it peeled him off the bottom and sent him tumbling. The current grabbed at him immediately, and he was soon bouncing along the bottom at a stiff four knots.

If he had any chance of being rescued, he needed to stay with the wreck. It was the only logical place Max would search for him. If he tumbled past it, there was no way he'd be able to fight the current to return. He didn't have anywhere near enough air to surface using proper decompression stops. And an ascent without them would lead to a fatal dose of the bends. His joints would constrict as the nitrogen in the tissue dissolved out, and he would die in unimaginable agony.

He managed to flatten himself into a proper swimming position. He knew he couldn't fight the current, so he didn't even try. Like someone caught in a riptide, he swam at an angle to the current instead of fighting it directly, vectoring off some of the brute force of the water rushing past him. He was certain that the current had already kicked him north of the hulk, but he had a slim chance of finding the wavering remains of the fishing nets that trailed off the ship like a bride's train.

His legs began to burn as he kicked with every-thing he had. He wouldn't let himself consider that the nets had been ripped clean off the old wreck by the second torpedo. He swam hard, battling a current he couldn't defeat, burning through his supply of trimix at a prodigious rate. He fought the growing agony of cramped muscles filling with lactic acid, groaning aloud inside his helmet. The rip and saw of his breathing filled his head with the sounds of desperation.

This was how he would die, clawing his way across the bottom, sensing the net was just outside of his visual range and feeling that if he could just keep going another handful of seconds he would reach it.

And then he actually saw it, waving in the current like the arms of a giant jellyfish. He could also see that he was approaching the very end of the ensnared mass of nets. He had only fifteen feet to swim, but there was only ten feet of net before he was swept past it. If he missed, death was the only option.

Cabrillo doubled down. His feet kicked in a flurry of motion, but not giving up any efficiency. He thrust with his arms, his gloved hands curled into perfect paddles that pulled him against the Gulf Stream. He adjusted his angle slightly, forcing himself to fight even harder in the face of the current but knowing he'd been coming in too shallow and would miss.

He reached out. Inches. That was all he needed. He roared as the tips of his fingers brushed the old netting just at its very end. They scrambled to find purchase, but the net was covered in marine slime that was as slick as grease.

There, he finally grasped the second-to-last opening in the net only to have the rotted line snap off in his hand. He clutched at the last bit of rope and prayed, because he could swim no more. The net would either support the extra drag of his body clinging to it or it wouldn't and he'd be lost.

He stopped kicking, and the old fishing net held his weight. He pulled himself up so he could grip it with both arms and willed his breathing to slow, and the adrenaline began to filter out of his bloodstream. He clung there, panting, knowing he was still in a precarious position but unable to find the strength to move. The net was floating, gently undulating, in the current, so when he felt a sudden jolt he knew something was wrong. He grabbed his more powerful handheld light and flashed it up the net. The lamp revealed it was tearing. His weight was too much for the rotten old sisal lines.

He started climbing up the net against the current, his head down and his shoulders and arms doing all the work.

The net lurched again as more of it parted. He was scrambling now. He recalled climbing cargo nets at the CIA's training facility as part of an obstacle course, but it was nothing like this. The press of the current against his body and bulky gear dwarfed the gravity he'd fought back then. And unlike those training sessions, he couldn't use his feet because his flippers would get in the way and he couldn't afford the seconds it would take to slip them off.

The net tore completely free just as he reached a still-stable section. The current sucked the detached piece out from under him. It snagged against his weight belt, and for a moment it pulled on him with the strength and tenacity of a pit bull. His grip was just about to slip when the net unsnagged and vanished behind him.

Not allowing himself time to recover, he continued climbing up the net, scrambling in a mad dash to the safety of the wreck's shattered remains. It was a two-hundred-foot climb. Once he felt the net was safe enough, he removed his flippers and clipped them to his dive harness and took a few moments to let his feet take the strain off his arms.

He gave himself just three minutes' rest before continuing on, though now it was his legs providing most of the heavy lifting and he made good time.

The mine tender was unrecognizable as a ship. The glow from his headlamp and his dive light revealed the ship had been blown into scrap by the first Russian torpedo, and a lot of its remains had been buried under a blanket of sand kicked up by the second. Chunks of hull plating lay strewn across the seafloor. He identified part of the ship's funnel only because of its distinct stovepipe shape. He saw no sign of the cage Tesla had enshrouded the ship with or the strange machine he'd discovered in the vessel's hold.

It was a miracle that the net had remained snagged on what little of the superstructure survived the explosion. He found a spot in the lee of a ruined boiler and settled to the bottom, finally able to take a proper rest.

Because the submersible acted as a relay for their communications, he knew it was pointless to try to raise the *Oregon*. The distance to the surface was just too great for his gear, but the main problem was that the mini-sub's hull section became deaf and mute once it detached from the propulsion sled.

He powered down his helmet light to conserve the battery. He was trapped on the bottom of the sea, as unable to change his predicament as an astronaut who becomes separated from his space capsule. Juan could do nothing but rely on his crew to save him. His faith in them was boundless, but rescues take time. They would need to recover the submersible first, and only then would Max discover that he was still down here. Next they would need to organize recovery gear and send down either *Little Geek* or the Discovery 1000, the second, smaller mini-sub the *Oregon* carried. It all took time.

The vast ocean crushed down on him from above, a lone man sitting on the seafloor among the rusted ruins of a dead man's dream, a lonely pinprick of light in a stygian darkness as vast as the cosmos. Juan, feeling the cold start to seep into his skin, finally looked at his remaining trimix supply, nodded grimly, and put out his dive light so that the black crushed up against his dry suit.

He had ten minutes to live.

17

Max Hanley continued to issue orders while Eric adjusted their heading once again.

'Mark, I want you and MacD down in the boat garage ready to launch a RHIB at a moment's notice. That means I want the outer door open and the engines warmed.' He keyed in the intercom to reach the techs in the sub bay. 'This is Max. Prep the Disco for SAR, and make sure *Little Geek*'s ready as well.'

The *Oregon* tore across the sea at a near-racing-boat's pace, driven as much by her engines as by Hanley's determination to rescue his people.

Mark Murphy was swinging out of his chair when he spotted something on his console.

'Max, I'm picking up the automated beacon from the Nomad. She's surfaced.'

'Over the wreck?'

'Negative. They've drifted almost two miles north.'

Eric Stone asked, 'Should I alter course?'

'Negative,' Max replied after a thoughtful pause. 'Keep us headed for the wreck site. Mark, get moving. Tell me when you and Lawless are ready to go. We'll slow the ship and you guys head out for the mini-sub.'

'We're on it.' He raced from the bridge while Max

put out a shipwide bulletin for MacD Lawless to report to the boat garage.

A mile from their destination, Murph reported they were ready to go. Max gave the order to back off on their speed, and when he deemed it safe, he told them to go.

Powered by a pair of massive outboards, the RHIB was an open-cockpit rocket ship for the water. Its sleek black hull and ring of inflated pontoons allowed it to survive in virtually any sea, and it could be configured for any number of missions.

The RHIB sliced through waves, bouncing and hammering over the taller swells while a white rooster tail erupted from her stern. It wasn't built for comfort – the two men stood behind the main controls on flexed knees, their bodies absorbing the shock of the rough ride.

Where Mark was nerdy and a bit doughy when he didn't focus on fitness, MacD Lawless looked like an underwear model, with a chiselled physique and a movie star's face. He was the newest member of the Corporation, having been rescued by them from Taliban kidnappers in northern Pakistan. He'd more than proved his worth in the ensuing months, and with his easygoing New Orleans charm and melodious Southern accent, he'd ingratiated himself with the crew.

Like a stone across the surface of a pond, they skipped their way across the Atlantic, pushing the RHIB past fifty knots. Behind them, the *Oregon* was just a dot as she raced to her own rendezvous. MacD steered the boat while Mark navigated using a tablet computer displaying a satellite relay of the Nomad's location.

It took them just a few minutes to reach the drifting hull, which to both men looked like a railroad tank car far, far from home. MacD sidled up to the mini-sub, and Mark leapt over with a painter in hand to tie them off. Lawless didn't wait for Mark to finish before he grabbed a swim mask, kicked off his Nikes, and dove into the water. Mark watched him go over with a slow shake of his head, not understanding why Lawless would do that when they could access the sub through the rear-mounted air lock.

Lawless had been hit by enough spray on their mad dash here to know the water was shockingly cold, yet he still gave an involuntary gasp as it leached through his clothes. He sucked in a deep breath and dove down and swam toward the front of the submersible. He pressed his mask to one of the three small portholes. The interior of the sub was pitch-black. Not a good sign.

He rapped on the glass with his LSU class ring, and, within seconds, a figure threw itself into the pilot seat and a light flipped on, revealing Eddie Seng. He had a bruise near his temple that was starting to swell up like a pigeon's egg. He quickly reached a piece of paper from a stack next to his control panel and held it up for MacD to read.

Lawless blew out his breath when he saw what Eddie had written and scrambled to the surface as fast as he could.

The instant his face cleared the water he shouted, 'Mark, stop!'

He heaved himself out of the water and up onto the bobbing hull in one powerful lunge. Lawless saw Mark kneeling over the air lock hatch, his bands poised to crack the seal. 'Don't open it.'

'Why not?'

'Because it's fully pressurized, and, if you do, not only will it blow the hatch into your skull but it'll turn Mike Trono into a meat bomb.'

Murph carefully pulled his hands away from the locking wheel and let out a breath he didn't know he'd been holding. 'What about Juan?'

'No idea. Eddie just held up a note saying Mike is in the air lock. It's got to be pumped up to about two hundred psi.'

'Hold on.' Mark leapt back over to the RHIB and grabbed another piece of electronics he'd taken from the *Oregon*. He uncoiled a length of wire from the device and handed its end to Lawless.

'There's a communications port directly above the auxiliary electrical port. Both are near the large external air intake port. Can't miss it,' Mark said with a grin and shoved MacD in the chest so that he tumbled back into the water.

MacD gave him a scowl and duck-dove with the cable in his hand. He surfaced thirty seconds later and shoved the swim mask up onto his forehead. 'Give it a go.'

'Eddie, can you hear me? It's Murph.'

'Never been so glad to hear your voice,' Eddie responded. 'You got the message?'

'Yeah. What's Mike doing in the air lock? And where's the Chairman?'

'Long story. As for the Chairman, he's still down on the wreck.'

'He was outside when the torpedoes hit?'

'Not the first one, but he went out to free us just before the second one exploded.'

'Is he alive?'

'Don't know. Listen, we don't have time for this. Mike's breathing off his own tanks. We need to get this tub back to the *Oregon* and get him some trimix so we can start decompressing him out of there.'

'Right. MacD and I are out here on a RHIB. The *Oregon* should be over the wreck by now. We'll tow you over and lift you aboard with the deck crane.'

'That's good. Mike and I have been chatting, using Morse code. He's kept his breathing shallow and figures he's got another half hour or so.'

'Tell him he'll be fine. Talk to you later.' Mark gave MacD a look, and the newest member of the team knew what he had to do. He pulled his mask back over his eyes and went to retrieve the cable.

Just a minute later, they took the Nomad under tow. The RHIB was designed for speed rather than torque, but they still managed to get up to fifteen knots pulling the ungainly hull through the water. Mark had radioed ahead, so when they motored under the shadow of the *Oregon*'s lee side, the most powerful of the ship's forward derricks had been swung out and lifting hooks lowered to the water.

The mini-sub was pulled from the Atlantic as easy as a babe from a cradle, water sluicing off its sides, dousing the two men in the RHIB.

Lawless gunned the motors to steer them into the boat garage as the mini-sub cleared the rail and was lowered into the main cargo hold. Once they were aboard, Murph grabbed a towel from a storage bin, dried his hair and face as best he could, and headed for the hold, figuring Max would handle the Chairman's rescue while he figured out how to open a particularly dicey can of worms.

Down in the moon pool, Hanley was securing two spare trimix tanks to *Little Geek* with nylon webbing.

'Okay,' he said at last, 'try it.'

A tech at *Little Geek*'s controls spooled up its three propellers and maneuvered them on their gimbals to make certain they didn't become fouled by the extra burden the ROV would carry.

'Looks good,' Hanley said, getting to his feet. 'Give me a hand.'

The two men lifted the two hundred pounds of robot and air tanks and lowered it on its umbilical down into the moon pool itself. It vanished as soon as they let go of the thick armoured cable, dropping down in an arc that swept it northward thanks to the Gulf Stream. The little robot would need to fight the current the whole way, but since she was tethered and being supplied power by her mother ship, it wouldn't be an issue.

The only issue now was if they'd gotten here in time.

Cabrillo couldn't believe the cold. It had crept up on him so insidiously that it was in his bones before he realized it. He had remained perfectly still, not generating any body heat – that was the culprit. In order to stretch out his air supply, he had to sit as quietly as possible, and yet that allowed in a killer just as deadly as asphyxia.

His hands shook so badly that it took three attempts to flip on his dive light. Its glow made the loneliness somehow more tolerable. Humans were, after all, a social animal. And to die alone was one of our species' innate fears. He turned his gaze onto his air readings. The ten minutes he'd given himself were up. He was breathing gas that was so amorphous that it couldn't be read by the tank's monitors.

He was feeling it too. Each breath seemed thinner, less substantive. No matter how deeply he tried to fill his lungs, he just couldn't get enough air. Again, panic gnawed at the edges of his mind, but he beat it back and tried to keep his breathing steady. Max just needed him to hold out for another couple of minutes.

The light dropped from his icy fingers, and he was so cold he'd gone beyond shivering. He kept trying to breathe air that simply wasn't there, and no amount of mental trickery could negate that fact. He'd rolled the dice and come up short. Juan never pictured it like this.

He'd always assumed he'd die in a gunfight. Statistically speaking, he should have been shot down years ago. But of all the bullet scars his body carried, not one was in a critical area. It was funny. To survive all that and die while on a dive.

He wanted to laugh at the irony, but there wasn't enough air, so he settled for an enigmatic grin and slowly lost his grip on consciousness.

'Come on, damnit!' Max barked. 'We should see it by now.'

He stood over the tech's shoulder, and both men watched the video feed from *Little Geek*. So far, they saw nothing but the barren plain of the seafloor. They were in the right position, but the wreck seemed to be gone.

'Are you sure you're on-station?'

'Yes, Max. I don't get it.'

The images were grainy, ill lit, and wavering but unmistakable in that there seemed to be no sign of the old mine tender. Both men stared until their eyes watered, trying to make out details that just weren't there.

'There, there!' Max shouted. 'Turn *Little Geek*, twenty degrees starboard.'

The tech worked the joystick while, four hundred fifty feet below them, *Little Geek* turned nimbly.

'Aha!' Max cried. Around the ROV was a debris field stretching far beyond the lights' perimeter. They had been off by a few feet, but in this kind of work that could be the difference between success and failure. 'Juan's around here someplace.'

'Won't he swim to the light?'

'If he can. Don't know what shape he's in.'

The little ROV threaded its way around the shattered wreckage, and this time it was the tech who saw a weak glow emerging from behind an old boiler. He guided the robot around the piece of machinery, and the light revealed the Chairman slumped up against the boiler, his hands resting palm up next to his dive light on the bottom. His head was canted over onto his shoulder in the unnatural pose of death. There were no bubbles emerging from his regulator.

'No,' Max whispered, and then repeated it a second time even softer. The third time he barely made a sound. 'No.'

He couldn't accept what he was seeing. He couldn't believe Juan was dead. That he'd failed his best friend.

This time he shouted, 'No!'

He reached over the tech's shoulder and grabbed *Little Geek*'s joystick and used it to ram the ROV into the Chairman as hard as its little motors could push.

Rather than fall over from the impact, Cabrillo's corpse straightened. His head rose off his shoulders, and an arm came up to grasp the micro-sub.

The tech gasped. 'Was he asleep?'

'Judging by how thin the bubbles are coming from his regulator, I think he passed out.' Max couldn't contain the smile plastered across his face.

Juan had been dreaming of his late wife, killed in a single-car crash while he was away on a mission for the CIA. He knew in his heart that her loneliness had turned her to drinking. Her blood alcohol level that night was twice the legal limit. It didn't matter that she'd been out with friends. And that they hadn't stopped her from getting behind the wheel. Her death was his fault. Period. And when he was especially down, her memory haunted his dreams.

Cabrillo jolted awake to a blinding light shining into his eyes. His predicament rushed in on him a moment later, but it took his air-starved brain another few seconds to understand what had happened. It was *Little Geek*. That was the source of the light. He reached out for the small ROV and felt the extra tanks Max had secured to it like a pack mule's panniers. Hanley had even positioned them so their umbilical air feeds were within easy reach.

Juan hadn't taken a breath in almost a minute, and his vision was narrowing to a central point surrounded by grey, but he had just enough mental capacity to unhook the air line going into his helmet and replace it with one from the fresh tank. Fifteen seconds passed and nothing happened, he still wasn't getting air. Then for some reason *Little Geek* barrelled into him again.

Max was trying to tell him something. What was it? He didn't know and just wanted to go back to sleep. His head sagged, and for a third time the ROV bounced off his chest. It pirouetted so the bulky trimix tank was right in front of him.

The valve. Juan reached out a hand and cranked open the valve. With a life-giving hiss, his helmet filled with breathable air, and he took it so deep into his lungs, they felt like they would burst. His confusion began to clear as his oxygen-starved brain rebooted. He took ten, twenty deep breaths, giddy at the feeling and never so thankful. He flashed a diver's OK sign at the camera mounted below the lights. In response, *Little Geek* spun three hundred sixty degrees, like a happy puppy circling after its tail.

Little Geek settled onto the ground next to him as if it wanted to be petted. It was then Juan saw the bundle Max had secured to the top of the ROV. He opened it and said a silent prayer of thanksgiving. Hanley thought of everything. His hands were numb to the point of uselessness, and he could barely guide a finger through the activation ring of a magnesium flare, but he managed.

The light was blinding white and would have scarred his retinas if he'd looked at it, but his head was turned away. He didn't care about the light the flare threw off, only about the way it heated the water there in the lee of the mine tender's boiler. He could feel the difference after only a few seconds. Also stuffed in the bag were chemical heat packets. He broke their seals to activate them and clamped them between his thighs and under his arms. Others he stuffed between his dry suit and buoyancy compensator directly over his heart.

He gave himself ten minutes to recover. By the time he was ready to go, the acrylic-domed Discovery 1000 with Eric Stone at the controls had joined him. Eric and *Little Geek* stayed with him during the mind-numbingly long ascent, hovering nearby as he went through hours-long decompression stops. Despite the cold and his exhaustion, he took it slow and safe. He knew he'd probably have to sleep in the *Oregon*'s cramped decompression tank with Mike, but one night was all he was willing to put in.

Most of the crew were lining the moon pool when he finally emerged from the ocean, and he was greeted with a standing ovation and wild cries and whoops. Max looked especially pleased with himself, and even the doc smiled over her professional concern for his well-being.

He was helped out of the water, and workers shucked his gear in record time.

'How are you feeling?' Julia Huxley asked, shouldering her way to his side. 'Any symptoms?'

'I'm cold,' he stammered through chattering teeth. 'I'm hungry, and I need a bathroom in the worst possible way.' He turned to Hanley, who was hovering right behind Julia. 'I never doubted you.'

'Why would you?' Max said, all nonchalance. 'I've never let you down before.'

'Thanks.'

'You can owe me.'

'Enough with the male bonding,' Hux cut in. 'Juan, you're going into decomp with Mike so I can monitor you both for signs of decompression sickness.'

'He and Eddie are okay?'

'Eddie has a possible concussion, and Mike's fine. This is only a precaution.'

'Did he keep the sample of that framework or was this all for nothing?'

'I don't know,' Hux replied, while, behind her, Max produced the sample with a conjurer's flourish.

'Ta-da. Mark already took a quick look and says he has no idea what it is.'

Juan took the foot-long rod as he was hustled to the decompression chamber at the back wall of the sub bay. It had a rough texture, but unlike anything he'd held before. If he had to give a single-word description of its texture, he'd say 'alien.'

He handed it back to Max. 'Get me some answers.'

'Mark and Eric will be up all night on this one, that I guarantee. Now get into your sarcophagus with Mike, and I'll have the kitchen send down some food. Should be interesting to see Maurice give white-glove service through an air lock.'

Juan stepped through the heavy door to the first section of the two-part steel chamber and had a seat on the thinly padded bench. The air pressure would be brought up to about half of what he and Mike had experienced on the bottom, and then he could enter the second chamber, where Trono now waited. The facilities were primitive and stark, looking like something out of a 1960s Navy training film, but, for safety's sake, Juan didn't mind putting himself through the tedium.

He cleared his ears as the pressure in the chamber rose, ran through what had happened over the past hours, and chalked it up as the luckiest escape of his life.

18

Dr Huxley released the two divers at seven thirty the following morning. Cabrillo went straight to his cabin, noting that the weather was picking up and causing a pronounced roll as he walked the corridors. He'd spent thirty minutes in the tiny shower closet in the decompression chamber to warm up, so he took another brief shower and shaved using the same straight razor his grandfather had used for forty years as a barber. After patting both the blade and his face dry, he threw on a touch of aftershave, dressed in chinos and a black mock turtleneck, and headed to the mess for breakfast. He stopped first at his desk for his tablet to check their position and noted they were making good time on their rendezvous with the Emir's yacht, the *Sakir*.

He took a table in the middle of the dining room and had barely settled before Maurice poured him coffee in a bone china cup.

'Good morning, Captain.' As an ex-Royal Navy man, the chief steward didn't abide by the team's corporate structure and never referred to Juan as Chairman. The *Oregon* was a ship. Cabrillo was in charge. He was, therefore, Captain. 'No ill effects from your adventure?'

'Other than a sore back from sleeping on a lousy cot, I'm fine. Thank you.' He sipped at the strong coffee with appreciation. 'And now I'm even better. Whatever you bring me for breakfast, double the amount of sausage, please.'

'Have you checked your cholesterol recently?'

'Hux cleared me for double rations of morning pork just last week.'

'Very good, Captain.'

Eric and Mark entered the sedate dining room with the propriety of charging rhinos, spotted the Chairman, and rushed right over. Both wore the same clothes they'd had on the night before and had the wired jittery look of people about to overdose on caffeine.

'Good morning, gentlemen,' Juan said broadly. 'What has you two buzzing like a couple of bees?'

'Red Bull and research,' Mark replied.

Cabrillo dropped his pretence of disinterest and asked, 'What is that material?'

Eric spoke first. 'Something that was just discovered a few years ago.'

'It's a metamaterial,' Mark said, as if that was an explanation.

'That means . . .'

'It's a material engineered almost at a nanoscale. Its design is what gives it its unique properties, like manipulating light or sound waves.'

'Think of the egg cartons garage bands put up to deaden echoes in their practice spaces. Multiply that by a hundred, and then shrink it down to the nanoscale. The material maintains the precise angles to deflect anything you want.'

'Would it deaden sound?' Cabrillo asked, thinking he understood.

'Absolutely, only in frequencies we can't hear.'

Juan realized he didn't get it at all. 'What's the point?'

'Their shape gives them properties that they wouldn't normally have. Like the reflective panels on the stealth fighter. Its shape, not the composition of its skin, gives it its stealth characteristics.'

'The skin has stealth properties too,' Mark corrected automatically, because any deviation from absolute truth drove him nuts.

'I'm trying to make a point, if you don't mind.'

'Fine.'

'So what does this particular metamaterial do?'

'No idea,' Eric said.

'Not a clue,' Murph chimed. 'The design of the entire frame determines its exact purpose. The metamaterial makes it happen.'

'Could it bend light around the ship? Make it invisible?'

'Possibly. Or it could work on an electromagnetic wavelength.'

'Even acoustic,' Stoney added.

'Any explanation about why nothing was growing on it down there?'

'Oh, it's loaded with cadmium. Absolutely toxic.' Seeing Juan's concerned look, Mark explained, 'Cadmium's mostly dangerous if inhaled or ingested. It's like mercury. You can handle the stuff, no problem, just don't let it get into your bloodstream.'

Maurice arrived and placed Juan's food on the table, lifting the silver dome with a flourish. It was an omelette exactly as Cabrillo wanted – loaded with sausage.

'Okay, you've told me what you know, now why don't you give me a little speculation.'

'When you met with Professor Tennyson, did he mention anything about the French?' Murph asked.

'Actually, he did,' Juan said, recalling the bizarre turn in his conversation with the Tesla expert. 'He said that Morris Jessup, the guy who popularized the story of the Philadelphia Experiment, was supposedly killed by French operatives in 1959, and his death made to look like a suicide.'

'Did he seem to believe that story?'

'That I can't recall. No, wait. I think he said it was a conspiracy theory, so he must have dismissed it.'

'Maybe he shouldn't have,' Mark said with relish. As the ship's resident conspiracy nut, he was in his element. 'Get this. In the spring of 1963, a game warden in Alaska found the remains of three people who'd died sometime during the winter. The bodies had been picked over by scavengers, so a straight identification was out of the question. Here's the thing. He found French francs in the pocket of one of them.'

'So?'

'I haven't told you the best part. The men were all wearing lab coats over shorts and T-shirts, and they were found lying on a patch of pure white sand in the middle of a boreal forest. By the time the ranger returned with a team to recover the bodies, animals had dragged them away. The only thing he could do was recover a sample of the sand.

'He sent it to a geologist at the University of Alaska in Anchorage, who realized that the sand wasn't pure silica but had a high concentration of ground coral in it. The ranger lost interest in the whole thing, but the geologist, Henry Ryder, kept on it.'

Eric cut in. 'It took him three years of asking around and comparing samples, but the sand they found in the middle of Alaska originated on an atoll almost in the exact centre of the Pacific Ocean called Mororoa.'

'Is that significant?' Cabrillo asked.

Mark said with delicious thrill, 'Mororoa is where the French monitored their atomic bomb tests. Back in the sixties, it had a sizable population of scientists and engineers. This Ryder guy contacted the French government and asked if they'd lost any scientists from Mororoa. He was stonewalled. This was all top secret, and the Cold War was at full boil. But he didn't let up. With the help of a woman in the university's French department, he made calls to the offices of France's top engineering schools and eventually deduced that three men –' he pulled a scrap of paper from his jeans – 'Dr Paul Broussard, Professor Jacque Mollier, and Dr Viktor Quesnel had all been missing since 1963, and that all three men were linked to France's nuclear weapons research.

'He reached out to their widows. Two wouldn't talk to him at all, but one admitted that her government had sworn her to secrecy. She would only confirm that her husband had been on Mororoa Island three years earlier and that was the last she'd heard from him.'

'Where'd you get all of this?' Juan asked, trying to wrap his head around it.

The two exchanged a sheepish look.

'Ah, conspiracy websites,' Murph admitted.

'So this could all be a bunch of bull?'

'Yes, except we called Alaska. Henry Ryder's long dead, and so is his wife. His daughter still lives in Anchorage and does remember that her father kept a vial of sand on his desk that she wasn't allowed to touch when she was a little girl.'

Stone cut in again, 'And he had a female friend who would come over from time to time who sounded like Catherine Deneuve.'

'Okay,' Juan said at length. 'That gives a little credence to the story. Where is all this heading?'

'Back to the Philadelphia Experiment being something real, just not how it has been reported, and that the French killed Morris Jessup to silence him once and for all, and that they continued the research at their most secure facility, and that maybe something went wrong, and that some lab jockeys and the sand they were standing on was transported to Alaska via some unknown force. The same way George Westinghouse's boat ended up in the Aral Sea years earlier.'

'I don't like science fiction,' Juan said in a warning tone.

'Chairman, cell phones were science fiction not too

long ago. Airplanes, rockets, nuclear submarines. The list is endless.'

'I'm putting my money on St Julian Perlmutter.'

'But why?'

'I asked him to look into the *Lady Marguerite*.' Perlmutter was a close friend of Dirk Pitt, and someone Cabrillo had come to rely on as well. The man possessed the largest privately held collection of maritime books, papers, and histories in the world, and he had a bloodhound's nose for solving mysteries. 'I can't bring myself to believe in teleportation devices. I think someone hijacked George Westinghouse's yacht and it eventually ended up in Russia. I've got Perlmutter trying to prove my theory.'

'But we already looked into it. There was nothing.'

Juan smiled. 'You guys are of the belief that everything worth knowing is already on the Internet. There is ten times more information in libraries than on the Web. Probably a thousand times. You two go way beyond Google searches, but you can't hold a candle to St Julian when it comes to tracking down answers to esoteric questions.'

Hali Kasim's voice came over the intercom. He was the *Oregon*'s communications officer. 'Chairman Cabrillo, please report to the op centre.'

Juan placed his napkin next to his cleaned plate and stood. 'If you will both excuse me. We'll talk later.'

Hali was seated at a console on the right side of the op centre when Cabrillo strode in. The Lebanese-born Kasim had a pair of earphones draped around his neck, but a line of crushed hair across his moppy head showed he'd been wearing them for a while.

'What's up?'

'You have a call from the number we gave to L'Enfant, but it isn't him.'

'Who is it?'

'Pytor Kenin. He asked for you specifically.'

Cabrillo felt a wave of anger sweep through his body that he quickly crushed down. Now wasn't the time for emotions. He took his customary chair and grabbed the handset jacked into one of the arms. He swung it up to his mouth and gave Hali a curt nod.

'Cabrillo.'

'Not calling yourself Chairman, eh?' Kenin said in Russian. 'And I know you can understand me, so do not pretend otherwise.'

'What do you want?' Juan asked in the same language.

'What I want is to know why I cannot reach the K-154.'

'That's because it sank about ten minutes after trying to kill me.' Cabrillo waited a beat to let that sink in. 'They slammed into the seafloor hard enough to open her up like a can of sardines. The US Navy's already received an anonymous tip about the accident, and I'm sure they'll have a salvage ship over her within another twenty-four hours.'

'What did you do?' the Russian shouted in rage.

'Kenin, you're the one who started this and you're the one who drew first blood, so don't act all incensed when we stand up to you.'

'You are meddling in affairs that do not concern you.'

'They started to concern me the moment Yuri Borodin died. I don't know what kind of games you're playing inside Russia's military establishment, and, frankly, I don't care. All I know is that I am going to stop you.'

'Delusions, Mr Chairman. You yourself admit you don't know what I am doing, so how are you going to stop me? Surely not the same way you stopped me from silencing Tennyson? You are now and always will be a step behind.'

Kenin obviously didn't know Tennyson was still alive and safe.

'You think that because you got to L'Enfant that I don't have other resources?'

'Ah yes, the enigmatic L'Enfant. Seems in the end he cares more about self-preservation than keeping his clients' secrets.'

'He withheld enough so that your sub commander made a fatal mistake,' Juan countered. 'And he's not the point. You are. Stop whatever it is you have planned and we end it here and now. Deal?'

'I'm afraid not. You see, you are already too late. In fact, your interference pushed up a scheduled test and made me change my target. I want you to take what's happened very personally. Had you left well enough alone, the Emir would still be alive, and so would the lovely Linda Ross.'

Juan went cold. 'What have you done?'

'Convinced my client that the toy I built for them works. Check your e-mail.' The line went dead.

Cabrillo was out of his seat and over Hali's shoulder a second later. 'Well?'

'He routed that call through just about every relay station on earth and most of the communications satellites in orbit, but I pegged him at a military airfield outside of Moscow.'

Juan put out a call over the ship's net for Mark and Eric to report to the op centre while Hali checked the general e-mail account for a message from Kenin. So far, nothing.

What had Kenin done? The question ricocheted around in Cabrillo's mind as his concern for Linda and the Emir turned his delicious breakfast into a molten ball.

Considering the resources Kenin had put into this operation, this had to be his last big score. He'd had the opportunity to go legit and vie for a cabinet position, or at least a command staff job, or continue to lie and cheat his way through the system. It appeared he'd chosen the latter, and now he'd have to disappear because whatever it was he'd stolen from the Russian Navy, they would doubtlessly want it back.

Stone and Murph arrived.

'Kenin just called and said he'd tested whatever it is he's been working on and has turned it over to his client. That means he's going to try to vanish. He's at the Ramenskoye Air Base. That's his jumping-off point. Hack your way in and find out where he's going. I'm going to call Langston and see if we can't track his plane using Uncle Sam's spy birds.'

'Juan,' Hali interrupted. 'It arrived.'

'Same routing?'

'Yeah. He doesn't know we back-traced him or he wouldn't have bothered.'

'Good job. That's our first leg up on Kenin since we hit the prison where they were holding Yuri. Put it up.' Juan nodded to Eric and Mark. 'You two stay for a second. I don't know what we're about to see.'

The e-mail contained an MPEG, which Hali opened. An image came up on the main view screen of a white ship on a rough sea; in fact, it looked like the vessel was facing the same weather conditions as the *Oregon*. The camerawork was jumpy, and it was obviously shot at long range from a helicopter. The time and date stamp showed this had been taken only moments earlier. The white ship was a mega-yacht, and it took Juan only a second to recognize it as the *Sakir*, the Emir's pride and joy. That ship was currently three hundred miles south of them and headed for Bermuda. By the size of her wake, she looked to be travelling at about fifteen knots.

Then off her port beam a weird blue glow grew out of the ocean like a bubble of gas escaping from the bottom of a swamp. The glow quickly engulfed the *Sakir*, yet it was still possible to see the three-hundred-foot supership.

With no warning, no dramatic yawl, the yacht simply flipped over as if it were a bath toy under the ministrations of a vengeful child. Water washed over her upside-down bow and raced along her length as her momentum continued to drive her forward while her twin ferro-bronze propellers beat the air.

The glow winked out a moment later. The men watching held their collective breath in anticipation of the huge yacht burying herself in the waves, but somehow she recovered enough for the water to pour off her red-painted bottom, and she settled into an unequal and doubtlessly short-lasting equilibrium. The video clip ended and reset itself to the opening frame.

'Helm!' Cabrillo shouted. 'Emergency full. Hali, get Gomez down to the hangar to warm up the chopper. I want to be in the air as soon as possible. Have Linc meet us there. Eric, go down to the sub bay and bring me full scuba gear including a suit. Mark, Engineering. I need cutting equipment, and from stores grab an emergency inflatable boat.'

A ship the size of the *Sakir* would have a crew of ten and a staff of at least twice that number. A single inflatable could only carry ten, but Juan didn't want to overload their helo and slow them down. Survivors would just have to take turns in the boat while the rest clung to its sides.

Survivors. Juan didn't know if there would be any. The weather wasn't ideal, so he doubted there were many people on deck when she capsized, and those trapped inside would be so disoriented that they might not be able to save themselves. Rescuing even ten was being overly optimistic. And if she sank before they arrived, this could turn out to be a total loss.

In that event, they would need the lifeboat for

themselves, because their MD 520N helicopter had the range to make it out to the stricken yacht but not enough to return.

'Go!' Juan ordered, and his people scattered.

Afterward they would parse the video to find out how a ship the size of the *Sakir* could be capsized like that. This was definitely new technology, something that dovetailed into Tesla's work, but what exactly it was and how it worked could wait until later.

Juan made a brief stop in his cabin to change into a leg better suited for swimming and grabbed some foul-weather gear. The *Oregon*'s rear hatch was open, and the gleaming black McDonnell Douglas helicopter sat on the hangar bay elevator like a bird of prey. Overhead, the sky looked pained as a storm continued to brew. Of course the weather wouldn't cooperate. At times like this, Cabrillo found, Mother Nature had a cruel sense of irony.

'Gomez, how are we coming?'

George Adams ducked his head out of the cockpit. 'You caught me with my pants down, Chairman. I just started swapping out a radio when Hali called. I need ten minutes to put the old one back.'

'You've got five.'

Linc and Mark showed up together. Murph pushed a handcart loaded with an oxyacetylene cutter and other gear while the ex-SEAL carried the eighty-pound inflatable boat in its hard plastic capsule on his shoulder with seemingly little effort. Hali must have told him what to expect because he was dressed in Carhartt's under a rain suit and steel-toed boots.

'What's up, Chairman?' Linc asked in his rumbling bass.

'Kenin somehow capsized the *Sakir*. We may need to cut our way in through the hull.'

'À la *Poseidon Adventure*?'

'Exactly.'

Next came Eric with Juan's dive gear. This time, he wouldn't bother with a bulky dry suit since he wouldn't need to dive very deeply to access the ship's interior. Hux arrived with a case of emergency medical supplies. She loaded the box into the chopper's external storage locker as Cabrillo finished suiting up. He wedged his back against the chopper's side so he could pull on his dive boots and then helped Eric load the rest of his gear on the chopper's rear bench seat. Linc had already stowed the capsule behind the pilot's seat.

'Gomez?' Juan questioned.

'One more minute. Might as well slow the ship now.'

'All right.'

There was an intercom mounted on the hangar wall. Cabrillo called the bridge, and almost immediately the sound of water gushing through her drive tubes changed as she went into full reverse.

Max is going to kill me for that, he thought to himself, not knowing that Hanley had meted out the exact same type of punishment when he was hunting the Russian Akula. As much as Cabrillo thought the *Oregon* indefatigable, she had her limits, and these sudden starts and stops wreaked havoc on her impeller blades and the motors that controlled their fine pitch.

'Saddle up,' Gomez Adams announced. He tossed a bag of hand tools to one of his hangar apes – the nickname for the men who serviced the helo – and settled himself into the pilot's seat. A hum grew from the equipment when he hit the master switch and started the takeoff procedure.

While Juan and Linc jumped aboard, the pilot jacked his helmet into the chopper's radios and did a communications check. 'Max, you in the op center yet?'

'I'm here. Talk about your rude awakenings.'

Cabrillo had his own helmet on and spoke. 'Have you seen the video?'

'Hali just showed it to me. You go get her, Juan.'

They would have reacted just the same had Linda not been on the *Sakir*, but her presence there made this rescue especially poignant.

'Don't you worry about that. Anything on the radar plot?'

'Nothing to be concerned with.'

'Keep an eye out. Kenin had to use either a ship or another submarine to pull that off. Ping active as you follow us, and watch for surface contacts. You know about L'Enfant?' Juan asked.

'Hali told me the little rat sold us out.'

'True, but he didn't spill that we could track Kenin's sub and had the capability to sink it. I don't think Kenin knows we have a chopper or that the *Oregon*'s the fastest ship in the world for her size.'

'Good point.'

'Kenin underestimated us once. Let's pray he does it again.'

'Understood. We'll keep an eye out.'

'We'll do the same.'

The crew never wished one another luck before a mission, so Max repeated his earlier plaint. 'You bring her back.'

'Roger.'

Juan curled his fingers in frustration while they waited for temperatures in the single turbine to reach the correct levels. Only then did Adams engage the transmission, and the rotor began to turn, lazily, at first, and then it vanished in a blur of motion. At the tail of the craft, rather than a second, smaller rotor, the chopper vented its exhaust through ducted ports for gyroscopic stability.

'Max,' Adams radioed, 'how we looking on winds across the deck?'

'You're clear,' Hanley replied.

'Then we're out of here.' He applied more power and eased up on the collective so that the angle of the rotor blades changed and they began to bite into the air.

The chopper lifted from the deck and barely cleared the fantail railing while the *Oregon* pulled away from under it. They adopted a nose-down attitude to pick up some speed and then rose steadily into the sky.

Occasional patters of rain pelted the windshield as they clawed their way up to a thousand feet and continued to accelerate southward.

'You did the calculations, right?' Juan asked.

'Yes. I put us over the target with fumes left in the tank if we maintain a speed of one hundred thirty knots.' Gomez glanced over his shoulder to look at Cabrillo for a second. 'Not to be the Negative Nelly of the group, but what happens if the yacht isn't there anymore?'

'We ditch and wait for the *Oregon* in this life raft here, and when we're saved, I deduct the price of the chopper from your stake in the Corporation.'

'I can follow you on the first two, but number three doesn't seem too fair to me.'

'He's pulling your leg,' Linc said. 'Otherwise, he'd have to deduct the cost of replacing the Nomad from his own share. Eddie told me the emergency ascent was the Chairman's idea.'

Juan grinned, thankful for the banter to keep him from dwelling on Linda's predicament. 'How's this? If we ditch, we'll call it square.'

'Sounds good.'

Linc spent most of the flight studying the ocean through a pair of powerful binoculars that even his massive hands could barely fit around. He would watch individual ships plying the Atlantic seaboard until he was certain they were no threat. Then something caught his eye, and he kept watching it far longer than any other target. He finally passed the binoculars over his shoulder and pointed to a spot about forty degrees off their route. 'Juan, what do you make of that?'

Cabrillo adjusted the glasses and looked to where Linc indicated. He thumbed the focus wheel until the image became clear. He saw a ship's wake where it was widening and flattening into the choppy sea. He followed its trail, but it vanished before he saw the ship making it. Confused, he scanned again. The wake was a white-foaming wedge on the ocean's surface culminating in absolutely nothing at all and yet its leading edge continued to move away from them.

The impossibility of what he was witnessing dulled his cognitive reasoning, and he continued to stare without comprehension or the ability to accept the reality of it.

A hundred feet in front of the flattened apex of the wake, occasional puffs of white water appeared, like the bow of a ship cutting through the swells, but between these two points was nothing but open water.

Juan blinked and looked harder. No, not open water, a distortion of what open water looks like, a facsimile of nature, not nature itself. Then the reality hit.

'Science fiction. Those two aren't going to let me hear the end of it.'

'You want me to get closer?' Adams asked.

'No. Keep true. Maybe they don't know we've spotted them.' Juan handed the binoculars back to Linc and keyed on his radio. 'Max, you there?'

'Standing by.'

'Go to encrypt beta,' Juan ordered, and Gomez

switched to the chopper's secondary encrypted channel. 'You still with me?'

There was a second delay in the rest of their conversation because the computers needed the extra time to decrypt the secure comm line. 'Still here.'

'I don't know how Kenin capsized the Emir's yacht, but I know how he got close enough to activate the weapon. We've got eyeballs on a ship's wake, only there isn't a ship making it.'

'Come again.'

'They have some sort of optical camouflage. The ship he used to target the *Sakir* is, well, it's invisible.'

'You sure this isn't a delayed symptom of the bends?'

'Linc sees it, or doesn't see it, too.'

'Juan,' Lincoln said urgently, thrusting the binoculars back at him. 'Check it out now. They must think they've cleared the danger zone.'

Juan found the wake again and again followed it to its source. This time, the ship was there, and what a craft it was. It reminded him of the US Navy's pyramidal *Sea Shadow*, an experimental stealth ship with a design based loosely on the F-117 Nighthawk. This boat was painted a muted grey that perfectly matched the surrounding seas, and it had sloped, faceted sides that met at a peak about thirty feet above the waves. Unlike the *Sea Shadow*, it wasn't a catamaran but a monohull, with a flat transom and a long overhanging deck above her bow. Function rather than aesthetics had gone into her design, making her the ugliest vessel Juan had ever seen.

He guessed she was making about fifteen knots, so more than likely if she was running from the scene of the crime, this was her maximum speed.

'So what do you want me to do about it?' Hanley asked.

At sea, the preservation of human life took precedence over everything else, there was no doubt about that. He couldn't order the *Oregon* to deviate from her course and intercept this bizarre new weapon. And none of their missiles had the range to hit it, but that didn't mean they were impotent.

'Give me a few minutes to figure out the vectors and relative speeds. I want you to be ready to launch Eddie and MacD in a RHIB to go after them.'

'That thing just capsized a three-hundred-foot mega-yacht. What do you think it would do to a puny RHIB?'

'I just want them to tail it. Once we're finished with the rescue, we'll track 'em down and handle it ourselves.'

'What about the storm?'

'There isn't a gale on this planet a RHIB can't handle.'

There was concern in his voice when Max cautioned, 'It might take us days to find survivors from the *Sakir*.'

'We're out of there as soon as the Coasties show up. You did radio them, right?'

'They're three hours behind us.'

'There's your answer. We do our thing for three hours and turn it over to the professionals. This is a good plan, Max.'

'A dangerous one,' Hanley retorted.

'Aren't they all? Load the RHIB with extra fuel drums, and I'll call when you're closest to this stealth boat's wake.'

'Okay,' Max relented. 'But I'm not sending those boys out without full survival suits and redundant GPS trackers.'

'I didn't think you would.' Juan had Max give him the *Oregon*'s relative position and speed and did the calculations. They would be on the *Sakir* when the *Oregon* was at its closest to the ship, so he radioed the time he wanted the RHIB launched and gave a relative bearing on their target.

'Juan,' Gomez said, 'we're approaching the *Sakir*'s last-known position. We could use extra eyes looking for her.'

'Okay,' Juan said, and over the radio to Max added, 'We're getting close. I'll call again when we find her.'

'Roger. Good hunting.'

'You too.'

19

They were lucky in the sense that they knew to within a couple of miles where the *Sakir* had been when she'd been attacked. All members of the Corporation team had GPS tracking chips surgically embedded in their thighs. The chips weren't powerful, so the signal was intermittent. But they had got a ping off Linda's chip when she'd ventured on deck twenty minutes before the *Sakir* was capsized, cutting down the search area tremendously.

They were unlucky, however, that the ceiling of clouds had dropped, forcing them to an altitude of four hundred feet and thus cutting how far they could see to the horizon. For ten minutes, as the chopper's turbine sucked gas like a drunk at an open bar, they crisscrossed grid lines Gomez had laid out on his knee-board chart. And they found nothing.

'I don't want to add to our woes,' Adams said over the chopper's communications net, 'but we've got about five minutes of fuel remaining.'

Linc didn't take the binoculars from his eyes when he said, 'Pessimist.'

And a moment later, he was proven correct. 'There.' He pointed ahead.

Juan leaned forward between the two front seats and accepted the glasses from the former SEAL.

Like a belly-up fish floating dead in the water, the capsized hulk of the once beautiful luxury craft lay lost and forlorn, with waves crashing along its length and remarkably little debris around it. As they drew closer still, Juan saw two people, who'd been sitting near where one of the propeller shafts emerged from the hull, stand up and begin to wave frantically. For a moment he was hopeful one was Linda Ross, but it quickly became apparent they were both men dressed in identical dark suits.

'Security guards,' Juan said. 'They must have been on deck when she flipped. They would have been thrown clear and then swam back to wait.'

Gomez flew them in, hovering over the yacht just aft of amidships. He timed the hulk's gentle roll and settled the helo with its skids straddling the *Sakir*'s keel. He killed the engine and powered down the electronics. The two guards rushed over to them, ducking below the still-spinning blades to reach the chopper.

Juan swung open his door. 'Is it only the two of you?'

'There was a third,' the more senior man said. 'He was with us on deck, but he never surfaced after the ship flipped over.'

'Any sign of other survivors? Have you heard anyone tapping from inside the ship?'

It was clear neither had thought to listen. Linc was already on his hands and knees sounding the hull with a giant wrench, his head cocked like a dog's listening for a response.

Juan began to gather up his scuba equipment. 'Let me get my gear out, and you two can sit in the chopper and warm up.' The guards were soaked to the skin and looked grateful for the opportunity to get out of the wind and rain. 'My ship should be here in another hour or so, and we'll get you some dry clothes and a hot meal.'

'Who are you?'

'Juan Cabrillo of the Corporation.'

'You're the outfit the Emir hired for additional security.'

'The irony isn't lost on me,' Juan told them.

Five minutes later, he walked down to where water pulsed and surged against the hull with his flippers in his hand. He bent carefully under the load on his back and slipped the fins over his dive boots, then settled his mask. He turned and walked backward off the side of the hull until the sea took up his weight and he was floating. He swam a few feet farther on so the waves wouldn't toss him back against the unyielding steel. He adjusted his buoyancy by dumping some air from his vest.

A moment later, he was falling along the edge of the hull. Ten feet down, where the water was much calmer, he passed the Plimsoll line where the red antifouling paint gave way to the snowy white livery the *Sakir* was noted for.

Cabrillo hadn't fully recovered from the stress and strain of yesterday's dive, and he wasn't diving with a partner, two cardinal sins, but if there was the slightest chance of saving Linda he would push on through to the gates of hell. He peered into a couple of portholes, encouraged when one of the rooms had only a little water on the floor – or what had been the ceiling. He tapped the glass in what looked like an officer's cabin but got no response.

Once he reached the inverted main deck, he was at a depth of thirty feet. He flicked on his dive light even though visibility wasn't too bad, considering the storm up on the surface.

The teak deck had been swept clean when the ship turtled. Gone were the chairs and tables, the piles of fluffy towels at the edge of the hot tub, and the cut-crystal glasses. Farther below him were the second deck and then the third, where the bridge was located. Down farther still were the ship's radar domes, radio masts, and her mammoth funnel.

Juan found a sliding glass door that had survived the violent forces of the ship's capsizing and forced it open. Because it was upside down, it didn't roll smoothly, and he really had to fight to squeeze through. The corridor went forward and aft. He arbitrarily started for the bow, checking rooms as he went. Each cabin was a flooded maelstrom of bedding, loose furniture, and clothing still swirling and dancing through the water.

He moved on and found his first body. It was a young woman dressed as a maid. She was floating in a cabin that she must have been servicing. Her cart lay on its side in a corner of the room, and extra sheets fluttered in the beam of his light like undulating sea creatures.

She was facing away from Cabrillo, so he swam closer and gently spun her around.

He blew out a startled breath that overloaded his regulator.

The poor woman must have hit a wall face-first because her features were distorted beyond recognition. Juan recalled the big ship's near-instantaneous flat roll and guessed she would have met her death when the wall smashed into her at better than twenty miles per hour. It looked no different than if she had been struck with a baseball bat.

He moved on, knowing that his task was only going to become grimmer.

Cabrillo found two more bodies on this level. One was dressed like the security detail, in a plain dark suit with tie, and the other wore a chef's white jacket and grey gingham pants. By the way their heads swivelled so loosely on their necks, he was sure both had died like the maid when they crashed into a bulkhead.

He reached the main stairs, a grand, sweeping affair that curled around an atrium which had once had a glass ceiling. Juan shone his light down on it, seeing that few of the panes remained in the ornate wrought-iron cupola. Below it, the ocean was inky black.

A sense of dread creeping up on him, Juan swam up the staircase. This level appeared fully flooded, but he couldn't take shortcuts on a mission like this. He laboriously checked every nook and cranny for someone who'd found an air pocket and survived their ordeal. He'd been aboard the *Sakir* on more than one occasion.

It was hard to wrap his mind around all this destruction when he remembered her as the epitome of opulence.

Sadly, there were more bodies. Juan recognized one of the men as the Emir's nephew, a likable teen who had ambitions of being a scientist. Particle physics, he remembered.

Each gruesome discovery made his anger at Kenin burn that much more, and the cut was doubly painful because these people were never the intended targets. Kenin put their deaths squarely on Juan's shoulders, and as much as Juan would have liked to rationalize away the guilt, he could not. These people's deaths were almost as much his fault as they were the rogue Russian admiral's.

The next deck, closer to the surface and thus the waterline, was the crew's area. Gone were the elegant silk wall coverings, the plush carpeting and subdued lighting. Here was a world of white steel walls, exposed electrical conduits and linoleum tile. The Emir had the money to give them better surroundings for when they were off duty, but leaving the space so stark was a not-so-subtle reminder that they were merely staff and he was the master. Sometimes the pettiness of the rich irked Cabrillo.

He expected to find a lot more bodies, but he didn't find any at all. Surely there had been some staff down here when the ship capsized, yet he found no one. He eventually located an entrance hatch to the engineering spaces. It had an electronic lock with a card reader, but when the ship lost power, the locks automatically disengaged. He swung open the steel door and swam up what was essentially a ladder because it was too steep to call it a stairway.

The main engine room was as clean as the *Oregon*'s own. The massive diesels, suspended from the ceiling, were painted white, while the floor had been green anechoic tiles. Juan found two bodies here, both in the overalls of engineering staff. He pushed on through to the auxiliary equipment room, where the ship's sewage and garbage were processed and fresh water was produced by a reverse osmosis desalinator.

He was dismayed that he hadn't found more victims and came to the sad conclusion that they had all been up on the second deck. Because of the physics involved in a ship flipping over, they would have all been killed by violent impact or so wounded that they could do nothing to prevent their drowning when water flooded into the ship. He was just about to go and explore the upper decks when he spotted a hatch overhead that had once been in the floor. It had to be bilge access. He swam up to it and tested the dogging wheel. It spun as if it had been oiled that morning.

The hatch swung down on its hinges, and Juan popped his head and arm into this new space, startling himself when he realized he had broken into a chamber free of water. He didn't think he'd reached the surface level, and a glance at his depth gauge confirmed he was still under eight feet of water. The air in the chamber was pressurized enough to stop the water from gushing in. He cast his light around what appeared to be an antechamber, because it was a small space, and there was another closed hatch to his right. There was only about four feet of headroom. He removed his tanks.

He realized that if the entire bilge was filled with air, it must be providing the buoyancy that kept the *Sakir* afloat. Eventually it would bleed out, but, for now, it was keeping the luxury cruiser from plummeting to the ocean floor.

He closed the first hatch and opened the next hatch, his dive light thrust out ahead of him. He was greeted with a tableau of death. There were thirty people stretched out along the walls, some clinging to one another, some off by themselves, others in little groups as if they'd been chatting before falling over. He had no idea how they'd gotten here or what had killed them. The air tasted fine, a bit musty and tainted with salt but breathable.

And as his light swept past one of the corpses, its eyes opened, and it screamed. In an instant, the rest of them came alive. They'd all been sleeping in the cloying blackness of the ship's bilge.

Two flashlights snapped on, adding their glow to the animated faces of people picking themselves up and rushing at Cabrillo. Several remained on the deck, and Juan could tell they were injured. Questions were hurtled at him in a half dozen languages, but one voice eventually drowned out all the others.

'About time you showed up,' Linda Ross chided him. 'Air's getting a tad thin in here, and I was bored. I lost my last cent playing gin rummy.'

Linda topped out at five feet two, had an elfin face with large eyes and a button nose. She had a few freckles that made her seem even younger and a girlish voice.

'What happened?'

'I was about to ask you the same question.'

Their conversation got derailed for a few minutes as the Emir, whose moniker stretched over eleven names and who Juan called Dullah, short for Abdullah, thanked him again and again for deliverance.

'We're not out of the woods yet, old friend. The *Oregon* is still a half hour away, and I'm afraid if we cut our way down here, the air in the bilge will escape and the *Sakir* will sink like a stone.'

He turned to Linda. 'What happened after you capsized? How did everyone end up here?'

'It was her,' the Emir said, beaming at Linda. 'She did it. She saved us all. When the ship rolled over, she knew to get us down here as quickly as possible. She knew that water would enter the boat and she rushed us here. You should have seen her, my friend. She was like a lioness protecting her cubs. I could barely pick myself off the floor, and your lovely Linda was organizing us so the strong could help the lame.'

Juan shot Linda an appraising look. She had a ghost of a smile on her lips, loving the emotional praise from the Emir but too coy to gloat.

'I tell her already,' Dullah went on, 'that I will pay her ten times what you give her to be my personal bodyguard. While my men wandered in a daze, she was saving our lives. I say it again, a true lioness. In all my life I have never seen one so brave, one so strong, one so . . .'

Dullah finally ran out of praise, so Linda said, 'You forgot the part where I turned water into wine.'

'I believe you could,' the Emir rejoined.

Juan looked at her. 'Linda, are you sure there's enough room in here for us and your ego?'

'Plenty,' she shot back saucily.

Good job, he mouthed to her, and then addressed the crowd: 'I need to speak with an engineer.'

One of the men stepped forward. 'Heinz-Erik Vogel, chief engineer.'

He was Teutonic, from the top of his blond head to the soles of his work boots, and stood as if at attention. Juan shook his hand.

'I'm Juan Cabrillo, Linda's boss.' He went on to explain his theory as to why the ship hadn't sunk yet, and the engineer heartily agreed, having come to the same conclusion himself. They agreed the best way to get everyone out was to breach the hull plates over the anteroom through which Juan had first entered the bilge. They could better prevent the air from escaping by using its access hatch like an air lock, opening it just long enough to get a group of people inside and then closing it up again while they were helped outside by Cabrillo's people.

A second hole would need to be drilled into the bilge and air pumped in at high pressure to make up for the expected losses when the hatch was opened.

They worked out the precise location of the ante-chamber as it related to the ship's propeller shafts, the only reference point Cabrillo would have on the otherwise bare hull bottom.

When they had settled all the details, Juan turned to Linda. 'I've got enough air for us to buddy-breathe back to the surface.'

She didn't consider his offer for a second. 'These are my people now. I'm responsible for them and I'm not leaving them until they're all safe.'

He bent and kissed her forehead. 'I knew you wouldn't. Close the hatch behind me. This should take about an hour to set in motion. We can start cutting now, and once the *Oregon* arrives, Max'll rig the air hose. When I tap on the hatch three times, that means I'm going to open it. Send through the first five people. Worst injured first, but they need to be quick, so have healthy people help them.'

'Got it.'

'Then we'll lever the hatch closed, clear the antechamber, let the pressure build back up inside here, and do it again.'

'Sounds good.'

'Okay, hotshot. See you later.'

It took Juan just ten minutes of quick swimming and a few minutes of decompression to reach the surface and drag himself back onto the *Sakir*'s hull. Linc was there in an instant to help him off with his gear. 'Well?'

'Linda saved all but a couple of them,' Juan said with a proud smile.

'Booyah!' Linc whooped. 'I knew my girl would pull through. What happened?'

'She got everyone down into the bilge after the *Sakir* rolled but before it completely filled with water. They're in there now, inside a bubble of pressurized air. I worked out with the ship's engineer how to rescue them and not have this tub sink from under our feet. What about the *Oregon*?'

'Launched MacD and Eddie twenty minutes ago, and, if you could see past the rudder, you'd know she's about ten minutes from pulling alongside of us.'

'Perfect.' Juan strode over to the chopper to open a line to Hanley. He laid out what they would need, and Max promised to have it ready by the time they arrived.

While Linc got the cutting torch ready, Juan changed out of his scuba suit, dried himself with a rag Gomez promised was clean, and threw on the outdoor clothes he'd grabbed from his cabin, complete with rubber boots that went up to his knees.

As soon as the *Oregon* was in position on the windward side of the *Sakir* so that her massive bulk shielded the work crew from the worst of the storm, a Zodiac shot out of the boat garage, trailing a thick rubber hose. Max was at the controls, and with him were some of his boys from the engineering staff.

There was no time for small talk. The storm was intensifying. Soon waves would sweep clear across the hulk and suspend any attempt at getting the survivors out. From the measurements Vogel had given him, Cabrillo marked out a three-by-three-foot spot on the hull, and Linc got busy with the torch. Molten metal was soon drizzling through the cuts he made as the torch slowly ate the inch-and-a-half-thick plate. Hanley had brought over a second plasma torch, and he was at Linc's side cutting with abandon. Farther along the hull, the *Oregon*'s engineers were preparing to drill a hole to insert the air hose. They had tubes of industrial contact glue ready to seal the hose into place once the nozzle was inside the bilge. Gomez Adams was warming the chopper for the short hop back to the hangar.

In all, Cabrillo's people were working like the well-oiled machine he knew them to be.

Juan had told Linda that they'd be ready in an hour. He missed that deadline by only two minutes and that's because he didn't factor in the time it would take Max to set up a hydraulic ram down in the antechamber. They would need its power to close the hatch against the pressure of air gushing out. Fortunately, it wasn't high enough to warrant decompression for those trapped inside.

Cabrillo gave her the signal, she tapped back that she was ready, and Juan opened the hatch. In the explosive blast of air, five people tumbled into the antechamber, sprawling on the ground in a tangle of limbs. One woman screamed when her already-broken leg was smashed against the far wall. Max activated the ram and it slammed the door closed, as promised.

'What do you think?' Cabrillo asked. The ship didn't feel like it had settled any deeper.

'How should I know? You didn't leave a barometer in there. Gunner's manning the compressor. He should be able to tell the back pressure. That'll give us an idea of when we can let out the next group. But truth be told, I think it worked like a charm.'

Juan grinned. 'Me too.'

By being patient and cycling air back into the bilge space, it took forty minutes for the last group, including Linda, Vogel, and the Emir, who had insisted on staying despite everyone's entreaties not to wait, to emerge from the bowels of the ship. Max dogged down the hatch while the last survivors picked themselves up.

Dullah shook Juan's hand again. 'Now we are, as you say, out of the forest?'

'Close enough, my friend, close enough.'

20

In an idealized, fictional world, the *Oregon* would have been over the horizon as soon as the passengers were rescued and on their way in pursuit of the stealth ship. But this was reality. And the reality was that the Atlantic is considered 'our pond' by both the US Navy and by the Coast Guard.

No more than a minute after the Emir crawled out of the bilge, an HH-60 Jayhawk helicopter, painted in the Coastie's traditional orange-and-white, thundered over the hulk at fifty feet, filling the already-stormy air with water kicked up by the rotor wash.

Juan had known this was coming and had already shut down the *Oregon*'s military-grade radar suite and had been tracking the inbound bird on the far weaker civilian equipment. If the chopper didn't have the gear to detect the differences, the cutter streaming in after her surely would, and that would raise questions the Chairman didn't want to answer. Another question he wanted to avoid was how a ship that had been seen loitering off Philadelphia had gotten this far south so quickly.

Max's latest invention would take care of that. He had recently replaced the steel plating on the *Oregon*'s fantail, where the ship's name is traditionally emblazoned, with a highly sophisticated variable electromagnet micro-grid. A computer controlled which of the tiny magnets that made up the array were energized. In this way, when a mist of iron filings was sprayed onto the plates by a retractable nozzle, any name Hanley devised would be spelled out. When he cut power, the old name and flag nation – in this case, *Wanderstar*, out of Panama – blew away on the wind. He'd typed in a new name, for which they had all the proper documentation, into the system and activated the nozzle. The magnets attracted the minute filings and spelled out *Xanadu*, from Cyprus, while the excess metal fell into the Atlantic. The system was so precise that from even a few feet away, it looked like paint that was flaking off in places, in keeping with the general shabbiness of the rest of the ship.

In the past, it took the crew up to thirty minutes to change the ship's name. Now it took less than ten seconds.

Cabrillo fished an encrypted walkie-talkie from his back pocket when the Coast Guard chopper had backed off to assess the situation. 'Talk to me, Max.'

'That bird's off the cutter *James Patke* out of Norfolk. She should be here in about a half hour. The *Oregon*'s now the *Xanadu*. Eric's up in the wheelhouse making the changes, both there and in the captain's cabin, should they want to board us.'

'I'll need my Captain Ramon Esteban ID,' Juan said. It was the identification that went with their Cypriot disguise.

'Stoney's putting it in the desk in your cabin.'

'We'd better make this look good. Lower one of the life rafts as if we planned on taking the survivors with us. Then jam up the davit controls so the Coasties will have to take them off our hands.'

'Already ordered,' Max shot back, then added with mild rebuke, 'Do you think this is my first time at this?'

'No. But it *is* our first time dealing with the US Coast Guard and not some Third World facsimile more interested in bribes than rescue.'

'Roger that. We'll be all right.'

The Coast Guard chopper approached again, this time with its side door racked open and a rescue diver seated with his legs dangling into space. When they were one hundred yards off the port beam of the wallowing derelict, and at an altitude of thirty feet, the diver slid from his perch and dropped like an arrow into the churning ocean. The helo immediately swept farther away to make the swim easier for their man. Max and his team took this opportunity to remove the hydraulic ram they'd installed and surreptitiously dump it overboard. With the air hose already retracted aboard the *Oregon*, this was the last bit of evidence that the rescue had been far more complicated than they were about to admit.

The diver reached the side of the *Sakir*, and Juan was there to give him a hand out of the water.

'Master Chief Warren Davies,' the man said as he pulled off his fins and attached them to a belt slung around his wet suit.

'Captain Ramon Esteban.'

'What's the situation, Captain?'

'This is a luxury boat,' Juan said with a melodious Spanish accent. 'I think it was hit by a rogue wave and obviously capsized. We were on our way to Nassau when we spotted the wreck. Two men had been thrown into the water, but we found them on the hulk. They told us that they heard banging from inside the hull. We used a torch from our ship to cut our way in and found all these people. We were about to move them into one of our lifeboats, but we are having trouble with the davit controls.'

Juan pointed to the *Oregon*. Her portside lifeboat hung halfway down her side, but was angled with its stern pointed toward the water and its bow skyward. A couple of deckhands appeared to be working on the controls.

'That shouldn't be a problem so long as this tub stays afloat,' Davies said. 'Our cutter will be here soon. What about injuries?'

'We are assessing that now. You have medical training?'

'Tons. Let's go check on the survivors.'

For the next half hour, Cabrillo played the part of concerned captain, all the while knowing his quarry was getting farther and farther away. Via walkie-talkie he got regular updates from Max, but idling in the area was driving him nuts. Finally, the *James Patke* appeared out of the curtains of rain sweeping the ship. She was a sleek, modern ship with a hunter's sharp lines. Her five-inch deck gun was mounted in a stealthy angular turret unlike the old domes of past generations. She could easily have passed for a Navy warship except for her white hull and blazing orange stripe. No sooner had she hoved to than two inflatables were launched off her stern deck and were shooting across the intervening distance ahead of rooster tails of churned water.

They quickly beached themselves on the *Sakir*'s slowly sinking hull – air was escaping from the bilge through the hole they had drilled – and since there was no place to tie them off, one sailor was detailed to hold their painter lines. The men aboard were medical personnel burdened with hard cases of gear, a couple of able seamen, and an officer who approached Cabrillo with an outstretched hand. 'Commander Bill Taggard.'

'Captain Ramon Esteban.'

'Master Chief Davies has already filled us in on what you've accomplished. Damn fine piece of work, Captain.'

'I loved the *Poseidon Adventure* as a boy,' Juan said with a disarming shrug. 'I never thought I would live it.'

'You said this was caused by a rogue wave?'

'Yes, we experienced it ourselves. A real monster that came out of nowhere. We were bow on to it, but I suspect this vessel took it broadside.'

'Strange, because we've contacted local shipping and no one reported any rogue waves.'

Cabrillo lightly tapped the hull with his boot. 'I think this is evidence enough, don't you?'

'Yeah, I guess you're right.'

Coasties began loading litters with the worst injured

into the inflatables for the quick ride back to the cutter. The rest of the survivors, cold and miserable, waited their turn on the shrinking hulk. Each minute saw the ocean eat up another few inches of deck space as the derelict continued to sink. Cabrillo's mind flashed to the painting of the survivors of the wreck of the *Medusa* as they huddled on their raft while it sank. If Taggard didn't speed up his rescue, he saw the same thing playing out here.

It took two more trips to evacuate the rest of the survivors. As they'd worked out earlier, the Emir gushed over Cabrillo's heroism and vowed to make him a rich man for saving his life. Cabrillo in turn acted the hardened sea veteran and said it was his duty and could not take financial reward for doing the right thing. This was all played out for the Coast Guard's benefit, and it seemed that Taggard bought the act. He didn't ask to board the *Oregon* or ask many questions about her at all. He had what he needed for his report, and though he couldn't promise the names *Xanadu* or Ramon Esteban wouldn't reach the media, he intimated that their role in the rescue would be downplayed. Budget battles loomed, and an operation like this made his service look good in the eyes of Washington.

The two shook hands, and while the Coasties returned to their cutter, Cabrillo and his team returned to the *Oregon*. The 'problem' with the davit had been rectified and the lifeboat was secured once again. They made a show of lugging their little inflatable up the lowered boarding stairs and stowing it on the cluttered deck. No sooner were they aboard than Max had them moving off deeper into the storm, keeping track with their stated destination of Nassau, the Bahamas. He kept to the course and a speed of just twelve knots until the threat detection gear showed they had steamed beyond the cutter's effective radar range.

Only then could they go after the stealth ship being pursued by MacD and Eddie in the RHIB. Cabrillo was still in the shower when he felt the engines spool up and the ship begin to pour on the power. They'd lost several hours on their target, and it felt as though Max intended on making it up as fast as possible. Ten minutes later, dressed in jeans and a Norwegian roll-neck sweater, Cabrillo entered the op centre.

'How are our boys?' he asked, taking his command seat.

'Still in pursuit,' Max replied.

'What's their fuel status?'

'If we can maintain forty knots, we'll reach them when they still have an hour's reserve.'

'That's a bit tighter than I like,' Juan remarked. 'If we're delayed, they'll need to break off the chase so they don't run out.'

'Not much we can do about that,' Hanley said. 'Coasties took their time reaching the wreck. Could've been worse if they'd wanted to board us and go over our papers.'

Juan didn't reply. What so concerned him was that in these seas, his men needed to keep headway in the RHIB to avoid being swamped by a wave. If their fuel load dropped to a certain point, they would need to slow down to stretch out their time under power. That meant letting the stealth ship escape.

Over the next hours, Cabrillo sat wordlessly drinking coffee while the plot showing the *Oregon*'s position and the blip representing the RHIB according to its locator drew closer and closer. Because they didn't know their quarry's capabilities, they were maintaining strict radio silence. Juan was relieved by the fact that they were maintaining a steady southeasterly course. The RHIB hadn't deviated more than a couple of degrees since the chase had begun nor had it changed speed. They'd also maintained a steady fifteen knots.

It was well past dusk when they had closed to within twenty miles of the RHIB and thus about twenty-one from the stealth ship. Juan judged they were close enough to have MacD and Eddie break off and return to the *Oregon*. He knew where his target would be over the next hour and wanted to be in a position to do something about it.

'Hali, open a line to Eddie.'

Hali Kasim, at the communications station, had been waiting for this for hours and had a channel open in seconds.

'Time to head home,' Juan said over the link. 'Reverse course. Eighteen.'

Eddie Seng clicked his radio in response and knew to turn back and expect to find the *Oregon* eighteen miles away.

Because he was no longer shadowing the slow stealth ship, Eddie would doubtlessly firewall the RHIB's twin outboards so the two vessels would have a closing speed in excess of eighty knots. The Chairman called down to the boat garage to inform them that the RHIB was inbound and should be off their beam in less than fifteen minutes.

It actually was just ten, but because the *Oregon* had to come to an almost complete stop in order for the RHIB to enter the hull, it was seventeen minutes until Juan could give the order for full speed again. Only, this time, he took the *Oregon* on a wide arc around their target so when they finally approached, it would seem that they were coming from the east and not like they'd been trailing the rogue vessel.

Linda Ross finally sauntered into the op centre, looking none the worse for her adventures.

'How are you doing?' Juan asked with genuine concern.

'Doc says I'm fine, and who am I to argue? Where do we stand?'

'Endgame's coming,' Cabrillo said. 'We're flanking them now.'

'Anything on radar?'

'He doesn't show at all,' Juan admitted. 'But he hasn't changed course or speed since fleeing the *Sakir*.'

As if on cue, Mark Murphy called out from the weapons station, 'Contact bearing forty-seven degrees. Range twenty miles.' Cabrillo had already figured out the tactical positions before Murph added, 'Directly in line with the stealth ship.'

'Rendezvous,' Cabrillo mouthed.

The situation had changed in an instant. Juan now had to get the *Oregon* between the stealth ship and this new contact before that vessel spotted them on radar. His ship had a much smaller radar cross-section than she should thanks to signal-absorbing materials applied to her hull and upperworks, but she was far from invisible.

'Helm, make your course three-three degrees. All ahead flank.' Like a hunter, Cabrillo knew to lead his target so that the bullet – in this case, the *Oregon* herself – arrived where the target would be, not where it currently was. Like before, he had the angles and speeds worked out in his head. Eric Stone would double-check them with the ship's navigation computer but as usual would find no error in the Chairman's calculations.

'Wepps, prep the main gun. Once he figures out we're coming, who knows what he'll do.'

'Not missiles?' Murph questioned.

'If that ship can produce a magnetic field strong enough to capsize Dullah's yacht, a missile won't stand a chance. Load solid tungsten rounds. Field won't affect them.'

Murph nodded at Cabrillo's insight while mentally chastising himself for not coming to the same conclusion and set about readying the 120mm cannon secreted behind doors in the *Oregon*'s bow. The smooth-bore gun used the same sophisticated fire controls as an

M1 Abrams main battle tank and could fire accurately no matter how the ship pitched or rolled.

'Curious, Juan,' Max said, fiddling with his pipe, 'how are we going to hit it if it doesn't show up on radar?'

'Easy. Launch a UAV.'

In minutes, the drone, little more than a large model airplane fitted with sophisticated cameras, was aloft and racing ahead of the *Oregon* at a hundred miles per hour. When it reached two thousand feet, its starlight camera picked up the stealth ship's wake, a dazzling line of green phosphorescence that sliced across the ocean like an arc of electricity. Its terminus was the ship itself. The ungainly craft was fighting the seas but maintaining its steady pace. The rendezvous ship was too far to see, but they would tackle that after dispatching their primary target.

'I've got bearings,' Mark announced, 'but we're still a little out of range.'

'He's going to see us soon,' Hanley cautioned.

Juan had to agree. He just didn't know what would happen.

'Twenty seconds,' Mark said.

Come on, Cabrillo silently entreated.

'Ten.'

The image from the drone changed. The angular hull of the stealth ship began to shimmer, and a blue glow erupted from its centre and spread outward. The ship blurred before vanishing altogether.

A second later, the feed from the drone turned to

static as it was swatted from the sky by an expanding dome of electromagnetic pulses.

'In range!' Mark cried.

'Fire!' Juan shouted as the wall of invisible energy slammed into the *Oregon*.

He didn't know if Murph got off the shot because a deafening blast of noise filled the ship as she began a rapid roll onto her port side, the red numbers on the digital inclinometer blurring to keep up with the list. Water was soon pouring across her decks and slamming into the superstructure. The combination of her speed and the pulse seemed to be driving her into the depths.

Then as suddenly as it started, the noise cut off like a switch had been flicked, and the ship began to right itself once again, albeit slowly as she had to shrug off hundreds of tons of seawater.

Cabrillo picked himself up off the floor, where he'd been unceremoniously dumped. Main power had tripped so the op centre was bathed in emergency lights. All the computer monitors and controls were dead, and he became aware that he couldn't hear the *Oregon*'s engines. 'Is everyone all right?'

He received a slow roll call of muted responses. No one was hurt, but they were all rattled.

'Max, get me a damage report. Hali, get ahold of the Doc, I'm sure there are going to be injuries. Mark, get another UAV in the air as soon as you're able. I want eyes on that ship. And for the record, I think you saved our lives.'

'Chairman?'

'You got the shot off, didn't you?'

'Barely.'

'In this game, barely counts. Nice shooting.'

It took twenty minutes for the engineering staff to reboot the power system and get the computers back online. But they were forced to use battery backup because the magnetohydrodynamic system was still down. Dr Huxley patched up one broken arm and diagnosed two concussions among the crew, and Mark Murphy utterly failed to get a drone into the air. As bad as the magnetic pulse was on the ship's hardened electronics, it destroyed those not protected. Small devices like PDAs, electric shavers and food processors had all been fried. The remaining UAVs were nothing more than toy gliders now. Cabrillo was forced to lead a team in a RHIB, and even that had to have its engines started manually with old-fashioned pull cords.

The going was tough as the storm intensified. Icy needles of rain pelted any exposed skin, though the sturdy craft rode the waves well. When they reached the spot where the stealth ship had been hit, they found a debris field encircled by a slick of diesel fuel that was rapidly breaking up. Cabrillo ran the RHIB to one of the largest pieces of flotsam, a section of composite material that looked as if it had been part of the ship's pointed prow. He and Eddie Seng lifted the lightweight chunk of debris into the RHIB and lashed it to the deck so they could examine it back on the *Oregon*.

'What do you think?' Eddie asked.

'I think when that shell hit, the boat blew apart like a grenade. Whatever powered the magnetic pulse generator had to be very unstable.'

'You think when the field failed it cratered the ship?'

'That's my guess. I'll run the idea past Murph and Stone to get their opinion, but I think I'm right.'

'What about the rendezvous ship?'

Juan looked around the darkened sea. 'Gone the instant they figured out what happened to their buddies here.' He added grimly, 'If we can't get the *Oregon* running in the next hour or two, we've lost them.'

They headed back home.

When the civilian radar finally came back online, the seas around them were empty, as Cabrillo predicted. The military radar came up a short time later, and its extended range showed a pair of ships, but neither was travelling in the right direction to be the rendezvous vessel. They were approaching, not fleeing. The main engines were finally refired five hours after the EMP blast. As chief engineer, Max insisted that they be brought up to full power in slow, carefully monitored increments.

As satisfied as Cabrillo was that the stealth ship had been destroyed, he was equally bitter that the trail was now going to go cold. With the damage they'd sustained, Hanley recommended some time in port so they could sort out all the problems and do a thorough systems check. Juan reluctantly agreed, and a day later they tied up at Hamilton Harbour's commercial pier.

What stores they needed for repairs that couldn't be bought in Bermuda could easily be flown in from the States. Max would see to that.

Cabrillo's job was to find two men who most definitely didn't want to be found.

21

They were called favelas. The slums of Rio de Janeiro were world famous. No one was quite sure why, but some had even become tourist destinations for the wealthy of the world to stare, agape, at the misery of others. While some of the slums clinging to the hillsides surrounding Brazil's second-most-populous city had been gentrified to an extent with running water and electricity, many of them had not and were still little more than clusters of shipping containers with crude mud tracks between them. These favelas, especially, were the homes of criminal gangs, usually drug dealers and professional kidnappers who would snatch people off the streets and hold them for ransom.

One such slum spilled off a hill like so much trash flung from a giant's hand. It was home to thirty thousand people crammed into a space not much larger than three city blocks. Dogs and half-naked children meandered the dirt paths that wound around the buildings. There were only a few of any permanence, cinder-block structures erected by one aid agency or other, with the intent of housing a few hundred people in tiny apartments. Instead, several thousand called each one home, many living in staircases or hallways or in tin and plywood shacks atop the roof.

Sewage ran in channels along the roads, and only occasionally would one of the cars lining the streets move. Most had been stolen and abandoned here and were stripped down to their shells, like the carapaces of dead beetles eaten by ants. The stink and squalour were appalling. It was a place of grey hopelessness where even Rio's perfect weather could not give joy to the inhabitants. It was also a place of oppressive fear of the drug gang that ran the favela with an iron fist. The police never ventured into the slum, and not once had the government tried to intervene in the region's internal affairs. Its leader was called Amo, which meant 'boss'. Nothing happened in his territory that he didn't know about.

The stranger looked like any of the thousands of peasants who flocked into the city from the countryside searching for work. He wore frayed tan pants and a simple cotton shirt. His sandals were soled with the tread of a truck tyre. On his head he wore a hat made from woven palm leaves. No one paid him any attention as he moved slowly up the hill, weaving between heaps of trash and kids roughhousing in the streets.

Finally, two young men with slicked-back hair and predatory eyes lifted themselves from the five-gallon buckets they were using as stools. One adjusted his shirt so the taped butt of an ancient revolver was visible. His partner hefted a baseball bat.

They approached the stranger and called out, 'What's your business here?'

They could see the man was in his sixties and had

a dim look in his eyes. He muttered a response that neither man understood.

'I think you should head back down the mountain, old man,' the leader of the two thugs suggested. 'There is nothing but trouble for you here.'

It was obvious the old man had nothing of value, so there was no sense robbing him, and letting him linger would mean one more beggar clogging the streets. Better to send him packing now than disposing of his corpse later when he died of starvation or dysentery.

'I want no trouble,' the man said in Spanish.

'He ain't even Brazilian, man,' the young thug complained. 'We can't feed ourselves, and some Bolivian expects to live off our charity.'

The kid with the gun spat angrily. 'Not your lucky day, pal.'

He grabbed the old man by the arm while his partner got him by the other, and they quickly marshalled him into a tight alley between two shipping containers that served as homes for dozens. A cat had been sunning itself on a tyre pile at the entrance of the alley, but its primal sense of trouble sent it fleeing. The ground was oil-soaked and packed as hard as cement.

They tossed the man into the side of one of the containers, but he turned so that he hit it with his back and not his face as they had intended. If either street tough realized how deftly the old man had moved, things might have ended differently. The space was too narrow to swing the bat properly, so the thug used its butt end like a ram aimed at the old man's stomach. He wasn't a big kid, and perpetual hunger did little to give him superior strength, but the blow would be enough to drop the old man to the ground with his lungs emptied of air.

The wooden bat hit the side of the container with an echoing thump. The man had dodged the bat, and then he went on the offense. He snatched the gun out of the leader's waistband before the man realized he'd moved and used it like a pair of brass knuckles. His punch broke the kid's cheekbone and flayed open the skin so that blood poured from the wound.

He howled in pain and outrage even as the old man turned his attention to the youth with the bat. He was still numbed from the unexpected hit against the unyielding container, so he could do nothing to defend himself as the pistol smashed into his nose, breaking it with the kind of force even the world's greatest plastic surgeon would have trouble repairing. He dropped to his knees, clutching at the wound. He keened like a siren, high then low. Next to him, the leader of the little duo of Amo's sentries was out cold.

The stranger finally took the time to notice the gun wasn't even loaded. When he'd first seen it, his instincts had been right not to try to fire it. He hadn't thought it was empty, just that it would probably explode in his hand if he'd pulled the trigger. He pocketed the gun for later disposal and hauled the still-conscious kid to his feet.

The camera was no bigger than a tube of lipstick, and its wireless router the size of a pack of cigarettes. It was mounted part way up a telephone pole.

The stranger pulled off his ridiculous hat and held up the kid's bloody face to the camera, saying, 'I know this guy is low level and that you've got better guards deeper in there, but you also know they're not going to stop me. I've tracked you this far and I'll keep going until I get to you. Admit defeat and no one else needs to get hurt.'

As he let him go, the kid immediately fell back to his knees, sobbing.

The stranger moved back out onto the main street. Nothing appeared any different. Some women were in line next to a truck that had carried water into the favela for sale. Some old men were sitting on a sofa left out in the elements so long, it was mouldy. Chickens tethered to a stick pecked at the stony ground near a hut. All was as it should be.

A few seconds later, a white pickup truck appeared at the head of the street. Though old and filthy, it represented real wealth in the favela. He waited as the vehicle ground its way to him. It came to a stop, and the passenger leaned out the window.

'He says to get in back. No tricks. He says you found him.'

The stranger nodded. There was an honour code at play here, one he knew he shouldn't respect, but he felt it was better to play safe than sorry. He vaulted over the fender and squatted in the bed as the truck laboriously turned around in the constricted street and began slogging back up the hill. The truck belonged to Amo, so no one dared look at it, yet people seemed to part like a shoal of fish breaking for a shark to get out of its way. It pulled up to a three-storey, cinder-block building. As soon as the stranger's feet hit the ground, the truck drove away. Lean-tos, running three deep, had been constructed around the building's perimeter, with the exception of the entry, so to reach it he had to walk down a tight alley of tin sheeting and sullen faces.

The building's front door had long been torn from its hinges. The concrete floor was filthy, and the air inside the building reeked of garbage. He did not know which way to go until he looked up the stairs to his right. What he saw startled him with its incongruity. It was a woman wearing a white nurse's uniform so crisp, it looked like she had just put it on. She was blonde and attractive, at least from this distance, and her legs, in the white hosiery of her uniform, were shapely. Amid all this misery and ugliness, she was like an angel sent from heaven.

She beckoned him with a finger and he mounted the stairs.

The second floor was also concrete, but it was painted a subtle grey and was impeccably swept. The walls were also painted and clean. There was only one door on this landing, and as he walked through, an alarm chimed. A man dressed as a security guard rose from behind his desk, a hand going for his sidearm in a well-practiced motion.

'Sir,' the guard said even as the stranger raised his hands.

'In a holster behind my back,' the man said and slowly turned. 'There's another in my pocket.'

The guard nodded to the nurse, who unarmed the stranger. The man knew the routine and stepped out of the room and back into the hallway. The door's threshold, though innocuous to look at, was a body scanner that had detected the taped-up revolver he'd taken off the kid and the FN Five-seveN pistol he'd been carrying. This time through, the alarm remained silent, and the guard relaxed his defensive posture. A phone on his desk rang. He listened for a moment before replacing the handset.

'Give him back his guns. He says that this one is just as deadly without them.'

The man took the automatic back from the pretty nurse and secured it in its holster. He made a dismissive gesture toward the broken-down revolver, so she kept it. The stranger finally took notice of the room. It was like the lobby of a discreet boutique hotel, one of those places in London or New York that were so exclusive there usually wasn't a sign out front. The floors were marble tile, the walls' wainscoting deep mahogany, and the lighting luxurious crystal fixtures. The view out of the two windows was what threw him for a moment. It should have shown the garbage-strewn streets of a Brazilian slum, but instead he was greeted by a cobbled road in what looked like an Eastern European town – the Czech Republic, maybe, or Hungary. The light streaming in appeared natural, and yet the two 'windows' were flat-screen displays with curtains so the people here wouldn't be reminded of the squalour outside. A far door opened, and another nurse, a virtual twin of the first, beckoned the newcomer farther into this surreal building.

The next rooms were even more luxurious than the reception hall. More flat-screen panels displayed views of the same street. An old woman was leading a horse on the opposite curb, and he felt as if the clip-clop of its hooves could be heard through the glass. He was finally shown into a sleek executive office with a fire-place and sofa cluster in one corner and a modernist glass desk at the far wall. In another corner were the closed doors of an elevator that would lead to an apart-ment on the third floor just as opulent as this room.

'Chairman,' the scarred and wheelchair-bound man behind the desk greeted.

'L'Enfant,' Cabrillo said back.

'I suppose if you had wanted me dead, you would have struck in the night and I never would have known it was coming.'

'The thought crossed my mind,' Cabrillo replied.

Two weeks had passed since the encounter with the stealth ship. The *Oregon* was still in Hamilton Harbour, her refit just about complete. He had given up tracking Admiral Kenin once he fled Russia. This had to have been his last big score, the one that would set him up for life. A man in that situation plans his escape down to the finest detail. He would be completely untrace-able ten seconds after implementing it. He would have a new identity that was unbreakable, a new place to live, bank accounts that had been in place for years. In all, a new life that was just as real – at least, to those looking – as the one he'd left.

'I must be getting sloppy,' L'Enfant said, waving his good right hand. 'First Kenin tracked me, now you.'

'The first time you were sloppy,' Juan agreed, 'the second you were just in a hurry.'

So rather than waste time tracking a man they would never find, he put Murph and Stone on locating the slippery information merchant. They had the advantage of knowing that he would have run soon after Kenin contacted him to get information on the Corporation. With that starting point, it still took twelve days of data-mining and fact-checking to discover another of L'Enfant's lairs, one in a most unlikely place.

Cabrillo added, 'You're also becoming predictable.' He shot a significant glance at the attractive nurse.

'Ah,' L'Enfant said, 'I wasn't aware you knew my penchant for pretty nurses.'

'Now you're deluding yourself. If it was just pretty ones, we never would have found you. But sisters who are also nurses are a rarer breed of cat.'

L'Enfant's single eye glittered as he looked at the nurse. 'My last ones were actually twins. Not identical, mind you, but twins nonetheless.' He clapped his right hand into the claw-like pincer of his disfigured left. 'Leave us, my dear.' When the nurse had gone, L'Enfant said, 'You have not tracked me here to discuss my medical staff, I presume.'

'You presume correctly.' Cabrillo waited for the shadowy man to figure out why he'd come.

L'Enfant studied him for a moment and finally asked, 'Why the disguise?'

'I needed to cross through some nasty neighbourhoods to get here. I didn't want to look like an attractive target for a mugger.'

'You always were a careful planner. Okay, what else may I presume? I have wronged you by speaking of the Corporation to Kenin, something for which I must atone.'

Juan nodded while L'Enfant adjusted the oxygen cannula under the ruin of his burned nose.

'I presume that my atonement comes in the form of tracking down Admiral Kenin for you.'

'Correct.'

'And you came to me in person rather than reaching me through more conventional ways in order for me to understand that if I fail to find him, my life is then forfeit.'

'Four for four. You should go into the soothsaying business. Do you know where Kenin went to ground?'

The man shook his reptilian head. 'No. Don't think I don't have feelers out there, but he knew what he was doing when he rabbited.'

'"Rabbited", really?' Juan said with a smile. 'Last time I read someone "rabbiting" was an old spy novel.'

'You prefer "on the lam"?'

'I prefer to know where he is,' Juan said sharply to

remind the information broker that this wasn't idle banter.

'I will find him.'

'Now call Amo and have him send the pickup. I'd rather not walk all the way back to where I can find a working bus that will eventually take me to a part of the city that has taxis.' It might have sounded like a joke, but Cabrillo had had to traverse ten miles of urban jungle on foot to get here because buses, let alone cabs, never ventured into this part of the city.

'I will do you one better. I have an old Mercedes that doesn't attract too much attention. Where are you staying?'

'The Fasano,' he lied.

'I figured a guy like you would go for nostalgia and stay at the Copa Palace.'

Had Juan not been a better poker player, he would have given away that L'Enfant had guessed where he was actually staying. He loved the stately deco-style Copacabana Palace Hotel and stayed there whenever he was in Rio.

'No matter. I will have my man drop you at the Fasano. No buses or taxis. It is the least I can do.'

Juan put a little menace in his voice. 'The least you can do is lead me to Pytor Kenin.'

22

The Container was in play.

That's what it was called, The Container. Capital *T*, capital *C*. The. Container.

That it was finally in play had sent bells ringing at the CIA, FBI, Homeland, Treasury, NSA, and just about every other acronymic entity in Washington, DC. Cabrillo wouldn't have been surprised to know his old friend Dirk Pitt and NUMA had been read in on The Container.

The rumours swirling around it were the stuff of legend and myth. No one was certain how or why The Container came into being or who was behind it, but from every souk and bazaar, from one end of the Middle East to the farthest island of Muslim Indonesia, word of its contents had spread.

In the first years of America's invasion of Iraq, massive amounts of cash were used to buy loyalty, as was custom in many parts of the region, though loyalty ran out when the money did or someone had a better offer. That left Washington in the position of having to pour unimaginable streams of cash into Baghdad, Başrah, and every hamlet up to the Kurdish border with Turkey.

Oversight of this bounty was thought to be foolproof but in actuality was an utter joke. Vast sums of cash were siphoned off by yet another layer of corruption in a corrupted society. The problem for those partaking of Uncle Sam's largesse wasn't how to get the money but how to get it out of the country. Sure, individuals could smuggle a few bundles of hundred-dollar bills, but what about those on top of the scheming and stealing? Packing a hundred K across a desert outpost was one thing. But what about the billion in hard currency that was unaccounted for? It would take a tractor-trailer to move it, or a container.

So that's what happened to it. It went into a conex shipping container and then it sat in a warehouse because those who stole it also knew the Americans would never stop looking for it. So they did what Arabs were especially good at. They outwaited their enemies. It took years, but eventually the US drew down its forces. Patrols no longer guarded every street corner and intersection. Tanks and up-armoured Humvees disappeared. Black Hawks and Cobras no longer buzzed over the cities in multitudes that rivalled a hornet swarm. After a decade, the Americans wound down their presence in Iraq until the crime bosses decided it was finally safe enough to move the cash. It would need to be laundered, of course, and a deal was struck with several banks in the Far East. To do it locally would set off alarm bells among the international monetary watchdogs.

So The Container would have to be shipped to Jakarta. The question arose as to who would smuggle it out of Iraq. American and other NATO warships still patrolled the Gulf and boarded vessels with disturbing frequency. They needed a smuggler. Several names were discussed in a heated exchange between the crime bosses who'd amassed the fortune until one was finally selected: Ali Mohamed. He was Saudi but could be trusted. He and his ship were away from the Gulf when the decision was made to finally move The Container, so there was a delay of two weeks before he could do their bidding. And then the day arrived when his ship docked in Iraq.

The Container was in play.

There was only one slight problem with their plan. They had underestimated their enemy's patience.

The Americans never forgot the money that had slipped through their fingers. Over time, they began to learn of the existence of The Container and made several logical deductions about its dispensation. They knew too that it couldn't be laundered in Iraq or any neighbouring country. It would need to be shipped overseas.

That was where they laid their trap.

Because the American Navy and her NATO allies controlled the waters of the Persian Gulf, they controlled which ships were boarded. Three ships were selected to go unmolested even though it was well known that they were smugglers. The ships made only infrequent trips up to Başrah, but their illegal cargos always reached their destination. Where other smugglers were caught in boarding raids or were forced to toss their cargos over the side while being pursued, these three cargo ships seemed to live charmed existences. They were never boarded, or, if they were, nothing illegal was ever found.

So it was little wonder that the crime bosses would choose among these three. To narrow the odds further so that the bosses would choose the one ship they wanted chosen, the American spymasters had played one more trick. The three ships and their legendary captains were one and the same.

Juan Cabrillo and his ship, the *Oregon*.

Without a doubt, this was the most sophisticated and time-consuming gambit the Corporation had ever pulled. It was the brainchild of Langston Overholt, Cabrillo's old CIA boss. Every few months, the *Oregon* would be reconfigured to look like one of three ships and sail into the deepwater port of Umm Qasr, Iraq. At first, CIA agents had to pose as the clients needing goods smuggled into or out of the country, but eventually the criminal underworld heard about these three smugglers who seemed never to get boarded. It took five years, but it worked. Whenever one of these three captains was willing to risk a run under the American's noses, there was a crime boss willing to hire him.

Now the years of preparation were about to pay off. The government would get its billion dollars back, and, just as important, should be able to trace which Americans had helped the Iraqis to amass the money in the first place.

Langston had taught Cabrillo years ago that for a democracy to flourish, it must have an incorruptible bureaucracy. This whole operation was about punishing someone who had profited from his position of power.

The *Oregon* looked like her old tramp freighter self, but with a red hull, cream upperworks, and a blue band around her yellow funnel. She appeared a little more shipshape than normal, but that was part of her disguise as the *Ibis*.

Cabrillo too was disguised as he stood next to the harbour pilot overseeing the final stages of docking the ship. His skin was darker than normal, and his hair and thin moustache were nearly black. His eyes were made brown with contact lenses.

The pilot keyed his walkie-talkie. 'Okay, snug fore and aft lines.' He crossed through the bridge to the starboard side, switched channels on his radio, and told the tug pressing the freighter to the big Yokohama fenders to back off. He turned to Cabrillo, extending a hand, 'Welcome back, Captain Mohamed.'

Cabrillo shook it, and the pilot pocketed the pair of hundred-dollar bills as smoothly as he handled the ship. There was no inherent need to bribe the pilot, since this is the last time the *Ibis* would ever dock in Iraq, or any other port in the world, but the Chairman liked to keep up appearances.

On the dock down below sat an eighteen-wheeler, with a container on its flatbed trailer, and two Toyota minivans that looked as though their odometers passed a hundred thousand about ten years ago. A sedan parked near them didn't look much younger. Towering over everything was a skeletal crane with a boom that could stretch fifty feet over the water. Lights rigged from it bathed the dock in an artificial twilight. This was an older section of the harbour. The cranes for unloading containers from the massive panamax freighters were farther up the roads. The tankers, which made up the largest portion of traffic coming into and out of Umm Qasr, were loaded out at sea using pipelines.

Juan had his own handheld radio, and he called down to the men near the gangway to lower the crane. It rattled through its chain fall and came to rest on the concrete pier. 'If you will excuse me . . .'

'Of course.' The pilot stepped aside to wait for the captain to conclude his business on the dock. He would then guide the ship back out into the open waters of the Gulf beyond the al-Baṣrah Oil Terminal.

Cabrillo took a second to square his uniform shirt into his black trousers and make sure his shoulder boards were even. Eddie Seng met them at the head of the gangway. He acted as first officer on the *Ibis*, while Hali Kasim played that role on the other two incarnations of the *Oregon* in this grand ruse.

The two men strode down the gangplank together. A customs official, this one truly corrupt, stood by as men piled out of the minivans. There were no visible weapons, but Cabrillo knew all of them were armed.

That was the other tricky aspect to this whole deal. Three different criminal syndicates collectively owned The Container along with their unknown American partner or partners. No one trusted one another, so there was tension on the dock even without the presence of a container full of cash. No one spoke as a few minutes elapsed. Then three more vehicles approached. They were all Mercedes SUVs, black with dark-tinted windows. Each would be as well protected as a bank's armoured car.

The bosses had arrived. More guards alighted from the vehicles when they stopped, and these men did nothing to hide the compact submachine guns they carried. Finally, the crime lords themselves exited from the backseats of their SUVs. They wore casual, Western-style clothes and looked as innocuous as tea merchants. Each was followed by a Westerner. These men were larger than their Iraqi hosts, and while they wore civilian clothing, each moved with military precision. They wore baseball caps pulled low and wraparound sunglasses despite the sun having set an hour before.

As Ali Mohamed, Cabrillo greeted the three crime bosses by name. He'd met two of them in the past and had dealt with the other's son on previous deals. That boss was well into his seventies and his son was about to take over, but for something as significant as The Container, he wanted to be here himself.

After the flowery exchange of greetings and displays of respect, the men turned earnest. Cabrillo pointedly wasn't introduced to the Westerners, and these men remained well back from the base of the gangway.

'I see more than four guards here,' Cabrillo said at length. 'That was our deal, four men only.'

'Do not worry, my dear captain,' the boss from

Baghdad said. 'Until this container is on the ship and away from port, we like to afford it extra protection. You will only have four men with it on the ship, as promised.'

'I wish them to be unarmed,' Cabrillo pressed. This had been a negotiating point from the beginning.

'I wish it too, but, alas, we must insist. What was it Ronald Reagan once said, "trust, but verify"? Four groups are represented here, four men on your ship, as well as four guns to, ah, verify, yes? Perhaps you will need their help if you are attacked by those mongrel Somali pirates.'

Cabrillo laughed and said truthfully, 'I think we can handle the Somalis. The last batch that attacked us fared quite poorly.'

'You know what is in this container, yes?'

'I have not been told, but I can guess.'

The boss, who had been convivial up to this point, lowered his voice and hardened his eyes. 'It would be in your best interest not to guess. Anything happens to it and everyone you've ever known and loved will die.'

Juan waited a beat to reply. 'There is no need for that. We have done business in the past and will continue to do so in the future. You pay me well for my risks. I pay my crew well. Everybody is happy. I see no need to add troubles to my life and theirs by upsetting that balance.'

The Iraqi kept his face stony before nodding and saying, 'Very good. I think we understand each other.'

'Yes, we do. I will be at dock 43C, Port of Jakarta, in

ten days.' Cabrillo added, 'As you trust me with this container, I so trust you that we will not be greeted by Indonesian police when we arrive.'

'No worries,' another of the bosses said. 'Our al-Qaeda contacts have reached out to their Jemaah Islamiyah brothers in Jakarta. Idiot fanatics, the lot of them, but useful. They will make sure your arrival goes unmolested.'

Juan could see that the guy from Baghdad didn't like the mention of their al-Qaeda connections, so he quickly filled the uncomfortable silence. 'Then I believe we are ready to load.'

The customs official came forward to sign off on the seals of a container he'd done everything in his power not to notice.

Juan watched the three Westerners shake each other's hands. One called just loud enough for him to hear, 'Good luck, Gunny.'

Cabrillo winced. He'd hoped the American armed guard would be of a higher rank than gunnery sergeant, because it would be easier to see who was above him on the military food chain. At least now he knew the man had been a Marine. The sergeant had a duffel thrown over a shoulder, and Juan could clearly see the outline of an assault rifle inside it. The Iraqi crime bosses conferred with their men, doubtlessly going over communications protocols for the hundredth time. Juan had to wonder at the trust it took to turn over a billion dollars to a subaltern who most likely resented your status even as he licked your boots.

The Chairman tried to shake each man's hand as they stepped onto the gangway, but none took up the offer or reciprocated when he gave them his cover name. The three Iraqis and the three Americans marched by in silence, though each man studied their surroundings with predatory eyes. Four tough hombres, Juan thought, and wondered how they would get along over the next ten days.

The boss from Baghdad threw Cabrillo an ironic salute and then waved his hand over his head. High above the pier, the crane operator had been waiting for this signal. The diesel generator that powered the crane's motors came to life in a bellow of exhaust smoke. In seconds, the cables began to pay out, and the lift cradle, designed to hoist the standard-sized container, descended on the parked semitrailer. It settled with a metallic thunk and then automatically clamped onto The Container's four corners. Cables were reversed and the box was lifted.

Juan took a second to study the bosses and the three Americans on the dock. All of them were watching The Container with the same rapt expressions of greed soon to be realized. They had sat for years on a fortune they could not spend. In just a couple of weeks they would be given numbered accounts that could buy them anything their dark hearts desired.

The crane operator shifted The Container out onto the boom so that it swung over the *Oregon*'s rail. The hatch had already been pulled on the number 2 hold, and The Container soon vanished inside. The semi had pulled away as soon as the trailer had been cleared, and another rig was in place with an identical container.

She was not built for the container trade, but the *Oregon*'s hold could still accommodate twenty of them in stacked rows. The others were empty and were being shipped back to the Far East, where they were destined to be filled with goods ready for export once again. For good measure, five more empty containers were deck-loaded once the hatch was back in place.

The bosses had retreated to their respective SUVs for the hours it took to load the ship. Cabrillo had watched the process from the bridge while the four armed guards were shown cabins that none of them had any intention of using. There was a single door into the hold, and even though the money was buried under a mountain of empty containers, all four intended to guard it for the week and a half it would take to cross the Indian Ocean.

Max Hanley joined the Chairman, carrying a thermos of iced tea and two glasses. Though it was cooler at night, the temperature still hovered north of eighty. Cabrillo would have preferred a beer, but he was playing a Saudi, and who knew how many men were watching the ship through sniper's scopes from the roofs of the nearby warehouses. He bet each of the bosses had at least two teams. He smiled to himself, thinking of when the last team to show up realized all the good spots to watch the transfer had been taken.

'Penny for them,' Hanley said, pouring tea over fresh lemon wedges.

'Sulky snipers.'

Max considered the non sequitur for a moment before getting Juan's joke. 'Kinda like which of the goons down in the hold gets to actually lean against the door.'

'I assume they'll take shifts.'

'Paranoid bunch.'

'Billion dollars, my friend. Wouldn't you be?'

'It would be awfully nice if Uncle Sam would let us keep it. I've even come up with a couple of ideas for how we could steal it.'

'Me too,' Juan admitted, then added with a larcenous grin, 'but merely as a mental exercise.'

'Of course.'

Both men knew that neither was serious. Oh, they definitely devised plans to get their hands on it, but neither would ever consider actually stealing the money.

'I just reviewed tape with Linda and the shots Eddie got with his lapel camera.'

'And?'

'We don't have much. The three Americans who stayed behind looked up only when the container was swung aboard, but they were in pretty deep shadow. Plus the hats and shades. Facial recognition might not even be possible. They never got close enough to Eddie for a decent pic.'

'I knew this wasn't going to be easy. What about the gunny?'

'Plenty of good snaps as he came aboard and was given the nickel tour of his cabin, the mess, and the door to the hold.'

'Have they come up with a name yet?'

'Pentagon is going through their database as we speak. Once we have his ID, they'll go through all his duty stations and former COs, and then we start looking up the pecking order. Do you give any credence to Overholt's idea that the American Mr Big will meet the ship in Indonesia?'

'He wasn't here, that's for sure. Mr Big wouldn't know a gunny from a hole in the ground. He's too high up for that. I'm guessing one of the guys here today was a major who served over the gunnery sergeant and the other is a mutual friend of both Mr Big and the major.'

Max thought about this. 'Ages seem right. Gunny and the major worked together, became friendly. They hatch the plot, take it to Mr Big's buddy to give them protection from above, and all of a sudden we've lost a billion in Benjamins. They'd still need a lot of help just to move that much cash.'

'Most certainly. That's where the Iraqis come in. They supply the labour while our little cabal of traitors supplies access to the money.'

'I should tell Langston to have the Pentagon concentrate on majors once we have the gunny's name.'

Just then, the harbour pilot returned from the head. 'Ah, and who is this, Captain Mohamed?'

'My chief engineer, Fritz Zoeller.'

Max greeted the man, using an outrageous German accent, before insisting that he had to return to his engine room as the loading was about complete.

An hour later, the ship reached open water, and the pilot transferred to a small boat to return to port. There was a full moon, so only the brightest stars shown from the cloudless sky. As usual, the waters of the sheltered Persian Gulf were as calm and as warm as bathwater. The radar plot showed plenty of activity. The big returns were tankers, ferrying oil out of the Gulf or heading north to have their monstrous hulls filled with crude. Other, smaller blips were the countless fishing vessels that plied these waters. Most now were modern craft, but a few lateen-rigged dhows still roamed the Gulf as they had for hundreds of years.

Radio traffic was heavy, with crews chatting with one another to keep awake during the long night watch. Not knowing if any of the four guards would venture up to the wheelhouse, Juan ordered it manned at all times. Cabrillo acted as officer on deck while Hali Kasim draped himself over the wooden wheel in an effort to stay awake. Juan enjoyed standing watch, even at night, while his communications expert was bored out of his mind. At midnight, just as if they were really conning the ship, they were relieved.

Over the next two days it continued like this, though there was really no point in maintaining the ruse on the bridge. The four men tasked with guarding The Container only left the hallway outside the hold to use the head. They must have formed some sort of loose pact, because they slept in shifts. Food was brought to them from the galley by one of the *Oregon*'s regular kitchen staff dressed not for the ship's opulent dining hall but in the stained whites of a short-order cook.

By now, they knew the lone American among them was Gunnery Sergeant Malcolm Winters USMC (Ret.). The Pentagon had e-mailed dozens of pictures of officers Winters had worked with over his twenty-year career, but neither Cabrillo nor Eddie could identify any as one of the other Americans on the pier. They were expecting more photos soon.

23

They came at sunup on the third day of the trip. Just as Cabrillo had suspected, there were three boats – low, cigarette-style powerboats – that surged out of the predawn darkness like sharks circling in for the kill. They had less than a foot of freeboard showing, so they had never appeared on radar. There would be another vessel out here with them, a mother ship waiting over the horizon that would have towed the powerboats to the ambush point. There were five pirates on each craft, coffee-skinned Somalis who had turned this stretch of the Indian Ocean into one of the most dangerous places on earth. Juan suspected it was the crime lord from Başrah who had tipped them off and told them what ship to stalk. Başrah was a port city, after all, so he would have contacts in the pirates' leadership.

Most of the men brandished AK-47s, but one on each boat carried the distinctive RPG-7 rocket launcher. They attacked from astern so the watch standers on the bridge never saw them, didn't know about them, in fact, until an RPG round slammed into the fantail just above the waterline in an attempt to disable the *Oregon*'s prop and rudder.

On any other ship, the explosion would have left them dead in the water, but the *Oregon* was hardened and armoured in critical areas so the rocket-propelled grenade did little but pucker the armoured belt and singe some paint.

Because they had to keep the bridge manned anyway, Cabrillo had decided to switch control to there from the op centre and keep only one person manning the high-tech room rather than the customary two. Seconds after the blast echoed throughout the ship, MacD Lawless leapt from the Kirk Chair where he lolled in boredom to the weapons station in the front of the room. Although he was the newest member of the Corporation, he knew *Oregon*'s systems as well as any of them.

It took him just a few seconds of channelling through camera feeds to spot the pirate boats. They were standing off about fifty yards from the ship, well beyond the range of fire hoses that some freighters deployed to protect themselves. They were waiting for their quarry to slow from the damage they'd inflicted with the RPG. If it did not slow, then another couple of RPGs would be fired into her. One way or another, they would not be deprived of their prize.

MacD at first considered using the ship's 20mm Gatling guns, but their four guests were all ex-military and would know the industrial whine of the Gatling rattling off at three thousand rounds per minute. Best he deploy a more likely weapon on a smuggler's ship. In one corner of the main view screen, a hidden camera showed the four guards down by the hold, paralyzed by indecision. They did not know what to do. Should they go topside and help defend the ship or should they remain at their post and be ready to make a last stand should pirates make it this far?

MacD activated a pair of M60 machine guns that Juan called their 'boarder repellants'. The guns were hidden inside oil drums welded to the deck near the ship's rail. The barrels' lids popped open, and the weapons emerged, muzzle first, before rotating to a horizontal firing position. He clicked the targeting icon on his computer screen, locking in the automated firing plots, and let the guns loose.

The guns fired a NATO standard 7.62mm round, and while not particularly large or powerful, this weapon made up for it in sheer volume of fire. The first cigarette boat was raked from stem to stern with fifty rounds before anyone aboard knew what was happening. The driver was killed instantly, two of the gunmen as well. The other two were tossed into the ocean when the out-of-control boat barrelled into a wave and flipped.

On the other side of the *Oregon*, the second gun had an even more devastating effect on another of the pirates' boats. This one exploded when gas from the punctured tank ignited off the hot engine. The fireball was something out of Hollywood. The third attacking boat took heed and raced for the horizon before the M60 could target it, but the mother boat, which had foolishly approached, either didn't see or didn't understand what had happened to their comrades. They held a steady course so that they could launch another RPG at their prey's fantail.

MacD hit the target icon again. On deck, the M60's barrel moved mechanically and aimed ever so slightly upward to compensate for the increased distance and a little windage. The computer even took into consideration the ballistic changes caused by the barrel being heated from the first barrage.

The gun chattered again just as the rocket man heaved the launch tube to his shoulder. He was hit multiple times but managed to pull the trigger before he died. The problem for his teammates was that the RPG was pointed straight at the deck of their own boat when the igniter engaged. The rocket blew through the bottom of the mother boat with barely a check in speed and sank quickly out of sight without exploding. The hole in the hull became a huge rend that would have doomed the crew even had the machine-gun fire not continued to pour in on them.

In all, it took just a few seconds from the opening shot to the last. Lawless blew out a long breath while crewmen surged into the op centre, Cabrillo being one of the first. He wore a pair of swim trunks under a cotton terry robe and dripped water onto the deck without noticing. He smelled of chlorine from the ship's pool.

'Pirates in cigarette boats. Three in total. Two were greased, while the last one ran for the horizon. Then the mother ship approached and took a powder too,' MacD reported without being prompted. He knew what the Chairman wanted.

'Damage?'

'One RPG to the stern. Awaiting a report from

damage control. Speed and course are unaffected. The guns are already stowed.'

Juan looked at the camera feed showing the four guards at the entrance to the hold. They were talking animatedly among themselves and finally reached some sort of decision. One of them shouldered his rifle and started for the nearest stairwell that would lead him to the main deck.

'I suppose,' Juan said, 'I should go tell him what happened. MacD, pop two of the guns out again. Linc and I will pretend we fired them.'

Max Hanley finally made his appearance.

'Damage?' Juan asked, for he knew Max would check on his beloved ship before anything else.

'We won't be changing our name any time soon. My magnetic sign is all messed up, but other than that we're good.'

'All right, we suspected this was coming. Now we'll wait to see if we get attacked again and prove once and for all there's no honour among thieves.'

Linda Ross was manning the op centre six days later as the *Oregon* was coming abreast of the island of Sumatra for the final dash to Jakarta. Juan and Hali had the topside con. Every few minutes, she would scan all the various computer screens and control panels for any sign that there was some sort of trouble aboard the ship. Then she would scan the main display. On it were shots of the sea, both fore and aft, as well as a radar plot refreshed by the repeater's swing arm. Another part of the screen was a cable news feed where talking heads were discussing heightened tensions between China and Japan over the discovery of a massive gas field near some disputed islands. Yet another was a peek into the hallway outside the hold where their four guests guarded the door. The men were unshaven, and the strain of maintaining vigilance over the past days showed in the hollowness of their eyes and the stoop to their shoulders.

She had to give them props. They were untrusting strangers who had held it together. Although the three Arabs now allowed themselves a half hour on deck each day, Winters never left his post.

She didn't see anything happen and only realized something was wrong after staring at the screen for another twenty seconds.

In all the days and nights since they'd boarded, only one of the guards slept at a time while the others kept watch. Studying the image, she took valuable time to recognize that three of the guards were sleeping and the fourth was gone. The resolution wasn't the best, but she quickly realized it was Gunny Winters she could no longer see, and the three men lying on the deck had each been shot execution style. There was remarkably little blood, but each had a bullet hole in their head.

She was about to call Juan up on the bridge and tell him what was happening when the engines abruptly cut off. Winters had had more than enough time to get from the hold to the bridge and take command of the ship. Linda was certain that he'd ordered Juan to cut power. The *Oregon* was now adrift under the command of a traitor and thief. And just like when the Somalis had struck, Cabrillo had predicted something like this too. And his first standing order when the next attack came was to simply wait it out and see where it headed.

Linda called Max to the op centre along with Eric and Mark. She kept helm control up on the bridge for now, but they would want the A Team in place when they retook their ship. She checked the radar repeater. There was a vessel about eighty miles away, and, as she watched, the icon split into two distinct returns. She knew in just a few seconds that this fast-approaching mystery ship had launched a helicopter and it was inbound at better than a hundred knots.

'Here we go.'

Cabrillo could have ended Malcolm Winters's mutiny in the first few seconds had he so chosen. Winters had been good, stalking his way to the wheelhouse, but Cabrillo had seen him creeping up on him in the reflection of an old coffee urn that sat on a shelf below the fore windows.

Instead of reacting, he'd sat seemingly unaware until Winters pressed the still-warm barrel of his Beretta against the back of Juan's head. 'Sorry about this, Captain, but there's been a change of plans.'

Hali, standing at the wheel, turned sharply with a quick intake of breath because he hadn't heard Winters until he spoke.

'Stand easy,' Juan said in Arabic.

'Yes, sir.' Hali fell into the role of frightened crewman.

'What is it you want?' Cabrillo asked, switching to English.

'Number one is, I want you to cut the engines.' Winters moved around so he could cover both Cabrillo and Kasim. An M4 assault rifle was slung across his chest.

Juan suspected a man like Gunny Winters, a veteran of three tours in Iraq, would speak at least some Arabic, so he gave the correct orders to Hali at the helm station. The beat of the engines, an artificial noise created to muffle the whine of the *Oregon*'s true power plant, eased down until the only sound was the subtle hiss of water floating past the ship's steel sides.

The morning was as beautiful as only the tropics can be. The sun was up, but the heat and humidity were still some time away. There was the merest of breezes, and the waves were long and ponderous and swelled no more than a few inches.

'What other weapons do you have besides the M60s you used on the pirates last Friday?' Winters asked.

Cabrillo had to admit he was impressed. Judging by the silver in his high-and-tight haircut, Winters was closer to fifty than forty. He had been operating on stress, caffeine pills and little sleep for over a week and yet he still looked pretty good. Yes, there was the beard, and his eyes were bloodshot, but he had lost none of his military discipline and little of his bearing. In a different world, the two of them would probably be friends.

'I keep a Tokarev pistol in the safe in my cabin, and my first engineer has a shotgun.'

'Tell your man to go and get them. He is to slide

them, breeches open, through the door at the rear of the bridge. If I see him or any other member of your crew, you will die. Understand?'

'Yes.' Juan relayed the orders, noting wryly that Winters did seem to understand because he nodded when Juan explained the safe's combination. Two minutes later, a sawed-off shotgun came sliding from the passageway behind the bridge, followed a moment later by a battered Tokarev pistol. The pistol's slide was locked back so it could not fire, and the double barrels of the shotgun were broken open so it was evident it was not loaded. Winters squinted at the pistol, satisfying himself that the magazine had been pulled.

'Toss them both overboard, please, Captain.'

Cabrillo picked up the two weapons, crossed over to the starboard wing bridge, and heaved the weapons over the side of the ship. He knew that Winters wouldn't be too concerned by the M60s down on the deck. In the close confines of the bridge, such a weapon would kill a hostage just as surely as the kidnapper.

Juan returned and stood by the helm. Winters had positioned himself well back from the windows in case he'd been lied to and someone had a scoped rifle. Again, Juan was impressed.

'Now what?'

'I want two crewmen to man that gantry derrick down on deck and start heaving the empty containers over the side.'

'What about your three companions? Surely they will have something to say about this.'

'They're dead,' Winters said bluntly. 'Now carry out my orders. And have your wheelman return to the hallway behind us for further instructions.'

Juan yelled through the back door to Hali and told him what to do. It took a little more time to organize a work detail. Eddie Seng and Franklin Lincoln soon strode out of the superstructure and made their way to the mast crane. Eddie fired up the diesel that powered the controls, and though it smoked as if it were about to expire, it ran as smooth as a sewing machine.

While Linc took the controls, Eddie scrambled up onto the first of the deck-loaded containers. He lugged a rusted wire sling that had four hooks, which could be attached to the four corners of a container, and a central loop for the hook coming down the crane's main cable.

By the time they had one of the containers dangling over the side of the ship, a new noise could be heard out over the water, the unmistakable beat of a helicopter's rotors. The noise grew until it filled Cabrillo's head. He could not see the chopper because it was coming up from the southeast and was soon hovering over the stern. He motioned to Winters that he wanted to see from the bridge wing. The old gunny nodded.

Cabrillo stepped out into an artificial gale kicked up by a Sikorsky S-70, the civilian version of the Black Hawk helicopter. The chopper's side door was already open, and as soon as the craft was stabilized over the fantail, a pair of thick ropes tumbled down to the deck. Two men followed them even before they had been fully deployed, dropping like stones until braking just before they smashed into the steel. Another pair followed a second behind them.

And then the chopper veered off and began thundering back south. The men were dressed in black combat fatigues and were loaded with gear and weapons. They had fast-roped with the precision of Special Forces, which was precisely what they had been.

'Your crew will remain inside the ship at all times,' Winters said from where he crouched. 'I don't care where just so long as they remain out of sight. If they venture too close to a doorway or window, they will be shot.'

'Hali,' Juan called.

'I am here, Captain. What was that noise?'

'Four more soldiers have boarded the ship. Pass the word that I want all crew members to go to the mess and wait there. No one is to go near the deck at any time. Is that understood?'

'Yes, Captain. We will wait in the mess hall until you come for us.'

Juan wondered whether he and his crew were meant to survive this ordeal or if Winters and his masters would eliminate them as potential witnesses. He suspected the latter. Not only was the crew witness to this hijacking, scuttling the ship would actually cover the theft from the crime bosses. A judicious SOS call, and a search and rescue that discovers the ship already well down at the head and beyond salvage, and, voilà, a billion dollars, free and clear, from your partners.

The empty container hit the water with a tremendous splash and bobbed like a red cube of ice in a drink. Eddie clutched the wire sling after detaching it from the container and was swung back on board.

Winters cursed when he shot a glance out of the wing window. He no longer feared a sniper since his men controlled the deck. 'I forgot to tell you to open the door so the containers sink.'

'I will pass that along.' There was an old bullhorn in a cabinet under the chart table.

'Go outside, Captain, and my men will kill you before you take two steps. Do either of your guys out there speak English?'

'Yes.'

The former Marine took the bullhorn and strode out onto the bridge wing. 'Hold fast. It's Winters.' His amplified voice boomed and echoed while down below two of his guards swung their guns up and took aim before relaxing once again. 'You two, working on the crane. From now on, open the container's doors so they sink. Raise your arm if you understand.' The Asian crewman who'd met with them on the dock back in Umm Qasr raised a hand in a nervous wave. Winters returned to the bridge. Though he'd spoken to the men outside, he'd never once taken his eyes, or the aim of his pistol, off the Chairman.

It took three hours to unload all the empty containers. By the time Eddie and Linc had finished, a boat had approached. It looked like a typical oil field tender with a boxy superstructure hunched over the bows and a long open rear deck. On the deck sat the Sikorsky helicopter that had dropped off Winters's men, as well as an enormous crane on crawler tracks. Between the two was ample room for The Container.

Cabrillo understood at once why they had brought their own crane. When the mission to steal The Container was laid out, Winters and his American partners didn't know if the ship chosen to smuggle the money out of Iraq had its own derricks to transfer cargo. Prudently, they had assumed it did not and brought their own crane with them on this high seas rendezvous.

'In case you are wondering, we are not going to kill you,' Winters said conversationally as he watched his partners steaming closer.

'I am not reassured,' Juan said.

'No. It's true. The way we figure it, there's no way you can show up in Jakarta with tales of us betraying the others. They might believe you, they might not, but they surely will make you pay for losing their money. Your only chance of staying alive is to sell this ship in some backwater port and vanish.'

Cabrillo said nothing.

'I've had a bellyful of killing,' Winters went on. 'Those three down below –' His voice suddenly cut off as a new sound enveloped the ship, the banshee scream of one of her 20mm Gatling guns opening up on the approaching tender. The rounds tore into her stern like a predatory cat rakes the haunches of its prey. Steel was shredded as easily as paper. The tender's rudder was shot completely off, and rounds destroyed the stuffing box where the single driveshaft passed out of the hull and into the sea. The shaft itself snapped under the onslaught, and her bronze propeller popped free like a rotten tooth.

Water began flooding her engine room in such volumes that the crew down below never stood a chance. The fusillade lasted just seconds, but it was enough to doom the ship to a fast-approaching death.

Juan had been expecting the blast from the Gatling. It had all been preplanned days ago as they gamed various boarding scenarios. Had a helicopter approached the *Oregon* where The Container could be hoisted off, it would have been shot down. They had left the Sikorsky unmolested because the empty containers had yet to be pulled free from the hold, and also because it did not have the lift capacity to carry off the cash-filled container.

If it was all in hundred-dollar bills, it would still weigh eleven tons. Twenty-two thousand pounds of money. It would be more if smaller denominations were thrown into the mix.

The distraction of the tender's destruction gave Juan no advantage. Gunny Winters nearly shot him in the face when Cabrillo charged. The old Marine had the reflexes of an Olympic fencer and the concentration of a Zen master. Even as the Gatling continued its dreadful wail, Winters was ready for a fight. Juan had barely pushed Winters's arm aside when the gunny cycled through four snap shots, the noise exploding in Cabrillo's ear. They crashed, chest to chest, and Juan felt like he'd run into a cement-block wall. Winters was about Juan's height, but under his loose shirt his body was thick with muscle. Winters smashed forward with his head like a striking cobra and would have crushed Cabrillo's nose had the Chairman not whirled back, maintaining his grip on Winters's gun hand. A lightning kick aimed for his groin came next, and Juan twisted his leg to take the massive blow on his thigh. His leg felt weak down to his toe.

Most fighters armed with a pistol would concentrate on using the weapon and ignoring everything else. Not this man. He came after Juan with everything he had. It was as if the pistol clutched in his right hand was meaningless. Meanwhile, Cabrillo opened himself up to punches and kicks as he was forced to maintain his grip on the gun hand.

The Gatling finally went silent, and smoke poured from the hundreds of holes shot into the tender's hull. The fight in the wheelhouse was in its seventh second when Cabrillo realized he was more than likely going to lose. And that set him off – the idea of defeat. He slammed Winters's hand into a window frame again and again until the pistol fell to the deck.

He released the hand, knowing it would be useless to Winters, and threw a combination of punches that the gunny expertly parried. Juan just had to buy a few more seconds. The plan called for his people to overwhelm the guards on deck and retake the bridge. Max would be storming through the door any second with Linc and MacD on his heels.

Winters's right hand should be worthless and yet he

managed to unsheathe a fighting knife he carried strapped inside his shirt. Cabrillo fought the natural urge to get away from the blade. Instead, he stepped closer, limiting Winters's ability to swing the knife. Winters flipped the blade and started to plunge it into Juan's shoulder. Juan grabbed at his wrist, but the former Marine had the better position and superior leverage, and the knife sliced into the meat of Cabrillo's trapezius muscle. Winters was angling the blade so it would eventually find the major arteries feeding the brain.

Hot blood poured from the wound and down his chest. Cabrillo roared as he tried to keep the knife from digging deeper while Winters tried just as hard to ram the blade all the way home.

It went in an inch. The deeper it was driven, the less Juan could check its remorseless plunge. He could sense his opponent gathering himself for one last effort, one last thrust, that would kill him.

He felt the spray of blood on his face before he heard the shot. Winters collapsed, lifeless, the knife ripping savagely from Cabrillo's body as he collapsed in a heap. Max stood in the doorway leading aft, a compact Glock in his hand still pointed at the ceiling, still smoking.

'The other four surrendered without a fight,' Hanley said.

'I had just about every advantage under the sun, and he still nearly killed me.' Juan peeled back his sodden shirt to look at his wound. It was a small slit, and little blood was seeping out.

'Better get Hux up here with her sewing kit,' Max remarked mildly.

'Your concern for my well-being is touching.'

'Ah, but I did just save your life.'

'A charge I can't deny.' Juan looked down at Winters's corpse. 'Tough old bird.'

'What do they say, there's no such thing as an ex-Marine?'

Within a few minutes, the bridge was crowded. Hux had Juan on a seat with his shirt off so that she could clean, stitch and dress the wound. Max was overseeing the rescue of the passengers and crew of the oil field tender. The boat was sinking by the stern so steeply that her bow was already out of the water. She was going too fast for them to launch a lifeboat, so men jumped free, with life jackets if they could find them, and started swimming for the big freighter they had come out here to rob.

Linda, MacD and Mike Trono, all armed, were near the lowered gangplank ready to welcome their new guests.

Cabrillo refused anything stronger than Tylenol and was back on his feet in time to see the crawler crane rip from its restraining chains and smash its way across the tilted deck and destroy the already-submerged helicopter.

'Someone's not getting their toys back.'

'Dollars to donuts,' Max said around the stem of his pipe, 'the tender and crane were rented, but that helo was owned by whoever financed this little caper.'

'I was thinking the same thing,' Juan agreed.

The tender's bow was now sticking straight up in a frothing roil of air bubbles escaping from the countless 20mm punctures. And then she was gone. The water continued to boil for a few seconds, but the hull planed off far enough that that too came to an end. All that remained was a small slick of oil and a few pieces of unidentifiable flotsam.

The first of the survivors reached the boarding stairs. Each was thoroughly patted down and told to sit on their hands in an open section of deck near the four men who'd choppered aboard.

Juan and Max went down to the deck to inspect their prize. As they had guessed, the tender's crew was hired help – in this case, native Indonesians who probably worked the oil fields off Brunei. They would be detained and questioned but ultimately released. What interested Juan were the four Westerners. Two of them, he suspected, were the two from Iraq. The other two were older, and while they looked like a couple of drowned rats after their unexpected swim, they both had a sage dignity and a predisposed haughtiness. He didn't recognize either of them, and they remained mute when he asked their names.

Cabrillo rolled his eyes. He took out his phone, snapped pictures of their faces and e-mailed them to Mark Murphy, who was still plugged in to the DoD databases. They got a hit right away, and the answer rocked Juan back on his heels.

'Max, do you know who we have here?'

'A rat.'

'True, but a former Deputy Under Secretary of the Army kind of rat.'

'Deputy Under? That's a real title?'

'Gotta love bureaucracies. Isn't that right, Mr Hillman? Don't know who your friend is yet, but I'm guessing you're the top dog here.'

'Who are you people?'

'Sorry, my party, I get to ask the questions. I think it's funny that you thought you would get away with it. You honestly thought the Pentagon would casually write off a billion dollars? A billion untraceable dollars. This money will be funding black ops for years, and you thought the military would simply forget about it.'

By the crestfallen look Hillman shot Cabrillo, that was precisely what he and his co-conspirators thought.

'They have been planning on recovering this money for years,' Juan continued. 'True, no one knew who had it, but they were damn sure they were going to get it back. We even knew you and your Iraqi buddies would turn on each other in the end. Had we made Jakarta, I fully expected a few hundred of al-Qaeda's finest there for the reception.'

'Where's Gunny Winters?' asked one of his friends from back in Umm Qasr, one of the men they suspected would be a former officer above Winters.

'He was one of your men?' Juan asked.

'I had the privilege of being his commanding officer on his last tour.'

'He was a good Marine?'

'The best.'

'He's dead.' The man already knew because he didn't react. 'Max shot him while he was trying to skewer me like a pig, and now that good Marine is going to be for- ever known as a traitor and a thief. I hope you are all proud of yourselves.'

'What happens next?' This from one of the guards who'd fast-roped down from the Sikorsky.

He looked too young to be part of the original cabal. Juan guessed he was a former soldier now working as a mercenary and had been hired on for this job. He prob- ably didn't know what was fully at stake.

'In a few hours, a Navy amphibious assault ship that has been following us since we left the Persian Gulf is going to steam over the horizon. They're going to send a boat to pick up the lot of you and a big Chinook helicop- ter for The Container. The four of you who fast-roped down to my ship will be charged, tried and convicted of piracy, while these lovelies will spend the rest of their lives in some unnamed allied country's worst prison, and most likely without the benefit of a trial. If I were a bet- ting man, I'd say Sub-Saharan Africa, where the HIV rate among inmates is close to fifty per cent.'

Hillman and the others visibly paled.

'You see, Mr Hillman,' Juan added, 'Uncle Sam won't acknowledge a theft of this magnitude took place. It makes our government look inept, and that means you are going to be quietly swept under the carpet.'

'Shows what you know,' the former DoD official sneered. 'They'll make a deal because I'm not the "top dog". I can name names, and then I'll walk away clean.'

Cabrillo leaned in close so that the man could see the depth of Juan's hatred and the joy he was taking in Hillman's defeat. 'That's a problem. See, you're top enough, in their book. You're taking the rap and the fall. Sing as much as you want, they're just going to ignore you.'

He and Max walked away. He had no idea if his threat was true, but it was nice to see Hillman really start to shake as he contemplated his fate.

Eddie and Linc pulled the last container from the hold, following the takedown, and set it on the deck. Cabrillo and Hanley walked around it once. The customs seals were still in place. Juan put a hand on the metal side of the box as if he could sense what was inside.

'Tempted?' Max teased.

'Don't start that again. But there's something I have to do. Overholt won't be too pleased, but I've got to at least look at it.' He cranked open the rear door, breaking the delicate seal.

What they saw were square bundles about the size of hay bales wrapped in various shades of coloured plastic. The bundles were stacked like any other commodity and ran almost to the ceiling. They could have been packages of tangerines or DVD players or any other commodity shipped in conex containers.

'Ho-hum,' Max said. 'What did you expect? Ali Baba's treasure room?'

Juan started at how accurate his friend had been. 'Never hurts to hope.'

Cabrillo wrestled one of the bales from the stack and slit open the plastic with the knife he always carried. Fresh pain erupted from his shoulder, remind-ing him that he would need to take it easy for a few days. He opened the tear enough to pull out some money, a four-inch-thick chunk of hundred-dollar bills.

'I read someplace that a stack of one thousand American dollar bills is a little over four inches thick. These are hundreds, so I've got a hundred grand here.' They both looked at the enormity of the cache and had a better understanding than just about anyone on the planet of exactly what a billion dollars really was.

He wedged the money back into place, and this time let Max put the bale back into the container. They closed the door, the locking arm coming down with a finality that ended an eight-year operation. Ironically, their fee would most likely come from this very stack of money once it made its way into a black budget account.

Hours later, after the dead Iraqis had been buried at sea and the prisoners and cash transferred over to the USS *Boxer*, the Chairman hosted a dinner for the crew in the dining room and, to rounds of raucous applause, detailed the money each member of the Cor-poration should expect for the successful recovery of The Container.

As fate would have it – and, in their business, fate dealt more hands than most – Juan had just poured his second glass of Veuve Clicquot when he felt his phone vibrate.

It was the duty officer in the op centre. 'Sorry to ruin the party, Chairman. There's a call on your private line.'

'L'Enfant,' Juan breathed. It had to be, and that could only mean the information broker had found Pytor Kenin. After this untimely but lucrative distraction, it was time to get back on the trail of Yuri Borodin's murderer.

24

Considering their destination, it made sense that Eddie Seng would accompany Juan for the scouting mission. L'Enfant had only provided an address. Mark and Eric had done their usual excellent research on the location, but nothing beat eyes on the ground. They flew commercial from Jakarta to Shanghai.

Neither man was particularly comfortable in Eddie's native land. Seng didn't like it because he'd spent much of his CIA career here, recruiting agents to spy for him, and he'd had more than his fair share of scrapes with the various security arms of the People's government. He suspected the dossier on him ran about a thousand pages. He looked nothing like he did in those days, the very best plastic surgeons the CIA's money could buy had seen to that, but, nevertheless, every time he'd returned here he felt that he was being watched.

Cabrillo was also a person of interest to the Ministry of State Security since he had once blown up a Chinese Navy destroyer called the *Chengdo*. Technically, Dirk Pitt had blown it out of the water, but he'd done so while aboard the *Oregon*. That wasn't what weighed on the Chairman. It was the fact that that particular battle had cost him a leg. He spent little time dwelling on the loss, which he'd more than made up for in so many ways, yet there were times when he felt it acutely.

Home to twenty-five million people, Shanghai was arguably the largest city in the world. As they rocketed through suburbs and sprawling acres of apartment blocks festooned with drying laundry aboard the Maglev train from the airport, Juan didn't doubt it. Eddie had been here on many occasions, this was the Chairman's first. Hitting speeds in excess of two hundred and fifty miles per hour, the ultrasleek train riding on a cushion of air took just minutes to reach the city's Pudong District. A cab would have taken hours to cover the eighteen miles.

Just a few years ago, Pudong, on the eastern side of the Huangpu River, had been sparsely populated, unlike the western bank, which contained the old sections of the city and masses of bland skyscrapers left over from the 1970s expansion. Now Pudong was the face of the city, with its iconic skyline of oddly shaped buildings, most notably the Oriental Pearl TV Tower, with its two strange globes stacked on top of each other, and the beautiful Shanghai World Financial Center. The streets had the hustle and noise of New York City.

They cabbed over to their hotel but checked in separately, since two men staying in one room would arouse suspicion. As luck would have it, neither room faced the right direction, so Juan had to play the ugly American and demand a different room. The second one was perfect.

The address L'Enfant provided was one of the newer skyscrapers in Pudong, a gleaming rectangle of black reflective glass that topped out at over four hundred feet. It wasn't the tallest building in the district, not by a large margin, but it was still impressive.

Eddie met Cabrillo in his new room with a view of their target tower. The hotel wasn't as tall as the building, but for now their view was fine. Eddie had entered China as a medical devices salesman so he could pack in some unusual electronics. Customs had gone over it, of course, but had seen nothing amiss.

He took one of the devices to the window, which opened a crack, and stuck a probe outside and aimed it at the nearby building. He watched a digital display as he aimed the probe at each individual floor, starting at the ground and working his way up. When he was aiming the probe at the second-to-top floor, he grunted at the display. The top floor showed him similar information.

'Well?' Juan asked.

The device was a laser that could read the vibrations on a windowpane. With the right software, those vibrations could be turned into the spoken words of anyone on the other side of the glass. They hadn't bothered bringing a computer to interpret the vibrations. They were only interested if anyone in the target building was trying to counter the use of such a laser detector.

'Top two floors have random-flux generators,' Eddie replied, putting the device back in its case. 'The panes are dancing like dervishes. Impossible for a laser to get a read on what's being said inside.'

Juan nodded thoughtfully. This didn't necessarily mean L'Enfant was correct, but it boded well that whoever occupied the top two floors was so security conscious. 'Okay, this is looking good. We'll split up now and find out all we can about the occupants of those floors.'

Eddie was already wearing his first disguise: a package-delivery boy. Later, he would change into a suit so he could try to talk his way into the building as a prospective tenant.

Juan was dressed as a tourist, complete with fanny pack, baseball cap, and a windbreaker with a panda logo. Thanks to an online photo-mapping service, they already knew the building had an extensive rooftop garden, and he had determined the best place to look down into it.

Four blocks from the black tower, Cabrillo entered the ornate lobby of another building, one so new it still smelled faintly of paint. There was an express elevator to the observation deck. A group of schoolgirls in matching skirts and sweaters talked and giggled and played elaborate hand-slapping games while they waited for the elevator. The two teachers chatted with a representative from the building's staff.

The elevator car finally arrived and the group entered. Juan gave the two teachers a goofy grin and they soon ignored him. They exited seven hundred and eighty feet above the street onto an open deck surrounded by a chest-high glass barrier. The vista was stunning. Far below, they could see ships in the Huangpu River and the famous Bund Promenade on the opposite side. To the north was the mighty Yangtze. And if one looked east, over the sprawl, there were the placid waters of the East China Sea.

The children oohed and aahed at the amazing views. For his part, Cabrillo was suitably impressed, but he had come here for one particular vista. He took a moment to check to see if anyone on the observation deck looked out of place. There was one security guard, who made a slow circuit of the deck like a shark patrolling one of those enormous aquarium tanks. The rest were tourists like himself or young couples playing a little hooky during the work-week. He approached the best spot for looking down on the rooftop garden but gave it no more than a glance before turning to look at the central structure that housed this tower's elevator machinery. He saw the security camera immediately, the only one on the observation deck. It was trained on the spot Cabrillo had seen was the best to study the target building. Someone wanted to know if they were being watched.

Juan hadn't reacted when he'd spotted the camera. He was too professional for that. He was also curious. He moved out of its range, strolling along like any typical tourist. He spent another twenty minutes looking at the view. The schoolgirls were gone, replaced by a group of German tourists on a package holiday. He estimated enough time had passed that no one would connect him to what he was about to do. He had already removed his baseball cap and reversed his jacket. It had been light blue with a logo. Now it was dark green and unadorned.

He moved under the camera and, when no one was looking, reached up to change its angle ever so slightly. He moved away to wait. It took ten minutes. The guy who arrived wore a suit, not the uniform of a typical maintenance man. He went straight for the camera and returned it to its original position. The man had a Bluetooth headset strapped over one ear, and upon instructions of whoever was monitoring the camera feed, he tweaked the angle of the camera another few degrees.

Cabrillo had already taken the first available elevator as soon as the man had made his move. Now he loitered on the sidewalk outside the building. He had to wait only a few minutes. Mr Fix-It didn't work at this building. He hit the streets with a long stride. Juan knew where he was headed, so he took off down a parallel street. He was just in time to see the man enter the black tower where L'Enfant said Kenin was holed up.

Yes indeed, the occupant of the top floors was very security conscious. 'Must be paranoid,' the Chairman muttered under his breath.

They hadn't really considered the observation deck as a suitable place to watch the black tower for the simple reason that it was closed at night. He had merely gone there to test his enemy's resolve. Juan returned to the building and spoke with a woman who managed leasings. Through a dummy front, the Corporation had already rented space on the sixtieth floor that gave them a perfect vantage. He was given keys to the suite of rooms but declined her offer to show him the space. Juan rode the elevator up.

There were three rooms, the first of which was an outer reception, with a secretary's desk and a seating area with a couch and matching chairs. A pair of doors led to the offices themselves. The offices were identically furnished – standard desks, credenzas, and chairs. There was even generic artwork on the walls. Cabrillo ignored it all. He removed a pair of compact but surprisingly powerful binoculars from his fanny pack and glassed the rooftop terrace four blocks away and two hundred feet down.

His view was unrestricted. Like this building, the target rooftop was surrounded by a glass railing, only this one was at least eight feet tall, and he suspected it was bulletproof. Entry to the terrace was from an elevator located in a pavilion on the building's southern corner. There was a long, shimmering pool surrounded by a teak deck. One end of the pool was piled high with rocks with water tumbling over them in an artful, natural display. Near it, and also set in rocks so it looked like a natural spring, was a hot tub with traces of steam rising off its surface. There were hundreds of plantings, and paths winding through the trees and shrubbery. The terrace looked like something Disney would create for one of their resorts, and Juan had to admit he was charmed by the effect.

Later, they would lug over their gear from the hotel. Juan's cover was photojournalist, and he had lenses many times more powerful than the binoculars he carried. To enter China, Eddie and he had had to list a hotel where they were staying, but from now on this suite would be their home.

Hours later, they were eating Kentucky Fried Chicken in one of the offices, discussing what they had learned. Cabrillo had just finished his report and used a piece of extra crispy to prod Eddie into telling his tale. They would have liked to have Max and some of the others listen in, but cell signals were too easily intercepted, and if the encryption was too tough for the government to crack, the police would be on them in minutes.

'There are two guards in the lobby,' Eddie told him. 'And unless you have a building-issued ID or an appointment, they won't let you loiter. All deliveries to the building go in through a back door. The packages are signed for, and internal security makes the delivery to the proper office. I talked to a couple of delivery boys. No exceptions.

'I got myself an appointment with an import/export firm on the twentieth floor. The elevators go up to the thirty-eighth and are unrestricted, but on each of them there's a key slot to go up one more level.'

'But the top *two* floors have acoustical security,' Juan said.

Seng nodded. 'Here's the kicker. I physically counted the floors from the outside. The building has forty-one storeys. The key-access-only floor is a buffer between the two-storey penthouse and the rest of the tower. From thirty-nine, you switch elevators to go to the top.'

'Are the elevators in the centre of the building?'

Eddie simply nodded.

'Then access to the penthouse is from the southern corner. At least there's an elevator there that goes to the rooftop.'

'We need to find someone with one of those keys,' Seng said.

'Won't do us any good. First off, I bet three of the key slots are dummies, and the access key works in just one elevator. And you can be sure security is going to be tight up there. Someone not authorized stepping off that car is going to raise the alarm. The elevator to the top two floors and the roof goes into lockdown, police are called or the guards handle the problem themselves.'

'Disguise?'

'Considering it,' Juan said. 'But that means figuring out who exactly has the authority to go up to thirty-nine and then up to the penthouse levels.'

Eddie shook his head. 'Only way to do that is to ride that elevator all day long.'

'And did it look to you like security is going to allow that?'

'No,' Eddie said miserably. 'Stairwells?'

'Will be blocked off at thirty-eight. We could pick the lock, but there will be cameras watching it. And before you suggest killing the power to the building, we both know they'll have battery backup and a generator.'

'We're talking as though this place is impregnable?'

'So far, it appears to be. Even if we can get into that one elevator shaft, it still puts us one floor below Kenin's.' This high level of security told Juan that he had indeed found the rogue admiral and he was the kind of man who planned his security thoroughly. 'I bet the ventilation system stops at thirty-nine and the penthouse levels have their own heating and cooling.'

'What about the structural chases for water and sewerage pipes?' Eddie asked.

'Too tight, and I would have a motion sensor installed on thirty-nine.'

'Well, we know he won't be leaving anytime soon.' Kenin would be undergoing cosmetic surgery to alter his appearance. The doctor would live and work inside the safe house. He might be allowed to leave on errands but would always be escorted. Kenin would rejoin society only when he was healed and looked nothing like his former self.

'Let's just keep our eye on the place for a few days and see what presents itself.'

At dawn the following morning, they saw the first stirrings of activity on the roof. The building's black glass walls remained as opaque as ever. A three-man security detail appeared on the open terrace. Juan watched them through a telephoto lens mounted on a tripod. One man remained by the elevator while the other two, guns drawn, checked every inch of the rooftop garden. They looked under bushes and around the waterfall. The pool lining was bright blue, so they could see it was clear. The hot tub lining, on the other hand, was dark, and one of the guards plunged its depth with a pool skimmer. They checked everything and missed nothing. And Juan could tell they kept in communication with one another at all times.

Solidly professional and deeply depressing. He had been thinking of somehow getting onto the roof and assaulting downward into the penthouse rather than coming up from below. These guys foiled that idea. As soon as contact was lost with one of the guards, the one by the elevator would go back to the penthouse and lock it down. By the time an attacking force breached the apartment, Kenin would be long gone.

He laid out that scenario to Eddie.

'So we flush him out and guard all exits, ready to snatch him off the streets,' Seng summed up.

Juan immediately saw the flaw . . . two flaws. Kenin could hole up in an office on a lower floor and wait out the attack. And, two, the police would be called as soon as the breach was discovered. Kenin had needed local help to establish his safe house, local help with serious pull.

The streets would be swarming with cops by the time he reached the ground floor. It would be impossible to follow him let alone stage a kidnapping.

For several hours, nothing happened. Eddie was studying the roof while Juan paced the outer office trying to come up with a plan. The same three-man security detail emerged again from the elevator and performed another scan, checking that nothing had changed on their isolated mesa of steel and glass. Eddie called in the Chairman so he could watch through his binoculars.

After the sweep, two of the guards went below while the guard posted at the elevator stayed where he was. Moments later, a woman wearing a plain white robe appeared. She looked Chinese and maybe a day past her eighteenth birthday. Apparently, Kenin liked them young but legal. When she reached the deck around the pool, she set down a wicker bag that she'd been carrying and shrugged out of her robe. Expecting a revealing bikini, Juan and Eddie were surprised she wore a sleek unitard swimsuit favored by Olympic swimmers.

She settled goggles over her eyes, dove in, and began swimming laps.

Cabrillo ignored her and watched the guard. He rarely glanced in her direction. Instead, he studied the surrounding buildings and the sky, looking for threats. Juan had to admit the guy was good. He never became fixated on any one spot, not even when a helicopter passed less than a half mile from the black tower. He watched it, yes, but it never became a distraction.

The girl swam for thirty minutes without taking a break.

It was nearing noon. A new guard came to spell the man at the elevator, and two others searched the rooftop terrace as if it had never been inspected before. One guard carried a sniper rifle with an enormous scope over his shoulder while the other cradled a Chinese Type 95 assault rifle. The bullpup design was the latest weapon in the People's Army. The fact these two were armed with more than just pistols was a new development. It was an elevation in threat protection that told Cabrillo to expect Kenin to make an appearance.

Next, a waiter arrived, pushing the kind of food trolley one sees in a hotel. He set out lunch at a table under an umbrella next to the pool. When all was ready, wine in a silver bucket opened and a last polish to the silverware performed, he stood back at a respectful distance. The girl pulled herself from the water with the easy grace of a river otter and towelled off.

A new figure emerged from the pavilion.

Juan felt his pulse quicken. He recognized Pytor Kenin immediately. He wore only swim trunks and rubber sandals so they could see the thick pelt of silvery hair that covered his bearish torso. He had typical Slavic features – a round head, firm chin, and deep-set eyes – and he moved with the vigour of a man twenty years younger. The girl offered her cheek and he gave her a quick peck. The little intimacy was almost believable. He must be paying her very well.

Juan noticed that one of Kenin's ears was bandaged and the other was red and swollen. The Russian was beginning plastic surgery to change his appearance and, as with everything else, he was being extremely cautious. Ears were as individual as fingerprints or DNA, and new sophisticated facial recognition software, coupled with the profusion of CCTV cameras in all the world's major cities, made it necessary to modify more than just the jaw, nose and brow. Juan knew of more than one terror suspect caught just by the shape of his ear. Kenin was sharp.

He ate leisurely, like a man without a care in the world. Retirement certainly suited him.

After the meal, Kenin busied himself with a laptop computer. Juan hoped he was using a Wi-Fi they could hijack, but the computer was hooked into an outlet by a thick, doubtlessly shielded cord. At one point, Kenin called over the waiter. The man vanished for a few moments, then reappeared with a humidor. The admiral selected a cigar and ritualistically snipped off the end with a gold cutter and lit it with a gold lighter.

They remained on the deck until around three. The girl had swum some, and for a time Kenin had lumbered about in the pool like a water buffalo, mindful not to douse his inflamed ears.

After the pair vanished back inside, the waiter tidied up, but it was the security detail that was the last to leave. They performed a thorough sweep, the fourth that day.

Eddie had taken pictures of all the guards' faces and uploaded them to his phone. He left Juan in the office to watch the deserted rooftop while he hustled outside. He found a good spot to watch the black tower's service entrance from under a parked car. If the driver returned, he'd have more than enough time to shuffle to the next in the string of automobiles lining the street. As each building employee left, Eddie checked his or her face against his database. He was forced to switch cars a couple of times, and by ten that night few vehicles remained on the street and he had to abandon his observation.

By then, no one had left the building for quite some time. None of the people he'd observed leaving the building had been among the guard staff. Like Kenin, they were locked in the building for the duration.

He returned to their rented office. Cabrillo was peering through the big telephoto lens at the darkened terrace. 'Any luck?' he asked without turning.

'Nada. I'll try watching the front doors in the morning, but I think they're holed up like their boss. You?'

'Zip,' Juan said sourly. 'Looks like they check the terrace each morning and again when someone's about to use it.'

Eddie and he ended up staying a week. The routines varied only slightly. Kenin would sometimes eat dinner out by the pool or stroll along the garden paths. The girl was replaced on the sixth day with another that looked little different apart from hair length. It would take a huge team to have been ready to follow her, a group so large that they would give themselves away.

They made other observations as well. Martial music played in most of Shanghai's public spaces, and patriotic posters were appearing all over the city. Soldiers were a common sight, and most had the people flocking around them to shake their hands. And in the skies over the city, fighter planes put on what seemed to be impromptu air shows.

In a country as tightly controlled as China, everything was done for a reason. The increased display of militarism was to get the people riled over the ongoing dispute with Japan about the ownership of the Diaoyu/

Senkaku islands. What had started as diplomatic brinks-manship was quickly escalating. Since the discovery of the gas and oil fields in the waters around the islands, the saber rattling in Beijing and Tokyo was growing louder. Ships had been dispatched, and planes had engaged in games of chicken, pilots from both sides flying so close to one another that an accident was inevitable. The fallout from such an event was incalculable but certainly dangerous.

The two men wiled away the boring hours discussing, and ultimately rejecting, idea after idea of how to get to Kenin. A chopper assault was out. The rotor sounds would alert the guards, and Kenin would lock himself inside. They talked about climbing the side of the building, but that would attract too much attention from people on the street. They considered a night HALO parachute drop. It had potential, but with the guards in constant communication, a sudden silence when the men were subdued would again alert the force still inside the building. Also, Chinese airspace was tightly controlled by the government, and an unauthorized flight would most likely be met by a couple of fighter jets long before they reached the Pudong District.

In the end, Eddie and Juan came to the same conclusion. Pytor Kenin had locked himself in the modern equivalent of an impenetrable castle and was more than prepared for a siege.

It was only when they got back to the *Oregon* and discussed their pessimistic assessment with the rest of the crew that new ideas were thrown at the project.

In a burst of inspiration, it was Juan himself who finally made the breakthrough. He needed only Max's mechanical savvy to pull it off. Hanley considered the challenge for a few seconds before agreeing. 'It's your neck, bucko.'

'It'll be a lot more than my neck.' The two grinned like schoolboys conspiring to commit mischief.

25

It took two weeks to get everything into position. Eddie had returned to Shanghai almost immediately with a small team to keep Kenin's penthouse under constant observation. The office also served as an address through which they could ship certain items into the country. The advance team also got to work on converting a small panel van they'd bought on the black market. Their final task was to find a suitable place to transfer gear from a submersible. They had lost the Nomad off the coast of Maryland, but they still had her smaller sister, the Discovery 1000. The *Oregon* would remain outside of China's twelve-mile territorial limit, and the illegal gear would be ferried in clandestinely. They would also use the Disco to get people out of the country as well.

Juan wished he'd have more time to practice with Max's brilliant piece of engineering, but the ship's decks were too dangerous, and using it over the water was suicide if something went wrong. He just had to content himself with the little bit of practice he got in the *Oregon*'s main hold. Keeping the contraption stable was tricky, but he thought he had the hang of it. If something did go wrong during the actual assault, he wasn't likely to survive.

He piloted the submersible himself. They launched from the moon pool an hour before sunset and dove deep enough that they couldn't be seen from above. Once it was dark, they could approach the surface. Linda Ross accompanied him. She would take the little four-man mini-sub back to the ship. All the equipment they were bringing was strapped to the top of the sub in a waterproof container.

'Can I ask you something?' Linda said as they started the slow crawl to a rendezvous at an unused pier along the Huangpu River.

'Shoot.' They were at a depth where there was just enough light to see feathers of biologic flotsam streaming by the thick domed canopy. The sub navigated through a lidar system – basically, radar with lasers.

'Why not just lob a missile down on to Kenin while he's sunning himself? Surely there are times he's alone.'

'If this was about revenge, I'd do it in a heartbeat,' Juan replied. 'But I want to get my hands on his stealth technology, or whatever it was, that made that ship disappear and capsize Dullah and you on the *Sakir*.'

'I assume you then want to sell it to your and my favourite uncle.'

'I whetted Lang Overholt's appetite while we were laid up in Bermuda. He said – and I quote – "Get me that and I'll hand you a blank check from the Treasury." I foresee a number one followed by eight zeros.'

It took Linda a second to imagine the figure. 'A hundred million. My my.'

'We just got them back their stolen billion. I think

they can afford it. Though Lang's going to grit his teeth handing it over.' Juan smiled at the thought. His old mentor was known as both a brilliant strategist but also the biggest miser in Washington, DC.

From time to time, they would rise close enough to the surface to get updated GPS signals to fine-tune the navigation plot. They were fighting the Yangtze's current, so the going was slow. Because Shanghai is the busiest container port in the world, an unimaginable amount of ship traffic thundered overhead. In the submersible the hiss of steel through water and the chop of propeller blades was an industrial symphony. It dimmed little when they made the turn to start following the Huangpu River that bisected the megalopolis.

They stayed close to the middle of the river. Juan knew on either side of them were mile upon mile of commercial docks. This was a city of industry, and its rivers were its lifeblood. When they passed the Pudong District, they were at a depth of forty feet but could still see the artificial neon glow of the numerous buildings cutting through the water. Twenty minutes later, they drifted toward their rendezvous. The site was in the process of renewal. A cement plant had once stood on a piece of real estate that now was prime for residential development. The towers that were to replace it would be home to five thousand people.

Now the plant had been demolished, but the quay where raw materials had once been imported still stood. Juan had one of their encrypted walkie-talkies. 'The Merman is here.'

'About time, Merman,' Eddie replied. 'For a while there, I thought you'd come to your senses and called the whole thing off.'

Juan surfaced the mini-sub in the shadow of the quay and quickly saw that he could slip it between the dock and a partially sunken barge. They would be invisible. Eddie was parked in a Chinese knockoff of a Toyota van. A fine rain was falling, blurring the lights of the city. Juan unstrapped himself, gave Linda's shoulder a squeeze, and made his way to the hatch.

'Take care,' Linda said.

'See you soon.'

Eddie had already released the straps holding the cargo pod to the sub's upper deck, and, together, he and Cabrillo lifted it into the van's rear cargo box. The pod itself wasn't much larger than those seen atop cars, and it weighed less than a hundred pounds.

Once they were clear, bubbles boiled around the Disco submersible and it soon plunged back into its natural element. Linda would be travelling with both tide and current, so she'd be back aboard the *Oregon* in half the time it took to get here. Eddie drove the truck to a commercial parking lot that was less than two miles from Kenin's tower fortress. They spent the next hour examining the items they had smuggled into China, making certain nothing had been damaged. Juan was trusting his life to this gear, so he was thorough and methodical.

It was too late to find a taxi so they walked back to the rented office that overlooked Kenin's penthouse retreat. MacD Lawless was watching the darkened terrace through the powerful camera lens. Mike Trono was stretched out asleep in the adjoining office. Cabrillo let him be and wrapped a sleeping bag around himself and curled up on the carpet. He was asleep in moments.

Next morning, the rain had intensified, and the forecast said it would continue for at least another day. The men remained holed up in the office. Eddie was reduced to the role of errand boy, going out to get their meals. They maintained the overwatch of the rooftop terrace because there wasn't much else to do. All of them had been on such stakeouts before and each had his own way to combat the boredom.

Thirty hours after sneaking into the country, Juan was with Eddie in the truck. The weather had broken. Seng was behind the wheel while the Chairman rode in the cargo bed. He was strapped in and ready to go. The roof panels had been cut and hinges attached so he could open them with the pull on a length of rope. They just needed to wait for Kenin.

Eddie found a parking space near where he'd spent part of a night watching the building's back door. He had to remain with the vehicle in case a cop wanted him to move. MacD was in position farther down the street ready for the diversion while Mike was up in the office with a radio to tell them when Kenin went out to enjoy the sunshine after so many days confined indoors.

The guards had done their dawn sweep, and at nine o'clock repeated it because the girl was coming out to swim. Mike relayed this information to the others using a predetermined series of clicks on their walkie-talkies. Not knowing the level of government monitoring made them prudently circumspect.

Juan heard two clicks from his radio handset. Kenin had made his appearance. Juan's stomach knotted. Minutes to go. He tightened his grip. He wouldn't open the roof panels until he heard that final single click in case anyone in the surrounding buildings looked down and became curious enough about an open-topped van to call the police.

He had to wait until Kenin was seated poolside. One guard would be standing outside the little pavilion that housed the elevator. But the real trigger moment would come when Mike saw the elevator guard switch frequencies on his radio and check in with the guards down in the penthouse suite. He did it every five minutes. A simple 'All's well.' Once he gave that, Juan had just those five min–

Click.

Cabrillo yanked on the rope, and the two precut sections of roof hinged downward, flooding the interior of the van in light. The truck shifted slightly as Eddie jumped clear and started making his way to another vehicle they had stashed nearby.

Down the street, MacD set the paper bag he'd been carrying in the space between two parked cars and casually blended back into the throngs of people on the sidewalks. After a ten-second delay Cabrillo knew was coming, the contents of the bag started to erupt.

It had been filled with tiny firecrackers. Ironically,

they had smuggled them in because they couldn't guarantee the quality of local fireworks from the nation that invented them. They lit off like echoing popcorn. Those people nearest the smoking eruption of tiny explosions stepped back smartly while nearly every other pedestrian edged forward to see what was happening. For half a block, all eyes were on the sparking and popping bag. No one paid the slightest attention to the van.

They never saw what emerged from the top.

The technology had been around since the 1960s. Max had found the design specs on the Internet. The only issue had been finding sufficiently pure hydrogen peroxide to fuel the contraption.

Cabrillo had spent the morning strapped to a jetpack. Now, with the crowded street distracted by the continuous string of firecrackers going off, he toggled the switch that caused the fuel to react with a silver catalyst and expand in an exothermic reaction that blew superhot gas through the pack's twin jet nozzles. The sound was like that of steam escaping from a loose fitting, but the exhaust was invisible.

Juan's first attempts at using the jetpack tethered down in the *Oregon*'s hold had been disasters. Seconds after lifting free of the deck, he would begin tumbling in midair, and had it not been for the ropes supporting him, he would have killed himself a dozen times over. But then came the eureka moment when he intuitively understood the dynamics of this kind of flying and he could keep erect and stable until the tanks ran dry and he would alight onto his feet with the grace of an eagle returning to its aerie.

Max had done the calculations, and Cabrillo trusted no man more than Hanley, but as he lifted out of the truck's cargo bed he knew he could be dead in thirty seconds. That's all the time he had to soar four hundred and twenty feet into the air and land precisely on the flat-roofed elevator housing. If he didn't make it, he'd be just shy of terminal velocity when he augered into the pavement.

Cabrillo came out of the truck with the majestic slow rise of a Saturn rocket, the weight of thrust tightening the straps between his legs and across his back. He wasn't going to bother with a helmet, but Max convinced him to wear it after mounting a camera so the *Oregon* could watch his progress as he climbed higher and higher. The world shrank beneath his feet, and he could tell that his launch had gone unnoticed as they'd planned.

There was nothing to be done about people in surrounding buildings seeing him. He could only hope they saw it as some sort of publicity stunt. Ten seconds into the flight, the top of the building looked no closer in the helmet's monocular display, and he'd burned half his fuel.

But as the hydrogen peroxide jetted through the exhaust nozzles, the weight dropped and his speed increased. His acceleration was geometric, and quite quickly his target appeared to be within reach. The countdown display calculating thrust time showed he had eight seconds of fuel, and he had only a dozen floors to go. More and more of the city opened to him the higher he rose along the skyscraper's sheer glass wall, but he took no heed. He concentrated on keeping his body still and his movement to a minimum. That was the secret of flying the turbo-vacuum, as Max called it. Stay nice and steady and keep corrective gestures small. He wavered only slightly as he shot higher and higher and knew that if he survived this, it would be an exhilaration he would never forget.

Four seconds left and he passed the thirty-ninth floor. He eased ever so slightly off the throttle control, slowing his assent. He didn't want to fly higher than absolutely necessary.

He cleared the last floor with a second of fuel remaining, then realized he still had to get above the glass wall that encircled the top of the building. He didn't remember if Max had included this final barrier in his calculations.

There was nothing he could do. He leaned in to launch himself at the wall and managed to clear it by kicking his legs forward. This threw off his aerodynamics, but it didn't matter. The last of the peroxide fuel spewed from the pack, and Cabrillo fell two feet onto the top of the elevator housing. He managed to land on his knees and not hurt himself thanks to pads built into the thermal protective chaps he'd worn.

He slapped the quick release for the belt and shucked out of the jetpack like it was a cape. Empty, it weighed less than forty pounds. He was on his feet a second later, an FN Five-seveN pistol in hand. It was fitted with a silencer and an extended magazine containing thirty rounds, plus the one already in the chamber.

The guard stationed at the elevator had heard something landing atop the building and was slowly walking backward away from the structure to get a better look. His pistol was only partway up. Juan got the drop on him. The high velocity and small size of the FN's rounds put the man down.

The Chairman took off the helmet and thermal chaps and jumped the eight feet to the terrace floor. He was closer to the southeast side of the building, so he took off into the artificial jungle. Cabrillo moved quickly, his veins buzzing with adrenaline. His senses were heightened to the point that he could hear traffic down on the streets even over the glass barrier. The second guard was the sniper, and Cabrillo saw him as he was scoping a high-rise about five blocks away. The way he held motionless and kept the weapon on one spot told Juan that this guy wasn't as professional as the others. The building he was looking at had balconies and he'd doubtlessly spotted one with a sunbather on it.

He died getting an eyeful.

Cabrillo still had three minutes before the security team downstairs was alerted that something was wrong. He should take out the third guard now, but he was close to what they had identified as the air intake for the penthouse's ventilation system. The mechanism was just an anonymous grey box nestled among the trees.

Juan bent to it, unclamping a side panel that gave access to the sophisticated filtration system. He pulled the racks of molecular filters until the air circulating downstairs was the same choking smog the rest of Shanghai's citizens polluted their lungs with every day. Next came the pony bottle of gas. It was a knockout gas similar to the one the Russian Spetsnaz had used to retake a Moscow theatre back in 2002, but much safer. Cabrillo opened the tap and let the ventilation fans draw the gas into the suite and distribute it to every nook and cranny.

Then he went hunting for the third guard.

Mike Trono had said the man was on the western side of the building. But that intel was four minutes old, and these were roving guards. He went west anyway, keeping off the paths and in the planted beds as much as he could. He avoided the swimming pool area entirely. If Kenin got a glimpse of someone slinking around his little urban oasis, he'd bolt instantly. The man had the instincts of a wharf rat and three times the cunning.

Juan found a spot where he could look down the entire western edge of the building but couldn't see his mark. He moved on, careful to disturb nothing. The man gave himself away with a sneeze. He was less than ten feet from Juan, hidden by a wall of ferns. Juan was about to take his shot when he heard Kenin's voice and the girl's reply. His hunt had drifted closer to the pool than he'd realized.

He waited. The guard did the last thing Juan expected. He came through the wall of ferns rather than stick to the path. Even silenced, the Five-SeveN made enough noise to carry to the pool. An assault rifle barrel parted the foliage. Cabrillo grabbed it, yanking the guard off balance even before he'd emerged from the artificial jungle. As the man's head came into view, Juan clubbed him with the butt of his pistol, and again as he slowed the unconscious man's fall to the deck. He checked for a pulse. It was there but weak. He would live.

The gas he'd released would reach maximum saturation in just a few minutes more. There was no use in delaying. He moved to the nearby path and slowly stepped out from the forest and onto the teak pool surround. The girl saw him first and screamed. Kenin looked up from his computer and startled. His sanctum had been breached.

'Hands up, now,' Juan ordered in Russian, and repeated the phrase in Chinese as Eddie had taught him. He gave them a half second to comply before shooting the pitcher of iced tea on the table between their chairs. Kenin's nubile companion yelped again, but this time both of them raised their hands.

'Tell her to get into the pool and stay there,' Juan said, still speaking Russian.

The Chinese girl must have understood the language because she rose from her chaise and jumped awkwardly into the azure water, her eyes like saucers and her pretty face ashen with fear.

Kenin regained some of his lost composure, his eyes hardened, and though his hands were still up, they were no longer comically stretched to their limit as they'd been seconds earlier. He demanded with hauteur, 'Who are you?'

'The best man at Yuri Borodin's wedding. And right now I am begging you to give me an excuse to put a bullet between your eyes.'

Understanding dawned on the rogue admiral. 'You're the Chairman. You are Juan Cabrillo.'

Juan saw motion out of the corner of his eye and reacted on pure instinct. He triggered off a half dozen rounds so fast, it was as though the FN were an automatic weapon. He glanced left and saw Kenin's butler stagger out from behind a big rubber tree. Five of the six shots had hit him centre mass; blood stained his white jacket. A MAC-10 machine pistol fell from his nerveless fingers as he pitched face-first onto the tile decking.

Kenin used the momentary distraction and took off running for the elevator. He had maybe a seconds-long head start and was closer to his destination by twenty feet. Juan couldn't afford to shoot him in the back, so he took off after the Russian. He was twenty years younger than Kenin, but the admiral ran with the drive of a cornered animal. He knew his life was on the line and put on a burst of speed he probably hadn't thought he was capable of.

Cabrillo still closed the gap. Kenin wore open-toed moccasins under his linen slacks and they slapped with each stride. Juan was readying himself to tackle Kenin from behind when the Russian stopped ten feet shy of the elevator vestibule, turned, and threw the punch he'd trained his entire life to throw.

Juan too had stopped short and reared back slightly but still took the most brutal punch he'd ever felt. Kenin knew his opponent was going down, though he hadn't yet fallen. Kenin had broken his wrist throwing that punch, but it didn't matter. What mattered was that he was about to escape. It didn't register that the man who had somehow breached his security swung the big pistol up just enough that when he triggered off a round, it took off the Russian's pinkie finger at the first knuckle.

Kenin clutched at his bloody hand when this new-found and sharper pain exploded over the pain of his cracked forearm. Blood sprayed the wall behind him while the severed digit landed in a flower bed to their right.

'Next one's in your heart,' Juan snarled. He was still woozy from the hit but recovering fast. He waved the gun to indicate he wanted Kenin to return to the pool.

The girl remained in the shallow end, clutching the edge, leaving only her dark eyes showing.

Cabrillo tossed a towel to Kenin to staunch the bleeding and closed up the Russian's laptop. He also pocketed a pair of cell phones from the table where Kenin had been sitting. Juan found another in the girl's wicker bag. There would be no useful intel on it, so, with an apologetic shrug to the girl, he flipped her phone into the water.

'Let's go,' Juan ordered. He and Kenin returned to the elevator. As a precaution against being overcome by the gas he'd earlier dispensed, Juan pulled a pair of filter masks from his equipment pouch and fitted one over his nose and mouth and threw the other to the Russian.

The elevator doors were open.

'Sit in the corner on your hands.' He waited to push the button to the thirty-ninth floor until Kenin was in the correct position.

Juan had him stay there for most of the trip, getting him to his feet just as the elevator car slowed. Cabrillo pulled him up by his injured right arm. Kenin sucked in air through his teeth from the pain.

The elevator dinged open. The Chairman studied the room beyond Kenin's shoulder, the barrel of his FN Five-seveN pushed into the Russian's spine. There were three guards dressed in matching uniforms. These were tier two protection, not the elites who had been upstairs. Two of them were huddled over a chessboard while the third had his feet on his desk and his nose buried in a magazine. Beyond them were plate-glass windows and the beautiful cityscape.

This floor must have been ventilated with the rest of the tower because these men were conscious. Juan pulled off his mask and bellowed in Russian, 'On your feet!'

The three men turned and saw their boss and assumed he had issued the order. They leapt guiltily and stood at attention. It was only then that Juan revealed himself. One man stupidly reached for his holstered pistol. Cabrillo couldn't afford to take chances now and put two in the overzealous guard's head.

The remaining guards threw their hands into the air and started begging for their lives. Juan had them give their pistols the old two-fingered toss and then ordered them to cuff each other to the desk with the plastic zip ties they carried.

He used one of the ties to secure his prisoner's hands as well.

Cabrillo was just pushing Kenin toward the door that would lead them out of this office when all hell broke loose. The door exploded off its hinges, and Chinese men in uniforms, like the one Eddie had described seeing in the lobby, came pouring through. They were armed but also very poorly trained, for when they saw Juan's pistol, they started firing like madmen. The windows behind Juan cascaded earthward after being ripped to shards by countless bullets. Kenin took a barrage of shots, his body jerked back by the impact. He lurched drunkenly as Juan dropped low. Kenin rolled over Cabrillo's back as the momentum thrust him through the gaping window frame. They were forty storeys above the street, and Juan just managed to see the shock and rage in Kenin's eyes before gravity pulled him from view.

Yuri would have loved the irony that the evil and malignant man who had ordered his arrest had died at the hands of his own inept guards. This wasn't exactly the revenge Juan had envisioned, but it was satisfying all the same.

Cabrillo returned fire. He still had more than twenty rounds in the Five-seveN, and he laid down a covering barrage that let him retreat to the elevator. He hit the button and changed out the spent magazine. This new one was his only spare. He could hear bullets impacting the outer door as he was lifted clear. The laptop had been hit in a corner, but it looked like nothing vital had been destroyed.

The guards who'd rushed in must have been stationed outside the main elevators on thirty-nine. They were the cannon fodder should anyone assault the floor via the building's main elevator. One of the guards in the inner office must have had a way to signal them and had done so without Juan realizing it.

Juan resettled his mask and rode up one level. The door opened to a utilitarian space. The luxury apartment would be upstairs. This area was for the guards and staff. A small side table was against the wall opposite the elevator. Juan dragged it over so it prevented the doors from closing to keep the men downstairs from using it. They wouldn't have access to this floor via the emergency stairs, but they would have them guarded so no one could come down. Juan was, essentially, trapped.

But had he been Pytor Kenin, he would have a third way, a secret way, out of the penthouse. He searched quickly. He found a few more guards and staff members unconscious in their rooms. And then he found the escape shaft he was sure Kenin would have installed. It was in a specially made phone-booth-sized room.

The ceiling was open so he could see into the top floor of the penthouse. Looking down, he saw nothing but a black abyss.

But right in front of him was a fabric escape tube with an inner elastic tube that would allow him to control his descent. Juan climbed into the constricting conduit, feeling a little like he was working his way through a whale's intestines. He wriggled and wormed his way down, not knowing how far this extended. He finally saw flashes of light down below his feet and, moments later, flopped out of the escape tube into a room with windows lining one wall.

Kenin had thought of everything. On the floor next to the door was a knapsack that would be his go bag, with essentials like spare IDs, cash, and weapons. If Kenin had extra time when fleeing his penthouse above, there were different changes of clothes on a wardrobe rack – a tailored suit, casual clothes, and uniforms for a janitor, a delivery driver, or a security guard.

Juan helped himself to a fresh shirt that was a little too big but was close enough. He stripped off any tactical gear he still wore. His pants were slightly dirty, but not so bad that anyone would take much notice. He went to the door and cautiously opened it. Beyond was a hallway like any other. It could be in an office building in any city on the planet. Reassuringly banal. On the door he could see that Kenin's escape chute had dumped him out in room 3208. He'd descended almost ten stories.

He regretted having to leave his pistol behind, so

from here on he'd have to talk his way rather than fight his way out of whatever came next.

Carrying Kenin's laptop, he stepped from the office and let the door close behind him. He walked past several closed office doors and politely nodded to the one person he saw, a middle-aged man who returned the nod and didn't seem suspicious. Where Kenin had punched him hadn't starting bruising yet. In an hour the spot would be a hideous shade of puce/black.

He found the elevator and had to wait less than thirty seconds. There were a few people on it when the doors whispered open. Juan got on, turned to face front like everyone else, and waited. There came a chime, and the doors closed. A few stops later, the elevator opened in the lobby. Everything appeared normal at first. Then he saw some of the security team huddled together at their station. They seemed agitated and unsure as they listened to a walkie-talkie, presumably from the men up on thirty-nine. Juan looked away. No need to draw attention. A police car pulled up outside. Cabrillo almost changed direction, but that would have been suspicious. Enough people must have called in about a guy flying up the side of a building that the authorities finally sent a patrol to investigate. He was opposite the two cops in the large revolving door as it rotated on its axis. He was out. They were in. Who knew what would happen when they sorted everything out.

He gave his two-way radio a click to tell Eddie to come. Moments later, their second van appeared around the corner. Eddie read the situation. The Chairman was alone, so there was no need to duck to the curb quickly so they could toss their prisoner in the back. He found a spot farther down the block and waited for Cabrillo to jog up to him.

'Let's go,' Juan said as soon as the door was closed.

'What happened?'

Eddie had some bottled water on the engine cover between the two seats. Seeing it, Cabrillo felt his throat suddenly dry and tight. He twisted off the cap and drank a half litre in one throw. 'Believe it or not, Kenin was shot by his own guards. Everything was going pretty much to plan. I had just neutralized the men at the bottom of his private elevator when the guards tasked with overseeing the building's main elevators came at us with guns blazing.'

'The Ruskies are going to be bummed,' Eddie observed.

'When I first got in touch with my guy in the Kremlin and told him I had a bead on Kenin, I got the impression that Moscow will be just as happy with this outcome. Saves them the hassle of admitting what he'd done, putting on a show trial, and shooting him themselves.' Juan held up the laptop. 'I just hope Murph and Stoney can get something valuable off this thing so this whole op will be worth it.'

'If it's on there, they'll get it.' They drove in silence for a few minutes. Eddie finally asked the burning question. 'How was it?'

'How was what?' Juan replied.

'Come on. It must have been amazing.'

The Chairman grinned. 'Amazing doesn't come close. I used to think skydiving was the closest I could ever come to being able to fly. It's nothing compared to the ride I just had. I think I want Max to build me another jetpack for Christmas.'

They cruised around until sunset and then made their way to the abandoned cement factory. Eddie, MacD and Mike were all in the country legally and would fly out the next morning, maintaining their covers in case they might ever need them again. Since Juan had snuck into China, this time he would have to slink out too. Eddie kept Juan company until the Discovery 1000 rose in the shadow of the pier. Cabrillo leapt onto the mini-sub's back and waited for the hatch to open. Hanley himself was piloting the submersible.

'How'd she fly?'

'What's the old line about having the most fun you can have with your clothes on?' Juan asked. 'That's it in a nutshell.'

They bantered all the way back to the *Oregon*, both men content in the afterglow of a mission gone right. It was especially poignant for Cabrillo. He counted few men in the world as friends, and Yuri Borodin had been one of them. Now he had avenged that friend. Yuri's soul could rest a little easier.

The Corporation had nothing lined up at the moment, and if Eric and Mark could crack the laptop, they were due a windfall from the American government along with final payment for The Container affair.

Cabrillo thought he should tie up the *Oregon* for a while and give his people a well-deserved vacation.

Fate was about to intervene once again. Far from vacation, the *Oregon* and her crew were about to enter the fight of their lives.

26

Max Hanley was a born pragmatist. He liked Cabrillo's idea of laying up the ship for a bit and letting the entire crew take a vacation. He also knew where they could get a replacement for the Nomad 1000 submersible and he figured its current location was as good a place as any to let the crew off.

He had been negotiating with a Taiwanese university that happened to have a Nomad they no longer needed. The school had once been a technical training facility for commercial fishing, and the submersible had been an unsolicited gift. Max could have always bought a new one from the manufacturer, but he was not one to waste a penny, let alone several million dollars.

Max choppered in ahead of the ship as it sailed for Taipei, to meet with university staff. His cover was that he was brokering the deal on behalf of a start-up oil exploration company, the industry that snapped up the lion's share of US Submarines' yearly production of Nomads and Discos. The *Oregon* was the freighter he had hired to transport the submersible to the offshore petroleum fields of the Gulf of Mexico.

The inspection went well. The school had moth-balled the Nomad properly and had checked on her frequently. The batteries took a charge, although Max already knew they'd need to be replaced. Certain things one didn't buy used. He had fresh ones aboard the ship. All the electronics and mechanical systems worked, and he found no corrosion or damage to any of the hydraulic lines. The only problem they found was the manipulator hand on the end of the robotic arm didn't work properly. To Max, it was a simple fix, but he got them to shave a few thousand off the price.

When the *Oregon* arrived, it captured the attention of hundreds of students. They gawked at the massive vessel that blocked their view of the bay and open ocean beyond. Max had arranged a customs inspector to be here from Taipei and he signed off on the loading.

Juan himself, dressed like a scruffy seadog for the benefit of the onlookers, was at the controls of the ship's main crane. Crewmen rigged the lift, using slings under the submersible's thirty-foot hull, and an hour after arriving it was lying crossways on the forward hold and the ship was ready to sail. Max had to stick to his role as broker, so he would drive to Taipei.

The Taiwanese capital was on the northern tip of the island, and they could have steamed there in about fourteen hours, but Cabrillo took the *Oregon* out of traditional sea routes, both for coastal vessels and those crossing the Pacific for ports in the Americas. And he needed the cover of darkness. A ship deploying a minisub, while uncommon, wasn't unheard of. The ship leaving the area without seeming to recover the minisub would raise questions.

Because the Nomad was untested, Juan would let no

one else make the initial dive. In the hours it had taken to reach a secluded spot of ocean, the crew had replaced the old batteries with new ones and had attached a system of inflatable bladders to the hull should the mini not respond to Cabrillo's control. There were safety divers in the water as well, and the area around the *Oregon* was lit with powerful spots above and below the surface.

After being lowered into the water and having its shackles removed, the mini-sub's tanks were slowly flooded by Juan. He blew them as a test when the seas overtopped his viewing bubble. He rose as pluckily as a toy submarine in a bathtub.

So then he went for it, diving down along the *Oregon*'s steel flank and then rising gently into the moon pool. More crew were in place to secure the lifting cables. In moments, the sub was safely stowed in its new home, and Cabrillo was heading to the dining room for a late supper.

He noted the asparagus he was served had come from a can. It was a good thing they were berthing soon. All their fresh provisions had run out, and he was told, when he asked the mess attendant, that they were down to three rather unpopular ice-cream flavours.

Juan couldn't sleep that evening, and it had nothing to do with fresh vegetables or butter rum taffy ice cream. Something nagged at his subconscious, some little kernel jabbing into his mind that exhaustion couldn't nacre over like an oyster encasing a bit of sand with pearl. At midnight, he resigned himself to wakefulness and got out of bed. He slipped on his leg and dressed in the clothes he'd discarded an hour and a half earlier.

He wasn't in the mood for a drink, and sitting alone in his cabin held no interest. Julia Huxley was one of those remarkable people that needed just a few hours of sleep per night. He sought her out and found her not in her cabin but down in medical. She was on the Internet as part of a service for people who had immediate medical questions but no access to doctors.

'Hey, Juan. Can't sleep?' she greeted when he paused at the door to her office off the main examination room.

Her office was a small cubical barely big enough for her desk and a spare chair. One wall was covered with framed diplomas and awards. She'd confessed once that her version of the 'ego wall' wasn't for her but her patients. Seeing her so lauded tended to put them at ease.

'Master of the obvious,' Juan smiled back and took the spare chair.

'Let me just finish up here. I've got a guy in Fiji who I think is having an attack of shingles.' She and her patient typed back and forth for another couple of minutes. 'There. Done. Poor fellow is in for a miserable time. So, what's on your mind?'

'I don't know,' Juan admitted. 'Something.'

'That narrows it down,' Julia teased with a grin. 'Okay, try this. How long has something been bothering you?'

'Just tonight. I've been on top of the world since escaping Shanghai and then when I went to bed tonight,

I couldn't fall asleep. I'm getting this feeling that I've missed something.'

Hux suddenly looked grave. 'You and I have been through a lot together.' Julia had overseen Juan's recovery from having his leg blown off. 'I know you, and I know when you think you've overlooked something that you are probably right. You have.'

'I know,' Cabrillo said. 'That's what's making this so tough.'

'We can assume this has to do with our past mission, so why don't we go through it together.'

And they did, from the very top when Yuri Borodin's aide-de-camp, Misha Kasporov, rang them to tell them about Borodin's illegal incarceration up to the moment the Discovery 1000's hatch closed in the Huangpu River for the ride back to the *Oregon*. She hadn't realized how close some of the calls had really been and rebuked him for being reckless. He took her remarks the way a lifetime smoker takes the advice of their doctor to quit. Great tip, but it ain't gonna happen.

'It has to be L'Enfant's betrayal,' Julia concluded for him. 'Everything else about this is pretty straight-forward, at least by your standards.'

'Obviously we can never use him as a contact anymore. He might have come through with Kenin's location, but the trust is broken. We both recognize that. And, yes, he's the best in the world at what he does, but there are others we can turn to.'

'So you're saying that isn't it?'

'Yes. No. I don't know.' Juan raked his fingers through

his hair, which was now the length of a Marine recruit's. 'Kenin deduced who we are after we rescued, well, almost rescued Yuri. He must have known our reputation because he immediately started eliminating any connection to his optically stealthed ship. He also leaned on L'Enfant to find out where we were going to be. He sent his ship out to capsize the *Sakir* and I assume sink us as well.'

Juan paused as something began to gel in the back of his mind. 'What do you think it cost to develop that stealth ship?'

'Who knows? Even if he had Tesla's formula for making a ship invisible and samples of his equipment, we're still talking a hundred million at least.'

'Exactly, and yet he risked it to go after a Sheik's boat and us. If he had access to a submarine, surely he had people in the surface fleet loyal to him. Why didn't he just launch a few ship-killing missiles at us and at Dullah's yacht?'

'We could have shot them down,' Julia pointed out.

'He didn't know that. He threw a hundred-million-dollar asset at a hundred-dollar problem. That bothers me. This was also his big score, his final act of thievery before leaving Mother Russia for good. It's inconceivable that someone was willing to pay that kind of money to kill an Emirate's sheik who happens to be our client at the time. That is too big of a coincidence.'

He grabbed the phone off Julia's desk and dialled Mark Murphy's room. Murph answered on the second ring. Juan could tell he was on speakerphone.

'How are you two coming with that laptop?'

'We just got it back from Linc,' Eric shouted over some godawful techno playing in the background.

'Turn that noise down,' Juan admonished.

'Noise?' Mark shot back with indignity. 'That's the Howler Monkeys.'

'I'm sure it is.' The volume thankfully dropped. 'Why did Linc have the computer?'

'You didn't get my e-mail?'

'Obviously not or I wouldn't be asking.'

'The laptop was booby-trapped with a packet of C-4. Eric and I figured it might be rigged, so we X-rayed it first. Good thing we did. We guessed the charge goes off after the computer is opened and the password's not entered within a certain amount of time. Linc needed until tonight to remove the detonator and explosives.'

'How long before you guys get anything?'

'We're just starting on the password now. After that, there's no way to know how many levels of encryption Kenin used. My guess is, a ton.'

'How long?' Juan demanded again, his tone harsh and accusatory.

'Days. Weeks. There's no way to say. Sorry, Chairman.'

'Twenty-four hours,' Juan snapped. 'That's an order.'

He slammed down the phone. Julia looked concerned.

'They work better when they think I'm mad and making unreasonable demands.'

'So that was theatre?'

'Partially,' Juan said. 'But we need answers quickly.'

'I don't understand,' she admitted. 'What's the rush?'

'You know that conflict between China and Japan over some islands?'

'Yeah, something about sovereign rights and newly discovered oil or gas or something.'

'I don't think it was a recent discovery. I think China has known about it for some time. I remember when I was rescuing Yuri he asked me about current events. I made some lame joke, but I mentioned that the civil war in Sudan was winding down.'

'And?'

'China was a major backer in that conflict because they were getting a lot of their oil from the region. They stopped funding the war because they realized they won't need to import fossil fuels from Africa if there are decades' worth right off their coast.'

'But the Japanese?' Julia said by way of roadblock.

'Could do nothing without our help. And what do we do in situations like this where two naval powers are butting heads?'

'Ask Max or Eddie. They're your military guys.'

'Come on, Hux. Everyone knows what we do.'

'We send in an aircraft carrier.'

'Exactly. Force projection at its finest. And it's not just a carrier. It's a whole battle group with several destroyers, a frigate, some cruisers and two submarines. They all act as a screen to keep the carrier safe. The system is so well designed that it's also considered impervious to attack. Back in the bad old days of the Cold War, the Soviets figured they would need at least a hundred cruise missiles to have a hope of taking out just one carrier.'

'O-kay,' Julia drew the word out. 'In comes our carrier, both sides back down, and crisis averted.'

'Think it through, Doc.'

And the horrifying thought that had nagged at Juan's mind until he'd talked it out with her too. She blanched. 'There's another of those stealth ships out there.'

'That's got to be it. The ship was conceived before the Soviet Union dissolved as a way to counter our carriers. The Russians don't need something like that anymore, but a burgeoning and increasingly hostile China would love to be able to take out a big nuclear carrier and do it in such a way that they can't be blamed.'

'Would they be so bold?'

'This has been coming for years,' Juan said. 'All the hacking into our computer systems and industrial espionage. We've been in a closet war with China for at least a decade. Now that energy independence is within their reach, they will do anything to fulfill its promise.' A fresh thought struck Cabrillo. 'Sinking the *Sakir* was a demonstration to the Chinese of the weapon's power. They must have been monitoring the sinking from the rendezvous ship that escaped us when we were dead in the water. Kenin chose Dullah's yacht to get back at me, and I bet he even got some Middle East faction to pony up some dinars for the hit on Dullah too.'

'What do we do?'

'I'll alert Langston but without anything concrete, like Kenin's computer having a file labelled "bill of sale", there isn't much he can do. The Navy won't act on anything so insubstantial.'

'Our vacation is going to end before it even starts, isn't it?'

Juan just gave her a look. He called the op centre and asked the duty officer to track down the location of the nearest carrier battle group. If it was called in to the region, he needed to know its route since the Chinese would place their deadly stealth ship directly in its path. He was relieved to learn ten minutes later that the *Johnny Reb*, as the USS *John C. Stennis* was nicknamed, had just left Honolulu en route to the Navy base at Yokosuka, Japan. They had a few days' breathing space even if the President ordered her into the disputed area immediately.

There were other practical considerations to take care of. Cabrillo thanked Julia and headed to the office just off his stateroom. He roused Max from his Taipei hotel suite to tell him the change in plans and to meet the *Oregon* at the Bali District piers the following day. They had already reserved a berthing space for the two weeks they'd planned for the Corporation-wide vacation. Cabrillo called the port authority to tell them they would only need it for a few hours.

The penalty for the change had been stiff, and Cabrillo wasn't sure if he was on the right track. Thanks to them being over the international date line, it was one o'clock yesterday afternoon in Washington, DC. He called Langston Overholt.

After explaining the situation, Cabrillo asked his old

mentor and the CIA's Spook Emeritus what he would recommend.

'This isn't actionable intelligence, Juan,' the octogenarian said. 'It's guesses and supposition. Which from you are usually enough to go to the Secretary of Defense, but on this, I'll need something more.'

'Like proof from Kenin's laptop?'

'That would only show that he had sold such a weapon to the People's Republic. Unless he also had their battle plans, I don't think we can do much of anything. Of course I will pass along a memo of interest and that might get a nonspecific threat warning to the carrier group's commanding admiral. But you must understand that if they do get sent in to intervene on this whole Senkaku/Diaoyu islands mess, they will already be at maximum alert status. Your crying "Bogeyman" won't change a thing.'

Cabrillo had expected as much. That was the problem with Washington. Bureaucratic inertia was measured at a glacial pace. The system wasn't designed for quick lateral thinking. The news was not all bad. Langston continued, 'I will talk with Grant down at the China desk to see what they've heard. We are aware that China is taking this much further than they have with other disputed islands, like their row over the Spratlys. Japan doesn't want to back down either, which is why we've dispatched the *John Stennis*.'

'I thought there is a carrier already based in Japan,' Juan said.

'The *George Washington*, yes. There was a fire aboard

her a week ago. A sailor was killed. They claim she's not fit for sea duty.'

There was an odd tone in Overholt's voice when he said this, and Cabrillo suspected he knew what caused it. Lang was a World War II veteran. They sent ships back into the fight just days after they took hits from kamikazes. Today, it would take months for safety inspectors and inquest panels and JAG attorneys to make the decision that the carrier was seaworthy.

'We are monitoring the situation,' Overholt said. 'Where are you going to be?'

'Trying to guard the entrance to the East China Sea.'

27

Cabrillo was sitting watch in the op centre when he got the call from Mark Murphy to meet in the *Oregon*'s boardroom. Juan checked the time on the main screen. His pet nerds had missed his deadline by only three hours.

They had already docked at Taipei's new port, nestling like an ugly duckling between two beautiful swans in the form of a couple of cruise ships disgorging passengers for a day of sightseeing in Taiwan's capital. The truck from the chandlers was already at the dock, and within an hour of their arrival, the crates of perishables and other food had been hoisted aboard.

Juan nodded to the navigator that she had the conn and made his way to the boardroom. Murph and Stoney looked like they hadn't slept since getting the computer back from Linc. Both men had red-rimmed eyes with bags sagging below them. But they also had knowing grins spreading from ear to ear.

'I take it there's good news?' Juan asked and took his seat at the head of the table.

'Oh yeah,' Mark said. 'We just finished cleaning out Kenin's last account. All told, he had fifty million in various banking centres all over the world – Caymans, Dubai, Luxembourg. You name it.'

'Well and good,' Juan said. 'What about there being another stealth ship? Did they build another one?'

'Sure did,' Eric Stone confirmed. 'China paid twenty million for it, plus picked up the tab for Kenin's luxury retreat in Shanghai.'

In most cases, Cabrillo delighted at being right about something. Not so today. The news sent a chill through to his heart because this meant China was likely emboldened enough to use this new weapon against an American target.

'They were built in 1989,' Stone added. 'Originally, the Russians wanted to build one for each of our carrier battle groups. But they abandoned the project after only two were constructed. They were in mothballs at a shipyard and appeared to be all but forgotten. Kenin discovered them two years ago and had them both refurbished, adding some improved technology discovered on Tesla's mine tender. He knew that the Chinese would be his only potential clients and courted them for months. They finally agreed to the deal at about the same time the disputed gas fields were first mentioned in the media.'

That timing seemed right to Cabrillo. The Chinese knew that if they stuck to their plan the US Navy would intervene. They needed something to counter an American flattop that wouldn't ignite World War III. In his opinion, he thought Kenin should have held out for more money. Then again, the Russian already had more money than he could spend in a lifetime, so why bother asking for something you'll never need?

'Are the technical specs on the computer?'

'Sorry, Chairman,' Eric said with an air of hangdog about him. 'We cracked every file on his laptop. He had a file describing the capabilities that he used to entice the Chinese, but nothing about how the weapon worked or what equipment he'd recovered off Tesla's ship.'

'We'll keep going over it, Chairman,' Mark replied, 'but it's not looking good. Kenin wasn't a nuts-and-bolts kind of guy. He didn't care how the ship functioned, only that it did function.'

'Okay,' Juan said. 'Thanks, you two. That was great work. Go hit the sack.'

Cabrillo pulled up a map of the China Sea on the big screen at the far end of the boardroom table and tried to place himself inside the mind of the man in command of the stealth ship. He needed to pre-position himself in front of the carrier battle group and let them come to him since his wake would be visible when the ship was in motion and would surely catch the eye of a pilot flying combat air patrol. It would all depend on the ability to track the unbound carrier group and project its course, a straightforward task because of the constellation of Chinese spy satellites.

Juan could get the battle group's course from Overholt, so he had the same information as his opponent. The real question was, then, how far out from the disputed islands would I want to take down my quarry? The farther away, the better. However, that decreases the odds of the ships remaining on the projected course. They zigged and zagged at random intervals even as they steamed in a steadily western direction.

He gamed a dozen scenarios and came up with a dozen places he'd lie in wait. It was fruitless yet telling at the same time. Fruitless because, after more than two hours of staring at the map, he was no closer to finding a solution, and telling because it showed how desperately important this was for the Chinese. If the carrier reached the region, any hope of taking the islands by force vanished.

The Chinese had been using the tactic of wearing down the Japanese fleet in hopes that they would abandon the area and thus their claim to the islands. As the world has witnessed with carriers rotating through the Persian Gulf for the best part of two decades, you just can't wear down the US Navy.

Captain Kenji Watanabe lined up the H-6 in his sights and ever so gently pressed the trigger on his joystick. Nothing happened. As he knew nothing would. He hadn't armed his F-16's weapons systems. He banked below the lumbering, twin-engine aerial-refuelling plane as it fed avgas to a J-10 fighter jet.

While the J-10 was a modern aircraft that looked like a cross between his own Fighting Falcon and the Swedish Gripen, the flying tanker was an old Soviet design from the 1950s. Like much of China's air fleet, it was a knockoff built under license and wouldn't last five minutes in a real fight. Even the J-10 was really no match for the F-16. It had limited range, hence the need for constant refuelling as the aircraft crisscrossed the skies around the Senkaku Islands, and the F-16 was far more manoeuverable.

Watanabe's real advantage was the fact he had probably ten times the cockpit time compared to the Chinese pilot.

He was seasoned enough to know to give the linked aircraft ample room to perform the tricky operation. The Chinese had only recently perfected air-to-air refuelling, so the pilots wouldn't have much experience. No sense causing an accident with his jet wash. Watanabe came around so he was behind the tandem planes. That way when the J-10 Vigorous Dragon detached from the flying gas station, he'd be on his six. The last Chinese fighter Kenji had done this to hadn't been able to shake him until he'd finally given up and broke for home base. The veteran pilot felt confident that this new Chinese wannabe ace wouldn't fare much better.

The swept wing H-6 suddenly dove as it hit clear air turbulence. The J-10 pilot should have backed off and broken connection with the tanker, but instead he tried to stay with the bigger plane and overcompensated. To Watanabe's horror, the two planes came together and then came apart in a mushrooming fireball that blossomed like a second sun. He threw his own aircraft down and to the left to avoid the devastation and still felt bits of shrapnel pepper the F-16's airframe. He couldn't tear his gaze from the awful sight. The wreckage of two destroyed planes finally emerged from the bottom of the explosion like discarded husks. No piece was much bigger than a sheet of plywood, and all of it was charred black.

There would be no parachutes.

Watanabe radioed in his report, hoping, praying that he hadn't been witness to the trigger event that would send his beloved Nippon to war.

Despite protestations of innocence from the highest level, including an invitation to inspect Kenji Watanabe's fighter jet to prove it hadn't shot down the two Chinese aircraft, Beijing couldn't be mollified. They insisted that this had been a deliberate act and demanded the Japanese withdraw all aircraft and ships from the Diaoyu Islands and cede their sovereignty at once.

China made preparations to send most of her fleet to sea, including troopships carrying over a thousand commandos to occupy the islands by force.

Diplomatic channels hummed with attempts to defuse the situation, but neither side was going to back down. Japan ramped up its own military presence on the islands by commandeering a hydrofoil fast ferry and rushing in troops. The American President had no choice but to order the USS *John C. Stennis* to the disputed territory. He also lit a fire under the Secretary of Defense's tail to see that the crippled *George Washington* was back in service ASAP no matter what the lawyers said.

Inside the week, unless America's calming presence could prevent it, the third Sino-Japanese war was about to erupt.

*

The *Oregon* patrolled the seaway leading to the islands like a restless bear in a cage. Back and forth she swept, radar set to maximum, her crew keyed up on caffeine and adrenaline. The weather was cooperative, allowing them to send up drone planes to enlarge their search area. Juan even convinced Langston Overholt to allow them access to satellite data, though, in truth, they didn't have the expertise it took to interpret the high-res pictures with any degree of accuracy. For that, everyone was relying on the experts at the National Reconnaissance Office, a group even more secretive than the NSA.

For his part, Cabrillo sat in the centre of the op centre, dressed in jeans and a long-sleeved T-shirt. He rode the gentle swells that rocked the ship with the ease of a cowboy on a long cattle drive, his body tuned to his environment so that the minor adjustments to posture came without conscious thought. The gimbled cup holder built into his chair was rarely empty, though Maurice secretly switched him to decaf after the third cup. The watch would rotate at regular intervals and yet the Chairman remained a fixture in the room, silently brooding while his eyes darted from display screen to display screen. He checked the radar repeater over the shoulder of the watch stander and the feed from the drones over the shoulder of the remote pilot. And far from being distracted, the crew took comfort in Cabrillo's steadying attention. As long as he was there, things would be all right.

He caught sleep when he could, usually when the

ship was at the far end of her patrol box and thus less likely to stumble on the stealth ship. He didn't bother with his bed but rather fell onto the sofa in his office and pulled up a woollen lap robe that had been rescued off the *Normandie* after she burned in New York Harbor in 1942. He would rouse himself after a couple of hours and use the ritual of shaving to convince his exhausted body he had received enough sleep. Then it was back to the op centre, where he would prowl tirelessly just as his ship did.

Cabrillo had just returned from a two-hour catnap when something on radar caught his eye. It was a blip. That was little surprise. Though war clouds gathered, these were busy shipping lanes and would remain so up until the shooting started. Hali Kasim was on watch as both communications officer and radar operator.

'Hali, that target to our north, what's the range?'

'Fifty miles, give or take.'

'How long has it been on our scope?'

Kasim typed into his keyboard for a minute. 'Looks like twenty minutes.'

Cabrillo did some calculating in his head, using the radar's range and the *Oregon*'s speed and heading. 'She's doing less than three knots. Does that strike you as odd?'

Hali agreed. He was still working on his computer. 'I've got one even odder. There was a target at this exact same location the last time we swept this grid.'

George Adams happened to be on duty, piloting the model airplane they used as an aerial surveillance platform. He said, 'Don't need to ask me even once. It'll take me a bit, though. I've got a bird already in the air, but she's fifty miles the other side of us.'

Juan kicked into overdrive. This wasn't the time to wait around. There was something off here, and Cabrillo needed answers. 'Tell you what, Gomez. Let that one ditch and send up another.'

'You sure?'

'I'll take the loss out of my share.'

Adams did as ordered, kamikazeing the one UAV and launching another off the deck. It still took the better part of thirty minutes for the four-foot plane to approach the target. Juan hadn't altered the *Oregon*'s search pattern, but he had slowed its speed so as to not break radar contact. Twenty miles out, Gomez dropped the drone from a comfortable altitude of five hundred feet to a wave-skimming twenty feet.

This was where his instincts and experience as a pilot paid off. They needed to remain below the target's radar coverage, lost in the acoustical backscatter of heaving waves. There was no finer pilot aboard than Adams, so no one on the mystery ship knew they were being stalked. The drone's camera showed the dark ocean seemingly inches below the little plane's landing gear, while ahead the setting sun was a pale blaze of yellow against the horizon.

'There!' Juan called when he spotted a boxy silhouette sitting on the line dividing sky from sea.

Adams, with his superior eyesight, had already seen it and had slightly altered the UAV's course to intercept.

It took just a few more minutes for expectation to turn into disappointment. This wasn't the stealth ship. This ship was nearly nine hundred feet long and shaped like a box. Only at her flared bows near the waterline was there any attempt at streamlining the vessel. Forward was a little pillbox of a bridge to break up the monotony of her flat upper deck, while aft her twin funnels were blunt fins clustered on her starboard aft quarter. There was a large, garage-style door amidships, and another on her flat transom. The whole vessel was painted a dull green.

Juan recognized the class of ship immediately. She was a car carrier, a floating, multilevel parking garage that could transport a month's worth of automobiles from a factory and ship them anywhere in the world. They were common in these waters, as both China and Japan were major car exporters. Why she was going so slowly was something of a mystery, but not today.

The feed suddenly cut out. Gomez cursed. Juan knew what had happened, and it wasn't the first time. The UAV had been flying so low that a rogue wave had plucked her out of the sky. Such were the accepted dangers of approaching at wave-top altitude.

'And that, my friends,' Adams said, 'is why we use unmanned planes and don't put my backside at risk in the chopper for routine recons.'

'Nothing routine about that.' Cabrillo was out of his chair and standing below the main view screen. 'Gomez, run the last few seconds of tape again.'

The chief pilot brought up the final twenty seconds

of drone footage. He saw nothing out of the ordinary, but Cabrillo made a gesture behind his back to play it a third time. Then a fourth. Finally, on the fifth viewing, just seconds before the wave smashed the UAV into the sea, Juan shouted, 'Stop!' He studied the screen shot. 'Advance slowly.' The picture turned choppy as it ran. 'Stop! What do you see?'

Adams saw the big car carrier at a ninety-degree angle as it was quickly filling the camera lens's angle. There was barely any wake at her stern and no frothing water at the bows, which meant she wasn't moving very quickly, but that was something they already knew. Again, he couldn't see what had so piqued the Chairman's interest. No one else on duty seemed to see anything either because the crew remained silent.

As if sensing the collective confusion, Juan said, 'Look about five feet up from her waterline. Does anyone else see a faint white line?' His question was greeted with a chorus of assents. 'Any thoughts on what it is?'

This question was greeted by silence. Finally, it was Gomez Adams who figured out what the Chairman had understood immediately. He leapt from his seat. 'I'll have the bird warmed up by the time you're ready.'

'People,' Juan said, 'that isn't a car hauler. It's a floating dry dock. That white band is a line of salt rime from the last time she was under ballast.' He keyed on the shipwide intercom. 'This is Cabrillo. Battle stations. Battle stations. We've found the at-sea base of operations for the Chinese stealth ship. Linc, Eddie and MacD to report to the chopper pad in full combat gear.

We're going in black.' He issued several other orders and then followed the pilot out of the op centre. Max was on his way to relieve his post in command of the ship.

Juan ran to his cabin, yelling for crewmen to make way as he hurried by. Any remnants of his deep exhaustion had fallen away. He switched prosthetics to what he termed his 'combat leg'. This was a veritable Swiss Army knife of weaponry. It had a built-in .44 caliber single-shot gun that fired out of his heel, and a place to secrete a Kel-Tec .380 pistol, a small amount of explosives, and a knife. Next, he drew on a black tactical uniform, made of a flame-resistant cloth, and black combat boots. He kept his personal weapons in an old safe that had once sat in a station of a long-defunct southwestern railroad. He spun the dials to open it, and ignored the stacks of currency and gold coins he kept in case of emergencies. They used to have a nice cache of diamonds, but the market had been right to convert those into cash.

The bottom of the safe was a virtual armory. He slipped into a combat vest and rammed a new FN Five-seveN into the holster. He clipped on a tear gas grenade as well as two flashbangs. His main weapon for this op was a Kriss Arms Super V. It was the most compact submachine gun ever built and resembled something out of science fiction, with its stubby foregrip and skeletal butt stock. Its revolutionary design allowed it to chamber the massive .45 caliber ACP round and gave the shooter unparallelled control over a notoriously difficult bullet to fire on automatic. Normally fed with a standard thirteen-round Glock magazine, Juan's was fitted with a thirty-round extender. He slipped spare magazines into the appropriate pockets.

Had this been an extended mission he would have carried weapons of the same caliber in case he needed more rounds for the Super V, but this was going to be a quick-and-dirty takedown, not a protracted gun battle. The combat harness was already fitted with a throwing knife, garrote wire, a med kit and a radio, so all he had left to take was a black ski mask and he was ready to go.

He threw open his cabin door and almost knocked Maurice to the deck. As it was, he had to steady the old Englishman to keep him from dropping his silver tray. 'You pad around as silent as a cat,' Cabrillo admonished.

'Sorry, Captain. I was just about to knock. I brought you some sustenance.'

Juan was about to tell him that he wasn't hungry, but suddenly he was famished. 'I don't have a whole lot of time.'

'Take it and go,' Maurice said, pulling the domed cover off the tray. Inside was a steaming burrito, the perfect food to walk and eat. 'Shredded beef and pork, and very, very mild.'

Juan grabbed the burrito and put the bottle of electrolyte-infused sports drink into the thigh pocket of his pants. He took off at a jog, calling over his shoulder before taking a monstrous bite, 'You're a good man, no matter what anyone says about you.'

'They actually say I'm a great man,' Maurice called back.

The *Oregon* had already slowed enough to launch the chopper. Gomez was at the controls when Juan strode out onto the aft deck and started for the aft-most hatch that was the ship's retractable helipad. The turbine's whine filled the air, so Juan didn't hear MacD Lawless run up behind him to tap him on the shoulder. Behind the cockpit, Cabrillo saw Eddie and Linc were already strapped in. Lawless threw him a big toothy grin. Around his neck hung a venerable Uzi, a gun little changed since it first appeared in 1950.

Juan nodded back.

MacD took the last rear seat while Cabrillo swung into the cockpit next to Gomez. The aircraft shook like an unbalanced washing machine as the rotors whipped faster and faster. The noise died somewhat when the two open doors were closed. Juan put on a set of earphones, Adams threw a thumbs-up to the deck worker to pull the restraining chalks that prevented the helicopter from sliding across the deck in rougher seas, and the MD 520N lurched into the sky.

That initial launch was the highest altitude they reached for the entire flight. Gomez kept them at wave-top height, though now he had peripheral vision to keep from being battered by a crossing wave like the one that took out the UAV. They were so low that the rotor kicked up spume that the windshield wipers could barely clear.

'How we looking, Max?' Cabrillo radioed.

'Looking good. There's not much traffic out here right now. I can't see anything within twenty miles of your target unless there's some small fisherman in her lee.'

'Okay.'

They flew hard for the sun as it continued to radiate over the skyline. True darkness in this part of the world was at least a half hour away. There was no need to talk about a plan. These men had fought and bled together enough to have an almost telepathic connection with one another. While MacD was the newest team member, he'd more than earned the trust of his teammates.

Gomez had swung them south so they would approach the ship from the rear, its blind spot. And with a shocking suddenness, the dot on the horizon blossomed into the ugly, truncated stern of the car carrier/dry dock, if Cabrillo's theory was correct. If not, they were about to perform an inadvertent act of piracy on the high seas.

The chopper stayed low until the last possible second. The ship's stern completely filled their field of vision. Juan studied the rear car ramp. It sure looked legitimate, and the white band he thought was salt was much less convincing in person. He felt a tickle of doubt.

It wasn't too late to abort the mission.

He pulled down his ski mask.

He stayed with his intuition and said nothing as Adams heaved the chopper over the boxy fantail, its skids clearing the rail by inches. He raced up the length of the ship and threw the helo into a hover just feet from the back of the antennae-studded pilothouse. The men opened their doors and jumped to the deck. No sooner were they clear than Gomez reversed course and quickly sank back over the rear of the ship, where he would await word for extraction.

Juan led the team over the railing that protected the path out to the ship's stubby flying bridges. He could see inside the bridge. There was a helmsman at a traditional ship's wheel. An officer and another crewman were heading out to investigate the thunder of the helicopter's rotors. All the men were Chinese. The officer finally noticed the armed men rushing toward the pilothouse and shouted to his companion. Cabrillo opened fire, deliberately shooting over the men's heads. The bridge door's glass inset disintegrated, and heavy slugs ricocheted off the ceiling and peppered the far wall.

MacD dove through the opening, shoulder-rolling up to his knees, and kept his weapon trained on the officer. Eddie came next. He covered the helmsman. Cabrillo was the third man, while Linc remained outside covering their rear.

The third crewman had bolted. Everyone was shouting – the ship's crew in fear and the Corporation team telling them to drop flat.

Juan went after the third man who had fled the bridge via an open stairwell at the back of the room. Cabrillo made it down a couple of steps before someone started firing up at him. At least one bullet hit his artificial leg with a kick like a mule. He quickly climbed back out of the shooter's line of sight and sent a flash-bang tumbling down to the next deck. He turned away and covered his ears, and still the effects were almost paralyzing.

This time, he put his hands on the shiny railings flanking the steps and slid submariner style down to the top deck. The gunman was fast. He was just vanishing through another door, his hands over his ears. Juan triggered off a couple of rounds but didn't think he'd hit anything. This told him that the sailor recognized a flashbang and knew how to abate its noise and intense light show. Another crewman was still there in what was the chart room/radio shack. He was seated behind an old marine transceiver, clutching at his head as the grenade continued to echo in his skull. Juan clipped him behind the ear with the Super V and the man's struggles ceased. He slid down to the floor. MacD would be mopping up after him, so he didn't waste time cuffing the man.

The shooter was headed someplace, and Cabrillo needed to find out where. But, so far, nothing made him certain he was right about this situation. Armed crewmen were rare but not unheard of. And maybe the guy watched a lot of action movies and recognized the grenade.

The exit led to a corridor lined with doors on one side. These would be cabins for the officers. One door flew open, the occupant no doubt alarmed by the noise. The guy was dressed in boxers, and he too had a weapon. Juan didn't give him the opportunity to use it.

He put a round in each of the Chinese officer's shoulders. It was enough to take him out of the fight but not enough to kill him. Cabrillo refused to use lethal force until he was positive.

He came to another staircase and used his last flashbang, rushing down even as the thunderbolt reverberated off the ship. He'd seen blood drips on the floor. He'd winged his man, and now the trail would lead him straight to his quarry.

At the bottom of the stairs was another grey metal passageway, with cables and pipes running along the ceiling. The blood looked black in the inadequate lighting, but it was enough to follow. Cabrillo went through the door to his right and stopped short, his mind reeling.

He was wrong. Way wrong.

Ranks upon ranks of sedans were lined up as tidily as cars in an airport's parking garage. They ran as far as the eye could see. All the colours of the rainbow were represented, and although they were dusty, they shone like jewels in the otherwise dank confines of the legitimate car carrier's hold. They had hijacked an innocent ship, and Juan had shot two simple sailors. The defeat and guilt were crushing.

He was reaching for his throat mic to tell the others that they had been mistaken when he recognized the decorative badge on all the cars' hoods. For an instant, he was back in Uzbekistan with old Yusuf, and they were looking at the car in which his brother had died when the ferry he was riding on sank. Like that rusted-out wreck, these cars had the distinctive Viking-ship-silhouette hood badge that Juan had looked up upon his return from the Aral Sea. These were Russian cars. Ladas. And all their tyres were flat. The meaning behind this discovery was immediate, and his respect for Russian war planners went up a couple of notches.

Cabrillo started running after the wounded sailor again.

In order for the Soviet stealth ships to be used in case of a war with the United States, they needed to stay close to the carrier battle groups at all times. The carriers were deployed all over the globe, and to shadow them without raising suspicion, the Russians disguised their support ships as car haulers, bolstering this camouflage by going so far as to load them with the iconic Russian car, the ubiquitous Lada. This was in case the ship was ever boarded by customs inspectors. The cars here were dusty and all the tyres flat because they'd been locked in the hold since the demise of the Soviet Union. Neither Kenin nor the Chinese had bothered to unload them.

The blood trail led Cabrillo down a spiralling car ramp. He slowed at the bottom to peer out onto this next cargo deck. More Ladas, more flat tyres, and so many years in the salt air had covered many of them with lesions of rust. A pistol shot pounded off a fitting next to his head, and a sliver of metal nicked him at the temple. Blood trickled down his jaw. He fired off the rest of his clip, blowing glass and bits of metal into the air, while the shooter crouched behind a Lada wagon. The onslaught was enough to make him break cover and run.

Cabrillo didn't want to kill the man. He wanted him to keep running and show him how to enter the secret parts of the ship, the ones, like on the *Oregon*, that customs men never saw. He changed magazines at a run, listening over the comm net to MacD and Eddie coordinate rounding up the rest of the crew.

The shooter descended one more level before making a beeline aft. Juan stayed on him like a scent hound, letting the man get far enough ahead that he didn't bother taking delaying shots at his pursuer. Finally, Juan saw him come to a door that looked as though it was in the ship's aft-most bulkhead. They should be directly over the propeller, and Juan should have been able to feel its vibrations through the soles of his boots. He quickly glanced toward the bow.

Cabrillo had an excellent sense of spatiality and knew immediately that the distant gloom of the forward part of the hold was considerably less than the nine-hundred-foot length of the ship. The closet was built into a false wall.

He looked back and could see over the man's shoulder that it was a storage closet. This was it. The *Oregon* had the exact same setup. Cabrillo ran, cutting the distance, dodging and weaving around cars, until he accidentally knocked a wing mirror off one of the rustier ones. The noise alerted the gunman. He had been fumbling with something on the closet's back wall. He whirled and raised his pistol.

Cabrillo already had the Super V tucked hard against his shoulder and cut him down with a quick pull of the trigger that unleashed a half dozen big .45 caliber slugs.

'Eddie, you there?' Juan said. Operational security demanded he not take his eyes off the body, but he knew the gunman was dead.

'Roger.'

'You guys secure?'

'Just the bridge and crew areas. Still haven't swept the engine room or cargo area.'

'Don't worry about that. Come aft on deck three. I think I hit the jackpot.'

Juan stalked toward the fallen man and confirmed he was dead. He let the Super V drop down on its single-point sling and dragged the corpse out of the way. He couldn't find the trigger mechanism that would give him access to the ship's secret area, so he rigged it with a block of plastic explosives.

'We're coming,' Eddie announced over the radio when he and MacD approached Cabrillo's location. No sense in getting killed by friendly fire.

'Any trouble?'

'Nothing a club over the head with the barrel of old Mr Uzi here couldn't fix,' MacD drawled. 'What's up? We swabbing the decks for them?'

'Watch and learn.' Cabrillo backed them away from the utility closet and keyed the electronic detonator. The blast was an assault on the senses, loud and concussive, and it carried, echoing up and down the rows of cars.

He had blown a hole through the back of the closet. Beyond was something out of a James Bond movie. The aft section of the ship, a good hundred and fifty feet in length, was a cavernous open space ringed with metal catwalks and staircases. Down below, water sloshed gently against a pair of piers that rose almost twenty feet. Thrusting out of the water between the docks was a cradle made of timbers that would secure the stealth ship, once it was in position, and the mother ship refloated to its proper trim.

To Juan's disappointment, the cradle was empty. The stealth ship was out there, hunting the *Stennis*.

Atop one of the piers was a small structure that had to be a control room. It had a big plate-glass window overlooking the floating dock. The three men took off running across the catwalk and down the stairs. The door to the control room didn't have a lock. MacD nodded to Juan, who opened it. As soon as it was ajar, Lawless tossed a flashbang, and Juan slammed the door to contain the blast.

The grenade went off with a roar that bowed the plate glass but didn't shatter it. Cabrillo threw open the door again. Two Chinese men, wearing mechanic's overalls, were staggering around, dazed and nearly half mad from the blast. Juan tackled one, MacD the other. No sooner were they down than Eddie had them cuffed.

Cabrillo studied his surroundings, finally taking a chair at what looked like the main controls. Everything mechanical was written in the Cyrillic alphabet, and then he noticed the room was painted that bland green the Soviets so loved. The computers were new additions. Mark Murphy had met up with the Chairman just before he'd stepped out on deck and handed over a standard-looking flash drive.

'Some of my best work,' he'd said with pride. 'Plug it in to a USB port and it does the rest. I call it the Dyson Oreck Hoover 1000, 'cause it'll vacuum up anything.'

Cabrillo slid the drive into position and, moments later, the dormant computer came to life. After that, there really wasn't much to see. Mark said a curser would appear on the otherwise blank screen and start to blink when his device had sucked all extractable information out of the system.

He wished they could use the ballast controls to scuttle the ship, but there would be mechanical fail-safes in place to prevent that. Better off just to set scuttling charges and be done with it. While he waited for the computer to do its thing, he split the rest of the C-4 he carried to Eddie and MacD to take care of that particular task.

'Linc, you copy?'

'Roger that.'

'Round up our prisoners and see to it they get to a lifeboat.'

'Gotcha.'

'Don't launch yet. I've got two more down here.'

'You find the stealth boat?'

'No, but this was definitely its base.' A curser started blinking, just as Mark had programmed. Juan plucked the drive from the USB slot and eyed it. 'And we might have been given a look under her skirts.'

Ten minutes later, the crew had been jettisoned from the ship in her encapsulated lifeboat. Eddie had found two more men down in engineering. One would go down with his ship, foolishly thinking he could kick a gun out of Seng's hands. The charges had been laid, and Gomez Adams had the chopper resting lightly on the deck. Though the craft weighed less than a ton, it had such a small footprint that it put tremendous pressure on whatever it landed on. Keeping the revs up prevented it from damaging the deck plate and potentially trapping itself.

The men climbed aboard the chopper, and Adams, wearing night-vision goggles, for it was now fully dark, lifted them away. They let Linc do the honours since his had been the most boring part of the operation. He thumbed the detonator.

The blasts were little more than bursts of bubbles from under the waterline, and it looked like something so puny would have no effect on the elephantine ship. But Eddie was a master at demolition, and MacD had been an eager student. Aiding them was the fact that Juan had firewalled the ship's big diesel engines. The forward momentum had water pumping through the strategic holes Seng and Lawless had punched through the hull. And as the speed increased, so too did the volume of water. This would keep going until the engines were swamped, but even then inertia would keep the water coming.

The car carrier would slip under the waves within the hour.

28

Under his flight suit, Slider had on a T-shirt with a picture of an F-18. Below was 'o to 60 in .7 seconds.' With the two turbofans shrieking behind him at max power, he threw a salute to the catapult officer and felt that acceleration for himself. *Johnny Reb*'s number two cat launched him and his F/A-18 Super Hornet down the runway and out over the bow. The sleek fighter jet was pushing 165 miles per hour when the deck vanished beneath it, and its swept wings generated enough lift to sustain flight.

Captain Mike Davis (USMC), call sign Slider, gave a little whoop as he was catapulted off the carrier and the plane was transformed from a helpless little bird that needed coddling by the deck crew to a deadly raptor that dominated the skies. He raised the plane's nose and roared into the dawn. In minutes he was at twenty thousand feet and fifty miles out from the *Stennis*. He and his wingman, who would launch just after him, were flying combat air patrol over the whole battle group.

Because they'd really poured on the atoms getting to the East China Sea, the group had been forced to leave behind its slower resupply ship, but the cruisers, destroyers and frigate were all on-station covering *Johnny Reb* from attack on all fronts. Below the surface lurked a pair of Los Angeles-class subs that had had no problems keeping up with the carrier's frenetic pace. The group was still three hundred miles from the Senkaku Islands, so Slider wasn't expecting much of anything to happen on his patrol. Closer in, he hoped things got a little more interesting.

For now, his radar scope was empty of aircraft not flashing the allies' IFF beacons. He knew that one of the planes up there with him was the E-2D Hawkeye AWACS, with its big radar dome on its back like the shell of a turtle. It gave those flying CAP a massive advantage in range over any other aircraft in the theatre. He'd see an approaching Chinese fighter not long after it left the mainland.

'Stinger Eleven, over.' It was a call from operations. On this sortie he was Stinger 11 and his wingman Stinger 12.

'Eleven, over.'

'Eleven, be advised we have a delay on Twelve, over.'

'Roger that.'

A problem with the catapult most likely was causing the delay. They would need to either fix it quick or hook Stinger 12 onto another cat. Either way, Slider didn't mind having the skies all to himself.

Though he had at his fingertips electronics that allowed him to see the virtual world for more than a hundred miles, Slider kept his head on a swivel, always looking around, scanning the instruments, looking at each section of sky, making sure someone wasn't hiding in the sun or behind him in a blind spot. He knew the Chinese were developing stealth technology, and if this turned out to be the Big Show – and the intel weenies said it might just be – then the People's Air Force would deploy their best toys. He searched for an aircraft his sensors might miss with unwavering vigilance.

Damn, he thought, I love my job.

And then he didn't.

Without warning, the F-18 yawed hard to starboard and dove for the earth. He'd been cruising at six hundred knots, well below the plane's maximum speed of Mach 1.8. The Super Hornet shattered the sound barrier even before Slider responded to the yaw. No matter what he did to the stick, the plane remained in a nose-down position, and chopping the throttles had no effect on his speed.

G-forces built, and his pressure suit constricted his legs and abdomen in an attempt to keep blood from pooling in his lower extremities. Still, his vision greyed. A godawful shriek filled his head. The altimeter unwound in a blur.

'Mayday, mayday. Stinger Eleven,' he gasped over the radio.

He couldn't wait for a response from the *Stennis*. He had to punch out now.

Slider pulled the handle for his ejection seat, and though the system had been hardened against EMP, the amount of magnetism slamming the airframe was simply too much for the hardware/software interface of the seat's sequencer. Not that it would have mattered. The shock of ejecting out of an aircraft hurtling toward the ground at twelve hundred knots would have killed Slider instantly.

He shouted as the ocean filled his field of vision. The plane shuddered. The engines were throttled back to zero, and still the F-18 raced earthward, accelerating all the way. The forces acting on the plane went beyond its design parameters, and chunks of its aluminum skin began to tear away. It started spiralling, shedding more of itself. A whole wing ripped free.

Slider mercifully lost consciousness.

The Super Hornet arrowed into the cool waters of the East China Sea with a surprisingly small splash, like a well-executed dive off the high board. The remaining wing and tail fins came off with impact while the stream-lined fuselage plummeted a hundred feet mere seconds after impact on momentum alone.

All this had been recorded by the *Stennis*'s circling AWACS plane. They had seen the fighter's dramatic flip and quick plunge to the ocean. The controller had tried calling the stricken plane but received no response. The crash was strange on many levels. Normally, if something catastrophic happened to an aircraft, it slowed, and yet Stinger 11 had sped up. It made no sense.

What would have made less sense was if there had been an actual eyewitness to the crash. Because they wouldn't have seen a thing. One second, a high-performance plane was flying high overhead and, the next, it had vanished as if it had never been there at all. Its snowy white contrail of water vapour streaked across the sky in a straight line, then ended abruptly, as though it had been erased by the hand of God.

The USS *John C. Stennis* was some sixty miles away from the spot the F-18 went down, and steaming hard.

'What just happened?' Max stood behind Cabrillo in the op centre. Eric was at the helm, Murph at the weapons station, and Hali and Linda manned communications and the sensor suite. They had all watched the jet crash on radar.

'They screwed up,' Juan replied, a fighter's gleam in his eye.

'The Chinese's stealth ship.'

'It looks like the plane experienced the same magnetic pull we felt when we took out Kenin's first stealth ship. The Chinese are too far out from the *Stennis*, and this crash means the area will be crawling with rescue choppers and one of the battle group's ancillary ships.'

'Meaning, he's going to have to bug out.'

'Stoney, why aren't we headed to the crash?' Cabrillo asked his helmsman.

The incident occurred well within the search box the Chairman had deduced. The only problem was, they had been caught out while patrolling the far edge, nearly fifty miles from where the plane went down.

'On it,' Stone said, and the ship came about and the cryopumps began to scream.

Juan now had to second-guess the captain of the Chinese stealth ship once again, and he was beginning to regret an earlier decision. He hadn't passed the data stick of information from the car carrier to Eric and Mark because he knew the two of them would have spent the night poring over it and he needed them fresh. Now he realized he needed to know a lot more about his adversary's capabilities.

He called down to the butler's pantry off the galley, 'Maurice, it's Cabrillo. I need you to do me a favour.'

The Englishman replied, 'I assure you, Captain, that anything I do for you is surely not a favour. You pay me handsomely for my services.'

'Fair enough,' Juan replied. 'In the middle drawer of my desk is a thumb drive. Could you please plug it into my computer?'

Eric and Mark both looked at him like a couple of dogs eyeing a T-bone. They had not been happy with Cabrillo's earlier decision and now they couldn't wait to get a look at what they'd got.

A minute later, the information had been fed into the mainframe, translated into English, and the two of them were glued to a pair of tablet computers.

Juan still had to make a call about where the stealth ship would reposition itself for another run on the carrier.

Linda broke his silent musings. 'Looks like a rescue chopper just launched off the *Stennis*. And one of the screening destroyers is breaking formation to investigate.'

Cabrillo also knew that the US Navy wasn't going to like the *Oregon*'s presence here. In fact, he fully expected to be told to leave, especially now they had lost one of their fighters. The old tramp steamer was the one wild card the Chinese captain didn't know was in the deck. He would have studied American naval tactics and doctrine and could anticipate responses to just about any scenario. But he didn't know the Corporation was gunning for him. Juan had to find a way to exploit that advantage.

'You're right about him screwing up,' Eric said, looking up from his tablet. 'When the magnetic field is activated, they lose their radar. With the jet flying in the clouds, they never knew it was inbound.'

'How big of a field can they put up?' Cabrillo asked. 'What's its range?'

'I'm reading that section,' Murph said. 'I need a little more time. There is some seriously funky math going on here.'

He tilted his tablet so Eric could get a look, and soon they were whispering about gauss levels, angles of incidence and terawattage. It was Greek to the rest of the crew.

Given the weather and lousy visibility, the Chinese stealth ship would only need to move a couple of miles away from the crash site to hide. It wouldn't need its magnetic screen at all, not until it made another attempt on the *Stennis*. Juan wondered if they wouldn't want to give themselves a bigger cushion. An Arleigh Burke-class destroyer had some of the most powerful radar systems deployed on any ship in the world. How much did the Chinese trust their vessel's stealth capabilities?

Were a couple of miles enough or would they back farther away?

If he were the Chinese captain, he'd give himself plenty of sea room and wait for another opportunity. They were still almost three hundred miles from the islands and at least two hundred from where the carrier battle group would position itself.

Cabrillo made up his mind. 'Mr Stone, take us another two points port, if you please.'

'Think he's bugging out?' Max asked, his unlit pipe between his teeth.

'Out, no. Off a little, yes. He's going to zig northeast and then zag southeast to get back into interception position.'

They were eavesdropping in on the Navy's rescue attempt. A Seahawk helicopter was over the area where the Super Hornet had augured into the sea twenty minutes after the event, but then the *Oregon* received a direct call.

'Attention to the ship at —' the female voice rattled off the *Oregon*'s exact longitude and latitude down to the second — 'you are about to enter a restricted military zone. Please be advised to alter your course.'

Before Juan could reply, Linda informed him that one of the patrolling jets had broken off its CAP and was headed their way.

'How long till he's here?'

'About three minutes. The honchos gave him permission to light the fires. His airspeed's close to a thousand knots.'

The inbound Hornet would need to drop out of the clouds for a visual and that meant he'd have to slow down also. That bought another couple of minutes. The *Oregon* was travelling at a hair over forty knots. That, in and of itself, was unusual. But that kind of speed from a broken-down rust bucket like her would raise even more hackles. He could bluff his way with the destroyer, since they were only looking at a radar return. Once the jet had eyes on them, the cat was out of the bag. Juan needed to slow, but he needed the speed in order to catch the stealth ship.

'It's variable,' Mark Murphy said.

'What?' Juan asked him irritably. He didn't need the distraction.

'The magnetic field. It's variable up to fifteen miles, but, at that range, the ship is still invisible – well, mostly – but the sheering forces we experienced after rescuing Linda are negligible.'

'Is the ship armed at all?'

'Not as far as I can tell, but there's a mountain of info here, and we're just scratching at the foothills.'

Cabrillo didn't think it would be armed. The magnetic field was the weapon and to work effectively it needed to get in close.

'"Foothills of data"?' Max scoffed. 'Wordsmith, you are not.'

Cabrillo was about to answer the radio hail when the woman's voice filled the op centre for a second time. 'Unidentified vessel, this is the USS *Ross*. We are a guided missile destroyer and you are entering a restricted military area. Turn back at once or we will take steps to compel you to leave this region. Do you copy?'

Juan knew this was mostly bluff. They were still a good distance from the carrier, although the *Ross* might be protecting the crash site as well as the *Stennis*. Either way, they were still a long way from resorting to any kind of violent confrontation.

'Chairman,' Linda cried, 'they just launched two more planes and they're vectoring on our position.'

The Navy was reacting a lot more aggressively than he'd anticipated. No doubt those two planes would be armed with antiship missiles, probably Harpoons. He keyed his mic. 'USS *Ross*, this is Captain Juan Rodriguez Cabrillo of the *Oregon*. Please repeat.'

Cabrillo didn't know how to handle this. He doubted he could talk his way into letting them pass, but he didn't think telling the truth would get him much either.

'You are about to enter a restricted military exclusion zone. You must turn at least ninety degrees from your current heading.'

'That F-18 is going to be here in about thirty seconds,' Linda informed him.

They still had miles to go before reaching where he thought the stealth ship would be hiding. It suddenly occurred to him that the ship had cloaked itself prematurely because its crew knew an American spy satellite was passing overhead. The new generation had no problem peering down from the heavens through cloud cover as dense as what they had hovering over them now. So the Chinese knew they would be spotted and had to cloak to avoid detection.

'Radar lock!' Mark Murphy called out.

'The *Ross*?'

'No. The first inbound fighter.'

Juan cursed. He'd been relying on the American reluctance to shoot first and ask questions later. Having the F-18 lock on weapons was no bluff, since a civilian ship wouldn't be able to detect it. They either thought the *Oregon* was a Chinese warship or they didn't care if they sank a civilian.

The mast camera zoomed in on a speck dropping out of the swollen sky that grew into the sleek fighter. She was just below the speed of sound, so her roar enveloped the ship a few seconds before the jet streaked over low enough that even down in the op centre they could feel it.

'This is Viper Seven.' The *Oregon*'s onboard computer decrypted the transmissions so quickly, it was almost like listening to the pilot in real time. 'It's not a warship but some old rust-bucket freighter.'

'Our radar shows it doing forty knots,' the flight controller countered.

'It's not lying,' the pilot called back. 'She's showing a huge wake and has one hell of a bone in her teeth.'

'*Oregon*, this is the USS *Ross*. Come about immediately. This is your final warning.'

'Linda, how far out are those other jets?'

'Five minutes.'

'Viper Seven,' said the air controller. 'You are

weapons free. Put a burst over her bows. That'll show these idiots we're serious.'

'Wepps,' Juan called to Mark Murphy, 'stand down.'

'Roger that.'

He knew Murph wouldn't respond to the upcoming strafe, but he couldn't help but give the order anyway.

The F-18 had already executed a tight turn and was on her way back when the order to fire came in. The pilot altered his course slightly so the plane would pass just ahead of the ship rather than over her bridge. At a half mile out, he toggled the six-barrel 20mm cannon in the Hornet's nose and unleashed a string of slugs that came so close to the old freighter's prow that the last two singed paint. He hit afterburners and screamed past in an angry display of military might.

They couldn't afford to play chicken any longer. 'USS *Ross*, this is the *Oregon*. Please do not fire again.' Juan went for broke. 'Listen to me very carefully. There is a Chinese stealth warship in these waters. It used a modified EMP weapon to take down your plane.' He wasn't going to try to explain it was invisible.

'Our aircraft are hardened against EMP weapons,' the woman aboard the destroyer responded. 'We will consider it a provocation if you continue on this course. Come about now or we will disable your ship.'

Cabrillo grew desperate. '*Ross*, I beg you. Do not fire. You have a real enemy out here who is trying to sink the *Stennis*.'

The woman – Juan guessed she wasn't the captain

but probably the *Ross*'s XO – came back, wariness in her voice. 'What do you know about the *Stennis*?'

'I know that she's about to be targeted by the same weapon that downed your jet.'

'I will give you one last fair warning to turn your ship about or the next time we fire it won't be for effect.'

Resigned to his fate, Cabrillo replied, 'As Pat Benatar so famously sang, "Hit me with your best shot."'

'I get it now,' Hali said.

'Why is the Navy being so aggressive? Would have been nice if Overholt had called to let us know,' Max said dourly.

'Damn.' Juan fished his cell from his back pocket and speed-dialled Overholt. With a little luck, he could get the Navy to back off this confrontation. The F-18 finished its turn and poured on the speed. She was coming hard, charging like a monster, but Juan knew this was a feint since the carrier hadn't given the order to open fire.

The phone rang a fourth time and went to voice mail. Overholt was like a teenage girl when it came to his cell. He was never without it and rarely in a place where he couldn't access a signal. Odd that he hadn't picked up.

'Lang, it's Juan,' Cabrillo said after the beep. 'I need you to call me ASAP. The Navy wants to turn the *Oregon* into Swiss cheese.'

The Super Hornet flew over the *Oregon* from stern to stem, flying low enough that the noise and vibration and the brutality of her jet exhaust shattered all the bridge windows in a cascade of shards that would have injured anyone who'd been up there.

'This is Viper Seven. I just blew out their bridge windows with my exhaust. That'll turn 'em.'

'Roger that, Viper Seven, but get into position for a real strafing run if this suicidal fool doesn't turn. Guns only.'

'Turning now. And I'm carrying air-to-air, not air-to-surface, so my missiles wouldn't do squat against a ship this big.'

Juan studied the radar plot showing up on the main screen. The two additional fighters off the *Stennis* were loitering about twenty miles away, but their missiles could cover that distance in seconds.

'Captain Cabrillo of the *Oregon*, this is Commander Michelle O'Connell of the USS *Ross*. Will you turn about now?'

Juan didn't respond. Let them think they'd killed everyone on the bridge. It would take the crew a few minutes to organize a new watch. That would buy more time.

'*Ross* to *Oregon*, do you read me?' O'Connell asked. There was a hint of concern in her voice. 'Is there anyone there? This is the USS *Ross* calling the freighter *Oregon*.'

Juan let her stew.

Over the military net, he listened in while O'Connell discussed options with the battle group's CO, Admiral Roy Giddings. In the end, the F-18 was ordered back around for a reconnoitre to see if there was anyone on the bridge. So the plane closed in, now flying at just above stall speed.

'Negative,' Viper 7 radioed. 'I didn't see anyone up there.'

'They've come close enough,' Giddings said. 'Viper Seven, strafe them at the waterline. *Ross* stand by to pick up the crew when they man the lifeboats.'

'Roger that.'

The fighter came down on them like an eagle, and as soon as it was in range, the 20mm erupted. The hardened shells hit the ship just above and at the waterline near the bow so that water frothed like she had been hit by a torpedo. None penetrated. The *Oregon*'s armour plate deflected all of the rounds. Had she been any other ship, this would have been a crippling attack, and at the speed she was running she'd be down by the head in minutes.

The old girl plowed on as if nothing had happened.

'Viper Seven, report,' Giddings asked a few moments later while the plane circled like a wolf around a wounded deer.

'Nothing,' Viper 7 finally said in dismay. 'Nothing's happened. I hit her good but she's not sinking.'

'Alert One,' Giddings called out. This would be the lead plane of the two additional Hornets they'd put up. 'You are go for Harpoon launch.'

Because of the time it took the *Oregon*'s supercomputer to decode the military encryption, the plane had already nosed around, and the ship-killing missile was off its rails.

'Wepps!' Taking a few rounds of 20mm was one thing. Nearly a quarter ton of high explosives was an entirely different challenge.

'On it.'

The Harpoon missile dropped down to surface-skimming mode as quickly as it could and accelerated up to five hundred miles per hour. Its radar immediately locked on to the one juicy target it saw and flew at it with robotic efficiency.

Mark Murphy dropped the doors hiding the *Oregon*'s primary defensive weapon and had the six-barrelled Gatling, a clone of the one carried by their attacker, spun up to optimal speed. Its own radar was housed in a dome above the gun that gave it the nickname of R2-FU because it looked like the cute droid from the *Star Wars* movies but had a nasty attitude.

When the inbound Harpoon was still a mile away, the Gatling opened up, throwing out a barrier of tungsten that the missile would have to fly through to reach the target. It was the old problem of hitting a bullet with another bullet, but, in this case, the Gatling had unleashed more than a thousand, all aimed directly at the missile.

The Harpoon exploded well away from the ship, and Murph silenced the gun. Pieces of missile plowed into the ocean while its fireball bloomed and distorted as it lost the force of the Harpoon's powerful rocket motor.

In the op centre, they watched the battle unfold via a camera mounted near the gun emplacement. The resolution hadn't been good enough to actually see the incoming missile, but they all cheered when the orange-and-yellow explosion suddenly appeared.

'Juan!'

'What?'

It was Linda. She was pointing to the bottom corner of the massive screen, the mast camera that had been slaved to tracking the first F-18. 'It just vanished.'

'What?'

'The plane. I was watching it and it just vanished like it faded out of existence. I just checked radar, and it's gone.'

Cabrillo's jaw tightened. 'Helm, plot a course of thirty-seven degrees. All ahead flank. Wepps, ready the main gun.'

'This is Alert One,' the pilot of the lead inbound flight reported. 'They have something like the Sea Wiz, the Gatling guns our Navy uses. They shot down my missile.' This had been reported by the pilot moments ago. 'And I no longer have Viper Seven on my scope.'

'Copy that, Alert One. Fire all. Again, fire all. You and Alert Two.' This time, it was Commander O'Connell aboard the *Ross* giving the order, and there was no countermand from the admiral aboard his flagship. 'I knew this guy was a black hat.'

Cabrillo felt the blood drain from his face. There was nothing they could do. Nailing one of the Harpoons with the Gatling was what the system had been designed to do. There would be seven missiles inbound. If they were lucky, they could take out four of them. Damn lucky at that, but three would still make it through, penetrate deep into the ship, and explode with enough force to peel her hull apart like an overripe banana. They had mere minutes.

But still they drove on, water blowing through the *Oregon*'s drive tubes with unimaginable force, the prow cleaving the sea, shouldering aside two symmetrical curls of white water.

'Chairman, I don't have a target,' Mark said.

'You will in just a minute.' Juan studied the display, noting the exact position Linda had seen Viper 7 disappear.

'You do realize we're between the proverbial rock and hard place,' Max said.

'It's going to get worse. I intend on hitting the rock.'

'We didn't fare so well last time,' Hanley reminded him.

Cabrillo keyed on the shipwide intercom. 'Crew, this is the Chairman. Prepare for impact.' He then looked over at his oldest friend. 'Last time, we grazed the field. That's its deadly power. At an angle, it will capsize a ship with no problem, but if we hit it head-on, we should slice right through it. Isn't that right, guys?'

Mark and Eric exchanged a few words before Stone deferred to Murph to answer. 'In theory, that's a good idea, but we're still going to feel the sheering effects. It won't capsize us, but it could drive the bows so deep that the ship sinks, driven under as if pushed.'

'See,' Juan said with an optimistic uptick to his voice.

The sound of canvas ripping on an industrial scale reverberated throughout the *Oregon* as the Gatling engaged one of the incoming Harpoons. No one was paying the slightest attention. Everyone watched the forward camera. They were getting nearer and nearer the invisible field.

Juan double-checked their position, calculating angles and drift, wind, and a few other factors. 'Helm, another point to starboard.'

The ship was just beginning to respond when the entire hull lurched as though the sea had been sucked out from under the bow. It was the sensation of going over a waterfall. They had reached the dome of opto-electronic camouflage hiding the Chinese warship, and as the *Oregon* passed through, the magnetic forces attacked the hull with varying degrees of intensity. The stern felt nothing, while the bow was being enveloped with unimaginable force.

Then the noise hit, a transonic thrum that drove deep into the skull. Juan slammed his palms over his ears, but it did little good. The sound was already in his head, it seemed, and it echoed off the bones, trying to scramble his brain. Above this came the high-pitch scream of tortured metal. It sounded as though the keel itself was bending. The angle grew steeper still. Max clung to the back of Juan's seat to keep from being thrown to the deck. Loose articles began to roll toward the forward bulkhead. The lights flickered and a few of the computer screens went dead, their circuitry not sufficiently hardened against the magnetic waves and other forces that came and warped light around the stealth ship to make it invisible.

The main view screen exploded without warning because the metal wall behind it flexed past the glass's tolerance. Mark and Eric were peppered with shards, but both had been bent over so the cuts were limited to a few on the nape of their necks.

The *Oregon* was pitched so far forward that her drive tubes came free from the ocean, and two great columns of water were shot into the air like massive fire hoses blasting with everything they had. Another couple of degrees more and the *Oregon* would be driven under with no hope of ever recovering. Juan had gambled and lost. His beloved ship was no match for the forces she had been asked to overcome. She'd given it everything she could, but it was just too much.

The motion was so sudden that Max almost hit the ceiling. The ship had bulled its way through the invisible edge of the dome of optomagnetic camouflage and popped back up onto an even keel with the frenetic energy of a bath toy. The sound that had so tortured them passed as though it had never struck. The *Oregon* lurched when the force of her motors was once again fighting the resistance of the seas.

Unbeknownst to the crew, the six remaining Harpoon missiles struck the barrier seconds later and all six experienced catastrophic failure due to electromagnetic pulse overload. They fell harmlessly into the ocean in her wake.

'Everyone okay?' Juan called out.

'What a ride!' Murph whooped.

When it was clear the op centre crew was okay and

Max was starting to evaluate the rest of their people, Cabrillo scanned external camera feeds on his chair's built-in miniscreen. Unlike their first encounter with the barrier, this time much of the ship had been hardened against EMP. There would surely be damage, but the engines hadn't died and the main power buses hadn't tripped. Just as he suspected, not a mile away sat the oddly shaped stealth ship. He could only wonder what its captain was thinking at this moment.

'Wepps, you seeing what I'm seeing?'

'Yes, sir,' Murph said wolfishly. 'Permission to fire?'

'Fire at will. And don't stop until there's nothing left to hit.'

The big 120 in the bow belched fire, and, a moment later, the solid shot hit dead centre. Another followed even before the smoke cleared. A third a few seconds later. It was that round that hit some critical piece of equipment – something discovered by Tesla and tinkered with for over a century, something that teetered on the edge of physics – because when it was struck, what was left of the stealth ship vaporized in a dazzling corona of blue fire and blinding flashes of elemental electricity. It happened too fast for the mind to grasp, and, even later, when watched on tape played at its slowest possible speed, the very act of destruction was nearly instantaneous. All that remained behind were tiny bits of the composite hull and a slick of diesel fuel.

The overhead speakers played the voices of a very confused group of sailors and airmen who had just watched a ship nearly twice the length of a football field suddenly blink out of existence only to reappear a few seconds later, not to mention the six missiles they had fired vanishing too.

'Commander O'Connell, this is Juan Cabrillo of the *Oregon*. We are standing down and awaiting further instructions.'

'Please explain what just happened.'

'Think cloaking device. I told you there was a Chinese warship lurking out here. Give me an e-mail address and I'll prove it.'

Mark took his cue and prepared a digital file of their one-sided gunfight with the stealth ship. The commander gave an address.

A few minutes later, O'Connell came back. 'Who are you people and how did you know it was out here?'

Juan's cell rang. It was Overholt. 'One second, please, Commander.' He took the call. 'Lang, I'm going to need your help convincing an Admiral Giddings that he and his people never saw a thing and have never heard of the *Oregon*.'

'Did you get them?'

'Yes, but the cat's out of the bag about our secret identity. We also have the specs on how the stealth system operates.' He could picture Overholt rubbing his hands together with delight. Those plans were going to buy a lot of clout in Washington.

'Whatever you need, my boy. Whatever you need.'

'You're a pip.' He killed the call and addressed the commander once again. 'In a little while, Admiral Giddings is going to radio you and tell you that this incident never occurred and that you have no knowledge of a ship called *Oregon*.'

'So the CIA has their own navy now?'

'If that is what you choose to believe, that's fine with me. Besides, you have a war to avert, so I'd put us out of your mind and carry on with your job.'

'Captain Cabrillo, I want –' Her transmission cut off suddenly. When she came back, her voice had a little bit of awe in it. Langston had outdone himself in record time. 'Have a nice day, Captain.'

'You too, Commander, and good luck.'

29

Two days later, the *Oregon* was tied up to one of the long concrete piers at Naha City on the island of Okinawa. They were on the civilian side of the port, not the military. Max had secured a berth for two weeks and called in a few markers from past crew members, having them return to guard the ship while the crew took its much needed break.

As expected, the presence in the region of the big carrier task force had calmed tensions. They were talking already about jointly exploiting the new gas fields.

Old Teddy Roosevelt had it right, Cabrillo thought as he worked at his desk: walk softly but carry a big stick, and sticks don't come much bigger than a nuclear aircraft carrier.

He was making out electronic money transfers and feeling good about it. Most of the crew were on their way to wherever they wanted to go. It was amazing how many were sticking together in groups of threes and fours. They worked and lived with one another every day and yet, given the choice of a little alone time, they hung around together even more. Then again, they were more than coworkers or crewmates. They were family.

Juan wanted to include notes with the money but

knew anonymity would be best. He was giving instructions to one of the banks they used in the Caymans to make donations from a dummy front company. Five million was going to Mina Petrovski. It would not compensate for losing her husband, but it would make raising her two beautiful girls a little easier. He didn't know if his guide, the old fisherman, had left behind any family, so he made a donation to a fund that supported pensioners left penniless by the destruction of the Aral Sea. MIT received a five-million-dollar gift to endow the Wesley Tennyson Chair of Applied Physics. He figured the dusty old professor would like that.

Juan would never forget any of them. Men dead, one woman widowed, and all so other men could kill more efficiently. It was a sad commentary.

'Knock, knock,' Max said from the open doorway.

'I thought you were already gone.'

'Cab will be here in twenty minutes. Have you figured out where you're going?'

'Lady's choice.'

'Lady?'

'I had Lang pull one more string for me. She was due to rotate off in a week, so I pulled in one last chit, and Commander O'Connell will be here tomorrow afternoon.'

Max was surprised. 'You don't even know what she looks like.'

Cabrillo smiled. 'Does it really matter?'

'No. I guess not.'

'Besides, she doesn't know what I look like either.

I had Mark do a quick background check on the commander, and I know she's not married and her first name's Michelle.'

'Mazel tov.'

'Before you go, would you like to know what Perlmutter e-mailed me tonight?'

'He was still looking into how the *Lady Marguerite* ended up in a landlocked sea?'

'Give that man a mystery and he's like one of the Hardy Boys.'

Max scratched at his chin. 'I have a feeling our two science-fiction buffs are going to be disappointed.'

'Give the man a cigar. The men Tesla hired to man her the night of the test were a bunch of thugs. They stole the boat lock, stock and barrel right after the test. It next appeared in Havana and was called *Wanderer* and was owned by a sugar plantation owner. He lost it in a poker game to a Brazilian cardsharp, who sold it to a Moroccan merchant. Anyway, on and on, it changes hands until it ends up in Sevastopol, on the Black Sea, in 1912. There the ship was broken down and transported, first by sea and then overland, to the Caspian and then on to the Aral. The guy behind it was a Turk named Gamal Farouk. His idea was to use the boat as a lure to get investors to buy into a scheme he had to raise fish in the lake. Aquaculture, we call it today. Back then, it was an idea ahead of its time, and St Julian thinks the whole thing was a scam.'

'He thinks this Farouk character spent that kind of money to get the boat all for a get-rich-quick con game?'

'You ever see the dredge barges they hauled into the Klondike during the Gold Rush? Those things were ten times as heavy as the *Marguerite*, and I bet the syndicates who footed the bill all ended up losing their shirts. As Barnum said, "There's a sucker born every minute."'

'How did they put it all together when it arrived at the lake? That's the stumbling block that almost had me believing Tesla had invented teleportation.'

'Clever and simple. Farouk used dynamite to dam up a stream. The boat was assembled in the streambed and refloated when the dam was removed.'

As an engineer, Max nodded in appreciation of such an ingenious solution to the problem. 'So what happened to our Turkish swindler?'

'The day they launched the boat, Farouk and two wealthy tribesman he wanted as investors went out and never came back. The boat sank and was only discovered again after the lake vanished. The men who reassembled the *Marguerite* were probably camel drivers and farmers. When they finished, she was as seaworthy as a concrete block.'

'I think I prefer Mark and Eric's explanation, but your story does have its charms,' Max said. He checked his watch. 'Ah, but what about their tale of the three Frenchmen found in Alaska?'

'Three possibilities,' Juan replied without hesitation. 'One, it's just an urban myth and there's nothing to it. Two, they were French, so it could have been the result of a practical joke gone bad.'

'Okay, and number three?'

'They were screwing around with a force Tesla discovered tangential to his work on bending light around an object, a force he could not tame, and he rightly left it alone.'

'Which one do you think it is?'

'One, but I think two would have been pretty funny, and three scares me because only God knows what other Tesla projects are kicking around out there. This one nearly caused a war. Next time, we might not get so lucky.'

He just wanted a decent book to read ...

Not too much to ask, is it? It was in 1935 when Allen Lane, Managing Director of Bodley Head Publishers, stood on a platform at Exeter railway station looking for something good to read on his journey back to London. His choice was limited to popular magazines and poor-quality paperbacks – the same choice faced every day by the vast majority of readers, few of whom could afford hardbacks. Lane's disappointment and subsequent anger at the range of books generally available led him to found a company – and change the world.

'We believed in the existence in this country of a vast reading public for intelligent books at a low price, and staked everything on it'
Sir Allen Lane, 1902–1970, founder of Penguin Books

The quality paperback had arrived – and not just in bookshops. Lane was adamant that his Penguins should appear in chain stores and tobacconists, and should cost no more than a packet of cigarettes.

Reading habits (and cigarette prices) have changed since 1935, but Penguin still believes in publishing the best books for everybody to enjoy. We still believe that good design costs no more than bad design, and we still believe that quality books published passionately and responsibly make the world a better place.

So wherever you see the little bird – whether it's on a piece of prize-winning literary fiction or a celebrity autobiography, political tour de force or historical masterpiece, a serial-killer thriller, reference book, world classic or a piece of pure escapism – you can bet that it represents the very best that the genre has to offer.

Whatever you like to read – trust Penguin.